BIRD OF PREY

DC BROCKWELL

Print ISBN 978-1-913419-77-6

ALSO BY DC BROCKWELL

No Way Out

To my long-suffering wife, Beks, (only half-joking) without whom I wouldn't have started writing. I love you more than you know. xxxxx

DAY 1
TUESDAY, 20TH MARCH

1

———

"That'll be eight-fifty, mate," the Turkish taxi driver said through the plastic safety glass.

Cara Mooney went to open her bag, put her hand inside and felt the plastic handle of her blade. It was calling her; it was nearly time. She was so excited, she could barely contain it. Feeling a hand on her wrist, she looked over at Ryan, her pickup for the night.

"Oh no you don't." Ryan pulled out a wad of notes rolled into a ball. "I'm getting this." He unfurled a tenner and passed it through the glass. "Keep the change, mate."

What a poser! she thought, closing her bag, before he saw what was inside. He was tall, about six-two, good looking – if you liked that kind of thing – with short dark hair, which accentuated his high cheekbones and prominent chin. Cara couldn't wait to get him inside; she'd endured him all night, his initial pickup banter – which wanted to make her puke – and his clutching at her every five minutes. If he told her she was gorgeous once more, she thought she might actually vomit over him, and that would put an end to the night sharpish.

"Come on, let's go inside so I can get you out of that," he said, looking at her dress. He took her hand and pulled her out of the black cab. He said it loud enough for the taxi driver to hear, who gave her a little knowing smile as she stepped onto the pavement. "It's not far; you don't mind a bit of a walk in those heels, do you?"

"I don't mind the exercise." She held his hand and walked next to him past a row of terraced houses. "Do you live in one of these?" The air was biting her. Cara chose the red dress she was wearing for a reason: she looked hot in it, and it showed off maximum cleavage.

"Are you shivering?" Ryan placed an arm around her shoulder, like it would warm her up. "It's one of these a bit further along; it's not far now."

Cara wondered why he hadn't asked the driver to stop outside his house. It seemed daft, given the fat wad he'd just shown her – he was showing off, that's what it was, she thought, as he walked her up to a door. About bloody time; her legs were turning blue. "This it?" He nodded. "And you live alone?"

"Yep." Ryan slid his key in the door to the end of terrace house. "All mine."

Once inside, she felt the warmth of central heating. It was a bachelor pad, she noticed, as Ryan walked her through the lounge, which had the biggest flat-screen TV she'd ever seen hanging on the main wall, where a lovely picture should be hanging. In the dining room, she saw a fully stocked bar – such a guy thing to have to impress the ladies. He clearly hooked up with girls regularly, living in a place like this, wearing a suit like he was.

"I can make you a cocktail, if you want," he said, opening the cabinet and showing off his extensive collection of spirits.

Itching to get upstairs, hearing it calling her, Cara replied, "Erm, no thanks. I had enough at the bar. If I have another I might fall asleep on you." Every hint of her West Yorkshire accent was gone, replaced with the southern fairy drawl of living for years in the city.

"And we can't have that, can we?" He sidled up to her, putting his hands on her waist, leaning in and kissing her. After he let her breathe, he said, "Tell you what, let's forget drinks and go upstairs, yeah?"

"Can't wait!" She meant it, only not for the reason he thought. Cara took his hand, again, and followed him upstairs to the landing. He showed her the bathroom, which was a man's bathroom, the spare bedroom, and finally the master bedroom. "You've got a lovely place here, I have to say." She slid her bag off her shoulder and placed it on the chair by his desk. "Have you lived here long?" Not that she cared.

"About a year." He stepped up to her and grabbed her tiny waist again; he seemed infatuated with it. Then he pulled her towards the bed and started kissing her.

When she couldn't bear it anymore, Cara broke the kiss and pushed him onto the bed. She delighted in the shock on his face. "Tell you what, how about I tie you up, and we have a night to remember, you and I?" When he nodded, giddy as a schoolboy on Christmas morning, she smiled down at him. "Have you got anything I can use?"

"In my wardrobe over there." He removed his shirt, then pushed himself up the bed, resting his head on a pillow, his arms up, ready to be bound to his bedposts. "You know, I had a feeling you'd be into this kinky shit the minute I saw you."

Cara opened the wardrobe and took out two ties; they were his posh work ones. "Will these do?" She held them up in front of her face, noticing he'd taken his shirt off. He nodded with vigour, excited. She walked over to his bed and climbed on, hovering over him while she secured his hands to the posts, making sure she triple knotted them. "There! Now you're all mine." She was sat on top of him, looking down at his eager face.

"What now, gorgeous?"

"Now," she replied, leaning over and pulling out the top drawer of his bedside cabinet, "we do this." She took out a pair of his socks and stuffed them in his mouth. He said something, not that she could understand it. "You've got to be the dumbest prick I've ever met. Don't let strange women you've never met before tie you up like this, you dickhead."

His eyes went dark, the blood drained from his face. It was the same expression Chris had had, just before she'd begun hacking him to pieces. How she longed for the elation she felt that morning; she had to get it back, even if it meant having to seduce pricks like this in order to do so. The freedom she felt that morning was a drug, far more powerful than alcohol, drugs and sex. "Now we're gonna have some fun." She got off the bed and walked over to her bag.

The blade in her hand, she turned to him, hearing him whimper; it only made her feel more powerful. "I just want you to know it's nothing personal, Ryan," she said, back on the bed, sat on top of him, looking down at his fear-filled eyes. "You just remind me of someone, is all. And I really fucking hate him, I mean, really hate him. He was a lot like you; he was all lovely to me at one time, and then..." She let it trail off.

John Wood, her ex-dealer. She'd seen the look on his face, the look of pure joy, as he'd raped her for six hours with two of his friends in his flat. Remembering how helpless she felt, Cara looked down at Ryan. "You'd do that too, wouldn't you? If I'd come up here, and changed my mind at the last minute, *you'd rape me too, wouldn't you?*" Without knowing it, her voice was filled with rage.

And as her arm lifted, the knife pointing down, her heart leapt, as she brought it down, digging into Ryan's belly. Up it came, and down, making deep puncture marks, blood dripping over her face as she brought it up again.

Beneath her, Ryan was screaming into his gag. Cara couldn't hear him; she was too busy stabbing him. Without realising it – everything seemed slow – she was moving up his body with her blows, stabbing him in the chest, neck and face, blood pouring onto the duvet. Yet, he was still alive. He was still screaming.

The killer blow tore through his eye, the blade embedding itself in the back of his skull. Cara sat on top of him, looking down at his distorted face, the handle of her knife sticking out of his right eye socket. She had to catch her breath. It was working; the endorphins were coursing through her veins, making her feel so powerful, she thought she could take on the world single-handed. It wasn't the same as with Chris; it was even better. Cara was out in the real world now; she didn't have Beattie's guards to help dispose of Ryan's body. She didn't have the bunker's furnace to make his body disappear. No, she was on her own, and it felt fantastic, the best she'd ever felt. Cara was now a Bird of Prey.

2

———

Nasreen Maqsood leaned on the basin. She felt the scar on her cheek when she splashed water over her face. The scar was angry and red; it was too visible, and in the worst place.

In the month since she'd helped destroy the Harrisons' brothel and torture house under their farm – where she'd received the cut to her cheek, courtesy of Beatrice Harrison – she'd felt very self-conscious of her scar. Everyone stared at it. Even friends and family members, who knew how she felt about it, stared at her cheek. She hated it. Now, every time she looked in the mirror, she was reminded of Beatrice Harrison, the one person she wanted to forget.

"He's ready for you, Nas," Detective Sergeant Hilary Farmer said.

"Thanks," she replied, throwing water on her face. Walking over to the paper towel dispenser, she ripped three pieces out, wiped her face dry and threw them in the bin. She was so nervous.

"For what it's worth, I'm glad you're back. The testosterone level here's been in overdrive."

Nasreen turned to her friend. "I'm not sure the super's going to feel the same."

Hilary Farmer was forty-eight and a veteran police officer, although a relative newcomer to CID, having joined only two years earlier. She had short dark hair, a pleasant face and a wily athletic physique with very small breasts. Nasreen hadn't asked, but assumed Hilary was gay. When they occasionally did talk socially, she never mentioned a boyfriend or girlfriend, or even a partner. It wouldn't bother her if Hilary was gay. Each to their own was her motto, though some of her Muslim friends would have something to say about that.

"Don't worry about Adams. We're all on your side, and God knows the press is too. Just go in there and get it over with; it might not be as bad as you think."

Nasreen sighed. "Maybe. Well, here I go."

Taking a deep breath, she walked to the door, pulled it open and stopped, turning back. "Thanks." Nasreen took one last look in the mirror. She looked really smart in her dark grey pinstripe suit and white blouse, the colours really complimenting her light brown skin.

"You're welcome! Now get going, you don't want to keep him waiting. He won't like that."

Out in the corridor, Nasreen passed her colleagues Simon Watts and Elliott O'Hara, who both gave discreet "good luck" thumbs up. She smiled and carried on along the corridor to her pending lecture from DCS Adams. Taking another deep breath as she approached Adams' closed office door, she breathed out, trying to steady her nerves.

Stood outside the door for what felt like an age, Nasreen knocked and heard him shout, "Come in!" With hesitation, she opened the door and stepped inside.

"Detective Maqsood, please, take a seat." Adams motioned towards a seat in front of his desk. "Close the door, please."

Taking yet another deep breath, she did as she was told, closed the door and walked over to her chair. Sitting down, she folded her right leg over her left and placed her hands in her lap, clasped.

Nasreen studied Adams. She thought his ears had grown, if that was possible? He had unusually long ears; they were the first thing she noticed about him when he'd met her. Maybe it was her imagination? Now, looking at him, she remembered the conversation she overheard him having in the stairwell. Before she heard it, she thought Adams was a good man, one of the good guys. Not anymore. Now, she knew he was bent; she was going to start looking into him. She'd vowed it when she found Danny alive in the bunker.

"So, tell me, how are you feeling? How's your wound? Is it healing properly?" Adams sounded genuinely concerned.

"All fine, sir. I had the stitches out about a month ago. The doctor says it's healing well, and he said the scar will fade in time."

Adams nodded. "Good. And how are you feeling about coming back to work? You've been seeing a counsellor, I believe?"

"Yes, sir. A force-appointed therapist. She specialises in PTSD; it's going very well, I think. I don't know, you'll have to see her notes, I guess."

"I'll take your word for it. Counsellor sessions are sealed. Nothing gets past patient-doctor confidentiality. And believe me, I'd look at your notes if I could."

"Sir?" She was confused by his tone; this was supposed to be a formal back to work interview. It wasn't that she was expecting to be welcomed back with open arms, far from it. She hadn't expected this tone either. "What do you mean by that?"

Adams leaned forward. "I mean that, if I could, I'd look at your therapist's notes. I don't trust you one little bit, Detective

Maqsood. If I had my way, you'd be relieved of duty permanently, or at the very least, back in a uniform on the street, not here in CID. But it's not my call. The top brass ordered me to induct you back in, so here we are."

Nasreen had to bite her tongue; there was so much she could say. Now wasn't the right time. How dare he talk about trust to her? She could feel her temper rising. "Look, sir, I just want to say–"

"Save it! I'm not interested in your excuses. Your behaviour was reckless and dangerous, not to mention selfish and unbecoming of a detective constable in this department."

"Selfish? I helped save twenty-four innocent civilians, risking my own life in the process. I almost died saving them, and you call me selfish?"

"Watch your tone, detective, don't forget where you are. You're not in front of your beloved cameras now. We all just loved watching you on *This Morning*, by the way..."

"And did I say anything negative about the force?"

"You didn't need to, the public already knew you'd been suspended. And now, they're all protesting outside the office, trying to get you reinstated. The IOPC might have caved in to the pressure, but that doesn't mean I have to."

"It seems it does, actually, *sir*," she replied, her hands trembling with anger. The way she said "sir" was dripping with disdain. "That's why I'm here, isn't it? The chief constable told you to take me back, and you have to play ball, isn't that right?"

"That's enough! You might think you have us over a barrel, but I can assure you, it only seems that way. I'm going to be watching you from now on. I've spoken to Terrence and he's going to be submitting reports on everything you do out in the field. You put so much as a foot wrong and you're out of here, press or no press, is that understood, detective?"

Nasreen nodded, her leg twitching up and down. "Understood, sir."

"Now, go and report to Inspector Gupta – he's waiting for you. Terrence's already on his way to the scene." Adams leaned back in his chair.

"Yes, sir," she replied dutifully.

"Now, get out of my office. And tell Terrence I expect his report on my desk before he goes home."

Nasreen stood to leave; her legs were wobbly – she hoped Adams couldn't tell. If she thought it was worth it, she would tell him she'd overheard him in the stairwell, put the fear of God in him. It didn't serve her purpose though. Deciding to keep it to herself, she walked to the door. "Arsehole," she muttered.

3

Cara opened the door to her flat, stepped in and closed it behind her. She felt great. She honestly hadn't felt so alive since she left the bunker well over a month ago. She bent down, undid her red high heels and kicked them off, not caring where they landed. Then she took off her coat and her dress and walked naked through her lounge and into her bedroom. Her legs and hands were freezing.

Since leaving Ryan's, she'd taken a long walk home. When she left, it was approaching four in the morning; it was now just gone nine. She'd been out walking all that time, and she actually watched the sunrise – she loved it.

Feeling sweaty after all that walking, Cara hopped in the shower. It was only a quick rinse this time, having showered at Ryan's. There was very little time to put her affairs in order. Now that she'd passed the point of no return, she had to leave the flat, and the sooner the better. She knew she had a little time, but she had to make sure she was long gone before the pigs came knocking on her door. And it would happen; it was inevitable.

The way she figured it, someone finding the body in Ryan's flat would take time. It could be as early as this morning; he could have a cleaner, who would let herself in and find the body. Hell, Ryan could have a girlfriend, she lets herself in and finds the body. It could be later; it might take days for someone to worry enough to break into his flat. But Cara was working on the minimal time taken.

Then the police would need to investigate, talk to friends and family. It would take a few hours, maybe a day for them to speak to one of his friends at Johanna's Bar. Then they would need to view the CCTV footage from the bar. That was where she came a cropper. The bar had cameras. Not that it really mattered, there were cameras everywhere. Cara didn't care; all she cared about was carrying out her plan, before the police found her. She didn't intend on getting away with it.

And Cara hadn't taken precautions at Ryan's flat, either. She could have cleaned up, wiped surfaces of fingerprints, washed up the wine glass she used after making her masterpiece, which would now have her lipstick on, and hoovered up any fibres. The thing was (a) no amount of cleaning would prevent them from finding trace evidence; she'd researched it. It was pretty much impossible to commit the perfect murder and get away with it, and (b) she couldn't be bothered. There was no fun, no joy in working to hide her masterpiece. Ryan *was* her masterpiece and she wasn't afraid to show him off.

At least she hadn't fucked him. There would be so much more evidence on Ryan's body if she had. Then there was the fact she had form; she'd been arrested so many times she'd lost count, so they had her DNA and then some.

As she stepped out of the shower, Cara thought she could wait here in the flat for the inevitable knock on the door. There were no witnesses to her slaying him. They had circumstantial evidence that she was in the flat, sure. Oh, but she kissed his forehead on leaving, so they'd probably pick up on that.

She could wait and ride the storm, get taken to a police interview room, deny everything and go to court and testify that she didn't kill Ryan. No, fuck that! Far too much effort, and she wouldn't get to have her fun if she did that. Cara had many more masterpieces to make yet. No, she would stick to her original plan.

Walking into her bedroom, Cara started her morning ritual of fifty press-ups, followed by fifty sit-ups. She'd abused her body so much with the booze and drugs that she figured she had to counter it by doing at least some exercise. She wouldn't keep her body – or her looks – by poisoning it with that shit, without exercise.

As she went up and down, touching the floor with her nose, she thought about Lucy. She wondered where her ex-girlfriend – ex-soulmate – was now. She wondered what she was doing, and with whom. It was part of Cara's ritual, while keeping fit. When she went on her long runs she thought about Lucy a lot too.

Lucy Davis was her first – and only – true love. Cara had been with so many men in her life she'd lost count. Unlike most girls, she'd started with her dad when she was just six. He used to come into her bedroom when he was drunk and get in her bed, his hands everywhere, telling her she was his "special girl". Her sorry excuse of a mum – a junkie – never tried to stop him. Bitch!

Cara lifted her body up and back down, with her arms crossed. She had fifty sit-ups to do. She remembered the first time she told Lucy about her abuse at the hands of her dad; Lucy had hugged her so tight in their room at the rehab centre. Thinking about it, that was also their first kiss, while she was crying on Lucy's shoulder.

When they'd finished their long embrace, their faces so close, Cara locked eyes with Lucy's and moved forwards until their lips met. After the shock of the initial kiss, they had both come together for something far more passionate. It was glorious.

She missed Lucy so much. Every day Cara woke up, rolled over in their bed and felt the empty pillow. It always took a couple of seconds for her to remember Lucy was gone; sometimes it took longer. It depended on how smashed she was from the night before. If she was only drinking it wasn't too bad, but if she'd injected heroin it could take ages for her to remember Lucy leaving.

Cara knew she should stop the junk. But life got in the way sometimes, and she had to drown the shit out somehow. Heroin did that for her, if only for a short while. But now, now she had a new drug, a new high that heroin couldn't compete with in a million fucking years.

When she'd finished her last sit-up, her body moist from perspiration, her face slightly red from the effort, Cara got up and started getting dressed. Needing to look casual, she chose some comfy light blue jeans, a thick purple jumper, tied her long blonde hair into a ponytail and threaded it through the hole in the back of a light purple cap. She had a pair of tan Caterpillar boots she would wear too.

Since she was leaving this shithole of a flat for good, she took one last look around. The lounge was covered with empty bottles of vodka, cans of lager, pizza boxes and other takeaway food containers.

Wading through the mess on the floor, Cara grabbed everything she thought she needed: food from the fridge, extra clothes, including a killer black dress for tonight, and cash from under her bed. She remembered her passports, one real, one fake, put it all in a red suitcase and pulled it to the front door.

Putting on her thick coat, she carried the suitcase down the three flights of stairs.

Outside, she dragged the suitcase around the back of her

block of flats to her car, heaved the heavy case into the boot of her red Nissan Micra and closed the door. She sighed, looking at her old home; she would never be back here again. All those memories of her and Lucy, gone. It didn't matter, she had a new life now, and it'd only just started. Cara had plans for tonight, another masterpiece to make.

4

———

Detective Sergeant Terrence Johnson stared down at the deep gash in Ryan Bentley's eye socket. One thing he hated about this job was wearing the PPE, the white coveralls, foot protectors and mask. He bent over and took a closer look. He felt queasy. "Just look at the amount of rage. How many puncture wounds do you count?" he asked Aldwyn Bishop, the pathologist at the scene.

"Twenty-four. Twenty-five if you include the eye."

Terrence looked at his colleague. "What do you make of it?"

"The way he's tied up, looks like we're dealing with a deeply troubled perp. And a powerful one at that. I'd place bets on this being a female."

"That's an awful lot of anger for a woman." Terrence looked the body up and down. The sheer volume of blood surprised him; it always did. More than the blood though, was the horrified expression on the victim's face, his mouth open, with the one good eye looking up at the ceiling, searching for a reason why. The puncture marks were red and angry, clotting blood present inside the holes. "Why couldn't it have been a man?"

"If it was a male suspect, the victim would be tied facing

down, if this was sexually motivated and the suspect wanted penetrative sex, that is. But looking at this, it appears there *is* no sexual motive, other than the victim being tied up with his shirt off. No, this is something else."

"If it was a woman, she's strong. The amount of energy it must take to stab someone twenty-five times. Someone's cut this bitch loose."

"I noticed a wine glass downstairs with lipstick on. My guess is the suspect picked him up at a bar somewhere, brought him back here, and had a drink before."

Terrence heard voices from behind him. He turned to find Nasreen and Detective Inspector Arjun Gupta entering the bedroom wearing their PPE. He turned back to the body. Poor bastard, he thought. "Good to have you back, Nas."

"It's good to be back, I think." She fiddled with her face mask.

"How'd it go with Adams?"

"Ask me later. I don't want to speak ill of the man in public."

"Don't mind us," Bishop said. "It doesn't bother me, does it bother you, Arjun?"

Terrence smiled when Inspector Gupta agreed that he didn't mind her badmouthing their super. He had very little respect left for Adams after the way he'd treated Nasreen. It was just unfortunate they couldn't get rid of him. "Nasreen Maqsood, Aldwyn Bishop, Aldwyn Bishop, Nasreen Maqsood."

He watched as Nasreen shook Bishop's hand. "Nas, Bishop, here, is a freelance forensic pathologist; he gets called out to cases like this by all the forces in the country, so it makes him a very busy man. We're lucky to have him assist us on this. Now that the introductions are done, let's get down to business."

"What have we got so far?" Inspector Gupta, the shortest man in the room, was a round Indian man in his early fifties. "Terrence?"

Terrence read from his notepad. "Right, the victim's name is Ryan Bentley. He's thirty-six, lived here for little over a year. According to the cleaner, who found him at nine this morning, he's an investment banker. He recently split up with his girlfriend, who lives over the other side of town. He's universally liked by all those he knows, like I said, courtesy of the cleaner, who's also a friend."

"Great. Thanks, Terrence," Gupta said. "What do we know about the crime scene?"

"May I?" Terrence asked Bishop, who nodded. "Bishop believes we're dealing with a female suspect. He thinks the victim met her at a bar locally, brings him back here, has a drink downstairs, before bringing him up here, promising some action, ties him up and goes to town on him. I have to say, I agree. The way he's tied up suggests it's a female."

"Really?" Nasreen pointed at the stab wounds. "You think a woman did this? How much rage must she be holding on to?"

"That's exactly what I said."

"Aren't female murderers rare? I mean, come on, just look at it." Nasreen pointed at Ryan's torso. "How many stab wounds are there?"

"Twenty-five," Bishop replied. "I've counted."

"Twenty-five? This woman stabbed him twenty-five times. Holy crap! Have you seen anything like this before, Bishop?"

"Once, in the States. It happens, but not so much here in the UK. We've all heard of Jillian Dempsey, right? Even she didn't stab her victims twenty-five times. No, whoever we're dealing with, she's physically strong, and she's very angry."

"Could be the victim upset someone." Terrence glanced at each of them. "We need to look into Ryan's background, see if we can find something there."

"The first thing we need to do, is find out where he was last night," Gupta corrected. "Did we find his mobile?"

"No, sir," Terrence replied. "We've looked all over."

"She took it," Nasreen said. "That's what I'd do. Take out the sim and destroy it. Why chance it, right?"

"We'll need to start with the next of kin then," Gupta said. "Okay, so here's what we're going to do: we'll leave the CS team to gather as much trace as they can. Nasreen, you and I will go door-to-door, see what we can learn about the victim from neighbours. Terrence, can you go to the station and run a background check on the PNC, also contact his family and see what they know? Aldwyn, do you mind staying on to carry out the autopsy? Okay, let's go!"

5

Assistant Commissioner Peter Franks was excited; he was putting information packs together for the first project meeting at the warehouse. He had thirty packs to piece together for his participants. His home office was the best place to carry out his task. He couldn't use the station office for this; he didn't want any unwanted eyes going over the sensitive information.

Since Lennox Garvey had taken care of Franks' William Rothstein problem, the project was back on track, where it should be. He had the supplier sorted and ready to go; he had his dealers in place, and he had his new importer on standby. In addition, he had all the seized narcotics from the UK sent to the warehouse, so the project had stock to use from day one. It was the Commissioner's idea to utilise narcotics scheduled for destruction, providing the quality was pure. Any samples with less than ninety-five percent purity were taken away and destroyed.

Although he was satisfied that the Rothstein problem was over, now he was concerned about Garvey. He'd hired one of Zack Astor's guys to take care of Garvey, but that hadn't turned out how he'd wanted. Instead of Garvey dead inside the boot of the car, it had turned out to be Astor's guy, which meant that Garvey was out there, somewhere, probably plotting his revenge. So far, though, there had been no sign of Garvey. Franks hoped Rothstein's number two had decided to go home, back to Jamaica, back to his uncle.

Franks placed the last thirty pieces of paper on the other stacks on the floor. All he had to do now was bind the thirty packs together and he was ready to drive to the Midlands for the meeting. He glanced at the clock on the wall and saw it was 15:38. That gave him time to drive to the warehouse and set everything up, ready for his guests' arrival.

Dressed in full Commissioner uniform, with his trousers neatly pressed, his shoes so shiny he could see his face in them, and his shirt neatly ironed, he walked over to his desk to grab the hole puncher. His burner phone rang. He picked it up and pressed the green answer button. "Hello, Clive," he said in a reasonably chirpy manner.

"Peter, we've got a problem."

"Oh, what now? I'm just getting ready to leave for the meeting. You're still coming, aren't you?" He could feel his temper rising. Bloody Adams was such a pain.

"I'll be there, don't worry. And it's not about the meeting."

"What then, what is it? Spit it out, will you, I'm busy."

"Nasreen Maqsood, sir."

There it was, that bloody name was really fraying his last nerve. It was bad enough that she'd messed up his original project, but then she went on TV talking about it. Fortunately, Nasreen didn't know what was going on, not really. She helped destroy the bunker, good for her and that NCA officer, but it had nothing to do with the project. "What about her, Clive? What's she done now?"

"She hasn't done anything. Can't we get rid of her? She's a

liability, disrespectful, not to mention reckless. Why did you force me to take her back?"

"How many more times? I've already told you we can't let her go, not with the press breathing down our necks." He looked at the information packs, wanting to crack on with the binding. "We'll wait for this shitstorm to blow over. She'll hang herself before long, I guarantee it. Nasreen won't be able to help herself. And when she steps out of line, you'll be rid of her."

"I've got Terrence monitoring her performance."

"Good, good. Mark my words, she'll be out of our hair before you know it. Keep Terrence on her; he'll come through for us, okay?"

"Yeah, sure."

"Is there anything else, Clive? I really must get on."

Fortunately, Adams didn't have any more pressing matters, so Franks said goodbye and hung up, placing his mobile on the desk. He got down on his knees and started punching holes, ten sheets at a time.

He was getting excited. Months of hard work, of clandestine meetings with colleagues and dealers was finally paying off. Soon, he would have a list of names to arrest; the dealers were going to hand over their first competitors this evening. When he had the targets, he would hand them over to the appropriate chief constables. Within a couple of months, each force would have their first high-profile detentions under their belts.

6

Nasreen hung her bag on the backrest of her chair. "That was a waste of time. None of Bentley's neighbours know anything about him. Not that they'd tell me, anyway. Have you had any luck?"

"I've managed to contact his parents; we're meeting them tomorrow morning," Terrence replied. "They're coming in to identify his body at nine. They own and live in a pub up north and can't get down here until then. The mum was inconsolable."

"I'll bet." She sat. It felt good being back behind her desk. If she was honest, she thought she would never be back in the office again. Her career had looked like it was in tatters only a month earlier, and here she was, turning her computer back on. "I never thought I'd miss this office."

"Yeah, I hear you."

Nasreen waited for her monitor to spring to life. Inspector Gupta adjusted his seat in front of her. She liked him, so far. Before she was suspended, there was talk of a new inspector starting. From what she had gleaned today, he was a consummate professional, taking his role seriously.

While they were knocking on doors together, he'd filled her

in on his career to date. Gupta started as a constable in the South West twenty-eight years earlier, when he was a young twenty-four-year-old. He'd moved around a lot over the years, having served in the South East, London, the North East and the West Midlands. He'd been married and divorced twice and was currently on his third fiancée. He told Nasreen that he was a glutton for punishment.

Gupta told her he thought she was very brave. He said he watched all the news coverage she'd received and watched her interview on *This Morning*. And while he said she was brave, he added that what she did was also very dangerous. She agreed.

She couldn't expect a professional police officer like Gupta to think that going into a bunker full of villains with a gun and without backup was a good idea. In hindsight, she thought it was dumb too.

"Still no sign of the victim's phone?" Gupta asked anyone.

"I don't think so, sir." Terrence's voice boomed. "I can check with the CS team, but I haven't heard anything from them, and I asked them to call if they found it."

"I'll speak to them now." Gupta picked up his phone. "Did you find out much about him on the PNC?"

"I've been too busy, sir," Terrence replied. "I had a meeting with Adams for an hour, and I was on the phone with Bentley's parents for an hour and a half. Sorry!"

"I'll log on now, sir." Nasreen accessed the Police National Computer and typed in "Ryan Bentley" in the search bar. There were twenty-two Ryan Bentleys on the system to wade through. She cross-checked addresses and found the file she wanted.

Ryan Bentley had a chequered past, it seemed. He was arrested for drunk and disorderly sixteen years earlier. Then there was an assault six years later, although not formally charged.

The paperwork showed that he was only involved on the

fringes, joining four friends in a fight with another group of young lads. It was a part of everyday life these days, she thought. And then in 2012 he was arrested for statutory rape; he slept with a fourteen-year-old girl he met in a nightclub. The Crown Prosecution Service took the case all the way through to the Crown Court, but his defence was strong. He met the alleged victim at a nightclub, where entry requirements were that guests had to prove they were eighteen or over.

Nasreen looked the case up on Google and found newspaper articles in *The Sun* and *Daily Express*. The case made national coverage. Bentley's defence also asserted that the alleged victim consented to leaving the nightclub and escorting Bentley back to his flat. They had intercourse consensually. According to the papers, it was only when the parents of the "victim" caught her in the act of trying to sneak back into the family home that the victim had burst into tears, saying that she'd been raped. The parents, quite rightly, prosecuted Bentley. After a week-long trial, Bentley was acquitted.

"Here's a possibility. He was tried for statutory rape six years ago. Could be worth looking into, couldn't it?" Nasreen looked to Gupta for confirmation.

"Right now, we need as many leads to follow as we can. Good work, Nasreen, do you mind following up on that?" Gupta waited for her reply.

"Please, call me Nas. Nasreen's what Mum used to call me when I was in trouble. I'll try calling the parents. The victim will be of age to speak to alone now."

Picking up the phone, Nasreen dialled the number she found on the PNC for the parents. When a male voice answered, she introduced herself and gave him the reason for her call. She explained that Ryan Bentley had been murdered and asked him if she could speak with his twenty-year-old daughter, to eliminate her from their enquiries. She explained that it was a formality, that all friends and family members would need to provide alibis too. She also explained that anyone who'd had dealings with the victim would need to be eliminated from their suspect pool. Finally, he relented and shouted for Julia to come to the phone.

"Julia Sandall?"

"Yeah, who's this?"

Nasreen reeled off her reason for calling and explained the situation.

"He's dead?" Julia's voice was a mixture of shock and sadness. "How?"

Not wanting to tell her over the phone, Nasreen decided she had no choice. It would be far better to see her reaction in the flesh, rather than listening to a voice. "He was stabbed multiple times in the early hours of this morning."

Julia gasped. "Oh my God! I don't believe it." Her voice quivered. "He was–"

"Can you come into the station and give a statement? It's just a formality."

"I never meant him any harm. It all just got... blown up... and snowballed." She sobbed, then sniffed. "Before I knew it... I was in court testifying that he raped me."

"You don't need to explain yourself, Julia. We just need to eliminate you from our enquiries. Can you come in for me?"

"What, now? Can't we just do it over the phone?"

"It depends, can you prove where you were this morning between 02:30 and 03:30?"

"Right here. I was in bed asleep. My parents will vouch for me. I had a bad day with my son yesterday; he's got whooping cough, so I was in bed by nine and stayed in bed until half six. I can put my dad back on; he'll tell you the same."

It wasn't like Nasreen really thought Julia had stabbed Bentley two dozen times. She was satisfied Julia was telling the truth; she sounded genuinely upset Bentley was dead. It was worth a punt, she thought. "If you could, please. I hope your son recovers quickly."

"Thanks."

The dad came back on the telephone and vouched for his daughter's whereabouts. That was that; there was no need for a formal face-to-face interview. Nasreen thanked him for his time and patience and hung up.

"No joy?" Gupta asked.

"Afraid not, she was kind of sweet. Clearly a tearaway when she was younger, but she's got a baby now. She was at home with her parents and baby this morning. I believe her."

"Make sure the report reflects that. The super's out for your blood, so everything needs to be a hundred per cent accurate, okay?" He said the latter part quietly.

"Hey, you won't get any arguments from me." She started filling out her interview form, knowing that if Adams found anything out of place, she was for the high-jump. Anyway, she shouldn't be worrying about her career; their victim had just had his throat sliced open. Nasreen hoped this wouldn't be a long drawn-out investigation.

7

Lennox Garvey drove past the gated warehouse less than a minute after the Assistant Commissioner, Franks, went inside. He'd followed the senior police officer's Peugeot for over two hours in his blue Honda Civic. As he drove past, he noticed the police sign on the front gate; it was an official police warehouse they were using.

Barkley, his best friend and ally, sat in the passenger seat next to him. He owed his life to Barkley, who rescued him from inside the boot of a burning car. Since fleeing the field where he should have died, Lennox had been able to move around freely, safe in the knowledge that Franks thought he was dead. However, now that the assistant commissioner had had the burnt body's DNA tested and knew the remains weren't his, he had to assume that Franks would be on the lookout for him. On his way here, the double-crossing prick hadn't seen his car behind him, or at least it seemed that way.

"Where're we going to park?" Barkley glanced at him.

Lennox carried on driving until he found a suitable place to perform a U-turn. The police warehouse was situated in the middle of a huge factory park with over three hundred separate businesses; it was a rabbit warren. To call it a maze was an understatement. "Look out for a good spot." He performed a U-turn and headed back in the direction of the warehouse. "We need somewhere with a good view."

"There, that looks good."

The factory he chose was on the other side of the road and to the left of the police warehouse. It wasn't perfect, but it had a good enough view. With binoculars, he would be able to see all the way up to the warehouse itself. There was a long car park. Barkley brought his digital camera, so they could take photos of the dealers Franks was working with and identify them.

Tonight's meeting marked the beginning of the conspiracy. Garvey knew that Franks had had gear shipped to the warehouse, so they had merchandise to sell to the dealers already. Garvey had watched pallets of cocaine being forklifted inside. At one point, he'd thought about putting together a team to break in and pinch the lot, but his uncle had talked him out of it. Since then, they'd formulated a new plan. What these police officers and dealers feared the most was exposure. The assistant commissioner wanted to bang up all dealers who weren't on their list, so that they could demonstrate how much safer and quieter the streets were when they finally came clean about the project. Lennox and his uncle had other plans; they were going to rain down so much carnage on these fuckers that they would regret double-crossing him.

Over the past month, his uncle had transferred enough money for him to arm his group, and then some. In a lock-up, he had an arsenal capable of taking on a small army. He had six Uzis, two Beretta M951Rs, two Heckler and Koch VP70Ms and five Glock 18Cs, all fully automatic machine pistols, with enough shells to take out said small army. He was looking forward to using the Uzis, having never fired one before, and he would get the opportunity tomorrow night. He had already chosen his first target.

Leaning back in his seat, Lennox watched the cars going past, one by one. It was dark outside, but the factory park was well-lit, with lamp posts dotted every fifty metres or so. He would take down the number plates of all the cars that drove into the police warehouse car park, and Barkley would try to get decent photos of the dealers and police. It didn't really matter either way, Lennox had someone on the inside: Amelie Desmarais. She was busy trying to get all the information he needed.

"Here's one now." Barkley motioned to a black car.

Garvey watched as the car pulled up to the gate; he couldn't see the model or make. He wrote down the number plate. Cars weren't really his thing; he knew a bit. It was a Mercedes, but he couldn't tell the model. A uniformed guard opened the gate manually, waiting for the car to drive through, before he closed the gate. Lennox noticed the guard wasn't a police officer; there was a red stripe on his hat.

When Barkley finished taking photos, Lennox leaned back in his seat again. They were in for a boring evening of surveillance. It was important to know who the key players were. He leaned forward and turned on the radio.

8

"What are you having?" The tall skinny barman eyed her up and down.

Cara asked for a double gin and tonic with ice and lime. She smiled and shouted "thanks" to the sleazy server. It was loud inside The Emporium, even at eight o'clock. Although the dance floor was empty, there were a number of large groups gathering. There was a line of revellers all along the fifty-metre bar, with seven bar staff busy getting them drinks.

The Emporium was predominantly a student nightclub. Located in a student city, they were a large demographic for the club. Tuesday nights were popular with the locals and students alike. It was nineties dance night, not that the students were old enough to remember the popular songs of the time, such as 'Rhythm is a Dancer' or 'Ride on Time', but she could, and she loved old-school disco. 'What is Love' by Haddaway played and she found her legs moving in time with the beat.

Since leaving her flat, Cara had driven for four hours to get here. She'd left her Micra in a car park not far from the club and she'd gone straight to a nearby pub and ordered food and drink. She'd taken a black lacey dress with her, and used the pub's loos to get changed. And she looked stunning in it, she knew. With a V-shaped neck, it was knee-length, sophisticated, and cost her just over a hundred quid.

When she'd walked downstairs to the bar, she noticed a few heads turn. And when she'd gone back to her table, a group of four blokes came over and chatted her up. She'd enjoyed the attention, trying to decide which one to make her masterpiece, but an hour later they left; they were on their way to a gig somewhere. One of them – the alpha, who loved himself, would have been perfect for her, a real masterpiece. Gutted, she had to move on.

"That's five-fifty, please, love," shouted the barman.

Cara paid him, picked up her drink and sucked her first sip through a straw. She turned and surveyed the land. It didn't take her long to spy a guy checking her out. She smiled at him. He was tall, with dark hair, young. He couldn't be any more than twenty. It didn't matter to her if he lived on his own, he was fair game. The only trouble: students generally lived in big houses with their mates, so she needed to focus on older, local men.

"I haven't seen you here before," came a voice to her left.

Cara turned to find a well-dressed tall bloke waiting for a reply. He had dark hair, was reasonably attractive, with a gap between his two front teeth, not that it detracted from his looks. She took him to be in his late twenties, possibly early thirties. "That's because I've never been here before." She took another sip through her straw.

"That's what I thought; I'd have remembered." He checked her out. "Are you local?"

"No, I live a couple of hours away. I'm meeting some friends here, I'm early."

"How about I keep you company until they get here? I'm Hayden, by the way."

"Chloe." She smiled as sweetly as she could manage. "Are *you* local?"

"Yeah, I live up the road." He shouted in reply, his face getting closer.

"Alone, or with friends?"

"On my own." He was standing right next to her.

Cara had a winner! He was perfect. He was cocky, arrogant and self-assured, just her type. She could tell he loved himself by his demeanour. He inched closer to her with every sentence. He would try to make out it was because the music was too loud, yet she knew better. He wanted to get her out of this lovely dress. Cara had other plans for Hayden.

9

———

Franks stepped forward. It appeared that everyone was here. The only person who hadn't made it was the Commissioner, who had an engagement to attend. That made him the highest-ranking police officer in the warehouse. It was fitting then that it be him to make the presentation. Although it should have been his boss who made the speech, he'd prepared one himself, for such an eventuality. He cleared his throat.

Stood around a large table were a mixture of Police and Crime Commissioners, Chief Constables and Chief Superintendents from all over the country on one side of the room. On the other side stood six drug dealers, each with an entourage of around three or four foot soldiers, and the importer, who had eight in his entourage.

Franks introduced himself, thanked everyone for coming, explained the reason for their visit, and explained the nature and scope of the project. On the table in front of him was a huge map of the United Kingdom. On the map, the different regions were all colour coded, the country split into six areas: South West, South East, London, Midlands, North East and North West.

He went around the room introducing the dealers and which geographical location they would be assigned; it was no surprise to the dealers, they'd all been informed prior to the meeting.

He spoke about the benefits of being the chosen few to spearhead the project. He told them how they would be free to run their businesses unchecked, providing they abided by a few set rules.

They were to only sell merchandise from this warehouse; they had to stick to the map and only sell within their boundary; they had to give forty per cent of their takings back to the police, and for that they received protection from police interference. And lastly, he explained that they had to hand over their rivals, which, to Franks, was the most important aspect of the project.

They required high-profile raids for the media to splash over their daily rags. The public needed to see their raids, to see the arrests and prison sentences for themselves, if the ends were to justify the means.

James Foster, who'd been given the South East, was the first to offer him his envelope. Inside the envelope was a list of names. Franks opened it and read the list. He smiled, knowing a couple of the targets.

Next, Zack Astor, who was in charge of London, handed an envelope to him. Franks recognised one name on the list. The target would be a huge win if they took him off the streets, almost as notorious as William Rothstein. Franks was looking forward to raiding his home and businesses.

He walked up to all six dealers, including Matthew Walker, who was given the South West, Ibrahim Sandhu, the North West, Omar Almasi, the Midlands and finally, he walked up to Margaret "Maggie" Hughes, who was chosen to run the North East.

Having looked through the six lists of names, he knew some, but the further up north the names, the less he knew. He had a long list of suspects to start surveillance on, so he was happy. When the time was right, he would give the names to the appropriate Police and Crime Commissioner, some of whom were stood to his right, and order them to start surveillance operations on the dealers. It would be a drip-feed process.

The warehouse was lined with six-foot pallets on both the left and right. Each pallet contained consignments of different narcotics, all class A or B prohibited. There were pallets of cocaine, heroin, MDMA, ecstasy pills and everything in between, all the way down to cannabis. Every brick of cocaine, every pill of ecstasy and every packet of cannabis had been seized by police and kept in storage for destruction; now they were in the warehouse, about to be distributed to a paying public.

Franks let the dealers take what they needed for their first month. Because the narcotics were seized, he didn't charge them. It made sense, the drugs hadn't cost them anything. On subsequent months, he *would* be charging them.

The dealers' entourages packed the narcotics into duffel bags and walked out of the warehouse to their cars. One by one, the dealers left, leaving only the senior police officers.

"I hope we're doing the right thing," said one of the Police and Crime Commissioners.

"It's a bit late to be having second thoughts now, don't you think?" Franks couldn't have negativity; it spread like a brush fire. "Anyway, this is the best thing for the country. You wait, soon the streets will be cleaner and quieter. And then you'll know."

10

Nasreen stared up at the ceiling. She could hear her daughter Mina's quiet breathing next to her. Since she returned from having her cheek sewn up, and after she collected Mina and their nanny Katerina from Nasreen's mother-in-law's house, Mina had become very clingy. Every night, after she'd put Mina to bed, about an hour later, her daughter came to her room, crying.

She couldn't turn Mina around and put her back to bed, so she let her sleep in with her. It wasn't the best idea; she rarely got enough sleep. Mina was a fidget in bed, like her dad used to be. Her daughter turned, snuggled deeper into Nasreen's armpit. She rubbed her daughter's back with the softness only parents understood.

One good thing had come from her friend Danny's disappearance, and her suspension: she had become more focused on home life. Gone were the days when she would go into work early and come home late; she didn't want to be a workaholic. She'd missed too much of Mina's life already – she was going to put Mina first from now on. Of course, she still had to work, but she had to get that work-life balance right, for both her and her daughter's sakes. Nasreen didn't want to wake up one day and realise that she didn't know her own daughter.

As Nasreen looked up at the ceiling, she wondered what would make someone stab a man twenty-five times? What would make them do it? She wondered what that person's life must have been like? And if it *was* a woman, like Aldwyn Bishop believed, what must she have gone through? Was she just evil? Had she enjoyed watching him die, watching him gargle his last breath? It was one area of life that fascinated Nasreen, abnormal psychology; she'd studied psychology A Level at college and loved the subject. Nasreen didn't consider herself an expert, unlike Bishop, who apparently had degrees and certificates galore.

Her mobile phone vibrated on the chest of drawers next to her bed. She picked it up and looked at the caller. It said "Unknown" on the screen, so she carefully took her free arm from around Mina and swiped the red symbol. She never took calls if they were unknown. It was probably a sales call, but, looking over at her alarm clock, she realised it was too late for sales people to be calling. She leaned over and put the phone back on the surface, next to her clock.

She missed Ashraf so much. He used to make her laugh all the time, and so effortlessly too. Nasreen thought back to how destroyed she was when he'd died three years earlier of a brain haemorrhage, about how she thought she would never recover.

Time was a healer, for sure, but she wasn't the same person today than she was before he'd died. There was a gaping hole in her heart which would never be filled. These days, if she went a day without crying, it was a good day. And that was after three years.

Anything she was feeling now would pale in comparison to

how Danny must be feeling, she thought. He was still in a psychiatric ward suffering from PTSD. He was tortured for days, prior to her finding him. They beat him so badly, his whole body was purple. And it wasn't only his body; more harmful was the mental torture they inflicted. She visited him as often as her life allowed.

11

———

"Here we are. Home sweet home."

Cara stood inside the hallway, while her pickup closed the door, before showing her through to the kitchen. He reached into a cabinet and pulled out a bottle of vodka, then into another and took out two tumblers. "Not for me, thanks." She placed her hand over a glass. "I've had enough. I feel quite woozy."

He looked at her, shrugged, and poured himself one. "Fair play." He swigged back a double measure. "Straight to it; I like that."

After he placed the glass in the sink, he walked back over to her and placed both hands on her waist. He stunk of booze and fags. When he went in to kiss her, Cara reciprocated, feeling his exuberant tongue in her mouth; it made her want to be sick. For the sake of appearances, she went along with it, feeling her blade calling her.

His hands went from her waist, onto her arse, pulling her in closer. It wasn't time yet, she thought, still kissing him, her eyes open. It was only when his hands made for her tits that she balked, pushing him back with her hands. "Too quick, Hayden," she said, baiting him. "Slow down! We've got all night."

Hayden didn't like being pushed away, she noticed by his narrow eyes.

He moved in for a second time, grabbing her arse and pulling her close again.

"Come on, baby, don't be like that."

His horrible breath offended her nostrils.

"You've been giving me the come-on all night. It's time to pay up."

She was delighted by his anticipated behaviour. To him, she was just a dumb blonde, a pickup for the night. If he knew what she was thinking, fantasising about, he would run a mile, she thought, her eyes scared as she looked at him. "Please, I've changed my mind." She felt his hands tighten on her waist. "I think I'm going to go home."

"The fuck you are!" he snapped. "You're staying here and we're having a good fucking time, bitch. That's why you're here, isn't it?"

Reaching inside her bag on her shoulder, she felt the handle. "I thought you were a nice guy," she replied, her eyes still scared. "Clearly I was wrong."

Hayden grabbed her throat. "Hey, I'm nice. I just don't like being played."

"I'm not playing you." Her voice sounded higher than normal. "I want to go home, please. Move out of my way!" Cara played possum, signalling weakness by leaving his gaze, looking down at the floor in submission.

Inside, she couldn't be more thrilled, knowing the time was near. Hayden was about to become her latest masterpiece. "Please, Hayden, let me leave. I'll scream."

Hayden's face changed, from angry to furious; his brow furrowed, his mouth contorted into a sneer and his hand tightened around her throat. "You fucking bitches, thinking you can fuck us blokes around. You knew what was going to happen when you agreed to come back here. And you knew what I wanted when I came and spoke to you at the bar. You think you can turn around now, and say no? Fuck you!" He squeezed her throat even tighter.

"Please..." She feigned distress. "I... can't... breathe."

"On your knees, bitch," he said, spit flying in her face.

Now it's time, she thought, pulling her blade out from her bag and plunging it into his stomach. It felt so good, as it slid into him. Cara applied more force, making sure the full four inches went through him. And it wasn't only sticking it inside him that felt good; it was the look of disbelief on his face, as he looked down at the handle sticking out of his belly, then back up at the smile on her face.

After he'd relinquished his grip on her neck, Cara placed both hands on the handle, and mustering all her strength, pulled the blade up, tearing through his intestines.

The power she felt dwarfed any positive feelings she used to get from drugs and drink. She was getting stronger and more confident with each hunt.

Smiling at the blood dribbling out of his mouth, Cara yanked the knife out of his stomach, as blood sprayed over her dress and chest. The warm liquid felt good. "This is why you should be careful who you bring home."

Hayden slumped onto his knees, his eyes rolling back in his head.

She grabbed his hair and yanked his head back, exposing his neck. "And if you do bring a girl back, treat them nice, yeah?"

It was the moment she'd waited for all day.

Taking the knife, she pressed it against his neck, and used all the force she could to slit his throat from left to right. At one point, she thought she felt the serrated edge clip bone.

Hayden's throat tore open in a torrent of crimson, covering her. It surprised her how much force the blood sprayed her with.

When she let go of his hair, Hayden fell face down on his kitchen floor, blood pooling around his head. She moved her feet out of the way. "Now, that was satisfying." She watched the blood gain on her shoe. "You were my favourite so far."

Stepping towards the sink, Cara poured herself a triple measure of vodka and slugged it back in one. Feeling the fiery liquid glide down her throat, she coughed. "At least you bought the good stuff." She picked up the bottle and, minding the puddle of blood, stepped over Hayden's cooling corpse. She felt like watching some TV.

DAY 2
WEDNESDAY, 21ST MARCH

12

Cara stirred. She was lying under Hayden's duvet, warm, covered in his blood. She sat up, looking around the room. The bedside lamp was still on. Her head hurt from drinking a half bottle of vodka. The alarm clock said it was 04:38. It was time for a shower.

Despite the hangover, which she would cure with a couple of painkillers, she hadn't felt this good in a long time; even after Ryan. It was as though she felt better after each hunt. Cara didn't need drugs to get high anymore; she just needed to hunt. It was all so clear in her mind: she was born for this.

If only she'd realised it years ago; she could've hunted her prick of a dad. There was no chance now that he was banged up. Or she could've hunted her skaghead mum instead. No chance of that, either.

In Hayden's obsessively tidy bathroom, Cara stepped in the shower and washed off the dried blood. It took several washes with his shower gel. The water turned red. She hummed a tune while she washed, not knowing what the song was; it was just a tune she made up. Everything about her felt great. Fit, healthy, looking good. Even the needle marks on her arms seemed to have toned down.

All the reminiscing made her think back to the last time she'd paid John Wood, her dealer, a visit. If there was ever a man who needed hunting, it was him. The last time she'd knocked on his door, she went with no money. That was her mistake. When she found him playing the Xbox with two friends in the lounge, he'd offered her a beer, which she accepted.

After a couple of minutes of small talk, he asked her what she needed. She'd said she was after some H. He asked for the money and she told him she didn't have any, so she'd offered to deal for him instead, do some odd jobs around the flat to pay for it.

Odd jobs weren't on John's mind. He stood, looked her up and down and ordered her to get in his bedroom, to take her clothes off and wait for him. When she tried to get past him, he blocked her way. He was a big man, six feet and muscular. John was known for being a steroid junkie. He was as wide as he was tall, or so it had seemed as he'd loomed over her.

One of John's friends had moaned that he was waiting to resume the game. John ordered her inside his bedroom again. When she shook her head, he slapped her, hard. Her lip bled. Then he'd grabbed her by the hair, forced her into the bedroom and pushed her onto the bed. When he shouted at her to undress, she'd done so without argument.

Scared, she waited for two hours for John to take his payment from her. John, drunk, finally entered the bedroom with his two mates. Naked, outnumbered and terrified, there was nothing she could have done. John punched her in the face three times. They each raped her twice. She'd arrived at his flat at 11:00 and didn't leave until 20:30. She'd been beaten and raped for over six hours.

As she stepped out of the shower, she could feel her anger rising.

She slunk off, while John and his two mates were sat in the lounge, laughing and joking, playing the Xbox. She'd not been able to walk properly for over a week; they'd torn her, damaged her. But no one was ever going to get the chance to do that to her again, not her dad, not John, not... No, she wasn't going to give *him* the satisfaction.

Back then, she'd been a mess, hooked on H. But she wasn't now; she was fit and healthy, probably the fittest she'd ever been. She felt stronger now than she ever had. Maybe it was finding her calling? Now she was a bird of prey, out there hunting. It had to be the reason she felt so great; it couldn't be anything else.

After she dried herself off, Cara walked through to Hayden's obsessively clean and tidy lounge. She switched on the huge flat-screen television and sat on the edge of the couch. The TV was so big, it practically covered the wall. She watched Sky News for an hour, to see if Ryan was mentioned. He wasn't. The police might not have even found the body yet; she'd read many stories where dead bodies weren't found for days, sometimes weeks or even months. Cara knew Ryan would be found soon though. And when he *was*, it wouldn't be long before she was identified.

She still had time before she had to take precautions. Cara walked through to the kitchen, leant on a sideboard, and studied Hayden's body. "It was fun while it lasted, but I've got to go now. See you in my dreams."

In the hallway, she dressed back into her jeans, jumper and cap. It felt dirty wearing the same clothes as yesterday. Now she was on the road, she didn't have much choice; she only had three changes of clothing. Deciding she would go shopping later, get herself some pretty clothes, Cara checked her purse.

She walked back into the kitchen, bent down and checked his pockets for a wallet. Taking out a hundred quid, she slipped the notes into her purse to use later. Rummaging around his flat, going through cupboards and drawers, Cara found a small bag of weed – which would come in handy for later – and a flick knife. She pocketed both.

Deciding it was time to move, she grabbed her bags and went to the front door. It was still dark out, which was the way she'd planned it. The less people saw her, the better. There wasn't much chance of being caught by a nosy neighbour at quarter past six in the morning. After she'd descended the stairs, she walked outside, into the cold morning air. She breathed in heavily and exhaled. It was going to be a good day.

"How long have you been up?"

Lennox felt Amelie's arms wrap around his shoulders. She kissed the top of his head. He finished gluing the letter onto the paper and turned in his chair. Grabbing her waist and pulling her onto his lap, he wrapped his arm around her. "Not long. I wasn't tired."

"It's early. Are you coming back to bed?"

Just looking at her beautiful face hurt. Amelie reminded him of a younger Thandie Newton, with shiny long black hair, flawless skin and lovely straight white teeth. "Maybe in a bit. I'm going to finish this first."

When she looked down at the desk covered in newspaper cuttings, he observed his work. There were individual letters dotted about in different fonts and sizes. He'd spent an hour cutting them out while wearing gloves. He gently stroked her hair.

"What's all this?" Her look of confusion brought a thought of this evening's plans.

"Getting ready for tonight." He leaned in and kissed her.

"So, it all starts today?"

"Yeah, we've picked our first target," he said to her look of trepidation. "There's still time for you to back out, you know. If you don't want to be a part of this, no one will think any less of you. You've already helped us more than you need to."

Amelie backed up and stared into him. "I'm with *you*, Lennox. You know that. These people deserve everything they get, especially the police. They ought to know better."

Lennox had learnt, in the short time he'd known Amelie, that she had no fondness for the government, or any of its agencies. She confided in him that her father had been killed when a coal mine partially collapsed, two days after the end of the miners' strike of 1984 – 1985. The fifth of March, her father's death day, was a sombre day for her, he knew; he'd spent the evening with her.

Amelie had told him that where she grew up, in a small northern town, her father was the only black man working the mine. She was born in early 1984, which meant she had only been alive for just over a year before he died. Amelie never knew her father. But his legacy had lived on in her home. Her father being a staunch Arthur Scargill supporter, the name "Margaret Thatcher" was a swear word in Amelie's house, especially after his death.

After her father's death, the family had had to find ways to make ends meet. Her mother, a pragmatist, had confided in a friend that she desperately needed money. The friend had suggested that she had assets to sell: herself. Only a month away from repossession, her mother took her friend's advice and began selling herself to wealthy men in the surrounding towns. Amelie grew up watching men coming and going as a child. Lennox saw how that had led to Amelie selling herself now.

He knew she was a whore before they officially met. Shortly after he'd escaped the boot of the burning car, he started a surveillance operation against Assistant Commissioner Peter

Franks. Tailing Franks had led Lennox to Commissioner of Police of the Metropolis Harold "Harry" Thomas, who was one of Amelie's "elite clients".

When he learned who Thomas was, Lennox started tailing him instead of Franks. It was while following Thomas that he had seen Amelie stepping off Thomas' boat, *The Albatross*, a luxurious recreational vessel. She made a big impression on him immediately, even from afar. When she stepped off the boat, his jaw hung, she was so beautiful. He took the binoculars from Barkley to take a closer look.

Wanting to meet her, he started following her. After two days, Lennox "bumped" into her in a coffee shop she regularly went to. They started a conversation that had led to a date. It wasn't until a week later, breaking a moment of passion, that she'd confided in him how she earned her money. He'd pretended to be shocked.

It took him an additional week to broach the subject of Commissioner Harold Thomas. He pretended that he'd seen them together going into a hotel; in reality he'd followed Thomas. Lennox asked her how she knew the Commissioner. Then he'd gone on to explain what the Commissioner was really up to, how he knew, and even what he did for a living, including how he used to work for William Rothstein. Surprisingly, she'd taken the new information in her stride.

"I didn't believe you at first, about Harry, I mean. I thought you were full of shit."

"I would too, don't worry about it. It's a bit far-fetched."

"But when I overheard him on the phone, I knew I had to pick sides. I'm with you all the way, whatever it takes to get these bastards banged up. They can't get away with this."

"You know there's no guarantee they'll get banged up, even if we get proof. They're senior policemen, blue bloods. Their rich and powerful friends will probably brush it all under the carpet."

Amelie looked confused. "So, why are we doing this?"

"Because," he kissed her gently, "we've got to try. Barkley and the guys are on board; there's nothing we can't do. And with your help, I'm sure we'll get the proof we need to give to the press, blow their whole world up."

"Okay then." Amelie kissed him back. "We're agreed."

Amelie stood, held both his hands and pulled him up. She walked backwards, pulling him through the lounge. She turned and walked ahead of him, holding one hand until they were through the hallway and in the bedroom.

14

———

"I'm so sorry for your loss, Mr and Mrs Bentley, I really am," Terrence said, his eyes meeting the husband's. "We're going to do everything we can to get the person responsible, okay? What will really help, is to find out where your son was on Monday night. Do you happen to know?"

He watched Mr Bentley shake his head.

Mrs Bentley was too busy crying to answer Terrence's questions.

First thing, at nine, he went with them to identify Ryan Bentley's body. The eye and stab wounds, while still visible, had been cleaned by Aldwyn Bishop. The curtain was pulled back and Mrs Bentley broke down. Mr Bentley looked down at the hotel room carpet, tears rolling down his cheeks. Terrence didn't want to interview them at the station, so he joined them in their room.

"We keep in regular contact, but with the pub..." Mr Bentley let the sentence trail off.

"I understand. Life gets in the way. Do you know many of his friends? Would he have been out with them, do you think?"

Terrence had his notepad out ready on the table, his pen poised. He hated harassing grieving relatives of lost loved ones.

It was a necessary part of police work, unfortunately. He could see Mr Bentley was fighting to keep from sobbing, his voice strained when he spoke. It was entirely understandable.

Terrence observed the couple, Mr Bentley was a short round man. He looked like he belonged in a pub, in front of the bar, not behind it. He had a big round belly that hung over his trousers.

Mrs Bentley, on the other hand, was trim. She had brown curly hair, was relatively attractive, in a white housewife way, not that she was his type. Terrence's wife was tall and athletic, black and beautiful, vibrant and witty. Terrence was a lucky man.

"He has lots of friends." Mr Bentley paused. "Why would someone want–"

"I don't know." Terrence shook his head. "We're doing all we can. But those names – your son's friends – will really help us."

Terrence watched his interviewees.

Mr Bentley wiped his right cheek, while Mrs Bentley had her face buried in his shoulder, sobbing quietly. Terrence really hated this part of his job. Maybe he should change from homicide to robbery? He couldn't do that; he loved his job too much.

"Sure. If you think it will help." Mr Bentley dug into his jeans pocket and pulled out his mobile. "I've got Ioan's number on my phone. If he was out with anyone, it will be Ioan. Sorry, I don't have anyone else's numbers."

"That's brilliant, thank you." Terrence took the phone from Mr Bentley. He felt better having a tangible lead to work on. "I know this is hard, and believe me, I don't enjoy asking these questions, but I have to ask, is there anyone you can think of who might harbour a grudge against Ryan? Is there anyone like that, you can think of?"

"No. Everyone loved Ryan. He was the life and soul. Just ask his friends!"

Terrence watched as Mr Bentley's lip quivered; he was close

to meltdown. He'd been strong enough to make it this far. "It's okay, I have enough to be getting on with. Again, I'm so sorry for your loss."

Standing up, he thanked them for their time. He walked to the door.

"Julia Sandall." Mrs Bentley's voice carried a harsh tone. "That lying bitch could have murdered our boy. Why don't you go ask her if she did it?"

He turned back to them. "The rape case?"

"Statutory rape, Detective Johnson, and it was consensual; Ryan would never rape a woman," Mr Bentley replied. "That girl lied to the judge, the jury. She lied about my boy."

Terrence nodded. He could understand why they might suspect Julia Sandall for their son's murder. "We're way ahead of you on this. My partner interviewed Julia and her parents last night. She was in bed early, nursing her sick baby at the time and her parents can vouch for her. We've eliminated her from our enquiries."

It took Terrence half an hour to drive back to the station, where he found Nasreen hard at work on her computer. He took his jacket off and hung it on the back of his chair.

"How did you get on with the Bentleys?"

"Good, actually. I managed to get a phone number of Bentley's best mate. We might finally be able to find out where he was on Monday night. Give me a sec, I'm going to call him now."

Picking up the receiver from his desk phone, Terrence dialled nine and then the phone number Mr Bentley gave him. He waited for a reply. After four rings, it went through to voicemail. "Shit!" He waited for the message to finish. "Yeah, hi, Ioan, this is Detective Sergeant Terrence Johnson, calling regarding

Ryan Bentley. I was given your number by Ryan's dad. I need to ask you a few questions about Ryan's whereabouts on Monday night. Please could you give me a call, on," he said, reeling off his mobile number, before hanging up.

15

Amelie Desmarais picked up Lennox's plate and stacked it on top of hers. She'd just made them both a full English breakfast, complete with hash browns and fried tomatoes. While she managed most of it, she left half a tomato and half a sausage.

"I'm going to finish off in the other room." Lennox followed her into the kitchen.

At the sink, she felt his arms wrap around her waist. "Don't, I feel fat," she jokingly grumbled, accepting his strong hug.

"Don't be silly. There's hardly anything to you. We're going to have to fatten you up if anything, girl."

She turned to him and smiled. "Over my dead body. You wouldn't want a fat girlfriend, would you?" She realised she'd just said "girlfriend" for the first time, silently cursing to herself. It was folly to presume that Lennox wanted her as his girlfriend, what with her occupation as a masseuse and fuck partner to anyone who could afford her high prices. She felt so stupid.

"Maybe a bit fatter." He winked.

She breathed a sigh of relief – he hadn't been funny with her. Lennox seemed fine with it. It was a subject they'd not

58

broached; they'd only been seeing each other less than a month, so it would take time. She'd never felt this way before about a guy though, so comfortable she could talk to him about anything.

The past three and a half weeks had been wonderful. Bumping into Lennox, even if he had planned it, was the best thing that had happened to her in years. It had been a roller coaster, to say the least, but she really liked him. Finding out his past had been a shock; she'd had to confess hers too. Not many guys would date a whore, and that's what she was; she couldn't dress it up any other way – she sold her body for money. It wasn't like she was ashamed of it, Amelie earned enough money to mortgage her luxury riverside apartment.

"I'll be in the other room, if you need me."

She watched him walk away in only his underpants, which were tight. She wolf-whistled at him and laughed when he shook his hips. He had a fantastic body; she really enjoyed him.

Amelie washed the dishes. The floor was cold. Stood in only a long white T-shirt, she found her slippers and put them on. Going back to the washing-up, she thought about her life and how she'd ended up here.

Growing up in a small northern town had been tough. She was the only mixed-race student at her primary and secondary school, so she'd always felt like an outsider. It was funny how boys at school didn't seem to notice the colour of her skin, only the girls. The girls she'd met through school were nasty; they'd bullied her relentlessly throughout primary and part of secondary, until one day when she was twelve years old.

Amelie stacked the plates in the drainer vertically and emptied the sink. She cleaned the kitchen and wiped the surfaces until satisfied she could come in and cook next time.

Walking through to the dining room – where Lennox was playing with the letters – she looked down at the piece of paper, the mixed newspaper letters spelt "Dirty pigs". He was busy gluing another letter. "Are you having fun?" Her tone was playful. She rubbed his hair, then kissed his head.

"I will later, when I give this to him."

Leaving him to it, she walked through to her bedroom and took off her T-shirt. She looked in the full-length mirror and tilted her head slightly, pulling her tits up with her hands.

Her mobile phone rang and vibrated on her bed. Picking it up, she noted it was Harold Thomas. "Harry. I wasn't expecting a call. Is everything all right?"

"Everything's fine, Ams. I was wondering if you're available Friday night?"

She turned and looked out of her window, at the river below and all the activity down there. "I don't know, I'll have to check. Hold on." Dropping the phone on her bed, Amelie walked through to the dining room. "Harry's on the phone. He wants to see me on Friday. Is that okay with you? Did we have anything planned?"

"Go for it. You might get a chance to look through his laptop."

"That's what I thought. I'll take a USB stick with me, in case I get lucky."

Having checked with Lennox, she walked back into the bedroom and picked up the phone. "I've checked, and it appears I'm free. Where will I find you? *The Albatross*?"

"I'll send a car for you. See you at eight on Friday then."

Amelie looked at the phone for a second. It was possible she might get the chance to look through his laptop. He always had it with him on board *The Albatross*. She had only managed to download one page so far. Fortunately for Lennox and his friends, it had been valuable information: a chart showing the names of the dealers and which areas they were supporting, six names in total. Lennox was very grateful when he saw it.

16

Detective Inspector Gupta replaced the receiver on his desk phone. "A friend of Ryan Bentley's just came forward. She's in interview room three."

"Finally!" Terrence got up from his chair.

Nasreen stood, as Terrence's phone rang. She waited while he answered it. When he said hello to Ioan, she knew it was Bentley's friend he'd left a message for, so he would be a while interviewing him. She mouthed that she would be in interview room three, to which he nodded his understanding, still talking to Ioan.

As the lift doors closed, Nasreen waited in silence with her new boss. It was awkward, so she asked, "How long have you known Aldwyn Bishop, sir?"

"Years. Aldwyn and I go way back. I was his best man at his civil ceremony. His partner wanted his best friend, so they flipped and Aldwyn won the toss."

"He's gay?" She hadn't seen that coming. There was no way she would have known that from what she'd already seen. Bishop wasn't camp at all. There was nothing outwardly gay about him, not that there was anything wrong with him being gay. Was she disappointed? She tried to shake that question away.

"As they come. He's been happily married now for, eight years, it must be. Wow! That's gone quick."

The lift doors opened, and Gupta let her out first.

Walking along the corridor, side by side, Nasreen asked, "So, what's his deal? Why is he visiting crime scenes, if he's a forensic pathologist? Shouldn't he be in a hospital or coroner's office?"

"He's so much more than a pathologist. He's up to his armpits in qualifications. He's a registered member of the GMC; he's studied medicine for five years; has a degree in psychology and another in criminology and criminal justice studies. And that's only scratching the surface. He worked over in the States for eight years as a criminal profiler. He only came back to the UK last year because Tom got a job here. We're lucky to have him. He got married a week before they left for the States; he could still be there now. He'd probably have ended up as the Director of the FBI."

"Wow! That's quite the resume he has."

They reached interview room three. "After you," she said to Gupta, who opened the door and walked in.

To say Ryan's friend was a punk was an understatement. Nasreen looked at the pierced and tattoo-covered girl sat behind the table – she had three earrings in each ear, a nose ring and lip ring. The girl probably had other areas pierced too, not that Nasreen wanted to find out. Tattoos covered her arms – sleeves they were called. She even had tattoos on her neck. Her hair was short and spiky, brown.

When she sat down next to Gupta, Nasreen noticed how pretty the girl was, even after she'd been crying. She had a dainty little button nose, big brown eyes and a delicate little mouth. When standing, she couldn't be more than five foot three. Dressed casually in a jumper and jeans, her clothing belied her love of punk.

Nasreen waited for Gupta to ask if it was okay to record the interview. When the girl nodded, Nasreen hit record on the tape recorder, an outdated piece of equipment.

Gupta made the introductions. "Hi! I'm Detective Inspector Arjun Gupta and this is my colleague, Detective Constable Nasreen Maqsood. I'm so sorry, but I didn't get your name from reception. Please forgive me."

"I'm Poppy Hayward," replied the girl, with her hands resting on the table. "I only found out about Ryan this morning. I can't believe he's gone."

Nasreen put her hand out and held Poppy's. "I'm so sorry for your loss," she said, her voice genuine and kind. "I promise, we're going to do everything we can to catch the person responsible for killing Ryan."

"Chloe," Poppy replied.

"Sorry, who?" Gupta took out his notepad and pen.

"We met this girl at Johanna's Bar on Monday night. Ryan saw her standing alone at the bar and went over to talk to her. He spoke to her for about half an hour and brought her over to join us. She said her name was Chloe and that she was with a group of mates, but I never saw her talk to anyone."

"Chloe." Gupta wrote it down.

"Please, Poppy, carry on," Nasreen said. "What can you tell us about this Chloe?"

"Ryan thought she was lovely; he spent most of the night talking to her and dancing with her. It was school disco night in Johanna's, so me and my girlfriend, Emily, were dressed up in our old school uniforms for a laugh. Chloe was dressed up in going out on the town gear, you know. Ryan was all over her; he was touching and kissing her all night, ignoring the rest of us. He was like that, though, when he met girls. Me and Emily hated Chloe on sight – there was something off about her. She was so false."

"And did Ryan leave with Chloe after the bar closed?"

"Hell yeah, he thought all his Christmases and birthdays came at once, he was so excited. I can't believe she killed him." She sniffed, a tear rolling down her cheek.

"Think back, what did she look like?" Nasreen needed a picture in her head.

"She was really pretty, with long blonde hair. She was wearing a red dress, the kind you only wear if you're going out clubbing, not to a little bar on a Monday night. That's why me and Emily hated her; she was trying too hard to pull, not that she had to try hard. Every bloke in the bar was watching her."

"Did she have any identifying marks or features?"

"She had a tattoo. I could only see the top of it. It looked like wings from a bird of some sort. Sorry! Most of it was covered by her dress."

"You're doing great, Poppy." Nasreen was still holding her hand. "What sort of time did Ryan and Chloe leave Johanna's?"

"We all left when it closed at one, I think; I was quite trashed by the time it closed, so I can't be sure. I think it was about one."

"And how did they get home? Did they walk, did they get a taxi?"

"They got a taxi. I can remember that because I remember moaning to Emily that Ryan could've offered to give us a lift. We only live around the corner from him, but he wanted to get a taxi by himself. They were snogging in the back when they left us outside Johanna's."

"Who else was with you that night we can talk to?" Gupta asked.

"Emily, Ioan and Nathan. I can give you their phone numbers if you'd like? We all found out about Ryan at the same time. Ryan's dad phoned Ioan when we were all out last night.

We're all still in total shock. I thought I'd come in and tell you what I know."

"Thank you so much, Poppy," Nasreen said. "You've been a big help."

"Just promise me something." Poppy's piercing eyes bored into Nasreen's. "You catch this fucking bitch."

Nasreen watched as Poppy's face crumpled – her head bowed, and her shoulders went up and down as sobs escaped her. She held Poppy's hand again, adding, "We will. You have my word on that." Needing to verify a few more questions, Nasreen continued questioning Poppy for another five minutes, while Gupta remained passive, scribbling everything down.

Having shown Poppy through the reception access door, Nasreen went back up to the office via the lift. In the office, she found Terrence ending his conversation with Bentley's best friend, Ioan. Gupta waited for Terrence to hang up the phone, and sat facing him on his swivel chair.

"How did it go?" Gupta barely gave Terrence the chance to think.

"We need to view the CCTV footage at Johanna's Bar," Terrence replied. "Ioan said Ryan left with a woman called Chloe, long blonde hair, body to die for. Red dress. Apparently Bentley left with her in a taxi at about one in the morning. What did you get?"

"The same," Gupta replied.

Nasreen glanced at the phone number on her screen and dialled. It was only ten in the morning, so the chances of anyone answering in the bar were slim. It didn't open in the daytime, so they might have to wait until the afternoon to be able to gain access to the popular night spot.

"Oh, hi! Sorry. I wasn't expecting anyone to answer this early." She was so embarrassed, she swivelled around so she couldn't see Terrence or Inspector Gupta. Finally, she regained her composure and very elegantly explained the reason for her call.

Hearing Terrence and Gupta talking in the background, the voice identified himself as the owner, and sounded genuinely upset to learn of Ryan's murder. The owner told her they could come over and take a look at the CCTV footage at their earliest convenience; the man said he would be there all morning. Thanking him first, she hung up.

"Someone was in?" Terrence was interested.

"We can go over there whenever." She stood. "Let's go."

"Can I help you with anything this morning?"

Cara looked over the hoodie she had up in front of her, at the cute, red-headed shop assistant. "Not right now, thanks. I'll come get you if I need any help."

The assistant smiled and stood in front of her for an awkward length of time, without saying anything, just smiling. Cara felt like asking her if she had a problem; instead, she turned the hoodie around, so that the front was facing the girl. She held it over her chest. "What do you think?"

"Cute but Deadly," the girl said, reading the writing on the hoody out loud. "I love that one. If you like that, check this one out."

Waiting while the sales assistant went through the rack until she found a hoodie, Cara watched as the redhead picked it up and showed it to her. In the centre was Jack Skellington's head, and around it were the words "Your Nightmare". Cara loved it on sight. "That's awesome!" The girl handed it to her, and she added it to her collection of five jumpers, two hoodies and two pairs of jeans.

"Looks like you're buying the shop." The girl took some of the clothing off her hands. "Are you looking for anything else?"

Cara followed the girl to the till counter. "Yeah, I need some boots."

"You've come to the right place." The girl stacked Cara's purchases by the till.

No one was this helpful, ever, thought Cara, knowing it was more than the girl just wanting to help her choose clothes. It was all in the smile and prolonged staring. Since arriving in the shop, she'd felt the girl's gaze. The girl fancied her. "Oh yeah? What have you got?"

The clerk promptly walked around from behind the counter and showed her to the far end of the shop, where there were at least fifty different boots to choose from, all on display on racking on the wall. Cara felt stupid. "I can't believe I missed them."

"What style are you looking for?"

"I'll know it when I see it." Looking through each of the boots on display, she found the ones she was looking for. "Found them," she said, taking the boot down from the shelf. "Can I try the other one too?"

Coming back a couple of minutes later with the left boot, the clerk waited with Cara while she tried them both on. "What do you think?" She turned around in front of the shop assistant. "Sexy, or what?"

"I think they're wonderful," the girl mused, like she wasn't quite there.

Cara sensed the tone immediately. The shop girl was daydreaming about her. "Great! I'll take them." She felt like clicking her fingers, snapping her out of it.

As she walked back through the shop behind the sales assistant, something caught her eye. Cara stopped and took a black crop top from the rack. She held it up and smiled. It had a picture of an eagle swooping down to catch its prey, just like her tattoo. On the back of the top, the words "Bird of Prey" were written in red. It was like it was meant to be! Cara fell in love with it on sight and added it to her collection of clothes.

"Great choice. I bought that the other day."

Cara smiled. She really didn't need to know that. Delving into her bag, she felt the knife handle, went deeper and pulled out her purse. Not wanting to use plastic, she had her cash ready, aware of the police being able to track her through digital transactions. "So, how much is this little lot going to set me back?"

Waiting while the assistant folded and bagged everything, she finally got the answer and handed over enough cash. She took the change from the sales assistant and smiled.

"Thanks for shopping at Grind Store." With her hand covering the side of her mouth, she whispered, "They make us say that."

"No, thank *you* for helping me," Cara replied, before she turned and walked away.

"Those boots really suit you," added the girl, a little too late.

Cara felt her desperation.

Seeing an opening, instead of walking out of the shop, Cara turned to the girl. "Actually, you might be able to help me." She returned to the counter with all her bags. The girl looked interested, eager even. "I'm new in town, I've literally just driven here this morning. I have no idea where anything is, could you recommend any cool pubs or clubs?"

"How about I show you?" The girl's eyes were wide, begging.

"Excuse me?" Cara had her wrapped around her little finger. "Oh no, I couldn't possibly impose on you." And now she was reeling her in.

"Rubbish. I can show you around. Me and my mates are

going to a couple of pubs and on to a club later, if you fancy joining us? It's no bother, really."

Looking at the girl closer, she kind of reminded Cara of Lucy. She had the same shaped face, nice lips. Her body was a similar shape to Lucy's too. "If you're sure? I really don't want to put you out..." She let her sentence trail.

The girl held her hand out. "Imelda."

"Imelda. I love that name. Hi! I'm Chloe."

Cara shook hands with Imelda and smiled. "So, shall I meet you here when you finish? There's so many decent shops in town, it'll take me all day to get around them."

"That'd be good. I finish here at six. Are you here for long?"

"I'm moving here in a couple of months, so I'm just down to look at flats for a few days." If this poor girl knew the truth, she would run off screaming.

"Where are you staying?"

"I haven't found anywhere yet. I'm going to find a B&B later on, after I've shopped some more."

"No need. I've got a spare bedroom."

The way Imelda threw that at her oozed of desperation. It was said so quick it sounded rushed, with no thought behind it. She pretended to be embarrassed. "Oh, erm, well, if you're sure it's okay with you? Thank you so much. You've definitely gone above and beyond."

"What are friends for, yeah? It's not like you're an axe murderer or anything, is it?" Imelda laughed.

"Oh no." Cara laughed hysterically on the inside. "I'm definitely not an *axe* murderer." Could this morning get any weirder?

18

———

"Please, come in, detectives." The owner of Johanna's Bar held the fire door open.

Nasreen stepped in first, followed closely by Terrence. She'd never seen inside Johanna's before, not that she had the need to. Too old for all this partying nonsense, plus she didn't drink or take drugs. And her sobriety wasn't forced on her by her religion; if she wanted to drink or use drugs she would. She was more interested in keeping fit and healthy. Nasreen tried to get some exercise every day, even if she failed some days.

The owner introduced himself as Owen Sanders. Nasreen figured him for late thirties perhaps? She wasn't great at guessing ages. He was tall with short dark hair, which was greying slightly on the sides, just above his ears. He was a good-looking man. She shook his hand and introduced herself, after Terrence said who he was.

Johanna's Bar was long. It stretched back over a hundred metres and was half as wide. The bar itself ran almost the length of the room, with only a small chill-out room preventing it being the entire length. Near the front doors were stairs leading up to the public toilets, the office and staff kitchen area. Halfway along the room, opposite the bar was a raised platform, its dance floor. It was decorated in browns and creams, with enough lighting to keep the blindest of moths happy.

"Nice place you've got here." Terrence looked all around.

"Thanks, we like it. So, I can assume you've never been here before?"

"Who, me? Nah, this scene isn't for me," Terrence replied. "I'm too old for all this."

"Oh shut up, Terrence," Nasreen joked. "I've seen your moves – put everyone to shame, you do." She looked around and noticed cameras all around the bar.

The owner led them upstairs and into a small office.

"How many cameras have you got here, in total? I saw a few downstairs."

"Only two, I'm afraid. Most are for show. One's behind the bar looking towards the dance floor and the other is above the DJ booth looking towards the bar. And I have to be honest with you here, our CCTV unit is quite old. I haven't had the chance of upgrading the system, so I apologise now for the grainy footage. I hope it helps, I really do. I still can't believe he's dead."

"It must be a shock for you. If you want to help us catch this person, you'll show us footage from Monday night, after eight in the evening all the way through to one in the morning. We want to see what this girl looks like."

"The one in the red dress, you mean?"

"That'll be her. I've just spoken to one of Ryan's friends about her. He was here on Monday too."

"What do you remember about her, Mr Sanders?" Nasreen asked.

She watched Sanders playing around with video tapes. He wasn't kidding when he said the CCTV unit was out of date. They were still using video cassettes, like in the old days. She watched him insert the cassette into the top slot of a double-stacked VCR and press rewind. This brought back memories for her; she could just about recall video cassette recorders.

"I can remember enough." Sanders turned to face her. "She stood out, that's why I remember her."

"How do you mean she stood out?" Terrence was keen to understand.

"I don't want to sound like some scumbag club owner, or anything, but she was a good-looking girl. I mean, we get great looking girls in here every night of the week, especially on Mondays with the school discos, but this girl was something else. I was on security, stood by the bar, helping the team assess potential problems, you know what I mean. I saw her come in, and she grabbed my attention immediately. Like I said, we get great-looking girls from uni here all the time; this one was off the charts though."

"Because she was wearing that red dress?" Nasreen asked.

"That dress! Man, she looked amazing in it. And it wasn't only my attention she caught; she could've had her pick of the blokes in that night. All these fellas were checking her out when she came in."

Nasreen stood out of the way, as Sanders moved forwards and pressed play on the VCR. She waited while the owner fast forwarded the video to eight o'clock. The camera was at the back of the bar, looking down at the bar staff and any customers stood in front, waiting to be served. The video showed a blonde-haired woman in a red dress waiting. Nasreen couldn't see any facial features because of the grainy footage; they wouldn't be able to enhance it either. Even with grainy footage, though, Nasreen could tell how pretty the girl, Chloe, was, just by the shape of her face.

She watched as Ryan Bentley approached Chloe at the bar. They were talking and making each other laugh. At the back of the bar, near the dance floor, she could just about see two girls watching Ryan and Chloe. When she looked closer, she could make out Poppy Hayward, so the other girl must have been Emily. Even from a distance on blotchy film, Nasreen could see the daggers Poppy and Emily were giving Chloe. Behind Poppy and Emily, she could see two fellas: Ioan and Nathan, she surmised.

"Okay, can you take us further forward, please, Mr Sanders," Terrence asked. "We'll be here all night, otherwise."

When Sanders pressed play again, it said 22:15 on the bottom of the screen. Nasreen could see Bentley and Chloe further back, near the dance floor. They were dancing, if you could call it that. Chloe looked like she was enjoying herself; she kept moving her head in to speak to Bentley, who seemed to find her very funny. For a psychopath, this Chloe was socially adept. "Look at her working the boys?"

"And the daggers the girls are giving her," Terrence replied.

"Definitely a sociopath."

"Psychopath, sociopath, what's the difference?" asked the owner.

"Sociopaths blend in more," Terrence replied. "People like them; they know what to say and when to get what they want. Psychopaths generally don't fit in."

"Which is why sociopaths are harder to spot." Nasreen made eye contact with the owner. "And why it's going to be difficult to catch this Chloe girl. She's playing the lads, and doesn't seem to care about the girls staring at her."

"She doesn't see them as a threat," Terrence said. "Look at her; she towers over the girls. She must be a good five-ten? My money would be on Chloe."

After Sanders had fast forwarded again, it was gone midnight. Bentley and Chloe were kissing in the centre of the bar, away from the dance floor. Nasreen couldn't see Poppy or Emily, or Ioan, or Nathan. In fact, the bar was fairly quiet. "Do you have any cameras outside the bar, Mr Sanders? Apparently, they left in a taxi."

"I'm afraid not. But the council have a camera a bit further down the road. It might have been facing this way at the time, you never know."

"You're right," Terrence replied, "we'll get on to that."

Nasreen had seen enough. This Chloe was going to be hard to apprehend, she could tell. The gorgeous blonde was socially adept and a total sociopath. It wasn't a good combination. It looked like she could take any man home with her – the list of potential victims was vast. This girl could be anywhere in the country right now; she could be chatting to her next victim at this very second. "What about fingerprinting?"

"Fingerprinting where?"

Nasreen looked at her supervisor. "I was thinking the toilets? We know she went to the loo while she was here."

"It's a nice idea, but so many more people have been through those loos since Monday night – we'd be lucky to get a print from someone here *last* night. And I'm not saying we've got the best cleaners in the world, or anything, but this place does get cleaned every morning. Her prints will have been wiped away by now, surely?"

The owner was right. It was a stupid suggestion. The thing was, she didn't know where they could go from here? They couldn't use facial recognition software with the footage they had. If the council's CCTV unit caught Chloe outside the bar, the quality might be better, so that was a possibility. They were still waiting for the crime scene analysis to come back. If that came up empty, they might have to wait for Chloe to strike again.

19

"I wasn't expecting that." Terrence clicked on an email. Since returning to the office from Johanna's Bar, he had phoned the council that owned the CCTV camera outside the bar and spoke to an administrator there. The woman told him that she would do her best to email him the requested footage, but that it may take some time. He'd explained the importance of the situation. Only fifteen minutes later, the email arrived, with an attachment.

"Is it here already?" Nasreen wheeled her chair by the side of him.

"Yep, here it is." He clicked on the attachment and opened it.

Terrence called Gupta over, who joined them at his desk and stood behind him. On his monitor, clear footage appeared. Excitement crept in as he fast forwarded the footage to 00:45. The camera was a fair distance up the road from Johanna's, but he watched as party goers left the bar. He didn't bother fast forwarding, so he sat there watching the comings and goings.

"There's Bentley." Nasreen pointed him out on the screen.

"That must be Ioan and Nathan." They watched the two lads join their friend.

"Can we zoom in on this?" Gupta asked from behind him.

"I don't think so. I think we'll need to do that from the council's computer."

"That's a shame. Maybe we can take a still shot and blow it up."

"Maybe." Terrence replied absent-mindedly. "Wait, there she is!" With adrenaline spiking, he watched as Chloe emerged, walked up to Bentley, then kissed him. So far, Chloe's face had only been in profile.

"Come on, turn," Nasreen said.

Terrence realised he wasn't the only one willing her to show her face. If they could get a good picture of her, even if it needed to be blown up, the facial recognition software would do the rest. They could have her identity in a matter of hours. Once they had that, they could probe her life – it was through fishing in her past that they were more likely to apprehend her.

He sat back in his chair, frustrated, when Chloe turned and faced the other way. She clearly knew the camera was there; she'd probably spotted it on the way to the bar. "Bitch!" Bentley had his arms around Chloe, his back to the camera, with her in front of him, completely out of the footage. It was getting worse.

The taxi pulled up and Bentley opened the door for Chloe. In profile, she stepped inside. Bentley followed her in and closed the door. Ten seconds later, the car drove away. "That's that then." He stabbed on pause.

"Don't be so hasty, Terrence," Gupta said.

"Sir? We can't get anything from this." Terrence turned to his boss.

"I've seen the software work from a profile picture before. It doesn't get a hit very often, but it has been known to work. Do you mind going down to the council office and seeing if you can zoom in on her? Get a good profile picture of Chloe and we'll see what the software can do with it. You never know, we might get lucky."

Terrence stood and nodded. "On my way now." He looked down at the time on his computer: 15:33. He only had an hour to get down there, tops. He had to get a move on.

"Sir, should I look for other cameras in the area? She won't have hidden herself from all of them." Nasreen wheeled her chair back to her desk while sat in it.

"Good idea," Gupta replied. "I'll come with you."

Terrence hated dealing with councils – everything was a pain in the arse to the administrators there, a real chore. He sighed audibly and put his jacket on, followed by his thick coat. It was still cold out, but he took delight in the fact the worst of the winter was over. He was looking forward to the summer.

20

"Before we go in, I have to warn you, it's not much." Imelda turned her key in the door. "But it's home. I really hope you like it."

Cara waited for Imelda to open the door. And when she stepped inside, she could see what her new friend meant. She was in a bedsit. It was a bedroom and kitchen, nothing else. It was worse than her shithole flat, minus all the crap on the floor. There were no pizza boxes, bottles of booze or cans of lager. It was pretty tidy. She looked up and noticed the damp in the corners of the room – dark stains creeping over the ceiling. She could smell it too.

"Like I said, it's not much, but it's all I can afford on my salary."

Carrying her handbag, and her carrier bags, Cara turned and told her she liked it, as genuinely as she could. Imelda liked to keep a clean and tidy place. "Is there somewhere I can wash up?"

She placed her shopping bags on the bed and kept her handbag on her shoulder. Imelda had told her she had a spare room. It didn't matter to her; she knew what Imelda wanted to do, so it was easier this way.

Imelda led her out of the room, down a corridor to the communal bathroom at the end of the hall. She thanked her new friend and closed the door, placing her bag on the windowsill above the sink. Feeling tired, she splashed water on her face and looked at her reflection in a small mirror on the windowsill.

What she really needed was somewhere to hole up for a couple of days. This shitty bedsit was perfect. What was her next course of action? Keeping an eye on police activity was vital, and she'd spotted a flat-screen TV on Imelda's wall. In spite of how rank the room was, it was perfect for her needs.

Cara left the bathroom, walked back to Imelda's room and closed the door. Imelda stood in the kitchen preparing them drinks. Accepting a glass of Prosecco, Cara chinked glasses with her host, smiled and took a sip. "Cheers!"

"I'm so sorry I said I had a spare bedroom. It was all I could think of to get you to stay. You can have the bed, and I'll take the fold up sofa, if you'd like?"

Cara looked at the double bed. Chinking glasses again, she replied, "The bed looks big enough for both of us," and kissed Imelda's lips, softly, slowly.

Imelda was a good, strong kisser.

There was a knock on the door.

Breaking their kiss, she opened her eyes to find Imelda's still closed. "Are you expecting someone?" Her host was becoming more attractive by the minute. Imelda brought back fond memories of Lucy.

Her host opened her eyes and looked up at the clock on the wall. "Damn! They're early – I said seven." She walked to the door. "You're going to love my friends – they're a great bunch, really."

Waiting for her friends to enter, Cara glared at the thought of having to be sociable, polite. "Do you mind if I put the news on?" She picked up the remote control from the duvet.

21

Lennox took out the A4 piece of paper with the message glued on it from his duffle bag down by his feet and folded it into an aeroplane. A fully loaded Uzi rested on his lap. Earlier that afternoon he had personally loaded thirty-two bullets into each magazine of the four Uzis in the car.

"Is that him?" Barkley sat in the driver's seat.

Turning in his seat, Lennox looked at the headlights coming towards them through the rear windscreen. As the car passed them, he just made out the driver. It was him. "Yeah, it's time. Masks." He pulled the mask over his face.

Lennox watched as Barkley, who was driving, pulled his mask down.

Bembe, in the front passenger seat did the same, followed closely by Khenan, who sat behind Barkley. Up ahead, Lennox watched as the target's car pulled up outside his house.

There was a car already in the driveway. "Windows down."

All four automatically opened at the same time.

He'd waited for a month for some payback. Tonight was just the beginning of what he knew would be a bloody war. He'd chosen this target well. He was about to declare war on the police, and the dealers they'd chosen to supply the country, pushing out all others.

His biggest goal for tonight was to wake the assistant commissioner up, let Franks know he was alive and out to cause chaos for the project.

In the last month, he'd followed Franks all over; he knew who he'd met with, where they'd met. He couldn't know what Franks had spoken to any of his colleagues about but judging by the clandestine nature of some of the meetings, it was likely to be about the project.

Lennox had photos of Franks meeting with notorious drug dealers, including James Foster and Zack Astor. Lennox really needed rock-solid proof of the project's existence. So far, all he had was photographic evidence of the commissioner meeting with people; it wasn't enough. He needed Amelie to come through with evidence he could use, real evidence.

As Barkley pulled the car out from the lay-by, Lennox hoisted himself up and out of his window. He sat on the window frame, his upper body out of the car. He rested the Uzi on the car roof with one hand and held the paper aeroplane with the other. Next to him, Bembe leaned on the roof, his Uzi out, ready.

Up ahead, Lennox saw the familiar figure open his car door. He had chosen his first target carefully – he'd seen him meet with Franks in parks and underground car parks. The target was also the same man who'd met him with Franks, when Franks had asked him to kill Rothstein. Franks was a high-ranking police officer, enough to make a big splash on the news and in the national rags – Lennox wanted publicity.

As they got closer to the target, Lennox felt the rush of adrenaline he'd come to expect. More alert than usual, he felt a pang of excitement.

Up ahead, the target stepped out of his car. He watched, only metres away, as the target closed his car door and pressed a button on his key ring. Lennox heard the bleep of the car locking. The target hadn't turned, hadn't seen him coming.

The car slowed to a stop.

Lennox watched as the target started walking up his driveway towards the front door to his detached house. The area they were in was an affluent suburb, filled with detached four, five and six bedroomed houses. The target had obviously done well for himself.

It was time.

Lennox had his finger on the trigger. "Hey, Adams!" He watched as Adams turned his head, followed by his whole body. He had a jacket in one hand and a briefcase in the other. Adams was curious; he hadn't seen the guns yet.

When Lennox saw the fear suddenly enter Adams' eyes, he pulled the trigger. His companions pulled their triggers a split second after him. It sounded like firecrackers going off, as the Uzis – all four of them – spat the contents of their magazines at Adams' chest and head.

Lennox watched as bullet after bullet hit the senior police officer.

There was nothing the bent cop could do; his body took hit after hit, his face taking at least five shots; but his chest taking the majority of the firepower.

Lennox saw Adams' body slump in a bloody mess on his driveway.

It only took five seconds for the Uzis to stop firing.

In total, a hundred and twenty-eight bullets were fired in five seconds, the shell casings littering the concrete around the car. Fortunately, they'd been close enough for the Uzis to be relatively accurate. A few stray bullets had hit the garage door and blown out Adam's car's rear window. "Let's go!" He threw the paper aeroplane towards Adams' body.

Lennox clambered back inside the car, as all four windows

wound back up automatically. The empty Uzis were hot and smoky. He could smell cordite, sulphur and oil. It was a smell he remembered well from back in Jamaica. Lennox had handled four drive-bys in his day, but he had to admit, this was his most gratifying.

22

Cara waited while Imelda opened the door to her bedsit, feeling the effects of the alcohol. To her surprise, she'd enjoyed herself, chatting to her host's friends, all of whom were women.

It was good to have a girls' night out, without men ogling her. That wasn't to say guys on tables nearby weren't staring; they were, however she'd ignored them, and settled back, chatting away to her new "friends".

She had to use that term loosely; they weren't her friends at all. If they knew who she really was, they would scream and run to the cops.

"Here we are. Home sweet home."

Déjà vu! Cara had to do a double take. Imelda mirrored Hayden, to the letter; he'd said those exact words when he'd let her into his place.

She stepped in and dropped her bag on the bed. "Shall we have another glass of Prosecco?" Walking through to the kitchenette, she opened the refrigerator and pulled out the leftover bubbly.

There was a calmness in her that she hadn't felt since before Lucy left her, back when they were in love.

Imelda made her feel calm, serene. Since meeting her, Cara hadn't felt the blade calling her, not once. Even when a couple of guys made lewd comments about her kissing her host outside the bar earlier, she'd shrugged it off. Guys were such pigs!

"What do you want to drink to?" Imelda took the glass she offered.

"To us. Long may it continue." She smiled.

"Long may it continue." Imelda took a sip and smiled sweetly back at her.

The silence didn't feel awkward. Not yet, anyway. It would if Imelda found out who she was; there was no denying that.

It was lucky Cara was good at fitting in; she'd be just another psychopath otherwise. No, she was a bird of prey, a hunter. But like every hunter, she needed her downtime. And where better to hide out than here, in this crappy damp bedsit?

"We can watch a bit of TV, if you want?" Imelda walked through to the main room and sat on the sofa, in front of the flat-screen. "It's still early."

Cara couldn't remember the last time she'd sat down to watch television. There was a time, back when she was with Lucy, that she used to watch certain programmes. Lucy loved comedies, whereas Cara preferred dramas. There were lots of ways she was similar to Lucy, and big ways they were polar opposites. And it was those opposites that caused the turmoil in their relationship.

Imelda stared at her. "Are you okay? You're quiet all of a sudden."

"I'm fine." She clinked Imelda's glass. "Thank you so much for putting up with me."

Cara lay her head back on a cushion, looking into Imelda's

lovely big blue eyes. They were so similar to Lucy's it was scary. The TV wasn't getting a look in. "You have such lovely eyes, has anyone ever told you that?" She stroked Imelda's cheek.

"So do you." Imelda kissed Cara's hand.

23

Assistant Commissioner Peter Franks pulled up to a scene of chaos.

Blue flashing lights lit up this usually quiet street. There was a wide cordon around Clive Adams' home. Uniformed officers were busy keeping an interested crowd from getting inside the cordon.

He stepped outside into the cold night air and wrapped himself in his thick coat.

Walking up to the cordon, Franks lifted it and let himself under. He could see two plain clothes detectives working the crime scene.

He knew Simon Watts and Elliott O'Hara, two good, reliable, and efficient detectives.

As Franks walked up to the driveway, the extent of Adams' wounds became more apparent, the closer he came.

Looking down at Adams' body, he couldn't recognise the man's face. Bullets had fragmented his head – it was mush, pulpy mush. He had no face.

There was so much blood on the clothes that he couldn't see the colour of the fabric.

Blood trickled down the driveway. In his many years on the force, Franks had never seen anything like this. It was what he might expect to happen in the States, with their lax gun laws, not here in the UK.

He needed to get more information. "Watts, O'Hara, over here!" They quickly joined him on the driveway. "What've you got so far?"

"It looks like there were four shooters." Watts, the senior detective, commenced the debrief. "Witnesses say that the shooting lasted for a couple of seconds, five max. We've counted a hundred and twenty-odd shell casings, so it had to be multiple shooters. We've got tyre tracks leading in a northerly direction. Neighbours didn't see a car, so we don't know the make or model at this time."

"Okay, anything else?"

"We found this by the body." Watts handed him the paper aeroplane with a gloved hand.

Franks opened it up and read it: "This is what happens to DIRTY PIGS."

That confirmed it: Garvey was the only one who could know of Adams' involvement in the project. He folded the A4 piece of paper in half and then half again and slid it inside his uniform jacket. "Right, not a word of this leaves here. I'm not risking smearing Adams' name over this. You two are running point from now on, and only this case, is that understood? I want these shooters brought in quickly and cleanly. Do me a favour and get these journalists behind the cordon."

He turned. "Collins, you know better than that. Get behind the line, you know the drill."

"Have you got any comments, assistant commissioner?"

"No comments at this time. When I do, you'll be the first to know." Franks hated these parasitic hacks. He had zero respect for journalists.

He turned back and looked down at the body of his former colleague. This wouldn't go unpunished. Franks needed to get ahead of this.

DAY 4
FRIDAY, 23RD MARCH

"I don't care how busy you are," Inspector Gupta yelled into his phone. "Your guys swept my crime scene on Tuesday, it's now Friday. We've got a suspect out there, stabbing people. Get me my report today! Is that understood?"

Nasreen was glad she wasn't on the receiving end of Gupta's dressing down.

Her boss was a nightmare when he needed to be.

"No, in fact, get me your supervisor on the phone, right now."

She listened to Gupta erupt at the forensics laboratory's supervisor next. Since Wednesday, her team had failed to come up with anything new regarding "Chloe". The profile picture Terrence had brought back from the council office came up empty; either Chloe wasn't in the system, which Nasreen doubted, or the facial recognition software failed. And her excursion to find cameras near Johanna's Bar had been a total waste of time.

Gupta had sent her and Terrence over to Bentley's neighbours' houses to re-interview them, to see if they'd seen or heard anything on Tuesday morning. They'd come back to the office with nothing to report.

Her colleagues, Simon Watts and Elliott O'Hara were now in charge of DCS Adams' murder investigation. They were strung out, on a case with national media interest. Since Wednesday, reporters had been stationed outside their building day and night.

Every time she went out on an errand, she was subjected to questioning about Adams' case, and when she replied "no comment" they would go on to ask her about how the Rothstein case was coming along. She didn't know – the NCA was in charge of that investigation.

Although she'd come to dislike Adams, his family didn't deserve this, and neither did he. She knew he was bent, but he didn't deserve to be shot eighty-three times.

It was reported in the papers that on Thursday morning, the prime minister had chaired a COBRA meeting, concerning Adams' murder. They considered the brutality of his assassination to be a matter of concern for national security. The papers had speculated that the government believed it may have been carried out by terrorists. The government neither confirmed nor denied it.

At first, Nasreen had wanted to be a part of the team responsible for investigating Adams' murder. Having seen Watts' and O'Hara's stress levels, she was glad no one asked her to help.

Nasreen wanted to catch "Chloe" now, although she knew it was going to be a long drawn-out case; she could feel it.

"There's been another one." Terrence handed her a file.

Opening the file, she found a photo of a young man lying face down on what looked like kitchen lino. The second photo, of the victim lying on his back – after being turned over – showed the extent of his wounds. He had a huge gash vertically from his lower stomach, all the way up to his sternum. And a deep stab wound in his throat.

A close-up photo showed how deep it was; it severed every artery and vein in his neck. "Is that bone?" She looked through the paperwork: the body was found yesterday. "And why are we getting this now, after the fact?"

"The responding detective must've missed Gupta's flag. It happens. Flags don't appear on the PNC straight away, and they're easily overlooked. The preliminary work's been done thoroughly though. Bishop's over there now."

"How did he get the nod so quick?"

"He was called to the scene yesterday, as per his contract." Terrence sat at his desk. "When a body's found, he's often the first person to get the call."

"We need to get over there."

"The crime scene's been thoroughly dusted for prints and checked for trace. It'd be a waste of time."

Instead of arguing, Nasreen thumbed through the investigation documents. The victim's name was Hayden Oates, a twenty-nine-year-old software development manager. Looking at a photo attached to the form, he was a good-looking lad. Poor guy. Probably went to a nightclub, thought he'd got lucky, and ended the night being stabbed to death by "Chloe", or whoever she was.

There were interview documents included in the file. According to friends of the victim, he'd met "Chloe" at a nightclub called The Emporium. And Nasreen was right!

His friends had all stated that "Chloe" was a great-looking blonde girl in a black dress. Oates had apparently spent all night chatting to and kissing "Chloe" before walking back to his flat, which was just up the road from the club.

"Here it is." Terrence sat at his computer. "Let's hope we have better luck with this."

Nasreen wheeled her chair over to his desk and sat next to him, staring intently at the monitor. The file he clicked on opened up.

From the camera's angle, Nasreen could see the tops of the bar staff's heads and the dance floor in front. The file opened up at exactly the point when "Chloe" walked to the bar and ordered a drink.

"She really is nice looking." Terrence paused the video.

"The software's got to work on this, surely."

They had a clear picture of what "Chloe" looked like now. All they had to do was print a picture of her and send it off to the lab, where the software was handled. It might only take a few hours, depending on how well the computer picked up the pixels of the picture.

Nasreen felt excited – they were nearer to finding out Chloe's identity.

25

"Please tell me you've got some leads on this, Simon." Franks sat behind Adams' desk.

He watched Watts squirm in his seat. The detective looked uncomfortable. He had bags forming under his eyes and he looked tired. His suit was crumpled, and his hair was dishevelled. Franks thought he looked like a heart attack waiting to happen.

"We're working every angle, sir. The CSU haven't been able to find prints on any of the shell casings. The tyre tracks have come up empty, too. The car they used had the most common tyres in the country, so it could have been any number of makes and models. Adams' estate has no cameras. The closest CCTV camera's half a mile away and we weren't able to find anything on it we can use."

That wasn't what he wanted to hear, officially. Franks had to appear as though he wanted Watts and O'Hara to find the suspects. Unofficially, he couldn't have them succeed – it wasn't in the project's best interest. "So, what you're telling me is that you don't have any leads, is that correct? You know I've got the Home Secretary breathing down my neck on this."

"Like I said, sir, we're doing everything we can think of. We're going to go back and re-interview neighbours. We're looking into DCS Adams' history as well. That note has to mean something."

"Be careful, detective. That note doesn't leave this station, is that understood? I'm not going to have a decorated officer's name smeared over some note, is that clear? Think of Adams' poor family."

"Of course, sir, we'll tread carefully. But it's an angle we have to look into, isn't it?"

"Go wherever the investigation takes you. All I'm saying is be careful. What I can't have is the press getting wind of it."

"Yes, sir. We're on it."

Franks dismissed Watts and O'Hara. He watched them walk out of the office and close the door behind them. He swivelled in his chair, so his back was to the door. He pulled out his burner phone and dialled.

He waited for five rings before he heard Zack Astor's voice. "It's me." Franks looked through the window to his left. "We need to meet. I was thinking the usual place at nine? Good. Can you get Jim to join us, please? Good. See you then."

He slid the phone into his uniform jacket inside pocket and swivelled back to face the computer. He hated this office and didn't want to be here for any length of time.

There was nothing for it, he had to find a replacement for Adams and soon. The thing was, he had to find someone with the right mindset, someone who would look after the project, someone involved.

The only problem he had was finding that person – Adams was the lowest ranking officer involved, so none of the Chief Constables or Police and Crime Commissioners would want to take a demotion. So, who could it be? He scanned his computer for potential candidates. And then he found him – he was perfect. Faisal Bukhari.

According to Bukhari's record on the computer, he was a chief superintendent and involved in the project. How had Franks missed him until now? Bukhari would gain Nasreen's trust, being of the same ethnic persuasion. He might even encourage Bukhari to engage Nasreen in an extra-curricular capacity. Franks smiled as he picked up the office phone.

26

"I so don't want to go to work." Imelda cuddled Cara under the duvet.

"So, don't." Cara hooked her leg over Imelda's. "Call in sick. We can have some fun." She had an amazing day with her host yesterday. She almost had as much fun as she used to with Lucy – in the early days – almost. And Imelda reminded her of Lucy in many ways.

"I can't," Imelda replied with a sorrowful smile. "I need to pay the rent on this shithole, and I can barely afford it on my wages as it is. Sorry!"

Cara rolled over and sighed. She hated it when people deserted her – Lucy had deserted her; more than that, her ex stuck the pigs on her. Bitch!

"I'll make it up to you tonight though." Imelda cuddled her from behind, holding her tighter. "And I've still got time now. I don't need to be at work until ten."

There was nothing for it; she would have to leave soon. Cara pulled the duvet back and sat up, feeling Imelda stroke her back. "Sounds good," Cara said, none too convincingly. "Guess I'll go flat hunting." She turned and looked down at her host. "I'd rather spend the day with you though." The guilt trip wasn't working.

"I would if I could but I'm already on probation; I took lots of sick days after I started. I'm sorry. I'll make it up to you, I promise. I'll bring some Chinese food and a bottle of wine back with me tonight, how's that?"

"Okay, it's fine. I'll amuse myself until you get back." Cara stood and walked to the kitchenette for a glass of water.

27

Margaret "Maggie" Hughes squeezed her husband's hand. She knew it wouldn't be long until he passed away; watching him wither to the shell he was now from pancreatic cancer broke her heart. "I'll be back tomorrow, Phil," she said, in her Geordie accent, leaning forwards and kissing his hand.

"Come on, Mum, let's get you home. The party starts in an hour." Frank, her eldest, waited patiently for her to get up.

Maggie stood, looked down at her husband of thirty years and thought this might be the last time she saw him. He was so thin, so emaciated, how could he go on any longer?

Her grandson's fifth birthday party had come at the worst possible time. Maggie didn't feel like celebrating – all she wanted was to be by Phil's side. She wanted to be there when he passed, not wanting him to die alone in this hospice. "I'm not going tonight." She sat back down.

"You've got to go." Frank put his arms around her shoulders. "Luke won't understand why you aren't there. He's only just accepted Dad won't be."

Looking up at her concerned son, she realised Frank was

right, she couldn't let Luke down on his birthday. She stood and blew a kiss at her husband's gaunt face, then let herself get escorted out of the hospice room and along the corridor to the exit.

At fifty-six, she wasn't supposed to be a widow. Maggie didn't want to be left alone to deal with her family. And was she ready to take over the business? Did she have what it took to steer her loved ones through crisis after crisis, like Phil had for the past thirty years?

Even with the relative safety of working with Assistant Commissioner Franks, could she make the hard choices when they were needed?

Finding herself in the passenger seat of Frank's Jaguar, she looked out of her window at the hospice. It was a lovely Victorian building set in acres of lush green land. The hospice had taken Phil in without payment, so she had written a cheque for ten thousand, which was a drop in the ocean for her family – the hospice had treated Phil so well, with so much dignity, that she thought she would give them another ten thousand after he passed.

"I'll bring you up here first thing in the morning."

He was such a good boy, she thought, tears welling up. They'd done a great job raising him. Frank was a devoted son, husband and father. And it was a job he took seriously. She was so proud of the man he'd become. "Thanks," she replied, stroking his cheek.

"Give over, will you. Let's get you back home, so you can get changed. The restaurant's booked for six."

"You didn't book the whole restaurant, did you?"

"Yeah, all sixty seats are for our family and friends," he replied, looking behind him as he reversed the car. "I still can't believe how many said they're coming – we haven't seen some of our cousins in years."

"You're a popular lad. I don't know why you're so surprised. Luke is too."

As Frank drove her home, Maggie stared out of her window.

It was spitting outside. On the way, she thought back to her younger days.

Thirty years. She'd been married to the same man for thirty years, and had never strayed, not once. She thought she should get a medal for that. It hadn't been easy, especially when Phil went inside for five years for drugs charges.

She'd run the business while he was away. She was so happy to see him when they released him, and she'd relinquished control back to him gladly. Maggie had done well, or so Phil said on a number of occasions. It hadn't been all that difficult, really.

Having her three sons heavily involved in the family business was a godsend now. Back then, when Phil was inside, she had to rely on Phil's mates and colleagues to keep their heads above water.

There were always territorial disputes to be resolved with rival families – fortunately, she was adept at handling people. And when her diplomacy and people skills failed to resolve an issue, it was handy having Phil's mates around to resolve them in their own way.

She only had to let them loose once. The police investigation into the deaths of two rival dealers got intense, yet nothing came of it in the end. And as far as she knew, their cases remained unsolved to this day.

And so, with Phil on death's door and her family entering into a new phase with Assistant Commissioner Franks, did she still have what it took to take the reins?

Did she even want the reins? It might be better to let Frank take over. But that wasn't how Phil wanted it; he wanted Frank to take a back seat – Phil didn't think his eldest son was ready for the responsibility.

Her husband wanted her to show their son the ropes. Who was she to deny her husband his dying wish? Luckily, Frank didn't want it either. He was happy with her being in charge in the interim, until he felt ready.

It wasn't surprising that she'd married a dealer. Growing up in this great northern city, there wasn't much for a young girl to do, other than meet friends and fool around with blokes, smoke weed, snort coke, or inject heroin. She'd drawn a line at injecting H, but she'd certainly had her fair share of everything else, back in her younger years.

She met Phil at the tender age of eighteen, when she was young and impressionable. They dated for a couple of months before getting engaged. They held on until she was nineteen before they married. She had Frank when she was twenty. Maggie could remember those days so vividly. The city had changed a lot in the intervening years, but one thing that never changed was the drugs.

"We're here," she heard Frank say.

Maggie got out of Frank's Jag, closed the door and walked along her driveway to her lovely six-bedroom home. Having lived in squalor when she was growing up, her family home now was a matter of personal pride.

She loved this Victorian mansion, just loved it. She kept it like a showroom, never anything out of place. Her OCD pissed Phil off; he wanted to live in the house, but she would fuss after him, making sure he used coasters and kept the place spotless. She wanted everyone to respect their home as much as she did.

Upstairs in her en suite bathroom, Maggie splashed her face with water. She hated growing older, hated the additional wrinkles on her face and neck.

Still, she wasn't bad looking; she had a pleasant face and pretty smile. She was proud of her body the most. Even at fifty-six, she had a flat stomach and a pair of tits that would make some thirty-year-old women jealous.

It was through looking after her body for years that this was possible.

"You ready?" Frank shouted up the stairs. "It's nearly time."

She changed into an attractive floral evening dress, slip on shoes and joined Frank downstairs in the hallway. She hated being rushed. Following her son, she grabbed her coat and bag and closed the front door.

28

"Fucking got you!" Terrence had a broad smile on his face.

He opened the email, clicked on the attachment, and read through the information. "Nas, we've got her! Her name's Cara Mooney. And she's got a hell of a sheet."

Terrence waited for Nasreen to walk over to his desk. She bent down behind him and read through the attachment. "She's twenty-eight, grew up with a paedo dad and drug addict mum. She's been arrested for solicitation, GBH, ABH, assault; hell, is there anything she hasn't been picked up for?"

"It says she testified against her dad when she was twenty. He's inside for a fifteen-year stretch. She's got a much younger sister, by the look of it, who's currently in a halfway house after a long stint in a psychiatric unit." Nasreen keenly took note.

"Cara's been under psychiatric evaluation, too, with a Dr Travis Denton. We're going to have to have a chat with him. It's going to take us ages to go through all this." Terrence was so excited they had her name now. It meant they were well on their way to finding her.

There was no doubt in his mind that Cara Mooney was their

suspect. They didn't need to speak to friends and family of the two victims. It was as open and closed as any case got.

The CSU had managed to retrieve four bloody fingerprints. That was practically admitting guilt – fingerprints around the crime scene could be explained, but bloody fingerprints were notoriously difficult to explain away. They had saliva and fibre evidence too. This was their suspect, without a doubt.

"Let's see what we can find out about Miss Mooney, shall we?" Nasreen returned to her desk and typed "Cara Mooney" into the search bar on the PNC.

Terrence was giddy. He kept reading the file that the facial recognition software managed to identify. He couldn't believe that they'd found their suspect through the software, before the CSU had even delivered their report.

It didn't reflect well on the CSU's efficiency.

Gupta would be pissed, Terrence thought, as he caught sight of him. "Hey, boss, we got her!" He waited for Gupta to walk to his desk. "Read them and weep. And this came from the FRS, not from the lab."

"I'll be having words with them." Gupta read Terrence's screen. "Good work, Terrence, let's see what we can dig up on Miss Mooney, shall we?"

"Yeah, Nas just said that."

"Great minds think alike," Gupta replied.

Bishop walked towards them, carrying a thick file. Terrence waited for him to join them. He noticed that the file Bishop had was the official lab report. It was a lot thicker than the FRS report. "How did you get that before us?"

"Lucky, I guess," Bishop replied.

"Are you going to share that?"

Terrence held out his hand and Bishop gave him the report. Bishop might have been an asset to their team, but he wasn't a detective, not officially anyway.

That meant he shouldn't be getting reports before they did. "Holy crap, she was groomed. She must've been part of that northern grooming gang probe that was all over the news. She was one of those two thousand young girls drugged and raped by that mainly Pakistani gang."

He read the report. "Sorry, Nas, I didn't mean to..." He let his apology drift off.

"It's okay, they *were* mainly Pakistani, you can say it," Nasreen replied.

"So, this is one deeply disturbed woman we're dealing with," Gupta said. "First, she was raped by her dad for six years, and then she gets groomed by a gang for years after that. She's got to have a seriously warped idea of what a relationship is."

"I've checked the CCTV footage of The Emporium, and I can tell you now, if we don't stop her, we're going to have a lot more dead bodies to process," Bishop said, his tone alarmist. "She's on the far end of the sociopathic-psychopathic spectrum, which isn't good for us. This has only just started for her."

"Come on, Bishop, what does that even mean? What spectrum? She's a psychopath, that's that. Let's get out there and catch her." Terrence wasn't buying any of this psychological profiling crap. He watched as Bishop found a whiteboard and a red pen.

Bishop drew a horizontal line and halfway along drew a vertical line dissecting it centrally. "That vertical line represents the most normal a person can be, with neither sociopathic, nor psychopathic traits. It's extremely rare to find anyone who sits there."

Terrence watched as Bishop drew two lines, one either side of the central vertical line. Both lines were equal lengths away from the central line, only on opposing sides.

"This gap here and here represents most people we know.

Everyone, and I mean everyone, will be a little sociopathic or a little psychopathic. Think of it like the autism spectrum."

Terrence understood Bishop's explanation so far.

"The problem we've got is that Cara sits right here." Bishop pointed at the end of the left line. "She's socially adept, intelligent and beautiful, which means we're going to have trouble finding her, much less catching her. We can see she's evolving too. She's trying out different things, trying to find her own MO. When we get her psychiatric notes from Dr Denton, which we'll need a court order for, I wouldn't be surprised if her IQ is in excess of a hundred and eighty."

Terrence sat back in his chair. "You sound like you admire her."

"I kind of do. We're dealing with someone who's both sociable, and psychotic. She's like a chameleon; people she meets will like her."

"Why, because she's hot?"

"That, and because she's likeable. And she's not going to come quietly, either, which means that when we do find her, we need to make sure there's no one else around, because she'll take whoever she's with down with her."

"Thanks for your analysis," Gupta said. "I think it's time for a press conference, don't you? Let's see if the public can help us."

Terrence looked at the time on his monitor and saw it was five. "You'd better hurry if you want to get the press conference in the six o'clock news."

29

———

Lennox watched Margaret Hughes walk into the Italian restaurant, followed by her three sons, their wives and six children, from the passenger seat.

Barkley pulled up on the opposite side of the road, outside a kebab shop.

At quarter past six, it was busy on the high street, especially being a Friday night.

There were two pubs either side of the Italian restaurant.

"Let's hope we don't see any traffic wardens," Barkley said, watching the restaurant.

"It's after six, Bark," Lennox replied. "They're off duty."

In the back were two associates, who his uncle had asked to help him. They were also from Jamaica, but had lived in this city for years. They had considerable knowledge of the area, and would come in useful when it was time to make their escape.

"I could murder a kebab," said the associate behind Lennox. "Lenny, how about it?"

"No way! Keep your eyes on the restaurant."

"Come on, man, we're starving," complained the other associate. "We haven't eaten since lunch. We'll be in and out."

With a sigh, Lennox caved in and let them get out and buy kebabs. He ordered a lamb doner, while Barkley ordered a lamb shish.

After the two associates had left the car, he leaned back in his seat and kept an eye on the restaurant. It was busy in there. He saw Margaret greet some guests and sit down in the middle table.

"Where does your uncle find these dickheads?"

"Someone probably thinks the same about you," Lennox replied with a grin. "They're all right, so long as they do their job when the time comes."

He nudged the duffle bag down by his feet, felt the weight. He leaned forward, reached down, opened it and looked inside. Four Uzis, four magazines.

While leaning forwards still, he slid all four magazines in the machine pistols and chambered the first round on each gun. He remembered to put the safety on each, not wanting the two dick-heads behind him to accidentally fire them inside the car.

That had happened to a friend of his in Jamaica – his friend was shot accidentally five times, four times in the back and once in the head. At the time, they were about to shoot a rival dealer outside his home.

"Everything set?"

"Yeah, we just sit and wait now." Lennox closed the bag and leaned back. "I don't suppose you brought a deck of cards?"

Barkley half laughed, which was more of a snort.

Hearing his burner phone, Lennox reached into his coat pocket and pulled it out.

It was Amelie. He hated talking to her in front of anyone. To him, it was a sign of weakness to talk soft in front of friends, or anyone.

He spoke to Amelie for five minutes, making sure she was good – she was staying with Harold Thomas on board *The Alba-*

tross tonight. Lennox hoped she managed to download information from his laptop; they needed it. He needed to know which police officers were bent before he could wage war on them.

His two associates came back loaded with white carrier bags full of kebabs while he was still on the phone. He accepted his lamb doner while saying goodbye to Amelie.

Barkley and his two associates started making kissing noises as he hung up.

Putting his mobile back in his pocket, he turned and scowled at all three of them.

"Did we miss anything?" the associate behind him asked.

"Only Lennox declaring his undying love for Amelie."
Barkley sniggered.

"Fuck you!" was the only reply Lennox could think of as he stuffed some shredded lamb in his mouth. This was why he hated talking to women on the phone.

"Who would have thought, the mighty Lennox could be whipped." Barkley laughed.

Lennox pretended to wind his middle finger up.

"No, seriously, man, I've never seen you with a woman for more than five minutes," Barkley said, his face serious. "I think it's good you found your 'one'."

"Oh, please, I'm eating here," the associate behind Barkley said.

The other associate made some funny noises and pretended to be sick.

"Fuck the lot of you," Lennox said finally.

30

"Cara, do you mind putting the plates in the microwave for me, please," Imelda asked, placing the Chinese takeaway on the kitchen counter and removing the containers.

"Sure." Cara opened the cupboard, took out two plates and placed them in the microwave. She hadn't told Imelda she was leaving tonight, knowing her host would take it badly.

"So, how was your day? Did you find any flats you liked?"

"Nah, not really." She removed the plates and, with a tea towel, took them over to the counter. When she placed them, Imelda started dishing up both plates.

"Ah, that's a shame. You know you can stay here for as long as you need. You know that, right?"

Cara thought that sweet. "Thanks, I know that."

"What? What is it?"

Cara paused, not wanting to upset Imelda, her new Lucy. "I have to go home."

Imelda looked disappointed. "You are, tomorrow, right? That's what you said."

"No, tonight, I'm afraid," she said, having decided it was for the best. "After dinner. I'm sorry. Something came up at work;

I've been called in early tomorrow morning, so I need to drive back tonight. I'm so sorry."

Imelda stopped dishing up, held the counter and rocked back and forth. To Cara she looked like she was about to cry. "Are you coming back? Am I ever going to see you again?"

Cara put her hand on Imelda's shoulder. "Hey, beautiful, I'll be back in a couple of days, I promise. I'm not going to be gone long, but I do need to leave tonight. I'm sorry."

"So, when are you going to be back? Sunday? Monday?"

"Monday, if you'll have me." Cara wanted to move away from this emotional shit. She wasn't great at it at the best of times. While she was good at imitating emotions, it took a lot of energy out of her. She had no intention of coming back on Monday. Pretty soon, Imelda would know who she really was, and then she would be grateful Cara left.

"I guess it's only a few days." Imelda forced a smile. "And you're staying here, with me, right?"

"Absolutely, as long as you'll have me."

Startled when Imelda grabbed her cheeks with her palms and kissed her forcefully, Cara kissed her back. She hadn't felt like this since she was with Lucy.

Maybe she should come back for Imelda? No, that was stupid; Imelda knew her as Chloe, not Cara. This thing – whatever it was – was built on a lie. She had places to go, people to see, masterpieces to make.

"Let's have a nice dinner then," Imelda said, back to dishing up.

"Let's." Cara picked up her plate and took it over to the sofa opposite the bed. She used a cushion as a tray, moving her handbag from her right, to her left, allowing her host to sit down.

"Thanks." Imelda sat down.

"What for?"

"Just being you," Imelda replied, after a long pause.

Ordinarily, she would feel sick after such a display, but with Imelda it seemed natural. Lucy used to say mushy things like that, and at first, she'd loved it. After a while it just sounded false, like Lucy was simply going through the motions. Maybe she had been, Cara didn't know. Lucy was a total mystery to her anyway. "Aww, you're so sweet."

Before she started eating, Cara picked up the TV remote and turned it to Sky News. She looked up at the clock and saw it was 19:00. She'd watched the headlines on the hour, every hour, just to make sure her picture wasn't splattered across the nation's televisions. Ryan Bentley and Hayden Oates had both been mentioned during the news, yet there had been no mention of her. For the moment, she was safe to move around.

"Again? What's it with you and the boring news?"

"What?" Cara had a mouthful of food. "It's good to know what's going on in the world, don't you think?" She hoped Imelda could understand.

Imelda shrugged.

When the seven o'clock news came on, the headlines were announced. The lead story was that two murders had been linked. The announcer said that a press conference was under way. Cara watched intently, still forking food in her mouth.

The camera settled on an Asian man in a suit. At the bottom of the screen, she read his name: Detective Inspector Arjun Gupta. Cara stabbed a sweet and sour pork ball violently with her fork.

"Hey, what's it ever done to you?" Imelda looked at her with a jovial smile.

And there it was: a picture of her. It was the fucking horrible arrest picture too.

Why could they never find a decent fucking photo? It made her so mad, she just wanted to stab something.

She breathed deeply, feeling Imelda's gaze.

Her host obviously hadn't seen the TV yet. She breathed out. "What's wrong with…"

There it was, the inevitable pause.

Imelda had just seen it. Please don't do anything stupid, Imelda, she pleaded internally; she really didn't want to hurt her.

But she could feel her blade calling her – it was hard to ignore.

"Is that?" Imelda stopped mid-sentence. "Is that you?"

Cara listened to the detective talk about the murders and about how they were looking to question her in relation to both deaths. The fucker then went on to warn young men between the ages of twenty-five and thirty-five in pubs and nightclubs to be careful – both victims had been murdered after taking this woman home. The detective didn't mention how Ryan and Hayden were murdered.

"That *is* you!"

Cara stared straight ahead at the television.

She could feel Imelda's gaze.

Instinctively, Cara put her left hand in her handbag and pulled out the knife.

Transferring it to her right hand in one smooth motion, she stabbed the knife through Imelda's neck. When it was stuck, she held her friend's head with her free hand and opened Imelda's throat, freeing her knife.

Blood sprayed over Imelda's dinner, down her top, as Cara listened to her gargle the last minute of her life away. "That was silly," she said, wiping the blade on her host's top. "I wasn't going to hurt you."

Imelda slumped, blood pooling from the gaping slash in her throat. She looked like she was hyperventilating and resting her head between her knees.

Cara continued watching the news while she finished her dinner, finally placing half a pork ball in her mouth.

She stood and looked down at Imelda's cooling body. "Suppose I'd better wash up, eh!" Then, she walked to the kitchen, where she washed both plates, wiped down the surfaces and generally made the kitchen look respectable.

Back in the bedroom, she picked up her handbag and shopping bags and walked to the door, but before opening it, she turned to her host's slumped body. "It was lovely meeting you. Thanks ever so much for having me; it was wonderful."

31

—————

Nasreen looked at the time and saw it was half past seven. Silently cursing, she picked up her desk phone and dialled nine, followed by her home phone number.

Apologising profusely to Katerina, her daughter's nanny, she said she would be back in half an hour to an hour, saying she had a couple of things to finish up. She asked Katerina to put Mina to bed if she wasn't back in time.

Eight o'clock was too late for a four-year-old really, but she'd found that any earlier than eight meant a greater chance of Mina waking up and coming into her room, which Nasreen was trying hard to prevent.

"Nas, the press conference worked," Terrence said excitedly. "Armed police are on their way to a bedsit now. Someone phoned in saying they know where Cara's staying."

"Where's the bedsit? Is it local?"

"Nah, it's about a two-hour drive. Are you coming?"

Nasreen didn't have to be asked twice. This was the part of the job that excited her, that made all the mundane questioning and research worthwhile. "Of course!"

She joined Terrence and followed him to the lift.

"Cara was in a relationship for three years, apparently, with a Lucy Davis." The lift doors opened. After stepping inside, the doors closed. "I've tried to find Lucy, but it's like she dropped off the face of the planet."

"What happened? She *was* in a relationship? Does that mean she isn't now?"

"Nope, not anymore. It ended badly by the sound of it. Lucy took out an injunction against her; she's not allowed within two hundred feet of her. And then Cara tried kidnapping her. Instead of prison, Cara was given time in a psychiatric ward. Apparently, Lucy pleaded with the judge not to send her to prison. Cara was released just over a year ago."

"Shit! That did end badly. And you can't find Lucy now?"

"Nope. I've tried everything, including Facebook and Twitter. She used to be a journalist with *The Telegraph*, so I guess we could go ask the editor what they know about Lucy and Cara. They might know where Lucy is."

The lift doors opened.

"We'll put it past Gupta, see what he thinks, but I can't think of any reason why we shouldn't." Terrence led the way through the corridors, to the rear exit and car park. "We'll be taking over from any detectives at the bedsit, if there are any. They'll know it's our case, so we shouldn't get any shit from the locals."

"Do they think Cara's still at the address?"

"No idea. All I know is, someone called in, saying Cara's staying there."

"I guess there's only one way to find out."

In the passenger seat, Nasreen suddenly thought she should phone Katerina and tell her she wouldn't be home for a while. This was the downside of her job, no downtime.

32

As she drove along the motorway in her red Micra, Cara couldn't get Lucy out of her mind. Every time she tried to forget about her, to put her somewhere hidden, Lucy's beautiful face appeared. She couldn't fight it anymore – she still loved her, even after everything that had happened – she wanted, no, needed her back.

Meeting Imelda had rekindled Cara's love for Lucy. They were so similar in lots of ways, yet also very different. Lucy had always been career minded, whereas Imelda was treading water, coasting through life, from what Cara could tell. But they were both beautiful independent women. It was too bad she'd had to get rid of Imelda; she'd enjoyed their time together.

There was only one person she could think of who would know where Lucy was. It was risky though; she would have to drive back to the city. That Asian detective was back there too. But, life was all about taking risks, Cara thought, talking herself into finding a slip road, turning around and heading south to find Dawn Weaver.

33

Amelie Desmarais thanked the driver as she stepped out of the taxi. The driver didn't ask her for payment but she gave him a five-pound tip anyway, which her client, Harry, would tell her was unnecessary.

It was cold out, so she wrapped her fur-lined coat around her and started walking towards the marina, where *The Albatross* was moored.

As she walked past the twenty-four-hour supermarket, she noticed a couple of lads in their twenties watching her. Feeling their stares, she walked past them. One of them said something about her. Amelie was used to stares and comments, especially in her line of work; she'd learned not to care, having far more important business to deal with.

The Albatross, a thirty-nine-metre luxury yacht, able to accommodate up to ten people within its five bedrooms, was moored at the furthest end of the marina. She'd stayed over at Harry's home so many times, the novelty of sleeping on board a boat had worn off. It was a sight to behold though.

When she first met Harry on board the huge vessel, she'd been so awed by its magnificence that she'd forgotten herself and had asked him how much it cost. He told her that he'd bought it with an inheritance, after his divorce – it was a steal, he'd said, at eight-hundred-and-forty-thousand. She remembered thinking, *Oh, how the other half live.*

Reaching the end of the marina, she saw Harry waiting for her on the stern deck. He had the hatch down for her, wearing an expensive suit and black suede shoes.

She smiled, even waved. As she reached the hatch, she quickly felt inside her handbag for the USB stick, making sure she hadn't forgotten it.

"You made it in good time." He held his hand out. "I didn't know how long it would take in Friday night traffic."

"The driver was very efficient." She took his hand and climbed aboard in her high heels. Harry liked her wearing high heels, even though she was taller than him in them. She wasn't a short woman, at five feet eleven.

She greeted him with her customary kiss and quick embrace.

"Let's get you warmed up, shall we?"

"Oh yes, please." She followed him inside. "Winter's not over yet."

Inside the main lounge, there were three sofas, one port (left), one starboard (right) and one on the bow (front). There was a mahogany table in front of the port and starboard sofas. There was a huge flat-screen television hung on the wall above the sofa at the front of the room, which was showing Sky News. It seemed Harry always had the news on.

Amelie accepted the glass of wine Harry poured her.

"Shall we?" Harry pointed at the port sofa.

Amelie sat down, her left leg crossed over her right. She sipped the Tignanello, Harry's favourite tipple. He said it tasted of chocolate, coffee and marmalade, but it was lost on a simple girl like her – all she tasted was red wine. Maybe she *was* the philistine that Harry joked she was.

"What shall we drink to?" Harry held his glass up in contemplation.

"To a lovely evening together?"

"To many lovely evenings together." He clinked her glass.

Drinking a medium-sized mouthful, Amelie was grateful for the release alcohol allowed before they got down to business. She smiled, hoping she didn't appear nervous.

"Which leads me on to the main reason why I asked you here." Harry turned slightly, so he was almost facing her.

"Oh? I didn't realise tonight was a special occasion."

"Seeing you is always a special occasion, but that's not what I wanted to say to you, or rather ask you."

She noticed how jittery Harry was; he looked uncomfortable, embarrassed. Who would have thought a successful police officer, the highest in the land, would get tongue tied around a woman, or rather a prostitute he'd hired for the night? "You want to ask me something? Should I be worried?" She made light of the comment by reaching out for his hand and holding it.

Scratching his head, Harry said, "You see, the thing is... The thing is I want to ask you–"

"Whatever it is, Harry, it's all right." She tried to encourage him to say it. She didn't know what to expect. "You can tell me!"

"The thing is, I want to ask you if you'd like to make this, us, more regular?"

"More regular? How do you mean?" She still had her disarming smile, with a hint of apprehension. "All you have to do is ask if I'm available and I'll see if I can fit you in, but I do have other–"

"I'm asking you if you'd like to move in here with me, Amelie," Harry said with a fluster. "I don't want to think of you working with other men – I have too much respect for you. Please, think about it."

Holy fucking shit! She could feel herself squirming in her seat. *She* felt flustered now. What the fuck was the appropriate response to that? She'd just been asked to move into a luxury yacht, this beautiful place.

Any normal girl would jump at the chance to stop tricking and move in with the most respected policeman in the country, but she wasn't normal. There was also the small matter of helping Lennox expose Harry and his colleagues. "I, erm, I don't know, Harry. There's so much to think about."

"I realise it must be a shock, Ams, but all I'm asking is for you to think about it. It makes a lot of sense. I'm offering you a new way of life, a new start. You won't have to ever sell yourself again – you can start up a massage parlour, I'll even give you the money to get it off the ground. Think about it: a real business of your own."

He was getting too excited for her liking. Her head was spinning. She took a large gulp of her wine, hoping Harry hadn't seen her hands shaking. "Okay, I'll think about it."

Amelie let him take her hand and kiss it.

"That's great. Take as much time as you need. I won't pressure you, I promise. Here, have some more wine."

Taking charge of the situation the only way she knew how, Amelie stood, took his hands and pulled him to his feet. "Now, how about a nice back massage."

34

Maggie Hughes was trying her hardest to enjoy herself. Every time she forgot about Phil in the hospice, one of her extended family members had to tell her how sorry they were, that they hoped he would recover soon.

Most of them didn't know Phil was terminal and mere days, hours or minutes away from dying; it was the way she wanted it – they didn't even see most of the people here from one year to the next, so why should they get inside consideration on this?

The restaurant was packed. Frank, her eldest, had done a fantastic job organising his son's fifth birthday party. It took a lot of planning to get this many people together, especially family members.

Luke, her grandson, was having a great time with his cousins and friends, which was the main thing. Sat at the centre table, surrounded by her three sons, her three daughters-in-law and six grandchildren, life wouldn't get much better than this, except she missed her Phil.

She missed him, and he wasn't even dead yet, so God only knew how much she would miss him when he did finally pass away.

Frank, as usual, made sure she was fine throughout the starters and main course.

Vincent, her middle son, took it upon himself to keep the kids entertained, and he did it so well – but she knew he was a big kid himself, so it wasn't too much of a chore for him.

And then there was Scott, her darling youngest. He'd spent most of the evening glued to his smart phone, bless him.

While Frank kept the family construction business afloat, with the help of Vincent, Phil had made it Scott's responsibility to keep the other side of the family business going.

And judging by how often he'd been called this evening, he was having problems with the street dealers. He could handle it – Scott could handle anything. And if it ever got too much for him, he knew he could call on Frank and Vincent for backup. Her three boys together were a fearsome sight.

She watched her boys around the table. Frank was the tall good-looking one, no doubt about that. He was also quite stocky, with all the heavy lifting he did on site. He had dark spiky hair and a killer smile.

Her Vincent was about an inch shorter than Frank, not as classically good-looking, with short mousy brown hair. He inherited her killer sense of humour.

And then her Scott was the shorter burly masculine one. Scott regularly worked out at the gym. His brothers teased him that the only reason he was so big, was all the steroids he took. She didn't believe he took them though; he was a hard worker.

She found it funny that Scott was the least good-looking of her three, yet he'd always had more girls than his brothers. She knew that women didn't see good looks as the be-all and end-all, it was all down to attitude and confidence. Scott had bags of both.

Seizing an opportunity between courses, Maggie stood and made her apologies.

She was gagging for a smoke. It was a shame that all she had was her electronic cigarette. It would have to do until she got home.

"We'll come with you." Scott signalled his brothers to join him.

"Really, Scott, stop fussing. I'm only going outside for a vape."

"We're dying for a smoke, so we'll come with you, if that's okay?"

She sighed. "Suit yourself." She meandered between tables and children running around. It was so bloody noisy in there. If anything, she was going outside to get some peace and quiet.

Outside, Maggie rested her back against the restaurant window. She took her vape out from her pocket and drew on it, blowing out the air vapour.

She had a massive sweet tooth, so it was no surprise she chose caramel as her flavour of e-liquid. She'd chosen a nicotine level of twelve, which was high, but not too high. In six months, she'd gone from twenty-four milligrams to twelve, which she thought was great. Next month, she'd decided she would cut down by half again and try six milligrams.

Maggie listened, smiling to herself, as Scott and Vincent ganged up on their elder brother.

35

Nasreen looked at the dashboard clock: 21:34. They were nearly there. She was so excited, mainly because she didn't know what to expect. Had Cara been detained?

There was no radio contact from HQ regarding an arrest, so she assumed Cara was still at large. Good news like that was quick to make its rounds, even stuck in a car.

Inside her suit jacket, her mobile vibrated. Taking it out, she swiped the green symbol to her right, answering it. "Sir, we're nearly there."

"Good," Gupta replied. "You're on duty tomorrow, aren't you?"

"Yeah, my first week back, I drew the short straw."

"Okay, I've scheduled an interview with a Dawn Weaver for nine tomorrow morning. She called in to talk about Cara Mooney. She knows her, and a Lucy Davis, do you know who that is?"

"Cara's ex-girlfriend. Nine o'clock tomorrow, that's fine with me. Hopefully I'll learn a bit more about Cara's past."

"If you don't detain her tonight."

"I haven't heard from anyone at the bedsit yet, so I'm not

129

holding my breath on that one, sir. We're only a half hour away. I'll update you when I know more."

"If you could; I'd appreciate it. It doesn't matter what time."

Nasreen hung up and relayed the information to Terrence, who was concentrating on driving. The blue lights flashing helped clear their path, but traffic jams were traffic jams, no matter how many sirens and blue flashing lights there were.

Interviewing Dawn Weaver tomorrow morning would hopefully provide some insight into Cara Mooney's recent murder spree. Nasreen only hoped the girl living at the bedsit was okay – one more murder and they were officially dealing with a serial killer.

36

Lennox was ready. He ordered his companions to put on their masks. They had their weapons in hand and the windows were down. He had Margaret Hughes and her three sons in sight, outside the restaurant.

Giving the order to the associate behind him to get up on the roof, Lennox hoisted himself out of the window, sat on the window frame. There were a lot of people milling around the high street, so he had to wait until there were no innocent civilians in their firing line, or cars that were going to obstruct their mission. "Now!" he shouted, pulling the trigger, as all four machine pistols spluttered to life.

37

Maggie was confused. Who was letting off firecrackers?

Frank shouted, "Mum!" and stood in front of her.

She heard two thuds, then something sprayed her face.

Glass smashed behind her.

It suddenly felt like someone had punched her in her upper arm; it was numb.

Maggie fell to the ground. Frank fell with her.

When she looked over at her two younger sons, she saw Scott dancing spasmodically, his arms flailing. Then she saw him fall on his back.

Vincent was already on the floor, his eyes staring up at the sky.

Then she heard screaming from behind her.

There was screaming all around her. She heard a whoosh, right past her ear. Then she heard car tyres screeching. Maggie didn't know what was happening. Why was she on the floor? She'd only come outside for a vape.

And then, in a split second, everything clicked in her mind; the confusion cleared. She couldn't move. Her arm hurt. She tried to move Frank, only when she did, she couldn't see his face. He had no face. "Frank!" she shouted, staring at the bloody mess that used to be her son. She screamed a feral, primal scream, which attracted onlookers.

38

Terrence stepped inside the bedsit in full PPE to find total chaos. There were four girls crying, with uniformed officers trying to console them.

Crime scene officers were busy trying to do their part, but with the four uniforms and four civilians in the tiny room, they couldn't get much done.

It looked like there was no one in charge. There were no detectives, no senior officers in attendance. "Who's in charge here?"

One of the uniforms turned to him. "I am, sir," she replied, a pretty black woman, with a petite frame and scared, out of her depth eyes. "Sergeant Johnson. I'm so sorry, I'm new to this area. My constables have been trying to help, but–"

"Don't worry about it. We need to get these witnesses out of here. We can interview them outside, or in the corridor. Can you do that for me? We need to secure the scene, give the CSU a chance to do their thing."

"Yes, sir. I'm so sorry."

He waited while the uniforms gathered the grief-stricken girls and walked with them into the corridor. He could still hear their wails in the background. Oh shit! He turned and saw why the girls were so hysterical.

"She's done it again." Nasreen stared at the body of Imelda, her voice muffled by the mask. She crouched down in her white coveralls.

"And not that long ago, by the look of it."

He joined his partner and crouched down. With his gloved hand he pulled her head up slightly, to reveal the ugly red gash in her neck. The blood was still dripping, so he was right: Cara had sliced her recently.

"What do you think?" Nasreen glanced around the room.

"This doesn't fit her MO, that's what I think. She kills men, not women. There's no sign of sexual intercourse. We don't even know this was Cara."

"The witness said the girl staying here with Imelda was Chloe," came a voice from behind him. "Imelda met her at the clothes shop she works in."

"Right, Chloe. Thank you, sergeant."

"What time did you get here?" Nasreen asked Sergeant Johnson.

"Half seven. One of the girls was already here, knocking on the door. She told us the victim's car was in the car park out back, so she knew she was home. When we didn't get an answer, I felt I had probable cause and kicked the door in. And this is what I found. Half an hour ago the rest of the girls arrived, and I was trying to get them outside."

"I'm just trying to get my head around the victim's position." He stood, looking down at the corpse. "The way she's slumped over like that is weird."

"Was the TV on when you got here?" Nasreen asked.

"Um, yeah, on Sky News."

"You don't think Cara was watching the press conference when–"

"When the victim saw Cara's picture and tried to run? Is that what you were thinking?" Terrence's eyebrows raised.

"Inspector Gupta couldn't get the press conference on the six o'clock news, so he settled for seven instead. It makes sense, it fits." Nasreen waited for his thoughts.

Terrence looked at the body again. There was something in the way she was slumped over. "I don't think Cara wanted to kill her." He imagined Cara sat next to the victim. He could see her sat there, watching the news. Then he saw the victim go to move and Cara pull the knife out and slit her throat. "I think she made a sudden move and Cara instinctively cut her. In fact, I think these two were sleeping together."

"That fits with the testimony I got from one of the girls outside," Sergeant Johnson said. "She told me she was out with Imelda and Chloe on Wednesday night. She said 'they were getting on very well', so I read between the lines."

"She's all over the place," Nasreen said. "It's going to make her even harder to find. She doesn't seem to have an MO, and her victimology's all over the place now too. There doesn't seem to be any connection between the three victims. The first two were male, sure; both were stabbed. But that's where the similarities end. Other than that, there's no connection that I can see. And now, with Imelda as the third victim, where do we go from here?"

Terrence sighed. "We pray we get lucky."

39

"Hello, Dawn," Cara said from the safety of the shadows.

Dawn gasped. Cara stepped out of the darkness, into the orange light provided by the porch. She watched Dawn drop the rubbish bag in the wheelie bin and close the lid slowly. Dawn looked both left and right, searching for someone to come to her aid.

Dawn Weaver lived in a block of flats on the first floor. Access to her house was via two flights of concrete steps, leading to a two and a half metre wide covered walkway, with ten flats per floor. Cara had waited outside flat six, in the refuse collection point, behind the grey landfill bin and the blue recycling bin. The walkway was surrounded by a five-foot wall, with recesses outside each door, where the residents kept their wheelie bins.

"Cara! What're you doing here? I wasn't expecting you."

She stepped towards Lucy's best friend, noticing her backing up, a pigeon step at a time. She had her hand inside her bag, fingers clasped around the handle of the knife. She wanted Dawn to try to make a run for it.

"You should've called ahead," Dawn continued, still walking

backwards, getting closer to her front door. "I'd have fixed you some dinner."

"How sweet."

When Dawn was two steps from the door, she tried to turn and run inside her house.

Cara was too quick, getting her foot in the door before Dawn could close it. Forcing the door open was no problem – she was far stronger, always had been. "That's no way to treat an old friend, now, is it?"

Inside the flat, she closed the door, her knife in hand for Dawn to see, to fear.

"What do you want from me?" Dawn was still backing up, getting closer to her closed kitchen door. "I'll scream."

"No, you won't." Cara grew closer to her frightened ex-friend. "Because if you do, I'll stick you with this, do you understand me?"

Cara smiled when Dawn reached the kitchen door and couldn't step back any further. She watched Dawn's hand slowly reach for the handle.

Having to move fast when Dawn managed to open the door, run inside the kitchen and try closing it on her, Cara rammed the door open so hard that it swung back and crashed into a wall. "Don't be so fucking stupid," she said, gaining on Lucy's bitch of a friend. "You're not going anywhere."

"What do you want? If it's money, I can get my purse."

"Fuck your money!" Cara grabbed Dawn's blouse collar and put the knife on her neck. "It's Lucy I want, not you, and I know you have her address."

"I don't, Cara, honestly I don't." Dawn gulped. "If I knew where she was, I'd tell you, believe me, I would. Nobody knows where she is, as far as I know."

"Liar!" Cara slapped Dawn with a backhander to the face. She took delight in seeing Dawn's face snap to the left. "You're her best friend, do you expect me to believe she hasn't told you where she's living? I'm not stupid, Dawn, so don't treat me like I am, okay?"

"I'm telling you the truth." Dawn's cheek was turning red. "Don't you think I'd tell you, if it got you out of my flat?"

"I don't believe you." Cara grabbed Dawn and pushed her into a cupboard, her head crashing into the wood. Looking down at Dawn's unconscious body, Cara bent down, grabbed Dawn's arms and pulled her back through the hallway to the bedroom.

40

"That was so good," Harry said.

Amelie lay there – Harry on top of her – for a couple of minutes, their bodies moist and warm. When they'd both recovered, Harry rolled onto his back, his breathing still slightly laboured. Reaching over to her cigarettes on the bedside table, she took one out and lit it.

"Can I have one?"

"You don't even smoke." She passed him her lit one, then picked up her packet again and slid another one out, lighting it.

"I do occasionally." He drew in a lungful and blew it out.

"Yeah, I really should quit."

"This would be great, though, wouldn't it?"

"What would?" She knew what was coming, the hard sell.

"Being able to do this every night." He sucked in another lungful. "Well, maybe not every night, I'm not sure my body can take it. But whenever we feel like it."

"Uh huh!" He promised her he wouldn't pressure her.

"Wouldn't it though?"

Amelie looked over at his happy boyish face. "I thought you

weren't going to pressure me? I told you I'll think about it, and I will. You're asking me to give up a lot."

"Hey, I'm giving you a great opportunity here."

"An opportunity to stop being a whore, you mean. You know I'm not some street worker, don't you? I'm not out there selling myself to anyone I can find. I decide which clients I take and who I don't. I might be a whore to you, but I love my life. And let's not forget who recommended me to you."

Harry had contacted her through an MP, the MP for Lewisham East. And she'd met him through a well-known businessman in the area. Recommendation, word of mouth, was how she met most of her "clients". To date, Amelie had serviced three MPs, two doctors, a well-respected solicitor, and now a top police officer. She wasn't out there, on the streets, offering herself to any old "Joe".

"I never said I think of you as a whore, did I? You said that, not me. And it's not every day I ask someone to move in with me."

Amelie sat up and stubbed out her cigarette. "Whatever!" She got out of bed and walked over to her bathrobe.

"Where're you going now?"

"To take a shower, is that okay with you?"

As she walked out of the bedroom, she heard Harry muttering something to himself. Closing the bathroom door, she de-robed, stepped into the shower and turned it on.

It was funny how life went. A year ago, had she been offered to move in with Harry, she would have jumped at the opportunity. She'd have given up tricking in a heartbeat, for a life of luxury, living on this grand yacht with him.

But now that she had Lennox, the thought physically repelled her. Knowing that Harry was a dirtbag cop didn't help either. All she really wanted was to be with Lennox, not that she would tell him that; not this early on in their relationship.

She knew Lennox had some issues he needed to deal with, so she would let him finish his business before she complicated things between them. Harry was merely a means to helping Lennox finish his business.

Stepping out of the shower and drying herself, she thought about her mission: Harry kept his laptop in the bedroom next door, which he had converted into an office. The problem was getting to it. The office door was locked, and Harry kept his keys in his trouser pocket. If she were to get to the laptop, she would need to get those keys and that meant waiting until Harry was asleep.

Naked, she walked out of the bathroom and into the bedroom. "Harry, listen," she said, stopping herself when she heard him snoring. He lay naked on his back, on top of the duvet, his mouth open.

Creeping, trying not to make the floorboards creak, Amelie bent down at the foot of the bed and picked up Harry's trousers. She felt inside his pocket for the keys.

DAY 5
SATURDAY, 24TH MARCH

41

───────

"What're you doing?" Harry's voice was sleepy...

"Folding your trousers." Amelie picked them up, making sure the keys fell out of the pocket onto the carpet in the process. "You don't want them to get all creased, do you?" She walked over to the desk and neatly folded them and hung them on the chair.

"Are you coming back to bed?"

"Yeah, I'm sleepy." She walked back to the bed.

She lay in bed, under the duvet, trying to slow her heart rate down by taking controlled deep breaths. She felt Harry's arm over her stomach.

He was falling asleep, yet his hand was going south.

He was going to want to go again. She had no choice – she was getting paid two and a half grand for tonight. All she wanted was to get into his office and download the file.

A quarter of an hour later, an exhausted Harry rolled onto his side, spent. Amelie lay awake, staring up at the ceiling, waiting for his heavy breathing to turn into snores.

She lay there for a while, listening to him fall into a deep sleep.

When she was sure he was out, she pulled the duvet back and snuck out of bed, wrapping herself in her robe. She tiptoed to the bottom of the bed, picked up the keys and tiptoed out of the bedroom, closing the door behind her.

Next door, Amelie used the key to let herself into Harry's study, where his laptop sat on the mahogany desk, switched on and open, with no passwords required.

Harry obviously thought it was safe to leave his computer on in his own home, especially when it was in a locked room. Too bad for him, she thought, locating the file she had seen once before.

On the screen, Amelie saw a list of files. She was only interested in one: Project Clean Sweep. She had already downloaded one file, which had given Lennox the identities of the dealers they were using. The file she needed was entitled, "Personnel". It was the one Lennox had asked her to retrieve.

When she opened it, a spreadsheet came onto the screen, with a load of names, police ranks, and which force they belonged to. There were a lot of names on the list.

By the number of rows, it looked like there were around ninety police officers involved in the project. That was ninety dirty cops. Retrieving the USB stick from her robe pocket, she inserted it into the laptop.

42

———

Cara scoured every drawer, every wardrobe in Dawn's bedroom, looking for something. Stopping for a second, she thought about where else it might be. Then it struck her to look in the bathroom.

Leaving Dawn tied to her bed, gagged and unconscious, she walked through to the bathroom next door. There was a cabinet, which she opened, and smiled when she saw a pair of hair scissors.

Her smile widened further when she saw a bottle of brown hair dye. It was silly to think that dying her hair would fool people, but it might buy her enough time to escape, if it came to that.

The police and public would be looking for Cara with long blonde hair, not the shoulder length brunette Cara she would emerge from here as.

Cara cut it shoulder length at the back and shorter around the sides, leaving a fringe. She scooped up the hair cuttings and dropped them in the bin under the sink. Then she used the shower head to dye her hair brown.

By the time she'd finished dyeing her hair, she walked into the bedroom to find Dawn awake, crying into her gag, attempting to break her ties. "What do you think?" She waited for a reply. "Yeah, that's what I thought."

It was half past one by the time she started searching through Dawn's bedroom again, this time looking for something else. Cara raided every drawer and every cupboard in the room. She found a sex toy in one drawer. "So, you do like sex." She grinned. "I did wonder about you. You never had a boyfriend or girlfriend in the time I knew you. I thought you were some asexual freak, but now, seeing this, maybe you are 'normal' after all."

Cara sat on the edge of the bed, holding the eight-inch sex toy in her left hand and her knife in the other. "Maybe we'll use this later." She smiled down at Dawn's fearful eyes. "You can lie back and think about Lucy, can't you?" When Dawn shook her head, Cara's smile faded. "I know you've got a thing for her, Dawn. And I know it was you who talked her into leaving me. It doesn't matter how much you shake your head, I know it was you, whispering in her ear, turning her against me. It was you. And I know you know where she is now."

Leaning forwards, Cara pulled the gag from Dawn's mouth.

"Please, Cara, I don't know where Lucy is, honestly." Dawn's voice was frail and frightened. "I have her phone number, take it, please. You don't have to do this, you don't have to kill me, please..."

"Kill you? Who said anything about killing you? You must think I'm some kind of monster. Nah, I'm not going to kill you, but I'm not leaving until you give me her address."

Cara laughed inside when relief physically flowed over Dawn's face; her body seemed to relax, and she stopped fighting her restraints. "So, tell me where she is and this will all be over."

When Dawn said she didn't know, Cara's patience wore thin. "Just tell me where the fuck she is, you fucking skanky bitch!"

Dawn protested again that she didn't know where Lucy was. Cara picked up the gag and shoved it forcefully back in Dawn's mouth, anger welling up inside her. "Fine, do it the hard way!" She thought how she could make her captive talk. "Look, bitch, I don't want to be here; you don't want me here. Tell me where she is, or I'm going to start hurting you."

The muffled reply Cara knew well. It wasn't what she wanted to hear. "I mean it, Dawn, I'm going to hurt you if you don't nod that you're going to tell me." She bent over her prisoner and looked her in the eyes. "Don't be stupid, yeah? Tell me!"

Dawn shook her head.

"All right, you can't say I didn't give you a chance." A part of her was pleased Dawn was playing hardball; Cara had never liked her – she'd just pretended she did for Lucy's sake. "Here we go."

Cara walked into the kitchen, took her serrated knife out of her bag and walked back into the bedroom, where she heard Dawn gasp, then close her eyes, tight. "This isn't going to be pleasant, you know that, right?" Cara leaned over and removed the gag.

"Please, Cara, I don't know where she is. I only have her phone number. She was scared you might come after her when you were released, so she left and didn't tell me where she was going, just that we could talk over the phone. I'm telling you the truth; please believe me. Why don't you try her sister, huh? She might know."

Listening to her helpless host, Cara almost bought it, almost. "I don't think so," she said, replacing the gag, attempting to miti-gate the noise, "Lucy can't stand that twat of a sister of hers. No way! You're trying to palm me off to Katherine. That's just nasty, do you know that? You'd rather I was doing this to Lucy's sister?" And without warning, Cara stabbed Dawn's upper left calf, not hard, but enough to draw blood into Dawn's jeans. She knew it was only a matter of time before Dawn caved into the pain.

43

Expecting Harry to walk in on her at any minute, Amelie waited for the file to download onto her USB stick. She waited and waited. "Come on, you slow piece of shit."

When she was sure it was safely transferred, she pulled the stick out and placed it in her robe pocket.

Then she closed the file and left the laptop on the screen saver, as she'd found it.

She couldn't wait to get out of Harry's office. Amelie knew what she was doing was dangerous – it could get her killed. If Harry found out she was working with Lennox, she *would* be killed, found in some shallow grave somewhere.

Picking up the keys, she hurried to the door, opened it, stepped into the hallway and closed it, taking the keys out of her pocket. As she went to lock it, she saw Harry walk out of the bedroom, naked, looking for her, only he was looking in the opposite direction.

"Amelie?"

Turning to face him, she walked forwards a couple of paces, away from the door. "I'm here, Harry," she said, as he turned to her.

"What're you doing out here?"

She slid the keys into her pocket and walked up to him. "Nothing, I couldn't sleep, so I went for a drink upstairs. You don't mind, do you? I'm just getting the lay of the land, if I'm going to move in here."

"Really?" His face lit up. "Have you decided? You're moving in?"

Fuck! Why had she done that? It was the only thing she could think of to placate him, his eyes too suspicious. "Now, it's not a hundred per cent, but let's just say, the idea's growing on me."

"You mean it?"

"I'm not a liar, Harry, so yeah, I mean it," she replied, kissing him. "But, like I said, it's not a hundred per cent. I've got a lot of things to work out before I commit."

His arms around her waist, Amelie breathed out a sigh of relief.

"You'll make me a very happy man, you know that?"

Amelie smiled, aware his hands were dangerously close to both the keys and the USB stick. "Let's go back to bed, yeah? I'm really tired now."

She had to find a way of going back to the office and locking it and getting Harry's keys back in his trousers. The only way to do that was by getting him to sleep again.

It was half three in the morning by the time she was under the duvet again. Harry had his arm around her. He wouldn't stop talking, like an excited schoolboy on Christmas Eve, which might be adorable if she didn't have to return his keys.

44

___

Nasreen arrived at the station at half eight, giving her half an hour to set her computer up, make a cup of tea and settle in before Dawn Weaver arrived for her interview.

With how badly the department had been hit by budget cuts, everyone had to work one in three weekends. When Nasreen arrived at the office, she saw Watts and O'Hara were working, and so was Hilary Farmer.

In the kitchen, Nasreen switched on the kettle. Once it had boiled and she'd added her tea bag and milk, she walked her mug back over to her desk. While she was in the kitchen, her computer loaded.

Bringing up Cara's file, Nasreen reread it, looking for any details she may have missed. During her time as a uniformed officer, she'd come to believe that the more she knew about a suspect, the better. It was surprising how much information she could get on any suspect, if they were in the system, which Cara was, in droves.

Expelled from three schools for misbehaviour, Cara left with five GCSEs in the important subjects: maths, English, science, history and geography. Considering she had such a horrible upbringing, she'd gained A – C grades, which was impressive. Impressive was an understatement. Bishop said that he expected Cara to have an IQ up to, or in excess of 180, so maybe he was right.

Having been sectioned twice in her life – once after trying to commit suicide when she was eighteen, and a second time after kidnapping Lucy – the hospital would have a wealth of information about her in her psychiatric file, which they needed, if they were going to apprehend her. As far as Nasreen knew, Gupta had requested a court order.

By the time Nasreen read through Cara's file, it was nine o'clock. She sat back and waited for the phone to ring from reception downstairs. According to Gupta, Dawn Weaver had information on both Cara and Lucy.

45

Amelie awoke to the sound of the shower going in the background. She looked over at the other side of the bed to find Harry was missing. The alarm clock said: 09:16. She still had to lock the office door and get Harry's keys back inside his trouser pocket.

She heard the shower stop.

Knowing this was her best chance, she rose and wrapped herself in her robe, walked out of the bedroom to next door. After locking the door as quickly as she could, she walked back to the bedroom.

"Morning, sleepyhead." Harry was drying himself. "I was going to ask you to join me, but I didn't have the heart to wake you."

"Thanks, I was pretty tired."

Shit! She still had to get his keys back in his pocket. Sat on the edge of the bed, Amelie put her hands in her pockets, wrapping her fingers around the keys.

Harry found a pair of boxers in his chest of drawers and put them on. Then, with her heart pounding, Amelie watched as he picked up his trousers and pulled them up, fastening them with a button and pulling the zipper up.

Taking the set of keys out of her pocket – while he was putting on a T-shirt – she bent down and put the keys on the floor.

"Where're my keys?" Harry put his hands in his pockets twice to check.

"They were in your pocket when I folded them up earlier," she replied, using her foot to slide the keys further under the bed.

"They're not in my pocket now. Where the hell are they?"

"Don't panic! They've got to be around here somewhere."

She joined Harry in searching for his keys. Joining him upstairs, they continued searching for the keys. Harry was getting angry by the time they were back in the bedroom. Amelie crouched down at the foot of the bed and looked underneath. "Here they are!"

"Thank God." Harry took them from her. "How the hell did they get under there?"

"They must've fallen out when I folded your trousers," she replied, matter-of-factly. "Sorry, Harry, I didn't mean for them to drop out."

Fortunately, his expression changed from suspicious to happy. She hoped her face didn't give away her relief.

She'd done it! He would never know she'd been in his office.

"No, I'm sorry, I didn't mean to get angry." He put his arms around her. "This isn't what I'm like normally."

"It's okay, I get angry too."

When he embraced her, Amelie felt nothing but relief. She gratefully accepted his cuddle, knowing she would be walking out of here in one piece. She didn't honestly know how Harry would have reacted had he caught her on his laptop. The danger was over, for now.

46

———

Cara looked at the clock: 09:16.

Frustrated wasn't the right word. Incensed, enraged; she'd tried everything to get Dawn to talk. Either she didn't know where Lucy was, or she was one tough bitch. Looking down at her captive's bloody clothes, she shook her head, trying to think of something else she could use to get her to talk. "I know you have it, so you might as well tell me, or..."

Bending down, her mouth over Dawn's ear, Cara whispered. Dawn's eyes bulged, as she started crying into her gag. It was the desired response. Standing up, she looked down at Dawn's tear-soaked cheeks. Why she hadn't thought of threatening Dawn's younger brother earlier she didn't know. "So, are you ready to tell me?"

Dawn nodded vigorously.

"If you scream when I take this off, I swear I'm going to stick this in your eye, do you understand? And then I'll find your brother and stick this in him too. All I want is her address, and I'll be on my way." And Cara bent over, taking out Dawn's gag, half-expecting her to scream, given what she'd just whispered.

Why hadn't she thought of this to begin with? Cara was tired; she managed a couple of hours between torturing Dawn, which she enjoyed more than she thought she would.

"Over on my hope chest, there's a notepad." Dawn looked over in the direction of the chest, desperation in her voice. "Please don't hurt him, Cara, please. He's all I have in my life." There was no bravado, no defiance left in her.

Cara went over to the hope chest and picked up the pad, looking for a pen. When she located one, she walked back to Dawn's bedside. "Go on! What's the address?"

She too was desperate; she needed to know where Lucy was. She wrote it down, ripped out the piece of paper and tossed the pad on Dawn's bed. "Scotland? What the fuck's she doing there?"

It made no sense. Lucy was a city girl, and now she was holed up in the arse end of nowhere.

"What're you going to do to her? Please, leave her alone; she's happy."

Those words hurt. Cara, her eyes narrowed, looked down at her helpless captive. "And what's that supposed to mean, hmm? Are you saying she wasn't happy with me? Is that what you're fucking saying?" The knife in her hand was calling her. "Is it?"

"No! That's not what I'm saying." Dawn shook her head, her eyes wide, scared, knowing she'd made a mistake. "Please, just go. You've got what you came for."

"I'm not going anywhere until you qualify that comment." Cara gripped the blade's handle tight. "What did you mean, Dawn? We were happy."

"For a while, you were, yeah." Dawn looked at the blade, then up at Cara's angry face. "Lucy loved you; she did–"

"What the fuck do you know about it?" Cara folded the piece of paper and slid it in her pocket. "It doesn't even matter now, does it? I don't give a fuck what you think. You were always jealous of me and Lucy. You caused all the crap in our lives, whispering in her ear, telling lies about me."

"I didn't need to tell lies about you. You crashed your relationship; I was there for Lucy like real friends are. She was scared of you towards the end, do you even know that? She couldn't wait to get away from you. Why do you think she's moved as far away as she can? Lucy hates you now–"

"Shut your fucking mouth!" Cara towered over Dawn. Through a red hazy mist, her arm went up in the air.

All she saw when she brought the blade down was Dawn's interfering face.

It went through Lucy's friend's cheek, erupting in a torrent of crimson, as Cara pulled it back up and down, again and again.

"Fucking bitch!" she spat at her victim. "Why couldn't you just leave us alone, huh? Interfering, whispering, lying about me." And she hadn't come here to kill Dawn; she only wanted the address. Dawn wasn't one of her masterpieces – far from it.

She could hear Dawn gargling the last few breaths of her life.

The pillow beneath her head was red, as was her torn face. "Why'd you have to say those things, huh? Did you want me to do this to you?" Anger consumed her, thinking of all those times Dawn had said disparaging things about her to Lucy.

Bringing the bloody knife up again, Cara brought it back down, the blade slicing into Dawn's heart, killing her instantly. Looking down at her host's corpse, Cara struggled pulling the knife out. When she finally managed to, she wiped the knife on Dawn's top and, hands shaking with rage, she took three long deep breaths.

Knowing she had Lucy's address in her pocket, she calmed down. Checking herself in the bathroom mirror, she saw blood on her face and clothes. There was no way she could leave the house looking like Leatherface's sister, so she stripped and jumped in the shower, feeling the warm jets soaking into her skin.

47

———————

"How's the investigation going, guys?" Nasreen sat on the edge of Watts' desk.

They looked exhausted, which wasn't surprising, given the pressure they were under for results. Watts was the senior of the partners, although they were both sergeants, and he looked like he had the weight of the world on his shoulders.

"Slowly," the portly Watts replied. "We've got literally nothing to go on. Franks wants results. There were no cameras nearby, no witnesses, the tyres of the car they used are the most common there are, so it could have been any number of makes and models. We're looking into his past, to see if there might be something there."

"Oh, really?" She tried to sound surprised – she wasn't sure if she'd succeeded. "What, do you think it might be about something he's into?"

"Don't tell anyone," O'Hara whispered, "but the shooters left a note. It hasn't been made official yet, so mum's the word."

"Of course. And? What did the note say?"

"This is What Happens to Dirty Pigs," she read out loud.

"Bloody hell! You don't think he was dirty, do you? Not Adams, surely?"

In a bit more than a whisper, Watts replied, "We haven't found anything to confirm it, but stranger things have happened. And especially in this department – it won't be the first time, let's put it that way."

"Nah, I don't buy it. Adams was a straight shooter, wasn't he?"

"That's what we thought, until we saw this. You never really know anyone, not really, so we'll take this investigation wherever it leads us."

"There's got to be a rational explanation, or they killed the wrong man. I really can't see Adams as being bent." Nasreen looked up at the clock on the wall: 09:38.

It didn't look like Dawn was coming, so Nasreen decided to go and find her – she would check Dawn's flat first. "Okay, guys, my interview hasn't turned up, so I'm going to try to find her. If she arrives after I've gone, let her through to interview room three, would you, please?"

"No worries, Nas." O'Hara stared back down at his paperwork.

Not wanting to waste any time, Nasreen walked back over to her desk, picked up her suit jacket and coat and dressed for cold weather, buttoning up her coat. She tried phoning Weaver, receiving an answerphone message. "I'm off to Dawn Weaver's flat, if you need me for anything?" Nasreen waited for the partners to acknowledge her before she headed off.

48

Cara finished drying herself and changed into a hoodie and jeans. She loved her new purchases from Imelda's shop. The hoodie said "Cute but Deadly", which was so ridiculously apt.

Cara went to tie her hair in a ponytail, forgetting she'd cut most of it off. Placing her cap and boots on, she was ready to leave Dawn's flat.

While wondering what Lucy was doing, Cara opened the front door.

She stepped outside onto the covered walkway, turned around and closed the door.

"Dawn? Dawn Weaver?" she heard from behind her.

When she turned, that fucking bitch detective, Nasreen whatever her name was, stood in front of her. The inner rage, which she expelled only half an hour earlier, swept over her. This pig killed Beattie.

Dropping her bags, Cara grabbed the pig bitch and ran forwards, full force, easily pushing her back. She pushed the pig into the recycling bin, where Cara managed to get her on the floor.

49

Nasreen felt the woman kick her in the ribs, before she was picked up like she was a rag doll. The woman was strong – Nasreen was no match for this woman's strength.

Now upright, but with the woman's hands gripping her blouse collar, Nasreen tried to punch her, but she was too quick, throwing her back.

"You fucking bitch!" the woman screamed. "You murdered Beattie."

With only a foot separating her from this psychopath, Nasreen looked at this brunette woman's eyes. After a couple of seconds, it dawned on her who it was. "Cara?"

Nasreen could kick herself for letting the length and colour of her hair fool her.

"Beattie give you that, did she?" Cara pointed at Nasreen's cheek.

Nasreen changed position, ready for a fight, although the strength that Cara had was staggering. Only a second later, she backed up four paces, as Cara moved forwards. "You're under arrest for the m–"

Before Nasreen knew what had happened, Cara ran at her, grabbed her and pushed her into the perimeter wall.

She managed to avoid her head hitting the bricks, but that was the least of her worries, she realised, when she felt herself being pulled up and over the wall.

Screaming, as she was hoisted over the wall, her body kept going, until she saw the ground coming towards her.

She managed to turn and land on her feet.

As she landed, her knee turned forty-five degrees. Nasreen felt sick, as she rolled onto her back, holding her knee. She groaned in agony.

<h1 style="text-align:center">50</h1>

Cara looked over the wall and saw Nasreen rolling on the ground. She was injured. Without thinking, Cara picked up her bags from outside Dawn's door, ran along the covered walkway and down the concrete stairs until she was on the ground, in the car park.

Her Micra was only fifty metres away from the flats, but she had to decide whether to flee or whether to finish that fucking bitch off. "This is for you, Bea," she said, dropping the shopping bags and taking her knife out of her handbag. "Come here, you horrible bitch."

She turned on her heels and headed for the injured pig, who she could see rolling on the ground, clutching her knee with both hands. "You're so fucking dead," Cara yelled, as she raised the knife and brought it down on the injured cop.

51

———

"Thanks for a lovely evening, as always," Amelie said, embracing him.

"Hey, I should be saying that to you." He hugged her tight. "Please think really hard about my offer. And I'll try not to pressure you, okay?"

"I will." She had no intention of accepting his offer.

It was cold out on the decking, but she was wrapped up in her jumper and coat, so it was only her face that bore the brunt of the late winter weather.

Safe in the knowledge that she locked the office door, the laptop was as it should be, and that her USB stick was in her handbag, she kissed him for the last time that morning. "So, I guess I'll see you soon then."

"I can't wait. See you soon, beautiful."

As she smiled and turned to walk along the gangplank, she saw a grey-haired man in a long charcoal coat waiting on the other side. She didn't recognise him. It was only when she heard Harry say, "Peter," that she realised it must be Peter Franks, the man who had set Lennox up, and who tried to have him killed. She hated Franks on sight.

"Come on over, Peter," Harry said, holding her by the waist to prevent her from leaving. "I've got someone I want you to meet."

Amelie stood aside for Franks to meet them on board. As Franks approached, he smiled at her – she didn't like his smarmy "I know something you don't" smile. It repelled her, yet she smiled back, until he was on the boat, facing her.

"You didn't tell me we were going to be joined by such a," Franks said, intentionally pausing, "beauty."

Amelie felt like puking. Did he really think that kind of slimy bravado worked on women? "Why, thank you." She let him take her hand and kiss it.

"You're very welcome," Franks replied, with a sly smile.

"Amelie's leaving. I'm afraid it's just you and me out there on the open water."

"Oh? That's a pity." Franks gave her hand back. "Are you going to introduce us anyway? It'd be nice to put a name to a face."

Amelie stood back, closer to Harry.

"Amelie Desmarais, this is Peter Franks. Peter Franks, meet Amelie Desmarais."

"I'm very pleased to meet you, Miss Desmarais."

"Likewise," she replied, with a short smile.

Feeling confined, all she wanted to do was to leave this wretched boat, needing to get the incriminating USB stick as far away as possible.

More than anything, she wanted to get away from Peter Franks, away from his horrible mannerisms. Creepy didn't even come close to how she would describe him. "Um, I'm going to leave you both to it."

Franks stepped aside and let her past. She walked to the end of the gangplank and turned to find them both watching her.

Harry waved, followed by Franks. She smiled and waved back. "See you soon, Harry."

It wasn't until she was off the dock that she could turn and look back at *The Albatross*. When she did, Harry and Franks had gone inside.

52

Nasreen put her hands up and caught Cara's wrist, the blade pointing down at her right breast. Fortunately, when Nasreen saw Cara approaching, she'd tried to crawl backwards and her knee had popped back in, with excruciating pain. The adrenaline and fear had drowned out the pain. She was in a fight for her life.

Looking up, she could see the effort Cara was putting into killing her. Her face was contorted, her eyes narrowed and focused.

Cara was too strong for her and had the upper hand, being on top.

The blade was getting closer to her with every passing second.

She couldn't hold Cara off much longer, feeling the strain on her wrists.

"You're going to pay for killing Beattie," Cara said, phlegm dripping from her mouth.

"Beatrice... got... what... she deserved," she replied, between breaths, the blade only an inch away from her chest.

She was losing the battle, possibly the war. "As will you."

Nasreen screamed, as she felt the tip of the blade cut into her breast.

"What the," came a voice from a distance away. "What the hell's that?"

Looking to her left – every molecule in her body fighting for life – she could see a group of people running towards them; they were a long way off.

Staring back up, she could see the panic in Cara's eyes. With every muscle keeping the knife from digging into her any further, Nasreen struggled to stay alive. The blade had to be an inch into her flesh.

"You were lucky this time, bitch!" Venom oozed from Cara's voice.

As suddenly as Cara had lunged at her outside Dawn Weaver's flat, she stood up and ran off. A wave of relief swept over Nasreen, as she lay on the ground. Blood was pooling into her blouse; she could feel it. "Shit! Shit! Shit!"

A group of six people – three male and three female – came to her aid. When the guys said they were going after her attacker, Nasreen told them not to bother, that she was too dangerous. "Please, leave it. This is a police matter."

"Stay still," said one of the three girls. "We've called for an ambulance."

"It's okay, I'm a detective."

"We know who you are," said another of the three girls.

"You're so brave doing what you do," said the third. "I read all the newspaper articles about you and watched all your interviews on TV. You're, like, the bravest person I've ever met."

"Or the stupidest," Nasreen replied.

"So, why do you do it?" asked the second. "It's dangerous."

It was a valid question. "Someone's got to," was the best answer she could give. All she could feel was the pain in her breast and squelch of blood dripping down her chest.

In under five minutes, the ambulance arrived. Nasreen protested at needing assistance. All she needed was to take off her blouse and stem the bleeding, and a knee support. The paramedics put her on a gurney and wheeled her into the waiting vehicle.

53

"Fuck! Fuck! Fuck!" Cara slammed her fists on the steering wheel.

She missed her chance to kill that cop bitch. If those arseholes hadn't started running towards them, she would be dead by now.

Frustrated didn't even cut it; she was so angry with herself for not following through, for not stabbing her in her black heart. Cara slammed her fist on the steering wheel again.

She had more pressing matters to deal with, she was in the heart of the city, in her own car, which was registered in her name, with the police not far behind her. Where could she go? Needing to ditch the car and pick up a new one, it had to be nondescript.

Not far from John Wood's flat, she had an idea. Her frown turned to a smile. She could kill two birds with one stone, so to speak. Yeah, that's what she was going to do. It was Saturday morning, quarter past ten. He would be in now, she thought, knowing that he would have had a heavy night last night. It was the perfect solution to her problem.

When she was just around the corner from his block, she

parked her car on a single yellow line – not caring that it would get a ticket – and got out, taking her bags with her. She had the two most important items in her handbag, the blade and the bottle of mace.

With her shorter brown hair, and baseball cap on, she felt camouflaged enough to walk the two streets to John's block of flats. It had been a while. Cara had to admit to feeling nervous about returning, after John and his two mates raped her.

This time it was different. This time she was in control, not John.

He wouldn't know what the fuck hit him, and when he did finally realise, it would be too late.

"So, how's the investigation going?" Harry asked, handing Franks a tumbler of whisky. "How are Watts and O'Hara doing?"

Franks accepted the glass of whisky and took a sip. It was the rank high street shop variety, probably a Bell's or The Famous Grouse. He tried not to show his distaste. "They're doing the best they can." He sat on the left sofa in the lounge. "They've not got much to go on, to be honest. Garvey's a clever prick. He used a common car with common tyres, and Clive's house is nowhere near any cameras."

"You heard about the shooting last night? Two of Margaret Hughes' sons are dead and the third is in critical condition. Fifteen people were injured in total, including Margaret. I got a phone call from Norris this morning, while I was in the shower; he gave me an update. It had to be Garvey, right?"

Franks nodded. He'd had the same phone call from PCC Norris, only last night, not this morning. He'd told Norris to sit tight, while he discussed the situation with Harry. "Yeah, I've heard. It's all over the news. Garvey's becoming a royal pain in our arses. I had a meet with Astor and Foster last night. I told them they need to find Garvey and whoever else Garvey's with. They objected, but I put them straight."

"Good, because Garvey could really fuck things up for us." Harry sipped his drink. "We need him gone, now. We can't have any more of these attacks. I had my arse handed to me by Embry at the COBRA meeting – that can't happen again."

Franks hated it when Harry spoke to him this way. His superior was basically saying this was all his fault for not handling Garvey properly before. "They're doing the best they can. Garvey's a ghost right now; he could be anywhere, planning anything."

"Yeah, I know, and that's what worries me. The press is all over this. You've seen it; this is having the opposite effect of the project. We're supposed to be making the streets safer, not more like the United fucking States, with all their drive by shootings. We can't have this in the UK, Peter, we just can't."

"I know, Harry." His temper quickened. "Do you think I want this? I want the press to be showing big fucking drug seizures, not this crap, but what the fuck else can I do? I've got Foster and Astor looking into it. Tell me, what more can I do?"

There was an uncomfortable silence. Franks sipped his shit whisky, trying not to show his anger. Harry was right about one thing: all these shootings were damaging the project's fundamental mandate.

He took his boss's silence to mean he didn't know what else they could do about Garvey. "Look, we'll get him eventually, but until we do, we need to limit the damage as much as we can."

Harry looked at him, then sipped his drink. "And how do we do that?"

"We don't need to worry about O'Hara and Watts catching up with Garvey. They're good investigators, but they're not going to find him, so we can relax on that front. Do you know who we have investigating the Hughes shootings?"

"I don't know. Norris didn't go into details."

"For what it's worth, my advice would be to speak to Norris and make sure he puts a couple of rookies on it. We don't want Garvey caught by our own."

Harry nodded. "Can I leave that with you? I'm liaising with Embry on this, and you know what a handful she can be."

Franks raised one eyebrow. Home Secretary, Suzanne Embry, *was* a handful. And he wasn't talking about her more than ample tits, either, although he imagined they were probably more than a handful.

Very unusual to fancy a politician in the UK, but Embry was lovely to look at.

That being said, why should he do everything? Instead of arguing, he replied, "Yeah, leave it to me. I'm on it."

"We'd better hope there aren't any more shootings, or Embry'll be crawling up my arse," Harry said, the gravity evident in his voice.

"Lucky you. I could think of worse women to have crawling up my arse." He watched Harry's grim face turn to an unwanted smirk. "Speaking of women, where'd you meet Amelie?"

Amelie screamed "whore" to Franks the minute he laid eyes on her. Tall, mixed race, beautiful, body to die for. Why would a woman like that be interested in Harry? It made no sense to him – she had to be a whore.

"We met at a friend's birthday party a couple of months ago."

Harry refilled his own whisky and offered Franks another.

"Oh? That's great. Good for you. You deserve a good woman after your, second, or is it third divorce?"

"Cheeky git." Harry laughed. "Second. Yeah, she's amazing."

"What does she do for work?"

"She's a mobile masseuse. She wants to open a parlour soon, but for now, she goes to her clients' homes."

Amelie Desmarais was so obviously a hooker, how could Harry not see it? She even had the cliché job to go with it. Franks sipped his awful whisky and decided he needed to know more about Harry's hooker.

55

Terrence closed his car door, as he saw Aldwyn Bishop pulling into the car park in his dark grey BMW i8 Coupe. Terrence walked past two rows of cars until he saw Bishop getting his bits together.

When Bishop got out of his car, wearing a light grey well-fitted suit, he thought, poser, once more. "Nice ride, Bishop," he said, with an impressed expression on his face.

"Thanks. She's new. My partner bought her last week."

"Someone's clearly getting paid too much here, is all I can say," he said in jest.

"How's Nasreen doing?"

A change of conversation, Terrence sensed Bishop was uneasy talking about money. Maybe it was because he had lots of it.

At Bishop's boot, Terrence accepted the protective clothing and put it on over his suit. A white coverall, shoe protectors, face mask and gloves. He checked Bishop's gear; Bishop inspected his.

When ready, he started walking towards the flats, through the car park, with Bishop close behind. "She's got a stab wound to her chest and a dislocated knee," he replied, professionalism taking over. "It's not serious, apparently. She told me to come straight here, instead of going to the hospital. Cara's a brunette now. Nas said she was attacked when Cara was coming out of Dawn Weaver's flat. Uniforms are already there; they've cordoned it off and the crime scene team are on their way."

"Good," Bishop replied, as they ascended the concrete steps.

When they reached Dawn Weaver's flat, Terrence looked over the wall and saw how far Nasreen fell. He whistled, not wanting to ever drop that far – he would probably break a leg or an ankle. Poor Nasreen had been through the wars recently.

Terrence showed his warrant card to two uniforms outside the front door of Dawn's flat. They let him pass. He walked through the flat, looking quickly in each room, until he came to the bedroom. "Oh shit!" Terrence looked at Dawn Weaver's bloodied corpse. "See what you make of this, Bish."

He let Bishop through the doorway.

Terrence walked to the far side of the bed, while Bishop stayed nearest the door.

"There was real hatred there," Bishop murmured. "Cara really didn't like her."

"That's no way to go. How many stab wounds do you count?" Terrence asked Bishop, not wanting to count them himself.

"Eight or nine facial wounds. But they didn't kill her. No, the stab to the chest killed her. She would have bled out from the facial stabs, but Cara finished her off, by the look of it. That wound to the chest killed her."

"Why would she end it quickly? It doesn't make any sense. Surely she'd want the victim to suffer for as long as possible?"

"I don't think she wanted to kill the victim. Cara kills men, right?"

"Yeah, except the victim in the bedsit."

"Cara didn't want to kill her. You said it yourself; she was caught off-guard, right? Her picture on the news startled the victim, forcing Cara to kill her. This one though, it's different. There's so much anger. This vic knew her, didn't she?"

"Cara's ex's best friend, yeah." Terrence looked down at the cuts on Dawn's face. "She was due to come into the station for an interview. She had something to tell us about Cara and Lucy. She won't now."

"If I had to guess, and it is just a guess, I'd say the victim angered Cara somehow. If Cara wanted to kill her, she could've just stabbed her in the heart and have done with it. No, with this level of rage, the vic either said something, or did something to rattle her cage."

"Okay, so, what?" Then it dawned on Terrence. "You don't think she came looking for something, do you?"

Bishop considered his comment. "She's looking for her ex!"

"That makes sense. Looking for payback for having her put in a nuthouse. Nas told me Lucy was responsible for that."

"Which means we need to find this Lucy, and soon."

"This really is one sick puppy we're dealing with. I'm going to enjoy putting this one down," he said, observing how Dawn Weaver was displayed, both legs bound to the footboard and both wrists to the headboard. "The only problem is, she's gone to ground. We can't find her. Nas has already tried."

"Cara's still evolving. She hasn't found her MO yet – that's why she's all over the place. Our best chance of apprehending her is finding Lucy."

Terrence loved the way Bishop was so alarmist. The language he used and the way he said it always sounded so urgent, so dramatic.

He could tell Bishop had just returned from the States – they probably all sounded like that there. "Level with me here, have you seen anything like this before?"

"Honestly? No. What worries me is that she's out there. She might not be far, but she may as well be in Australia."

"Let's hope someone spots her and calls it in."

"Agreed, the only problem is people are going to be on the lookout for a long-haired blonde, not a shoulder-length brunette. It's a primitive disguise, but an effective one."

"I know, but there's not a lot we can do about that until Monday morning. I'll get Gupta to organise another press conference first thing Monday."

"It could be too late by then, Terrence. Think how many victims she could have murdered by Monday morning. We need to inform the public now."

56

———

Cara ran up to the communal door to John's block of flats, opened it and quickly stepped inside, hearing the police helicopter nearby. Stabbing a police officer would do that. She wished she'd succeeded in killing that fucking cop.

Security in this shithole block of flats was a joke – there wasn't any. Anyone could come and go; there was no lock, no passcode or card swipe machine, nothing, just pull and it opened. John would regret that soon enough though.

Carrying her shopping bags and handbag, she walked up the stairs until she came to the second floor. It was covered in graffiti, and smelt of piss. It was a real crack den. Looking at the dirty walls and floor, she pitied anyone who had to live in this cesspit. And this was just the stairwell – she dreaded to think what the flats were like inside. Having said that, she didn't remember John's being too bad.

Fortunately, she hadn't passed anyone on her way up.

Outside his flat, Cara put her shopping bags on the floor and knocked on his door, one hand on the mace inside her handbag. "Come on, you fucker, answer," she muttered.

There was movement from inside.

When she hobbled out of John's flat six months ago, bleeding and crying, she'd noticed he kept a baseball bat next to the front door – she hoped it was still there. John Wood was a big bloke; she would need help.

"Yeah?"

Cara smiled sweetly. He didn't recognise her at first. It didn't help that he was still half asleep. His short dark hair was everywhere. She didn't know short hair could be that messy. She tried to look desperate, like she was still a smackhead. "John, I need some H, man," she said, her voice low and drawn. "You can help a girl out, can't you?"

"Who the fuck are you? Who told you where I live?" Wood went to close the door. "Get the fuck away from my flat, you junkie bitch. The cozzers are fucking everywhere this morning."

"Come on, John, you remember me, don't you?"

It was only when he really looked at her face that he recognised her.

Cara smiled again, hoping he would let her in.

She didn't want to do anything out here in the hallway.

"Cara?" John smiled smugly. "Never thought you'd be back, girl. You must be the dumbest skaghead ever. Why the fuck would you–"

Pulling out the can of mace, she pressed the button, as the liquid shot into his face.

She laughed as he screamed in pain, backing into his flat, his arms up, protecting his eyes. Following him inside, when she was far enough in, she used her free hand to close the door, still firing the liquid at him.

"You fucking cocksucker!" She picked up the baseball bat he'd conveniently left for her. "This is for raping me, you bastard!"

John thrashed about wildly, making it hard for her to use the bat. He was blind and in excruciating pain, but wounded animals were often the most dangerous – she knew this well. The hallway wasn't wide, so she had to come at him with the bat over her head.

With John screaming, she only had a small time-window. Raising it, she brought it crashing down on top of his head.

It was a lucky shot, but not enough to be effective.

He was on the floor, flailing, trying to stop her.

She hit him again, this time rendering him unconscious.

Cara threw the bat down, bent over and grabbed his arms. She heaved him along the hallway and into his bedroom. By the time she'd dragged him to the bed, she knew there was no way she was going to get this steroid junkie on the bed.

Cursing under her breath, she had to bind him, but how? There were cable ties in her handbag. Cara looked around the bedroom for something to bind him to.

57

It was midday by the time Amelie arrived back at her riverside apartment. She'd paid the taxi driver a tip, the fare being taken care of by Harry. She opened her front door, stepped inside, and closed it with a sigh.

The first thing she noticed when she took off her high heels, were Lennox's trainers by the front door. They weren't there when she left last night. It was feeling more and more like a relationship. She took off her coat and hung it next to the door.

Lying on his front under the duvet, with his face on its side, was Lennox, fast asleep.

Amelie, exhausted, walked over to the bed and sat, unzipping her dress.

"Hey, beautiful," came Lennox's voice.

"Hey!" She stood and took off her dress. She so couldn't be bothered to fold it, so she launched it to the corner of the room. "I'm done in," she said, falling back on the bed, on Lennox's legs. "What a night."

Amelie closed her eyes. "I need a good night's sleep."

Lennox pulled back the duvet. "Come here, you."

She forced herself to accept his offer and climbed under the duvet, her head resting on his shoulder. With no effort, she could have drifted off there and then. "I managed to get the personnel file for you."

"You're kidding. That's fucking awesome."

"Yeah, I nearly got caught twice, but all's good. I'll try to get more when I'm next over there." She closed her eyes. Lennox kissed the top of her head. It was the little intimate touches that made her smile the most. "Thanks, baby. The USB stick's in my bag if you want to have a look. I'm going to sleep now." She rolled onto her side and rested her cheek on the pillow.

"Night, princess."

58

"Detective, the suspect's red Micra's been spotted," the uniform whispered.

Terrence turned his attention back to the camera. "So, if you're out clubbing, or just in a bar for the evening, keep a look out for this woman. If you see her, do not approach her, she is armed and extremely dangerous. Cara Mooney has already killed four people that we know of. If you see her, call this number, thank you."

When Bishop said they needed to inform the public now, he'd had a brainwave. Like clockwork, members of the press were waiting outside the flats, having heard on their police scanners that an officer had been stabbed. He made use of the Sky reporter and had offered to give her a comment on camera.

"Thank you, Detective Johnson, that was great," said the pretty reporter. "You said 'that you know of' just now, does that mean you believe there are more bodies waiting to be found?"

"It's a possibility, Danni, that's all. I'm really sorry, but I've got to get going." He made his excuses and walked back up the concrete stairs, along the covered walkway and into Weaver's bathroom, where Bishop was crouched down by the bin. "We've got to make a move. We've found Cara's motor."

59

———

Nasreen looked at her watch: 12:37. She winced as the doctor finished stitching the gash in her left breast. She never felt comfortable showing her body in public, but, luckily, she had a female doctor who pulled the curtain around, so that no one could see her topless.

"You were lucky, detective," said the doctor, packing up. "Any deeper and you might've needed surgery."

"I get told that a lot, how lucky I am, I mean."

"You can put your top back on now. I'll go and get you a knee brace. You'll need to come back to have the stitches out in a few days. I'm signing you off duty for a week to let it heal..."

"Oh, come on, doctor, you can't do that. I've got to get back to work. I'm right in the middle of a murder investigation. Don't sign me off, please."

She waited, as the doctor sighed. "I can only recommend. If you ignore my advice, there's nothing I can do about it. But I would advise working behind a desk for a few days. You need to give the wound time to heal."

Nasreen's blouse was soaked through with blood, so she used a hospital-owned T-shirt that the doctor had brought with her. It was tight when Nasreen put it on. It was one size too small, but it was better than wearing her bloodied top. "Thank you, doctor."

While she sat waiting for her doctor to bring the knee support, Nasreen pulled out her mobile phone and called Terrence. It was answered after three rings and it sounded like he was using hands-free equipment. "Are you driving?"

"Yes, we are. We're on our way to look for Cara. We've found her car, and it's not in a nice part of town."

"Nas, we're going to find her," Bishop said. "She won't get away with stabbing you, I promise. We've got two helicopters out looking for her, not to mention as many uniforms as we could get – she's not getting away."

"That's lovely of you to say, Bishop, but we all know how hard it's going to be to find her, much less take her in. So be careful if you do find her; she's dangerous."

"How are you doing, Nas? Are you still in A&E?"

"That's affirmative. The doctor wanted me to take a week off, but I put her straight."

"You need to take a couple of days, at least!" The reception was getting worse and Terrence found he was shouting. "And you're rostered off tomorrow and Monday, anyway. When you're finished at the hospital, go and spend some quality time with Mina, okay? I don't want you back to work until Tuesday at the earliest, understood?"

"But–"

"No ifs or buts, Nas, go home and recover. I'll keep you updated on any developments, okay? We've got to go, I'll call you later."

Rude! Terrence hung up on her.

She tried standing, slowly shifting off the A&E bed. When she put any weight on her knee, a searing pain shot to her brain.

The doctor said it would pass. Nasreen knew all about knee

injuries. Her first dislocation happened just before Ashraf died; she'd jarred her knee during a sparring session, and her kneecap had turned forty-five degrees. She really hoped it wouldn't put her out of commission for too long – she wanted to help apprehend Cara Mooney.

Picking her mobile up, Nasreen dialled home, and Katerina answered after five rings. She explained that she needed to be picked up from the hospital. Her nanny said she would drive over, and would be less than an hour. Nasreen didn't know what she would do without Katerina.

60

Cara looked down at the street below. So far, she'd seen ten police cars racing about; it was swamped with pigs out there. Helicopters could be heard above her. Having just stabbed a cop, it was no surprise there was a big reaction.

John said something into his gag, not that Cara could understand him. "What was that, John," she said, looking down at him, "watch the news, you say?"

Stepping over the bound lump, she picked up his remote. Sky News came on the TV automatically; she didn't even need to search for it. On the wall, the television displayed a picture of her with shoulder-length brown hair. It was a good likeness too. "Fuck!"

She heard him snort through his nose, laughing at her. "And fuck you!" She bent over and took the gag out of his mouth. "Have you got something to say to me, huh? If I were you, I'd be more worried about what I'm going to do with you than what's going on out there, you piece of shit."

"It's only a matter of time, whore. And if *I* were *you*, I'd worry more about getting out of here alive than getting even with me."

"On second thoughts..." She gagged him again. "You really are a horrible bastard!"

Picking up the knife from the bed, she crouched down and cut his T-shirt through the middle until it was severed, then whipped it out from under him.

Then she unbuckled his belt and yanked it out, throwing it behind her. She could hear him cursing her, when she cut his jeans off, leaving him in nothing but his pants. The way she had him bound, his wrists to the legs of his bed and ankles to the feet of a heavy wooden chest of drawers, made him look like a star. There was no way he was getting out of those cable ties. "I wonder which piece of you I'm going to start with?" She smiled when he looked up at her with scared eyes. "I think you know, don't you?"

Cara turned her attention to the hallway, when she heard the front door close.

"John? Where are you, babe? I've got something for you," came a voice.

Ducking behind the bedroom door, Cara watched John and put her finger in front of her lips. He screamed into his gag, trying to warn his visitor. Cara grinned down at him from her hiding place, excited. "Shh!"

"John? What the fuck?"

Coming out from hiding, Cara stood behind the young girl.

Cara listened as John tried to warn the girl.

Her name was muffled.

The girl turned around and faced her. It took the girl a couple of seconds to register that she was there. When the girl's eyes bulged, and she was about to scream, Cara plunged the knife into the girl's belly.

With her hand on the girl's shoulder, she forced the knife in until it couldn't go any further. "It doesn't pay to be your girlfriend, does it, John?" Cara laughed.

It was the look of disbelief on the girl's face that Cara loved the most.

Yanking the blade out, Cara grabbed the girl by the neck and twisted her round, so that she was facing John. She slit the girl's throat, blood spraying over the bed. Mostly, it sprayed, and then gushed over John. The girl's body slumped on top of him.

He was shouting, screaming, "No," into his gag.

With the girl sprawled over John, Cara bent down and rolled the heavy woman over, onto her back so that she was lying next to him.

She watched the girl's last moments, waiting for the eyes to die. "You know, you should try this. It's such a buzz, John. Oh wait, you're not going to, are you?" With the bloody knife in her hand, Cara forgot about the girl and turned her attention to her new almost-naked masterpiece.

61

Maggie was numb. Two of her beloved sons were dead, lying on a morgue slab, while her youngest, Scott, was hooked up to machines. The doctors weren't holding out for much hope – they'd been very clear on their diagnosis.

She held Scott's hand, her head down, hoping, praying to God that He spare her last remaining son. She needed Him to answer her prayers.

Her arm was throbbing. She'd been shot, but the bullet had only grazed her. It hurt like hell. She kept thinking back to the previous night, to seeing the muzzle flashes of the fully automatic machine guns firing at her and her sons. If only she could see the faces of the men holding those guns; she couldn't. "Please wake up, please wake up."

"Maggie," came a low voice she recognised, "there's a call for you from the hospice."

She looked up at Darius, Scott's best friend, who was holding a phone out for her to take. Darius was Scott's right-hand man – he knew the family business as well as any of her boys. Maggie took the phone from him.

Tears rolled down her cheeks, as she was told that her Phil

195

had passed away. The woman explained that they'd been trying to contact her all morning, to tell her that it was nearly time, to tell her to say her goodbyes.

All she had left now was her youngest son. If he died, which was expected, if not guaranteed, she didn't know how she would go on living. In five seconds, no longer, her entire world had collapsed. What could she do now?

Maggie thanked the woman for contacting her, hung up and handed the phone to Darius, who took it and sat down in a chair at the back of the room.

"Please, Scott, come home," she whispered, willing him to open his eyes.

He'd been shot five times, in various places. How could a man survive that? With God's help he could, she thought, putting her head down and praying. Until her Phil was diagnosed with prostate cancer, Maggie had never been a religious woman, never attending church, or any formal religious gatherings – it was only when Phil had cancer that she'd started praying regularly. She was never going to be a frequent church-goer; she believed religion should be a private affair between oneself and God.

Maggie didn't know what she should be doing. Should she be with her dead husband? Should she be with her dead sons? Or should she be here, by the side of her living son? There was so much she should be doing, she didn't know where to start. The police hadn't helped much – they'd come and asked her questions about last night, not that she was in a fit state of mind to be answering them.

It wasn't just her sons who'd been hurt or killed. Fifteen people had been shot in total, two of those fifteen killed, and thirteen injured. These animals didn't care who they hurt. One of Phil's nephew's sons had been shot, and he was only six. The hours directly following the shootings were chaotic. At least ten ambulances and as many police cars arrived outside the restaurant.

Everyone had been brought to the NHS hospital, which had a great Accident and Emergency ward. She'd consoled her daughters-in-law, while at the same time, trying to get to grips with the gravity of the situation herself.

Maggie spent over eight hours in the waiting area, while her son was in surgery, having the bullets dug out of his body. She had all her daughters-in-law with her, and over half of the extended family, some of whom had relatives here, who'd also been shot.

At three o'clock, she'd finally been allowed to see her only son. The doctor told her that Scott died on the operating table three times, although they were able to revive him each time. The doctor also told her that while he was a fighter, not to get her hopes up – Scott had had his spleen removed, and the chances of survival from injuries as severe as his were negligible. She'd prayed for him since.

She heard a phone ring and heard Darius talking – she wasn't listening. Her mind was too busy asking questions. Why were her sons dead? Who were the four men in that car? So many questions, she had, and so far, no answers.

"Maggie, you have to take this," Darius said. "It's important. It's about last night."

Although she didn't want to talk on the phone, Maggie dragged herself from her son and held the phone to her ear. "Yes?"

"Margaret Hughes? I'm Police and Crime Commissioner Charles Norris, ma'am. I've been asked to give you a call by a mutual colleague, Assistant Commissioner Peter Franks. First of all, I'd like to offer my condolences on your tragic loss – I know your grief must be great, so I won't keep you long."

She wasn't listening to the voice.

"Peter and I thought you would like to know we have positive picture identification of two of your attackers from last night. We have photos of them, taken from a kebab shop they visited opposite the restaurant. I would like to send you these photos, so you can make a head start before my officers investigate."

He'd suddenly gained her interest. He was offering her a chance to administer justice, street style. This commissioner must be part of the project. "You've found them?"

"We've identified their faces, but not yet their names. They're not in the system, which means it will take time for us to formally identify them through talking to witnesses and other investigative techniques, which will give you time to do your thing."

"Send them over," she said, quickly, desperately. "I'll pass you over to Darius, who will tell you the email address to send them to."

She handed the phone back to Darius, who took it and talked to the commissioner. Murderous thoughts flashed in her mind. These four feral animals would regret hurting her family. She had so many varying ways of murdering them in her mind, none of which were quick or painless. The longer it took to kill them, the better.

62

"What're you doing?" Amelie wrapped her arms around Lennox's shoulders and looked down at the laptop he was working on. On screen was the information she'd extracted from Harry's laptop, a list of the personnel involved in Project Clean Sweep.

Lennox grinned. "This is what we were waiting for. It's a who's who of bent cops. It even tells me where they're based and what rank they are. This thing goes right to the top of the police and further."

"So, I did good?" She kissed the side of his neck.

"I couldn't have asked for more, beautiful."

"There's more on Harry's laptop, a lot more." She hugged him tight. "It'll take me time to get it though. The laptop's in his office, and he keeps it locked."

"You've done enough, seriously. I don't want you getting hurt."

He turned in his seat, encouraging her to sit on his lap.

Amelie obliged and sat down, her arm around his neck.

"I don't think I could live with myself if you got hurt because of me."

She kissed him softly. "I've got something to tell you. About last night."

"Oh? What's up?"

There was no easy way of telling him. "Harry asked me to move in with him on *The Albatross*. He was serious too. He wants me to stop doing what I'm doing and commit to him, only him."

There was a long silence.

Amelie thought Lennox would object. Why would he want her living with another man? Whatever she decided to do, she would keep her apartment, no matter what. She loved this place – it was her haven, her paradise.

"And what did you say to that?"

"I told him I'd think about it. I don't want to, it's not as though I like him. But I could easily get the information you need if I was living on the boat. He'd have to leave me alone there at some point."

"I don't want you anywhere near that guy."

"Come on, that's not going to happen. He's my best paying client. The more I think about it, the more it makes sense to move in with him. I could have the information you need a lot sooner."

"I don't know, it's dangerous."

"Yeah, I know it is, but I can do this for you. Please let me. I want to help you get this guy, and the rest. What they're doing, it's wrong. Let me help you."

"Okay, okay, but the minute this gets too much, leg it, do you understand? I can't be the cause of you getting hurt, or worse."

"I'm doing this because I want to, not for you, okay?"

63

It was getting dark. Cara heard John crying into his gag. She'd just carved "RAPIST" into his chest with her blade. The deep gashes were bleeding freely, pooling around the curvy and straight letters. "Shut the fuck up! You big baby. If you think this hurts, just wait."

With her adrenaline peaking, she took the blade and made bigger letters on his stomach. His taut abs tried avoiding the blade, as he breathed in, but the knife easily sliced through his tissue and muscle, forming the word "SCUM". The word dripped down his side, onto the carpet. "If you think this hurts, try being raped by three men."

There was a knock on the door.

John tried calling out for help but he was too far away from the door for anyone to hear him. "I told you to shut the fuck up," she said quietly, angrily, putting the blade under his chin. "Another word and I'll stick you with this, got it?"

There was another knock.

Cara stood and slowly walked out of the bedroom, along the hallway until she came to the front door. Without making a sound, she looked through the peephole, to find two uniformed police officers waiting outside.

She crouched, her back against the door, waiting for them to leave.

When the officers knocked a third time, she got jittery, panicked.

She took several deep breaths.

There was movement outside.

When she stood and looked through the spyhole again, they were gone. With a sigh of relief, Cara walked back into the bedroom, where John was still crying, tears of pain streaming down his cheeks. "You fucking disgust me, you know that?"

When she straddled him, she thought about him entering this room with his two mates. She thought about him on top of her. Her screams reverberated in her mind.

She raised the knife above her head.

Every laugh, every taunt, every comment he'd made about her flashed in her mind, as she brought the blade down. The first blow stabbed Wood through his right eye.

Not satisfied, Cara raised the knife again, bringing it raining down on his face and neck time and again, until she was out of breath. Knowing the police weren't far away, and with adrenaline spiking, he was her most satisfying masterpiece yet.

DAY 8

TUESDAY, 27TH MARCH

64

Lucy Davis walked past the fat detective and sat on a plastic chair behind a scratched and battered table, which had been heavily scrawled over. The room was small, plain and depressing. She took her phone out of her bag and rested it in front of her. She hated having to be here.

"And what can I do for you today?" McGrath sat his fat frame on the chair in front of her. He studied her for a second. "Are you okay? You look pale."

Lucy coughed. "I'm fine, I think I'm coming down with something." She picked up her phone and pulled up a text message. She turned the phone around and slid it across the table, waiting for McGrath to read it.

Acknowledging her comment about feeling ill, McGrath picked up her phone, reading her message. "Hi Juicy, long time no speak," he read aloud. "I am a bird of prey now. I have so many things to show you, amazing things. I'll be with you for your birthday. Speak soon. Love C XXXXX."

Sat watching the sweaty detective, Lucy bit her lip nervously. "Juicy?"

"Cara's nickname for me," Lucy explained.

"Cara?" His accent was harsh Glaswegian. She had difficulty understanding him.

"Cara Mooney, my ex-girlfriend. She's wanted by the English police for those murders on the news. I don't know if you've heard about that, or not."

"Aye, we heard about it. But how does a girl like you end up with a girl like that?"

The way McGrath spoke was with disdain. He didn't like that he was talking to a lesbian. Lucy could tell she was talking to a homophobe. "What does that matter?"

"I'm just curious, how a cute woman like you, picks a psychotic bitch like that? I mean, you seem like an intelligent woman, how does that happen?"

Lucy felt like storming out of the interview room, or asking to speak to his supervisor. "She wasn't like this when we met. She was wounded, sure, but we all were. It goes with the territory when you're in rehab."

"You met her in rehab?"

Lucy knew she'd get a remark at that. It might not have been sensible getting involved with someone from the same clinic, but back then, Cara was vulnerable, like her. They formed a bond during their treatment. Sharing a room with Cara made her feel safe and cared for. "Yes," Lucy replied, her tone frosty.

"And you thought that was a good idea?"

"In hindsight, maybe not." Her vision was blurring. She felt sweat forming on her forehead. "But here we are. Look, can we skip the getting to know you part, and just get to the part where you tell me what you're going to do about Cara stalking me?" She folded her arms defensively. She didn't like McGrath, not one bit.

"Okay, Miss Davis, let's keep this civil, shall we?" McGrath held up his hands. "What would you like us to do about it?

We've got an abundance of money and officers, so you tell me what we can do for you."

His sarcasm was duly noted. "I don't know, what do you normally do when someone asks for help when they're being stalked?" She coughed, which turned into something far nastier. She accepted the glass of water McGrath offered her.

"Stalked?" He picked up her phone again. "This isn't stalking. Have you seen her?"

"Well, no."

"Has she been inside your home, or tried on your clothes while you're out? Have you noticed any of your belongings missing?"

"No, no, and no," she replied.

"Then I'm glad to say, you're not being stalked. She's getting off scaring you, is all. Honestly, Miss Davis, she's not on her way here."

Lucy tried not to show her contempt, however it must have been obvious. "First off, detective, she's abducted me before. Then I testified at her trial. Because of me, she was sectioned under the Mental Health Act. And because of my testimony, she was ordered into a psychiatric unit. I moved here to get away from her. I've only given my mobile number to one person, my best friend, Dawn Weaver, who Cara has murdered, and now she's sending me texts saying she's on her way. Doesn't that seem like an extreme to go to, just to frighten me?"

"And you think she knows where you live?"

"I asked Dawn not to write it down, to memorise it, but who knows? She might have told Cara where I live before she was murdered. So, yes, I do."

"And she might have been murdered because she didn't tell her where you live. You don't know that she got your address and is on her way here now, do you?" He sat back in his chair with his arms folded.

This was getting her nowhere. How could he be so blasé about it? She had good cause to ask to speak to McGrath's supervisor, an inspector, maybe. "No, I can't be certain, but the evidence speaks for itself, don't you think?"

"Look, Cara Mooney's a very wanted fugitive in England, okay? There's not much chance of her getting past the police down there, is there? But I'll tell you what I'll do, I'll speak to the lead detective on the case, for you. Will that satisfy you?"

"Yes, it will. I only came here to let you know what's going on."

"And I appreciate that, I do. But honestly, you don't need to worry about this. Cara will be apprehended before she ever sets foot in Scotland, I promise you. Later on today, you'll probably be watching the news and find out she's in police custody."

Lucy shook hands with McGrath. She hoped he was right. After all she'd been through with Cara, she wanted it to be over. When she heard the judge order her ex into a psychiatric unit, she'd known back then that Cara would be out sooner rather than later, which was why Lucy had relocated here.

Following McGrath to the reception area of the station, Lucy thanked him again for his help, and walked to her green MG Classic convertible. When she sat behind the wheel, she thought about Cara, thought about how happy they were together for the first year.

Starting the car, Lucy reversed out of the space, turned and accelerated towards the exit. Out on the road, she thought about their shared time at the rehab clinic. They shared a lot of themselves over the six weeks they'd been there; she'd opened up to Cara about her past, and she'd learned a lot about Cara's tragic upbringing.

Lucy had to admit that she was attracted to Cara from the first time she saw her, when she'd arrived at the clinic. Cara was so very charming and charismatic, or so Lucy thought – now she knew it was all an act, that Cara was a sociopath, able to say things she knew people wanted to hear. And it hurt to think that their three-year relationship was all a lie, that Cara never really felt anything for her, she couldn't, unable – how had she not seen it?

After a half hour drive, Lucy pulled into her driveway. She lived in a secluded house on a two-acre piece of land with her girlfriend, Helena. It was a lovely eighteenth-century property, small but full of character. It was white on the outside and full of wooden beams and very rustic on the inside. She loved it. She and Helena chose it together.

Lucy killed the engine and sat back in her seat. What must Helena think about all this? The poor woman just wanted a quiet life, to live happily in their lovely house, and now Helena had to deal with Cara, every bit as much as she did. She'd apologised to Helena so many times now, that it had lost all meaning.

Her mobile sang a tune. When she looked at the screen, she could see she had another text from Cara. Her heart stopped for a second. Lucy didn't want to read it. If she ignored it, maybe it wasn't real. Then she opened it.

65

───────

Nasreen limped out of the lift and into the office, where Gupta, Terrence and Bishop were sat around a whiteboard. There were photos of Cara's victims stuck on the board. There was also a line drawn horizontally across in black marker. Each of the photos were placed along the line in a chronological order.

"Sorry I'm late everyone," she said, carefully sitting on a chair left for her. "I've just had my stitches out. I won't be late again."

"How're you feeling?" Gupta asked, with genuine concern.

"Better than I was a couple of days ago, that's for sure."

"Good, I'll keep you on desk duty for the next week or so, until you've recovered."

"That's not necessary, sir. I'm fit for field work. I'm not going to sit here while you lot go out and get Cara Mooney. I need to help."

Nasreen noticed there were a lot of glances between her three colleagues. She knew being injured would make them baby her, but she wasn't about to let them do that. "I'm fine, honestly. I can still contribute, okay?"

"We'll see, Nas," Gupta replied.

"So, where were we?" Terrence stood next to the whiteboard.

"I was just saying that victimology's not helping us much on this one," Bishop replied. "There's no connection between victims that I can see. It looks like the first two were random pickups in bars and nightclubs, so ordinarily I would suggest staking out clubs and bars, but the rest of the victims aren't in keeping with that MO."

"Imelda wasn't tied up, so she doesn't fit," Nasreen added.

"But Dawn Weaver was, so she fits, but Cara knew Dawn. She didn't know the first two victims, or the third that we know of. You see where I'm coming from? Cara's all over the place. I would say she's evolving, but I don't think she is. I think she's playing this by the seat of her pants. She's making it very difficult to profile her."

"So, she's either crazy, or very intelligent," Terrence added.

"We know she's crazy." Bishop turned to the whiteboard. "And the jury's still out on how intelligent she is. But my guess is she's way up there. Arjun, have you got the court order yet for Doctor Denton's notes? It'll help us enormously to know what Cara's been through."

"Came through by email this morning," Gupta confirmed.

"Then can I suggest we go and pay the good doctor a visit?"

"I booked an appointment for midday."

"Sorry to ask, but what did we find at Dawn Weaver's flat?" Nasreen felt behind on the case after having to leave on Saturday.

Terrence passed her a file. Nasreen opened it and looked at the photos inside. She could see that Weaver died from a frenzied knife attack, much like the first two victims. It was strange for suspects to switch like this. "Was she sexually molested?"

Terrence shook his head. "Nope. No signs of molestation."

"But Cara knew Weaver, right?"

"Correct. She was coming in to tell us about Cara and Lucy Davis' relationship."

"So, why would Cara target Weaver?" Nasreen said this to everyone, throwing the question out to all. "She didn't know any of the other victims. Why change it up now?"

"We think she was there trying to get her ex-girlfriend's address," Bishop answered.

"Have we had any luck locating Lucy Davis?" she asked.

"Nope," Terrence replied. "It's like she vanished into thin air. I think Lucy's the key to all this, though. I think Cara's going after her, which is why she targeted Weaver."

"That could be her endgame," Bishop added. "She's not stupid, she knows we'll catch her eventually, and that she has limited time left, so she could have an endgame in mind."

"And what endgame would that be?" Nasreen asked.

"To find Lucy, and probably kill her," Bishop replied.

"Okay, here's what we're going to do," Gupta interjected. "Terrence and Bishop, you go and visit the good doctor, see what info you can glean from his notes. Nas and I will visit Weaver's flat again, see what we can find."

"Arjun." The team turned to find Franks in the doorway. "Can I see you for a second, please."

Franks had a piece of paper in his hand. Nasreen knew what that meant: they had another body. She tried to listen to what Gupta and Franks were talking about.

After a couple of minutes, Gupta walked back over to them.

"I stand corrected. Nas and I will visit the doctor. Terrence, you and Bishop are visiting a new crime scene. Cara's murdered a local drug dealer, a John Wood."

66

———

Lennox had the addresses of all twenty-nine Police and Crime Commissioners on Harold Thomas' list. He had a place to start; these were the top-ranking police personnel in the country.

Lennox put the USB stick into Amelie's laptop and downloaded it, adding it to the rest of the information already on it. He had enough intel on the stick to make people ask questions, to make life very difficult for the assistant commissioner.

Hearing the front door close, he looked up from the monitor to see Amelie.

He had everything ready. "Did you get them?"

"Yeah, I got the last two they had." Amelie hurried over with two plastic boxes containing USB sticks.

"Okay, we're making an insurance policy," he said, ripping the plastic packaging apart. He slid one into the USB port on his laptop and transferred all the files onto the first stick, then the second. "This way, if either of us are caught short, we'll have some leverage. I hate having to do this, but it's the only way to safeguard ourselves."

"Here." Amelie handed him two envelopes. "Where do you want me to keep them?"

Lennox handed an envelope with a USB stick in it back to her. "I don't want to know where yours is. Give it to a friend, relative, whoever, but make sure it's someone you trust. And I'll do the same with mine."

"Won't we be getting them involved too?"

"Not if they don't know what's inside," he replied, not quite believing what he was saying. "When you give it to them, tell them to keep it safe and only send it if something happens to you. Here, the address to write to on the envelope is here."

He waited while Amelie wrote the address on the envelope.

"Are you sure about that? Is this the best place to send it?"

"Where else are we going to send it?"

"The police, I don't know," Amelie said, a little confused.

"Baby, how can we send this to the police? We've got evidence on here of a massive conspiracy involving the highest-ranking policemen in the country."

"Shit, yeah, sorry, I wasn't thinking."

"That's okay." He smiled. "This company will know what to do with the information, if they need to. Remember, this is just an insurance policy. They won't play fair, if they do find us. This will make them think twice about hurting anyone, okay?" He saw the look of concern on Amelie's face. "Come here."

He held her tight, knowing how much danger he'd put her in by involving her. The last thing he wanted to do was hurt her, but he needed her help. They still had a lot of information to retrieve from Harry's laptop. Lennox hated the thought of her moving in with that bastard, Harry, but it was a necessary evil.

"All of this will be worth it, right?" she asked, her cheek on his shoulder.

"Yeah, of course it will, Am," he replied, certain it would

work out eventually. "These fuckers will get what's coming to them."

"And what about us? Will we get what's coming to us?"

He pulled away from the embrace. "What does that mean?"

"Those poor people you shot up north," she said, her chin crumpling, tears forming in the corners of her eyes. "You shot a kid, Lennox. He was only six."

Yeah, that had been a shock when he'd seen it on the news. "That was an accident, sweetie. None of us wanted that."

"But it happened." Tears were rolling down her cheeks. "I thought we were the good guys in all this. But we're not, if kids are getting shot – and the police won't stand for it, you know, they'll come after us harder now."

Lennox pulled her in for a hug again. "You're right. They'll try harder, which is why we need this insurance. If we get caught, we've got them by their balls, and they'll have to deal with us."

"Promise me you'll only get those responsible. No more kids, Lennox, please. I need to know we're the good guys."

"I promise, we'll be really careful from now on, okay?"

Lennox let Amelie go and get changed. He had to be on the road in less than half an hour. Leaving her apartment via the fire exit, to be sure he wasn't seen, he would be picked up by Barkley. They were going back up north.

67

Terrence showed his warrant card to a uniformed officer. Bishop followed him through the hallway and into the bedroom, where the Crime Scene Unit were busy dusting for prints, taking photos and all manner of other evidence gathering duties.

"Oh my dear God," Bishop said, stopping at the corpse of the female victim, his voice muffled by the face mask.

Looking down at the clothed girl, who was lying face up, surrounded by congealing blood, Terrence could tell she wasn't the intended victim. "The girl interrupted her?"

"That would be my guess," Bishop replied. "Cara dragged her body from where it fell over Wood, to where it is now."

"Yeah, I can see the drag marks." Terrence crouched down and studied the body.

The level of anger was apparent. When he looked down at the girl's body, he saw a nasty belly wound, and her neck had been slashed. "Okay, so the way I see it, this girl comes in, Cara waits for her, probably behind the door, the girl sees Wood tied up, then Cara comes from behind, the girl hears her, turns and Cara stabs her in the gut."

"Right," Bishop said, sounding impressed. "And then Cara turns the girl around, slits her throat and lets her drop on top of Wood. Then she drags the body back to where it is now."

"And then she goes to work on Wood." Terrence walked over to where Wood lay face up, both his eyes gaping red wounds, his mouth mangled, presumably by Cara's blade, and his neck a straggly mess. He looked down at the chest stab wounds, noticing how deep they were.

"And now she's started carving words into her victims." Bishop crouched down. "She's all over the place."

"I think we're safe to assume she knew him. RAPIST SCUM, is some message. It doesn't fit with her previous MO though, does it?"

"Like I said, she's all over the place. It's going to make finding her all the more troublesome. And look at how deep the letters are carved into his chest and stomach – the knife's practically scratching bone."

"I'm surprised she didn't cut his dick off. It's the kind of sadistic thing I imagine she'd enjoy."

"If she'd done that, he'd have bled out within minutes. No, she took her time with this guy, played with him, scared him. She knows better than to inflict a major injury too early – she enjoys the torture too much."

"When do you think she offed this guy?"

"Judging by lividity and colouration, I'd say forty-eight hours plus. Saturday evening, if I had to guess."

"And we were in this area on Saturday." Terrence was pissed off they hadn't caught her.

"Did we send uniforms to this block?" Bishop asked.

"Yeah, we did." Terrence put his hands on his head. "Fuck! She was right here, and we let her get away. And I'm not saying this guy didn't deserve being punished – he *is* a scumbag – but not like this. No one deserves this."

"If there's one thing I've learned working serial cases, is that the Caras of this world have the upper hand. We can't blame ourselves for not catching these people. The odds of us catching them straight away are low, to say the least. It takes a while for us to build up a picture of the suspect, giving them time to keep doing what they do. It's the nature of this kind of investigation, I'm afraid."

Terrence knew Bishop was right, but it didn't help much; he wanted Cara caught now – he wanted to make sure no one else was butchered like this poor guy, as much as he thought Wood was a scumbag. The previous four victims certainly didn't deserve to be murdered.

He looked around the room. Cara had ransacked the place – she'd been through every drawer and cupboard there was, left all the doors open. The contents of said cupboards were strewn over the carpet.

When he looked closer at the walls, he saw that there were two air vents with their fronts unscrewed and left on the floor. He walked over to one and put his hand inside. Right at the back, he found a small plastic bag of white powder. "Three guesses what she was looking for." Terrence held up the bag for Bishop to see. "There's no way of knowing how much was in here originally."

"So, she could have a large quantity of cocaine."

Terrence thought Bishop was right to sound grave – a murderer with a large amount of coke could be a nightmare combination. Cocaine made the user feel invincible, which Cara didn't need more of.

On the carpet, underneath the second vent, Terrence found two bullets. There was an oily rag nearby too. "Oh shit! That's not good." He held one of the bullets up with his gloved hand.

"No, that's not good. We're in trouble."

In addition to being coked out of her head, Cara was also

carrying a firearm. It was probably a small calibre gun, judging by the .22 calibre bullet Terrence was holding – it didn't matter, though; she could still do a lot of damage with it. He had to inform Gupta.

68

Franks shook hands with his interviewee, Faisal Bukhari.

He was taken by Faisal's looks. It wasn't just that he looked smart in his uniform, which was pressed, ironed and looked immaculate, he had a very symmetrical face. He had dark eyes and chiselled features.

Faisal had a firm handshake too, which pleased him. He didn't trust men with weak handshakes. "Thanks for coming today. I know you've driven a long way."

"Thanks for seeing me." Faisal sat opposite.

"Now, I can see from your file you've been a superintendent for eight years, and chief superintendent for two of those." He looked at his computer.

"Yes, sir. I was a chief inspector for five years and inspector for four years prior to that. You can ask any of my supers for recommendations."

"I've already taken the liberty of speaking to a couple of them. You'll be pleased to hear they all thought very highly of you. They said you're an exemplary officer, which is what I need here."

"Thank you."

"As you're probably aware, you'll be taking over from Clive Adams."

"Yes, sir. That was a shock to everyone. How's the investigation into that going? Have they found any suspects yet?"

"Unfortunately not, but we'll discuss that later. You understand that this meeting is a formality, don't you? I think you're perfect for the job, so all you need to do is put in your transfer papers and work your notice period. How do you feel about taking over CID?"

"There's only one thing I'm concerned about, sir."

"Your experience working criminal investigations?"

"Yes, sir."

"You don't need to worry about that so much. Your role is supervisory, so you won't be out in the field with the rest of the team, but we will put you through all the exams, so you're up to speed. We let the inspectors and sergeants take on the field side of the investigations. But there *is* something I need to discuss with you."

"Sir?"

"Are you up for a little walk?"

Franks led Faisal through the office, introducing him to his new team one by one. He noticed the looks Faisal received from some of the admin women. Of course most of the detectives were out of the office, conducting field work, but he managed to introduce him to Watts, O'Hara and Hilary Farmer, who were all hard at work on their computers.

Then he walked Faisal down the stairwell, out of the station and through the car park. From there he walked his new recruit to a park across the road. At just after eleven in the morning, the park was largely deserted, bar a few young mothers pushing their toddlers along the path. Franks invited Faisal to sit with him on a bench.

"It's nice here." Faisal gestured at the little pond with swans swimming on the surface.

"So I've been told." Franks wanted to get to it. "Anyway, the reason I've brought you out here is to discuss something a bit sensitive."

"I'm all ears."

"Nasreen Maqsood," Franks said, as though Faisal should know the name.

After her bout of television, newspaper and magazine interviews, every person and their dogs knew the name Nasreen Maqsood.

"I'm looking forward to meeting her."

"Good, I'm glad. The thing is, I need you to keep an eye on her for me, Faisal. The project can't afford to have her sniffing about, do you understand?" Franks watched Faisal's reaction. "I'll need you to keep her in check. She's on her final warning; if she so much as puts a step wrong, she's out. And I don't care how much the media breathes down my neck. So, I'm charging you with monitoring her, understood?"

"I can't see that being a problem, sir. Is that why you want me here, sir? Because I'm Pakistani?"

"Cards on table time. Partly, but mostly because I think you'll be good for the team. New blood's always good for morale, Faisal, don't you think?"

"I do, sir. So, when do you want me to start?"

"As soon as your papers come through."

Franks sat and chatted with Faisal for another fifteen minutes, before walking back to the station. He was confident that his new chief superintendent would work out well. Faisal was an efficient, hard-working and dedicated officer.

69

Nasreen walked with Gupta through the front doors of Welbury Lodge, the psychiatric unit of the Royal County NHS hospital. It was approaching midday and Gupta had arranged an appointment with Doctor Travis Denton, Cara's doctor.

It was busy in the reception area. When they arrived at the desk, Gupta spoke to a female receptionist and told her that they were there to speak with Denton.

Listening to the woman's directions, they were asked to walk to the Richmond Ward, which was located at the rear of the building. Once they had followed the directions, Gupta checked them in.

Nasreen noticed how clinical and cold it was, with brown wooden floors, white walls and lots of separate rooms with closed doors. There were barred windows throughout, and every door was protected by card readers.

There was a recreation room, if it could be called that. They were asked to enter and wait for the doctor. Recreation was obviously a loose term – there was a knackered old television in one corner of the room and a table in the middle of the floor, with a stack of magazines dating back to the previous year sat on top.

"What a depressing place," Gupta said, sitting down.

"I know. I doubt it'll improve the patients' mindsets."

Nasreen sat two seats down from Gupta, looking around at the bare walls and the dated box television; she would be surprised if it worked, it was so old.

"Detective Inspector Gupta?" Doctor Denton shook hands with Gupta.

Nasreen was introduced by her boss, but Denton failed to acknowledge her presence. Observing Denton in his white coat, he looked sleazy, with round glasses, studious face and a thin wily physique. He was sweaty, or maybe just oily. Nasreen was glad she didn't shake his hand.

"Do you have the court order?" Denton asked, getting down to business.

Gupta brought out the A4 piece of paper and handed it to Denton, who read it, to be sure. There was something off about the doctor.

"It all looks in order." Denton folded the paper into quarters and slid it inside his white coat pocket. "What do you want to know?"

"Everything there is to know about Cara Mooney. You're probably aware why we're interested in speaking to her."

"Where to start? Cara was ordered here a little over a year ago by the judge at her trial. She kidnapped her ex-girlfriend, and when she was caught and sentenced, her ex begged the judge to be lenient. The judge believed the kidnapping was a cry for help, which I still believe it was."

"Can we see your notes, please?" Gupta asked.

"Of course. Let me show you around the facility, while we talk."

Nasreen followed the doctor, while walking beside Gupta.

They were shown around the ward, which had twenty-five rooms, twelve for female inpatients and thirteen for male. Each room had a bed with ankle and wrist restraints attached to them, a bedside cabinet and nothing else. It really was depressing. "Are inpatients strapped every night?" she interrupted the doctor talking.

"For the first couple of nights. If they are well enough, then they're allowed to sleep unrestrained. You have to understand, detective, we're dealing with very emotionally disturbed, sometimes violent, patients here most of the time, so restraints are a necessity, and save lives." He was trying to justify their use.

When they'd walked around the ward, the doctor stopped at the reception desk and asked one of the receptionists for Cara's notes. Gupta accepted them, but immediately handed them to Nasreen to read. She went and took a seat in the recreation room, which was empty, and opened Cara's file.

The first thing she noticed was how thick it was. There were lengthy session notes between Cara and Doctor Denton, along with her personal information. The interesting, useful information was inside the notes.

When Cara arrived, she'd been sedated, restrained and kept immobile in bed for twelve hours. Doctor Denton first reviewed Cara the following day, after which he'd prescribed her aripiprazole, or as it was more commonly known, Abilify, an antipsychotic drug. According to his notes, Cara became less prone to violent outbursts a couple of days after starting her medication.

Once she'd calmed down, the sessions started. A month after being admitted, Cara had opened up to him about her childhood, about being molested by her father from the age of six, until she was eleven, when her father abandoned her and started visiting her sister's bedroom instead. According to the notes, Cara hated her sister for taking her father away.

Instead of lashing out at her father and sister, Cara sought love elsewhere. At the age of twelve, she met Karim Ravani, an eighteen-year-old Pakistani boy, who had shown interest in her, and plied her with cigarettes, booze and cannabis. She spent days in his flat. He was her first love, according to Cara. She played truant so much during that time that she was expelled from school.

According to the notes, when she was fourteen, Ravani introduced her to some of his friends, who'd paid Ravani to have sex with her. Her boyfriend told her that in his country, friends shared their girlfriends, which she had believed.

For him, because she loved him so much, she'd let his friends have sex with her, which became a regular occurrence, only with more and more friends, always in the flat, always with Ravani present.

By the time she was sixteen, Ravani introduced her to cocaine. Her time in Ravani's flat from sixteen to eighteen involved drinking alcohol, smoking cigarettes, snorting cocaine and having sex with at least twenty of Ravani's friends, sometimes as many as five a day. When she tried leaving the flat, Ravani reacted violently, hitting her repeatedly in the face until she was unconscious.

The first time she was sectioned was at eighteen, when she found a bottle of painkillers in Ravani's flat, and took an overdose. The next thing she could remember was waking up in hospital. With no one to love, she fell into a deep depression.

Cara spent nine months at a psychiatric unit, where her therapist, Doctor Victoria Sadler, helped her cope with her tragic childhood. The first kind person she'd ever met, it was Sadler who encouraged Cara to initiate criminal proceedings against her father, while at the same time administering antidepressants, counselling and kindness.

When released from Sadler's care, Cara moved into a halfway house, where she was regularly visited by Doctor

Sadler. At twenty, Cara testified against her father for child sexual abuse. Her sister, Tara, flatly refused to testify; instead she opted to defend their father, saying he'd been nothing but loving towards them. With testimonies from former schoolteachers, and indecent images taken from his laptop of naked children, her father was sentenced to fifteen years in prison. Tara was taken into care at the age of fourteen.

When Cara was twenty-one, she moved into a halfway house down south, away from her past. Cara had to learn to fend for herself. Doctor Sadler set her up with a job in a café, where she thrived serving customers. And in the evenings, Cara spent her time socialising with her fellow halfway housemates. It was at the halfway house, where she met Francesca Neal.

Both deeply damaged, Cara and Fran – as she preferred to be called – struck up a close friendship, which inevitably turned into something far more toxic; they were bad for one another. Fran introduced Cara to heroin, and it was at this point that their relationship unravelled.

Fran became obsessed with Cara, which bred jealousy and anger. When Cara told Fran the relationship was over, Fran flew into a rage and beat Cara until she was unconscious. Cara awoke in the hospital.

On her own once more, Cara moved back into the halfway house, with the help of Doctor Sadler. She started a new job at a factory, which she excelled at. A company with an active social scene, she struck up friendships within a group of drug users. While there, she continued to use cocaine, until she crashed her car into a tree.

At twenty-four, Cara was ordered into a rehab clinic, where she met and fell instantly in love with Lucy Davis. Cara was besotted with the talented journalist, and shortly after leaving rehab, met her for a coffee. The two damaged friends soon moved in together.

Happy for the first time in her life, the first year was a dream come true for Cara. It was only after Lucy started taking her career seriously that Cara knew it was over and went out of her way to show Lucy she was still there. She met Lucy for lunch, met her after work to walk her home; she even met Lucy's work colleagues for drinks.

Cara grew upset when Lucy suddenly moved out of their flat without telling her. She found Lucy living with one of her work friends, and tried to discuss their relationship, but Lucy phoned the police. Cara was arrested. Then she received a court ordered injunction, stating that she wasn't allowed within two hundred feet of Lucy.

Feeling foolish and angry at the way she'd been treated, Cara waited for Lucy near the work friend's home, with the intention of talking to her, to reason with her, but their conversation turned physical, and before she knew what was happening, she had Lucy in the boot of her car. Desperate and scared, Cara broke into an empty log cabin in woods nearby, where she tried to discuss her relationship with Lucy.

Two days later, the police found them; she was arrested and three days after that, Cara found herself in front of the judge, where she was sectioned under Doctor Denton's care.

Nasreen closed the file. The poor woman had been abused or betrayed by practically every person she'd ever met, bar Doctor Sadler. It was little wonder Cara behaved the way she did.

"Are you ready to go?" Gupta asked her, breaking her concentration. "I didn't get much from Denton. Did you find anything in the notes?"

"A lot. Are we allowed to take these?"

"No, I asked him that. I'll ask the receptionist to send over a digital copy. We have to hand the originals back."

When Nasreen stood, she felt a sharp stabbing pain in her

knee. She shuffled her knee support under her suit trousers and joined Gupta.

"How bad is it? Your knee," Gupta asked. "I still think you should be riding a desk."

"Stop worrying; I'm fine. And knowing me, I'd fall off a desk and hurt myself anyway." She smiled at her little joke.

Handing the file back to the receptionist, Gupta asked for the notes to be emailed to him, to which the receptionist agreed. Terrence, Bishop and Gupta needed to read them, to understand where Cara was at. Nasreen felt she understood Cara more now; she hoped it would help them catch her.

70

———

Maggie awoke with a start. She'd fallen asleep with her head on Scott's hand, beside his bed. How long had it been since she had any real sleep? She couldn't say. If she had to estimate, about two days, maybe.

"You know there's a bed for you just down the hall, Mrs Hughes," said the nurse, her hand on her shoulder.

"Thanks," she replied, her head fuzzy, "but I'm not leaving my son until he wakes up."

"I don't wish to sound harsh, but it could take days, or weeks. You need your rest, or you'll be no use to your son when he wakes up."

She looked up at the nurse's kind face. "You believe he will, don't you?"

"If you'd asked me that a couple of days ago, I'd have said don't raise your hopes, but now, I can't see why he won't. He's a fighter, your son. You hang in there. But, please, you need to get some rest, or you'll be admitted here too."

Maggie looked back down at her only living son. "At least I'll be with my boy." She felt a pat on her shoulder. Her eyes felt gritty. "Thank you, though, for your kindness."

Holding Scott's hand, the burner mobile Darius gave her rang. Darius was at home, getting some much-needed rest, so she had to answer it. To her surprise, it was Darius calling.

"I've got one of them. Stupid bastard only went back to his house, didn't he! What do you want me to do with him?"

"Hold on to him for me. Find out where the other one is, and when you have them both, call me. I want to meet my sons' murderers." She had an afterthought. "And if they have girl-friends or boyfriends, bring them along."

When she hung up, she found she had so many dark thoughts tumbling around in her mind; so many disturbing, murderous, sick things she wanted to do to these animals, these feral animals. Putting them down was too kind – she had much more painful plans for these two bastards.

When she saw the photo Darius had shown her, she didn't recognise either of them.

She'd received information from Darius that a man called Lennox Garvey was responsible for the attack, but she didn't even know who that was. The two black bastards she'd seen photos of were simply hired help, but that didn't matter to her – they would suffer.

Her hand shook from the anger and rage she felt inside. If she didn't get the chance to expel it, she might explode. She held Scott's hand tight.

"Hi, Maggie."

She turned to see her neighbour, who continued speaking. "It's okay, I'm here now. I'll keep Scott company; you go and get some rest – you look done in."

"Did the nurse put you up to this?"

"Put me up to what? I'm only here to help."

Maggie was tired and grouchy. Maybe she *should* have a nap – a small kip. "I'm sorry I snapped. I've had it from every direc-tion, is all."

"It's because we care about you. Really, I'm here to stay with him. Go and put your head down for an hour or so. If there's any movement, or anything, I'll come and wake you up, okay?"

Maggie got up and walked down the hall to a room with four beds in. When she opened the door, she could see Stacey, Scott's wife, asleep in one bed. Closing the door – in the dark – Maggie took the bed furthest away from Stacey, not wanting to disturb her. Maggie got under the duvet and lay down, closing her eyes.

71

Cara felt weird being back in her hometown. She hadn't been here for seven years, not since she was twenty-one. She hated the town, despised it; it brought back so many bad memories, memories of the childhood she wanted to forget.

It brought back images of Karim, of his lies and betrayal. She even hated the accent, the Yorkshire accent, she'd spent years trying to rid herself of.

There was only one good thing about this town: her therapist, Victoria Sadler. Sat across the road from Vicki's home in Wood's car, she watched a couple in their seventies or eighties walk past. She was crap at guessing ages, especially in elderly people.

Connecting her burner phone to the car, she charged it.

It was four o'clock. Sadler probably wouldn't be back home from the hospital until after dark. Cara couldn't sit in the car until her ex-therapist arrived – neighbours might get suspicious having a woman sat in a car for hours. She decided to go for a drive. She was only twenty minutes away from her old family home.

After a short drive, she found herself driving past her family's house. Cara wanted to stop and observe, but she couldn't – there were two police cars outside.

Fortunately, they were empty, the pigs must have been inside the house. She smiled to herself; did they really think she would turn up there? Her family didn't even live there anymore, for fuck's sake.

Knowing where to go next, she carried on driving until she came to a familiar block of flats. He lived there, Karim, her "ex-boyfriend". She parked across the road and watched school children walk past in their little uniforms.

In two hours, she'd not seen him. She wondered what he was doing, who he was corrupting, where he was. An anger pooled in her gut, thinking about the way he'd betrayed her, the way he made her think she loved him. What poor girl did he have up in his flat?

When a young mum pushing a pram looked at her through the window for a little bit too long, Cara turned the key, put the car in gear and accelerated forwards. She wasn't here for Karim, not yet.

"How'd it go with Denton?" Terrence asked, as Nasreen and Gupta sat at their desks.

Terrence had crime scene photos in his hands – he and Bishop were discussing the murder while waiting for Gupta and Nasreen to return. Bishop had just left, needing to get home for an important dinner.

They spent three hours talking to neighbours. One remembered seeing a blonde woman walking down the stairs about six months earlier, bloody and bruised. When asked why he hadn't reported it, the Asian man said he kept himself to himself – no good ever came from interfering in other people's business, which Terrence could understand.

Several of Wood's neighbours knew what he did for a living. He had a fearsome reputation in the area, which prevented local residents from speaking out against him. He beat one neighbour so badly, he spent two weeks in hospital; that was according to another neighbour.

"I didn't get much from him," Gupta replied, "but Nas struck gold with the notes."

Terrence turned his chair around, so that he didn't have to

twist his neck. "Is there anything in there we can use, Nas? John Wood's murder complicates things."

"Absolutely! I've just read her life's story." Nasreen got up from her desk and handed him the file. "We've got a few people we need to talk to."

Terrence accepted the file and opened it. He scanned rather than read it, hoping Nasreen would fill him in. It was getting late and he really wanted to go home. "So, who do you think we need to speak to?"

"We discussed it on the way over here," Nasreen said, "and we think we need to talk to Karim Ravani, her groomer. We think he might be her next victim. He did some horrendous things to her, so it's a good bet she'll want to harm him."

"I agree. John Wood raped her, by all accounts. A neighbour claims to remember seeing Cara all bloodied, walking away from his flat. She carved out the words "RAPIST" and "SCUM" on his chest and stomach – they were deep cuts too. She stabbed both his eyes, stabbed him in the mouth, his neck, chest and stomach – some fifteen that we counted. Here, see for yourselves."

He handed the photos to Nasreen, who flipped through them one at a time, pulling faces of distaste as she did so. He read briefly about a doctor. "So, who's this Doctor Sadler?"

"Cara's first therapist, back when she was in her late teens, early twenties," Nasreen replied. "From what I can tell, she was about the only person who was nice to her."

"Another killer with a tragic childhood, huh?"

"You don't know the half of it."

"I can't find Karim Ravani on the PNC." Gupta turned his chair to join the conversation. "We're going to have to go door-to-door when we get there."

"Where?"

"Cara's hometown," Gupta replied. "We can interview

Doctor Sadler at the same time as look for Ravani. Nas, can you look up Tara Mooney for me? If she's still there, we can kill three birds."

"Yeah, no problem," Nasreen replied. "I'll look up Francesca Neal while I'm on there. See if we can get anything out of her too."

All these names. Terrence couldn't help but feel a bit out of it. "Anyone care to fill me in? Francesca Neal?"

"One of Cara's exes," Gupta replied. "Didn't end well, apparently – she put Cara in hospital when Cara tried to end the relationship. Lovely girl, by all accounts."

"Tara Mooney lives right here," Nasreen said. "I've got her home and work addresses. Strange that she would move down south, where her sister lives, don't you think? There's no love lost between them."

"It's a big city, Nas," Gupta replied. "You can go years living in this town without seeing friends you know who live here. It might be like that."

"Yeah, maybe. I've got a funny feeling about Tara though. I think she'll be able to help us."

Terrence read about Cara testifying against her father. "Tara's in care because of Cara? That's cold! Probably no love lost there then."

"Francesca Neal lives locally too," Nasreen said.

"Okay, it's getting late, people," Gupta said, standing. "Here's what's going to happen. Tomorrow, Terrence, you'll go with Bishop to speak with Lucy Davis' editor at *The Telegraph*, Tara Mooney and Francesca Neal. Nas, you and I'll be taking a trip up north. I'll call ahead and let the local constabulary know we're coming."

"Are you going to ask them to look for Ravani?" asked Nasreen.

"Yeah. Sounds like a plan."

73

It was seven thirty by the time Doctor Victoria Sadler pulled up outside the gate to her house, opened it and drove along her driveway. Cara waited around the side of her house for her to get out of her car, having scaled the perimeter wall earlier.

As Sadler reached her front door, Cara whispered, "Hey, Vicki."

Lit only by a lamp post down the road, Sadler jumped and looked to her left.

Cara rounded the corner of the house and revealed herself. As she stepped up to her old therapist, she smiled. "Hello, Vicki, long time no see."

"Cara! What are you doing here?"

"I've come to see you," she replied, feeling disappointed Sadler wasn't pleased to see her. "Why, don't you want to see me?"

Looking around her, Sadler opened the door and ushered her through.

Inside, with the door closed, she turned to Cara. "Of course I want to see you, but you're all over the news. The police are out in force looking for you."

Cara nodded. "Let them." She noticed how afraid Sadler looked. "Why do you look so scared?" She put her hand out to stroke Sadler's cheek, but Victoria shied away. "Hey, I've come to see you."

"All those people you've murdered," Sadler replied, her face fearful. "Have you come here to kill me too? After everything I've done for you?"

Cara was hurt. She trusted this woman and had done since the day she'd met her. "Of course I haven't come here to kill you. I love you – why would I want to kill you?"

"Because I failed you." Sadler was crying. "I'm so sorry, I've failed you."

They weren't tears of sorrow – Sadler was scared, Cara noticed. This wasn't the woman she'd come to love. "Don't talk like that! You haven't failed me. I'm fine, look."

"You're a serial killer, for crying out loud." Sadler backed away from her. "It's all over the news. You've killed six people in as many days."

Without thinking, Cara slid her hand inside her handbag and wrapped her fingers around the knife's handle. "Stop walking backwards, Vicki, I mean it."

Sadler turned and ran through her hallway.

Cara pulled the knife out, as she sprinted behind Sadler, who reached the kitchen door. With a sense of déjà vu, Cara stopped, one hand holding the knife out, and the other up, with her palm facing Sadler, in submission. "Stop, please, I'm really not here to hurt you."

"You've got a knife in your hand, Cara."

"Look, I'm putting it away, okay?" She slowly placed the knife back in her bag. "Come on, let's just sit and have a chat, yeah? Let's act like two old friends who haven't seen each other in years – let's have some wine."

"You mean it? You're not going to hurt me?"

She nodded. "Have you got any wine in?"

"I'm a psychiatrist, Cara, of course I've got wine in. I wouldn't be able to do my job without it."

Finally, there was a smile. Cara followed Sadler into the kitchen. She took a wine glass from her therapist and sat down at the kitchen table. When the wine was poured and Sadler sat down, Cara asked, "So, how have you been?"

"How have I been? This is so weird. We don't talk like this at all."

Cara smiled. "What do you mean? We talk!"

"No, Cara, we fuck. I can't remember the last time we actually talked. Not since before I seduced you, I guess."

"I don't remember it like that." Cara wistfully spun the wine round in her glass.

"Have you spoken to Lucy since you got out?"

She shook her head. "No, I haven't even tried. Maybe in my head, but it never goes smoothly. Get that, even in my head we have a blazing row."

Sadler changed the subject. "You know, I'm sorry for how I treated you. It wasn't professional of me – I shouldn't have taken advantage of you like that."

Cara took a sip of her full-bodied red wine. "What're you talking about? You didn't take advantage of me – you couldn't make me do something I didn't want to do."

"Come off it, Cara, you've been made to do things you didn't want your whole life. And I'm no different – I shouldn't have seduced you. I'm your therapist."

"No, you *were* my therapist. We got together after I left the asylum. We could do whatever we wanted."

"It was a hospital, not an asylum. And it was still unethical." Sadler took a sip. "I could be struck off by the GMC and hauled up in front of the Medical Practitioner's Tribunal Service. Anyway, I'm sorry, for what it's worth."

"Hey, I enjoyed it. Would that make a difference to the tribunal service? And if it helps, apology accepted."

There was an awkward silence, as Cara thought about that first time with Sadler. Her therapist was so gentle, so caring, like she was professionally. Her therapist came to see her at the halfway house, the door had been closed, and before Cara knew what was happening, she was lying on the bed, with Sadler on top of her.

"What do you want to do now, Cara?"

Cara drank the wine. "Fancy going upstairs? For old time's sake?"

74

—————

Lennox sat in the car park of The Old Trafalgar pub.

From the car, he could see the beer garden, where Ibrahim Sandhu and his crew were sat having a beer. There were six Indian men with Sandhu, all dressed in Western style clothing, rather than the Indian style they normally wore around their area.

From the information Amelie had secured from Harry, Lennox knew that Sandhu was the project's North West dealer. He'd done his homework over the last couple of days; he'd found out Sandhu's address, where he conducted his business, and, using his uncle's resources, found out where he liked to drink. His uncle had associates in every major city in the country, including this one.

"Are we going in?" Barkley asked from the driver's seat.

"It looks like they've settled in."

Lennox put the binoculars in the glovebox. "Let's go get a drink."

Picking up the Uzi, he slid the clip in and chambered the first round, keeping it hidden from any customers driving into the car park. Barkley had parked as close to the garden as possible, to make exiting easier. He knew this was the most dangerous mission they'd embarked on yet – they would be out in the open, exposed for the first time.

Holding the gun under his jacket, Lennox walked with Barkley through the car park to the side entrance of the pub. It was busy, even for a Tuesday, with diners sat around tables, drinkers stood around the long bar. At the far end of the pub, there were three pool tables, all in play. There was a dartboard in use, with six blokes using it.

At the bar, Lennox ordered a pint of Stella for Barkley and a pint of Old Speckled Hen for himself. He paid, keeping hold of the gun pressed against his stomach, and they took their pints through the pub and out to the beer garden. There were ten tables outside, all capable of seating eight people, but only six were in use.

Considering Amelie's request that no more innocent civilians get caught up in their affairs, Lennox asked Barkley to move closer to Sandhu's lot, making sure all the other patrons were behind them. They were four tables away from the seven Indians. Lennox could hear them talking and laughing – he hated their Mancunian accents.

Putting his ale glass on the wooden bench, he kept his back to his target. Barkley was facing him, so he had a good view of Sandhu. "Stop staring," he muttered. "We want to do this on our time, not when they take offence to you staring at them."

Barkley turned so that Sandhu was to his right, but Lennox kept seeing him turn his head to get a better look.

"Which one's Sandhu?"

"The one in the red shirt and black leather jacket," Lennox whispered back. "Stop staring, yeah? The last thing we need is them noticing us."

He'd had no more than three gulps of his beer when he heard, "What the fuck're you staring at, mate?" When he turned, he saw all seven Indians were stood, glaring at Barkley.

Lennox put his glass down on the bench.

75

"You're still an expert at that," Cara said between breaths, as Sadler lay next to her on top of the duvet. Cara let Sadler cuddle up to her.

"I should be, I've had a lot of practise."

"Where's your girlfriend tonight?" Cara looked at the ceiling, her chest rising and falling. Being with Sadler was familiar, comfortable. It wasn't mind blowing, like it had been with Lucy.

"I'm between wives. She moved out last week."

"I'm sorry. I didn't know. I didn't even know you were married. You never said." Cara stroked Sadler's hair, while thinking about her Lucy, wondering what she was doing, and with whom. Dawn said she was happy now. Did that mean she'd found someone? Had she been replaced?

"Sorry I brought back bad memories."

"You don't need to apologise. I'll get over it; I've been married twice. I guess my job's not compatible with long-term relationships." Sadler sighed. "I understand where they're coming from, though; the hours I work means I'm rarely home. You're lucky you caught me tonight, actually."

"Me? I'm the lucky one? Hey, you're the lucky one. I could be halfway to find Lucy by now. I had to stop by and say hi though."

Oh bugger! She hadn't meant to say that. Now Sadler knew where she was heading. Although, she didn't know Lucy's address, so she guessed it was safe to talk about.

"You're going to meet her?"

It was alarming – Sadler's interest raised Cara's awareness. Was her therapist playing her? Was she gathering enough evidence to try to help the police later? "Honestly? I don't have a clue where I'm going; I'm making this up as I go." She decided that if Sadler kept on asking about Lucy, she might have to get rid of her. For one thing was certain: she wasn't going to let anything stand in her way of seeing Lucy.

Lennox reached inside his jacket, prompting Barkley to follow suit.

All seven Indians were moving forwards, approaching.

When he pulled out the Uzi, he saw the wave of fear hit them simultaneously. Their eyes grew wider; their mouths opened.

"Shit!" Sandhu shouted. "It's Garvey!"

Without waiting for them to clamber in different directions, trying to escape the onslaught that was to follow, Lennox raised the machine pistol to eye level and pulled the trigger once, as three shots were fired.

He heard screaming behind him, as civilians sat around the pub benches fled in different directions.

In front of him, one Indian was hit twice, once in the chest and once in the neck. His body was the first to fall. The next to fall was hit by three of Barkley's bullets, three in the chest.

A hail of lead tore through the remaining three Indians, as one by one, they fell. Lennox saw Ibrahim Sandhu dive behind a pub bench, while his associates' and friends' bodies fell around him.

Lennox moved forwards, knowing he still had rounds left in his gun.

He saw one of the Indians crawling along the paved ground. Lennox put two more in his back.

Barkley finished off one more, before Lennox saw Sandhu clinging on to the bench, his eyes wide in fear.

"Please, I'll stop doing whatever it is you don't like." Sandhu put his hand up, as though it would stop a bullet tearing through it.

Lennox looked down at the sorry excuse for a human being, lowered his aim and fired three times, one bullet tearing through Sandhu's left eye and out the back of his skull, one in the neck and the third in his chest.

Taking one final look behind him, the bloody bodies littering the patio were still; Lennox couldn't see any movement. A couple of legs twitched.

The screaming continued. He turned and ran, with Barkley slightly ahead. When he reached the car, he jumped in and waited for Barkley to fire up the engine. "Come on, let's go, let's go!"

Out of the car park, Barkley steered the car left and they were on the road. Lennox put the hot smoky pistols in a duffel bag on the floor by his feet. He could smell sulphur and cordite. "Let's get the fuck out of here," he ordered, as Barkley drove them south. They were heading back to the city, back to Amelie.

"I can't sleep," Mina whined, rubbing her eyes. "I had a bad dream."

Nasreen got off her bed and approached her sleepy daughter. She could let Mina sleep in with her, as she had done every night for the past month, but she'd had enough of restless nights, being woken up by Mina's fidgeting. "Come on, you, let's get you back to bed."

She took Mina by the hand and walked her back to her bedroom next door. Luckily for her, Mina climbed in bed willingly, with no griping or crying. She pulled the duvet up to Mina's neck.

"You know, they're just bad dreams, Mina," she said, stroking her daughter's forehead. "They can't hurt you. You're safe here, with me and Katerina, you know that, right? Nothing's going to hurt you, I promise." She bent forwards and kissed her daughter on the forehead.

"You promise?" Mina's eyes were wide with hope.

"I promise, sweetheart. Now, close your eyes and think of nice things. That'll keep those bad dreams away."

Mina obeyed. Looking down at the little person she'd

brought into this world, Nasreen felt such love for her. "Night night, baby girl, sweet dreams."

She walked quietly to the door and turned to look back at her baby one last time. She really was adorable, when she wasn't being a madam, which was happening more and more frequently the older she got. Closing the door, Nasreen wondered what Mina would be like as a teenager, Allah help her. Mina would either be a real darling, or a complete monster – Nasreen really hoped for the former.

And now, she wouldn't be able to sleep. She decided to go to the kitchen to make herself a cup of cocoa. In the kitchen, she switched on the kettle and prepared her "Best Cop" mug that Ashraf bought her.

"Where are you going?" Cara watched Sadler get up.

"To the loo." Sadler sat on the edge of the bed. "Is that okay with you?"

"Of course." Cara lay back, watching Sadler's buttocks as she walked out of the bedroom. She looked over at the alarm clock and saw it was 23:50. She felt like she'd had a good workout with Sadler – she felt strong and motivated.

Lying there, Cara thought about Lucy.

Looking back at the clock, Cara saw that eight minutes had passed. *Where did that time go?* Pulling the duvet back, and forcing her legs out, she hoisted herself up.

Naked, she walked out of the bedroom, along the landing to the bathroom, which was empty. Creeping, Cara walked down the stairs to the kitchen, where she found Sadler hovering over her bag. "What're you doing?" She saw Sadler jump.

When Sadler turned, she had John's small pistol in both hands, aimed at her chest.

DAY 9
WEDNESDAY, 28TH MARCH

Lucy sat upright in bed, her T-shirt soaked with sweat.

She thought she was going to throw up.

"Lucy, honey, are you okay?" Helena asked. "Did you have another dream about Cara? I think that detective was right; she'd be mad to try to come here."

"She is mad, remember? She's a psychopath."

Helena put her hand on Lucy's forehead. "You're burning up. I'll get you a cold compress – you might be coming down with something."

"I'm fine, really. It was just a nightmare."

Wiping her sweaty face with her hands, Lucy edged out of bed, feeling the cold wooden floorboards with her bare feet. She pulled the wet T-shirt over her head and threw it in the laundry basket, before walking to the bathroom next door.

The nightmare was so vivid, so real. She was back in the cabin, tied to the chair. Cara had her knife out, waving it about, yelling at her for being such a bitch. Then Cara ranted at her about a suicide pact that she'd agreed to. She woke up when Cara slashed her face.

In reality, that never happened. Cara had ranted at her about a suicide pact, but the police siren spooked her, and then Lucy had managed to beg and plead Cara to put the knife down and give herself up. Waiting to see if Cara decided to surrender or kill them both would go down as her scariest moment.

"Here you go." Helena, wearing a long T-shirt, held out a rolled cloth. "Put this on your forehead. I really hope you're not coming down with the flu. It's your birthday in a couple of days."

"I'm fine, honestly, stop fussing," Lucy replied, suddenly feeling queasy.

She swallowed saliva, but it kept coming back up, so she swallowed again, and again. Then without warning, her stomach contracted, as she heaved and threw up in the sink.

Lucy threw up three times, feeling Helena's loving hands rubbing her back.

She didn't feel right at all.

"Let's get you back to bed, Lucy," Helena said, guiding her. "I think it's flu."

Feeling light-headed, Lucy wrapped her arm around her girlfriend's neck and Helena helped her back to the bedroom and into bed.

When Lucy looked up, the room was spinning. She heard Helena come back into the bedroom. With her head swimming, she leant over the edge of the bed and vomited into a bucket Helena just managed to place.

"Oh shit!" Helena used the cold compress on her forehead.

"I'm fine now, Mum," she said, deliriously. "I just need to go to sleep."

"Get back!" The gun shook in Sadler's hands. "I mean it. I will shoot you!"

Cara took a step forwards. "No, you won't, Vicki, you don't have it in you."

Sadler looked sexy holding the gun. The thought turned into something far more sinister. Who did she think she was? "Come on, give me the gun, before you shoot me by accident. Look at your hands shaking."

"I mean it, Cara, don't take another step. Be on your way. I don't want to have anything to do with you anymore. You're a murderer. And you're not killing me. Now, get out of my house, before I call the police."

Without thinking, Cara took another step towards her host.

Sadler stepped back.

"If we keep doing this, you'll bump into the cooker. Come on, hand it over. I'm not going to hurt you, I promise."

"Just go, now." Tears streamed down Sadler's cheeks. "Please, Cara, I don't want to kill you." She backed up another step.

"I'm not going anywhere until you calm down." Cara stepped forward again.

"You're not leaving me any choice here." Sadler closed one eye and tilted her head. "I will shoot you, if you don't stop moving."

Impulse took over; Cara disobeyed Sadler and stepped forwards.

As soon as she did, she heard the click of the gun hammer, the sound of the trigger being pulled, and saw the look of fear on Sadler's face, as nothing happened.

A red haze enveloped Cara.

Sadler pulled the trigger once more, her face telling Cara she wanted it to fire.

Before Sadler could pull the trigger a third time, Cara flew at her therapist, grabbing the gun and so easily knocking Sadler to the floor, it was like she was made of air.

Straddling Sadler, Cara grabbed the pistol by the barrel, raised it above her head and brought the handle of the gun crashing down on Sadler's forehead with such power that she cracked her skull. "Safety was on, you fucking bitch!"

A red line started pooling blood. She raised it again, and brought it crashing down for a second time, but this time on her cheek, which caved in immediately. "You're just like all the others," she cried, raising it again. "You don't love me; you just want to use me!"

Cara smashed Sadler's face a further ten times, before she stopped, breathless.

While she was trying to catch her breath, she looked down at her ex-therapist's distorted, broken face. Her one good eye was looking up at her. Sadler's mouth was moving, but no words were forming. Cara guessed that her brain was dying – her forehead had a huge dent in it.

Blood trickled out of Sadler's ears, which, in itself, wasn't a good sign.

Cara was relatively clean. She stood, looked down at Sadler's eye and walked over to her bag on the table. She took out the knife and went back over to where Sadler's eye was still searching.

"That was stupid, bitch, I wasn't going to hurt you!" she yelled, stabbing Sadler through her good eye so hard that the blade stuck in the back of the therapist's skull, just like it had with John.

Sat on her dead therapist's belly, Cara felt sorrow for the first time in as long as she could remember. A single tear rolled down her cheek. She really had loved Sadler.

Now that she had killed her therapist, she stood and rifled through drawers and cupboards, looking for anything useful she could take to her next destination.

Cara turned the whole house on its head, emptying drawers onto the floor. She found an electric stun gun in Sadler's lounge cabinet, which she hadn't had a chance to retrieve.

Nasreen awoke suddenly, thinking she'd heard the landline phone. She couldn't hear anything but her daughter's gentle breathing. Mina was snuggled into her armpit.

Carefully, she freed herself, leaving Mina asleep in her bed. She got up, wrapping herself up in her dressing gown. With her slippers on, she went into the bathroom and shed her clothes, stepping into the shower.

Under the powerful jets, she thought about Cara. The poor woman had had a rough childhood and traumatic teenage years. Still, having had a bad childhood didn't excuse her recent violent behaviour – Nasreen so badly wanted to bring her in unharmed, to have her committed to a high security psychiatric hospital, which was where she truly belonged.

By the time she'd dried off, changed into her navy suit and white blouse, it was quarter to six. She'd agreed to meet Gupta at the station at seven, which meant she had to get a move on – it was a forty-five minute drive to work, although at this time of day, it would take half that.

Wanting half an hour on the PNC to look for Lucy Davis

again, Nasreen got ready as fast as she could. She still couldn't figure out why she hadn't found her yet?

When she was ready, she heard Katerina getting up. Chatting to her briefly, letting her nanny know that she planned on being back a bit later than usual, as she had a four-hour drive to Cara's home town and back again, she asked Katerina to put Mina to bed, if she wasn't back in time and not to give in to Mina's desire to stay up until she was home.

Nasreen left the house, locked the front door and walked to her car. Once inside, she fired the engine, accelerated to the end of her driveway and stopped, looking left and right for any cars about that shouldn't be there. There weren't, just her neighbours' cars.

82

Cara unwrapped the towel from around her head, shook her hair and looked in the bathroom mirror. Her red hair looked amazing, even if she did say so herself.

Cara walked through to the bedroom, put her knickers on and looked around for the rest of her clothes. When they'd gone upstairs to the bedroom, Sadler had practically torn her clothes off. Locating them, Cara put her bra on, then jeans and hoodie.

Downstairs, in the kitchen, she looked down at Sadler's corpse. "Thanks for a great night. Haven't enjoyed myself this much in ages." She collected her bag, which contained a knife, gun and stun gun, which she imagined would come in useful soon.

Knowing Sadler drove a decent car, which was preferable to Wood's horrible drug-dealer mobile, Cara would have to transfer her luggage from John's to Sadler's. It was 05:50 and still dark outside. Cara wanted to be on the move by the time it was light.

Outside, around the corner from Sadler's home, she took her bags from John's boot and walked them back to Sadler's Range Rover, where Cara put everything she owned in the whole world in the boot. She wouldn't get another chance to go shopping, not now her face was all over the news, even with gorgeous red hair.

When she was on the road, Cara knew exactly where she was going. She had one more person to visit while she was back in her hometown: Karim. And she had something special lined up for him. Pleading to a higher power for him to be in, she gunned the engine.

After visiting Karim, Cara had to drive eight and a half hours to visit Lucy in Scotland. She'd managed to get directions from Sadler's computer.

"Oh fuck! Fuck, fuck, fuck," Cara yelled, smashing her palms on the steering wheel, remembering she'd left Sadler's computer on. And worse, it was left on Google Maps, showing her travel plans.

Cara contemplated turning around and rectifying the problem, deciding against it, thinking the police, when they arrived, which could be in a couple of days, might not even look on Sadler's computer, and even if they did, Cara would have found Lucy and be on her way by the time they arrived. It was okay, she could work with it, providing her visit with Karim wasn't prolonged. She had no reason to think that it would be.

83

"Is everything okay? You're really quiet this morning," Gupta asked, driving.

"I was just thinking about Lucy. It's strange that I can't find her anywhere. I've looked on the PNC, I've looked through her financials."

"And what did they tell you?"

"The last time she used any plastic was almost a year ago, when she had seventy-five thousand transferred into her account, and that same day she withdrew it all. Since then, nothing. She's not on the PNC, she's never been arrested, so I can't find any info on her at all. Isn't it weird that someone involved with such a volatile psychotic as Cara has no form?"

"I can't say." Gupta stared ahead, concentrating on the road. "Let's go through it. Grab my laptop from the back seat, would you?"

Nasreen unclipped her seat belt, reached behind her and grabbed his laptop case. Opening it and switching on the computer, she typed "Lucy Davis" into the search bar. There were two hundred entries for Lucy Davis.

"Go into the DVLA page and look her up," he said, still focused.

Nasreen flipped the screen to the DVLA site and typed in the name. Four-hundred-and thirty-eight entries. "Done! Now what?"

"Filter them out by postcode."

Obeying, she had Cara and Lucy's flat postcode written on a piece of paper in her pocket, she typed it in and when she pressed enter there was only one entry left. "Got it!"

"Okay, so we know that's the Lucy Davis we're looking for, right?"

"Yeah, we know she exists, sure. That's a start, I guess."

"Does it state if her file's active? Is she still using the same car?"

"Classic MG convertible, yeah."

"Nice." Gupta nodded with approval. "Maybe we can trace her through her car. I think we should wait and see what Terrence and Bishop can get out of Lucy's editor. I'm not sure Tara Mooney's going to be much help to us with Lucy though, nor is Francesca Neal. If only we could find out who her relatives are."

Nasreen switched back to the PNC again. "Hang on a sec," she said, having a brainwave. "Cara kidnapped Lucy, right? There was a police investigation, right?"

"Right, but we've seen all that information on the PNC under Cara's file. Lucy doesn't have one," Gupta said, overtaking a lorry.

"No, wait, there must have been newspaper articles about it. It might have been big news, and Lucy was a journo for *The Telegraph*, so they would've covered her story a lot, would be my guess."

Without hesitating, she typed "Lucy Davis journalist" into Google and waited for the search engine to change screens. "Got it." She clicked on the first *Telegraph* entry that mentioned their Lucy Davis. When it changed, an article popped up on the screen. She scanned it, looking for names of people she could look up.

Gupta looked over at her. "Anything?"

"Hang on a sec," she said, excitement still in her voice. "I've got something. Lucy's mum was interviewed, Siobhan O'Malley." She switched back to the PNC and typed "Siobhan O'Malley" in the search bar.

Not as many entries came up, but she still had to wade through file after file, until she came to the correct one. "I've got a mobile number here." She noticed the time: 07:45. "I'll give her a call now."

Letting it ring, praying for Siobhan to answer, Nasreen cursed when it went to an answerphone. The message was long. Siobhan's lovely Irish twang said that her and her husband were out of the country until the beginning of April, upon which time she would call everyone back. "Shit! She's out of the country."

Nasreen left an urgent voicemail, once she heard the beep, asking Siobhan to call her on her mobile number. It was a long shot, although there was a small chance Lucy's mum might pick up her messages while she was away. "I think that was our best chance."

"We tried, Nas," Gupta said, overtaking a motorcyclist. "You never know, Terrence and Bishop might have better luck later."

84

"We're here to talk to Tara Mooney." Terrence showed his warrant card.

"Tara!" shouted the male coffee shop worker, inspecting his badge.

Terrence turned his back and inspected the premises. It was busy, at nine in the morning. It was an independent coffee house, not part of some big chain, like Caffè Nero or Starbucks. There were around twenty tables of varying sizes inside and ten tables outside.

Every table was in use by a mixture of old and young patrons, so he and Bishop would've been out of luck had they wanted to sit down.

When they spoke to Tara, they would have to go outside.

"Yeah? I'm Tara," said a voice from behind him.

When he turned to face the counter, he was met by a moody-looking, twenty-two-year-old Cara, although she wasn't as pretty as her older sibling. Tara Mooney had piercings in practically every part of her body possible; her ears, her nose, her lip, her bottom lip, her eyebrows. If he'd had a magnet on him, she'd have shot over that counter. He dreaded to think where else she'd had metal inserted. Half her face was covered by her shoulder-length blonde hair.

"Hi, Tara, my name's Aldwyn Bishop, I'm a consultant with the police and this is Detective Sergeant Terrence Johnson," Bishop said with a friendly smile.

"Let me guess, you want to talk to me about Cara?"

"You've guessed it," he replied, equally as sarcastic. "Is there anywhere private we can go to talk? Or shall we just sit outside in the cold?"

"You can go out the back," Tara's male colleague interjected, "if you don't mind a bit of mess. It's delivery day, and I haven't finished crushing the boxes yet."

Terrence thanked the young barista, who was busy using the coffee machine, steaming a cappuccino. He waited for Tara to show him the way, which she did sulkily. He could tell this wasn't going to be an easy interview.

In the staff-only access rear of the shop, Tara led them to a small kitchen, which Terrence presumed was the employee food preparation area.

There was a small table with four chairs around it. The only way he knew it was a kitchen was by the presence of an old microwave, a sink and a kettle. There was no cooker, hobs, or anything else kitchen related.

"Let me save us all the bother." Tara sat and took a cigarette out of a box. She lit it, sucked in and blew out a plume of smoke in his direction. "I don't know where my sister is, okay? And even if I did, I wouldn't tell you."

Terrence used his hand to blow the smoke away from him. "That's your prerogative, of course, but you should know that six people are dead so far, and there's likely going to be more if we don't find your sister. We really need your help, Tara."

"I don't know where she is."

"When was the last time you saw her?" Bishop asked.

"I don't know, two weeks ago, maybe? I'd have to look at my calendar." Tara drew on her cigarette again.

"You're on speaking terms now then?" Terrence asked, surprised.

"Yeah, why wouldn't we be? We *are* sisters."

"Oh, I don't know. Maybe because she was responsible for you going into care? Some might say that's not a very sisterly thing to do."

"She got me away from Dad, which I would say was the most-sisterly thing she's ever done for me, actually."

"Touché," Terrence muttered. "You testified for your dad, didn't you?"

"I did. But back then I thought the way Dad acted was normal. It was only during therapy that I realised how wrong it was, and that Cara was looking out for me. I hated her for a long time, but we made up after Cara met Lucy."

"Lucy Davis," Bishop said. "Tell us about her."

"What do you want to know? She was the best thing that ever happened to my sister – it broke Cara's heart when Lucy left."

"Which is why she kidnapped her," Terrence said.

"I'm not going to sit here and defend Cara. What she did was stupid, but she only went to talk with Lucy. It got physical, things got out of hand and Cara ended up taking Lucy to a cabin. She didn't mean for it to go the way it did."

Terrence sat back in his chair and studied the moody sister. "Your sister stuffed Lucy in the boot of her car and drove her to a secluded cabin, Tara. That's not a normal thing to do."

"Yeah? Cara's anything but normal."

"Listen, we have reason to believe your sister's looking for Lucy right now," Bishop added. "She's in danger. Do you have any idea where she lives?"

"I haven't spoken to or seen Lucy since Cara's trial." Tara

stubbed out her cigarette in the overflowing ashtray. "I liked Lucy; I thought she was great, but after she ditched Cara, I didn't see her again, until the trial."

"And Cara hasn't told you where she is?"

"My sister doesn't know *where* she is. It drove her nuts, not knowing."

"Can you think of anyone who might know?" They really needed a break. Lucy was their best lead, their best chance of finding Cara, or so everyone thought. It might be that Cara wasn't looking for her, but it was pretty much all they had, that and Karim Ravani, who Gupta and Nasreen were looking for. "Did you meet any of Lucy's friends or colleagues?"

"The only friend of Lucy's I met was that woman, Dawn, I think."

"Dawn Weaver," Terrence stated. "Who your sister murdered."

He was thinking they weren't going to get anything from Tara. He hadn't expected much anyway, so it wasn't a massive deal. He hoped Gupta and Nasreen were having more luck up north.

"You know, detective, it hasn't been proven that Cara murdered all these people. It says on the news that you're wanting to speak with her, but you don't know for sure. It could be someone else, you know."

"It's highly unlikely it's not your sister, Tara," Bishop said. "We have her on camera with two of the victims, we have her fingerprints at every crime scene, bloody fingerprints at that; we have trace evidence coming out of our ears. We know it's her we're looking for; we just need to know where she's going and why. We thought you might be able to help us with that."

"Sorry to disappoint you, Mr Bishop, but we weren't super close. We've only been friends for three years or so, and we didn't meet up every day or anything like that. I have my own shitty problems to deal with, without adding Cara's to the list."

"Do you know how she knew John Wood?" Terrence asked.

"*Him?* He was her scumbag drug dealer. About six months ago him and two of his mates raped her. Cara went round to Wood's to score some H and they kept her in the bedroom for over six hours. They took turns, the sick pricks."

"And she never pressed charges or spoke to the police about it?"

"Cara? The police? Get real! She hates your lot." Tara snorted. "I can't say I'm too taken, either, but hey."

"Okay, point taken," Terrence replied.

He and Bishop spent another five minutes questioning Tara, but she really couldn't tell them much more. It looked like the only person who might have known of Lucy's whereabouts was dead – which was just great! They still had to speak to Lucy's editor at *The Telegraph*, and Cara's ex, Francesca Neal, so who knew, they could strike it lucky.

85

———

Amelie placed a cooked breakfast in front of Lennox, who kissed her, before thanking her. She walked back over to the counter and picked up her own plate, joining him at the table.

Having him back lifted her spirits; it always did.

The news was rife with theories about who was behind the recent spate of shootings, including the most recent pub shooting up north.

Having discussed the benefits of moving in with Harry, Lennox had talked her into accepting the offer. If she had ready access to *The Albatross*, she would be able to download all the files they needed. Amelie didn't want to; she'd been putting off calling Harry to give him the "good news".

While tucking into her breakfast, her mobile phone vibrated on the table. Mid-mouthful, she glanced at the caller: Harry. "Damn it! What does he want?" Amelie moaned, swallowing her food.

"Answer it." Lennox sliced a piece of sausage. "You can tell him."

"Do I have to?" she grumbled. "I don't want to live with him."

"We've talked about this, baby. It's the only way. Everything we need's on that laptop." He begged her with his eyes.

Picking it up, sighing, Amelie put the phone to her ear and greeted him in her usual cheerful manner, raising her eyebrows at Lennox. "Yeah, Harry, I wasn't expecting a call?"

"Are you free Friday night? I know it's short notice."

"I can be free, yeah. It's funny you're calling this morning, though, I was going to ring you later.

"Oh?"

"I'd like to accept your offer, if you still want me to move in?"

"Really? You're moving in?"

"Yep," she replied, almost hearing him whoop. "So, Friday will be a good chance for me to measure up wardrobe space, if that's okay with you? But I'm warning you, I come with a lot of baggage. Are you prepared for that? Oh, and I'm not selling my apartment, is that understood?"

"I'll start making you some space. You're so not going to regret this, Amelie. You've made me a very happy man. We'll talk about other stuff on Friday, okay?"

"Looking forward to it." She hung up after saying goodbye. She put her phone back on the table. "Done!"

It was dangerous. Amelie hoped she wouldn't live to regret it.

86
____

Maggie looked up at the clock on the wall: 10:37. Scott had made it through another night, to her delight. She'd had visits from family and friends, with more cards and get well balloons arriving by the day.

She'd seen three nurses so far this morning, all of whom told her that his vital signs were strong, that there was hope.

It was so encouraging; she just wanted him to open his eyes, or move a little, something, anything, to show her that her prayers weren't falling on deaf ears.

The machines bleeped, whirred, and told the nurses her son's blood pressure and heart rate – she wanted to see a finger move, or something.

Walking over to the window, Maggie looked down at the car park. She watched cars coming and going, and the people getting in and out of said cars.

She liked to make up stories about the people she watched from afar. None of them had stories as harrowing as hers, though; in fact, the stories she came up with were mundane in comparison.

Thinking up these stories was a distraction, a way of not

thinking about her two other boys, dead, shot and killed by these fucking... animals.

After ten minutes of staring out of the window, she turned back to Scott, lying there so peacefully. She walked to his bed and sat down, her head lowered, praying silently. *Come on, Scott, wake up.*

She held his hand. What was taking so long? He'd defied the doctors' predictions. "Come on, Scott, open your eyes, you can do it."

When she lifted her head and looked across Scott's bed, she saw a finger move.

"Nurse! Nurse!" Maggie shouted, getting up.

One of the three nurses she'd seen already, she couldn't remember her name, came rushing in. "Everything all right?"

Maggie couldn't speak, her heart wouldn't let her, so she pointed at his hand. "Moved," was all she could get out.

"What moved? His finger?"

She watched as the nurse saw to her son's needs. She checked his vital signs, just as she had earlier in the morning. She picked up Scott's arm and counted his pulse rate by holding his wrist. "I'm sorry to dash your hopes, Maggie, but it looks like there's no change."

"His finger moved," she managed to blurt out.

Her Scott groaned, moving his head slightly. When she looked down at his lovely rugged face, she saw his eyelids moving. He was waking! She felt like jumping up and down; she felt like kissing the nurse.

"He's coming around," said the nurse, to a colleague, who had just entered the room. "Go and get the doctor, will you, please?"

There were no words to describe the pure joy Maggie felt, no way of expressing how much love she felt for her youngest son. Her boy was alive!

Inside, she willed Scott to open his eyes.

His lids were moving. "Come on, Scott, you can do it, just open your eyes, honey."

From a distance, behind the nurse, she saw him slowly open them.

The nurse shone a thin torch in both eyes, one at a time. When he flinched against the light, she knew, as only a mother would, that he was going to be okay.

She knew he would need time to recover, but he would recover, fully, she hoped. Maggie put her hands over her mouth and heard her own gasp.

For the last couple of days, it had felt like she'd been living outside her body, looking down on herself... Now she was back.

At the rear of the room, she sat on a chair and put her face in her hands.

For the first time since they were shot, she cried, full-on sobs wracking her body.

As she thought about Scott waking, those sobs slowly turned to laughter.

Her mobile phone rang. Maggie picked it up and walked outside in the hallway, not wanting to disturb the nurses, who were busy working on Scott.

When she answered it, she knew it was Darius. "My love, great news, Scott's going to pull through. He's going to make it. He just opened his eyes."

"That's the best fucking news, Maggie. We'll be celebrating tonight. Do you want some more good news?"

Maggie stopped, turned, and looked to see who was around her. When she saw a grieving couple sat weeping outside the next room, Maggie walked a little further down the hallway, out of earshot. "Go on, I'm listening. Have you got them?"

"You'd better believe it. And their girlfriends. They're all tied up and awaiting your arrival. What do you want me to do?"

She pondered the question. "Keep them entertained for me," she said, imagining what she was going to do to them. "I'll be along as soon as I can. We really are going to be celebrating tonight."

Maggie hung up. She had lots to do, so much to organise.

There were three funerals to start planning. Tears formed in the corners of her eyes. With praying for Scott, sitting by his side since she arrived here, she hadn't even thought about funeral arrangements, but she had to now.

First, though, she was going to focus on meting out justice, her kind of justice.

87

Cara had waited outside Karim's block of flats for hours; she was bored of waiting in Sadler's Range Rover. Looking at the time – 11:07 – she checked she had everything she needed in her bag, before opening the car door and getting out.

As she walked across the road, she passed a young mother pushing her kid in a push chair; the bitch looked at her for longer than was normal – it wasn't just a passing glance. What if the bitch recognised her?

Cara needed to make this quick, if she wanted to stay ahead of the cops. She would rather take her time with this one. Cara cursed to herself as she approached the door to the flats.

Being back in this block was weird – it was the same as she remembered inside the foyer. It was covered in graffiti, grubby. Outside the lift, she let an elderly couple get out, smiled at them and stepped inside, waiting for the door to shut.

On Karim's floor, she stepped out of the lift, turned left and walked along the corridor until she came to the door she remembered well. With her hand inside her bag, fingers wrapped around the stun gun, she knocked and waited.

There was movement from inside.

When the door opened, she was met by a face she didn't recognise. The man had a dark slightly greying beard all over his face, and he was wearing a taqiyah prayer hat.

Cara felt like laughing in his face, realising it was Karim under all that facial hair. "Hi, Karim," she said, pulling out the stun gun, quickly holding it to his chest and firing. Karim screamed and fell to the floor in the doorway. "Remember me, you fucker?"

She looked in both directions of the hallway – there was no one else around. She stepped over her comatose host, bent over and grabbed his wrists. Then she pulled him backwards along the hallway, towards the bedroom.

When he was fully inside, she closed and locked the front door, before pulling him the rest of the way to the bedroom she recalled well.

Using all her strength, she managed to get him on his bed, before cuffing his wrists to the bedposts using cable ties. Cara was excited, it wasn't going to be pleasant for him.

Looking down at his hairy face, memories of him and his friends flashed in her mind. How could she have ever thought she loved him? For six years, she'd lived in this flat, in his bedroom, servicing him and his friends. Anger boiled inside her.

Taking the knife out of her bag, she climbed on the bed with him. Karim was unconscious, lying there looking peaceful.

Sat on top of him, she sliced a sleeve off his shirt and stuffed it in his mouth. "Wake up, prick!" She slapped his face, hard.

Slowly, his eyes opened; it took him a little while to focus.

Cara slapped him again, getting his attention.

He was fully awake, screaming something into his gag.

"I'm not the same girl you used to know, Karim," she said, glaring down at him.

His wide, scared eyes pleased her. Instead of unbuttoning his shirt, she sliced it with her blade. "I've changed, you know. I'm a bird of prey now."

Ripping his shirt out from beneath him, she threw it on the floor. "Like you preyed on me for six years, I'm going to prey on you."

While he was trying to free himself from the cable ties, Cara unbuttoned his trousers and slid them down his legs. "It's a dirty job, but someone's got to do it," she said, whipping his pants down around his ankles. "I still can't believe you used to do it for me. What the fuck was I thinking? I must've been on drugs, or something." She listened to his muffled pleas. "Oh, wait, I *was* on drugs, wasn't I? *Your* drugs."

His pleas turned to crying; tears rolled down his cheeks onto the pillow beneath him.

Cara felt so powerful; he was hers to do whatever she wanted with. Climbing on top of him again, she looked down at his tear-filled eyes. "Remember when I tried leaving you that time? Do you recall what you did to me?"

Still holding the knife, her fingers wrapped around the handle, she narrowed her eyes with images of Karim's fists flying at her flashing in her mind. Cara brought the handle of the blade down on his face, hard. It felt so good.

88

———

"Shit!" Nasreen hung up. "There's no point driving to the hospital, Arjun. Sadler's not turned up to work and the receptionist says it's very unlike her."

Focusing on the city traffic, Gupta replied, "Try her mobile. See if you can get her."

Without arguing that the psychiatrist was more than likely dead, Nasreen dialled Sadler's number and waited for an answer. "Nothing. Shit! She's killed her. We're too bloody late." Nasreen smashed her fist against her window.

"Hang on, we don't know that for sure." Gupta was the eternal optimist.

Nasreen didn't believe him. She stayed quiet, as Gupta drove them to Sadler's house in one of the only wealthy suburbs in the city. It really was a shit town, Nasreen noticed, looking at all the beaten-up buildings around.

Fifteen minutes later, they arrived outside Sadler's gated home. The gate was closed. Gupta, for once, cursed. It was the first time she'd heard him swear. "What now?"

"I don't know." Gupta killed the engine and got out of the car.

There was a key code security system next to the gate. Nasreen walked up to it and inspected the high-tech device.

It had a card slot attached to it. There was an intercom button at the bottom, which she pressed. "Nothing," she said to Gupta, after three pushes.

There was no way of getting inside. She knew Sadler was there, even though there were no cars in the driveway.

"Let me make some calls," Gupta said.

As soon as Gupta dialled, a clapped-out Ford Fiesta pulled up behind them. Nasreen left Gupta on his mobile, while she approached the driver. "Can I help you?"

"You're in my way," the female driver replied. "I'm Doctor Sadler's cleaner. Can you move your car, please?"

Nasreen pulled out her warrant card. "Detective Constable Nasreen Maqsood. Do you have a key to the house?"

The driver looked shocked, and a little nervous. "Yeah, of course."

Nasreen caught Gupta's attention and he walked up to them. She explained who the driver was, and that she had a key. "Let us in, please."

At the front door, Nasreen told the cleaner to remain outside. Nasreen followed Gupta inside, and as soon as she entered, she knew they would find Sadler's body – the only question was, how badly mutilated would it be?

The last room they checked on the ground floor was the kitchen; it was always the way. "I'll go and get the evidence kit," Gupta said, leaving her there with Sadler's corpse.

"I'm so sorry," she whispered, crouching down to inspect the body.

When Gupta returned, he handed her a pair of latex gloves. Nasreen pulled them on and joined Gupta around the body.

There was one single stab wound in the eye, which would have been the kill blow, but the rest of her face had been badly beaten. Sadler's forehead was smashed in, but it wasn't with a fist; it had to be a blunt object, to cause that much damage.

Again, Cara had changed her MO – she'd not beaten any of her previous victims to death, so why Sadler? What was it telling her? She wished Bishop was here.

"SOCOs are on their way." Gupta stood. "We'll let them do their thing. Let's take a look around, see what Cara was doing here."

When they walked around the house, they saw that Cara had been through every drawer and cupboard in the place. The floors were littered with Sadler's belongings.

In the bathroom, upstairs, Nasreen saw there was an empty bottle of red hair dye. In the bedroom, she noted that the bed was messy, with two pillows used. Considering Sadler was naked, it made her wonder what was going on between Cara and Sadler.

"I think we need to find out what the relationship was between Cara and the good doctor," Gupta said, reading her mind. "She wasn't tied up, but her being naked, I think it's safe to assume their relationship was more than just doctor-patient."

"I was thinking the same thing," Nasreen replied, taking her mobile out of her suit jacket pocket and dialling Terrence's number. "Terrence, it's me. When you visit Tara Mooney, can you ask her what the relationship was between her sister and Sadler, please? Sadler's dead, but she wasn't tied up, so we're thinking maybe they were lovers?"

Nasreen waited for Terrence to explain where he was at. He and Bishop were on their way to see Lucy's editor, and had already spoken to Tara, not that they got much from her. Terrence said they would stop by the coffee shop later, which she thanked him for.

"Nas, come and take a look at this." Gupta looked down at

Sadler's computer in the corner of the bedroom. "I think we might have a lead."

When Nasreen joined him by the computer, she saw it had been left on, and what's more, it had been left on Google Maps. The destination required was the furthest point north west of Scotland – Nasreen had heard of the town, which was really a village. The most prominent feature of the destination was that it was near a lighthouse called Cape Wrath. "Do you think this is where Cara's heading?"

"It's remote; if you wanted to get away from the city, it would be a good place." Gupta zoomed in on the map, noting down directions.

"You think this is where Lucy is?"

"Could be. Then again, it could be Sadler's travel plans."

"There's only one way to find out." Nasreen took her mobile out and dialled a number she'd written down on a piece of paper while in the car. "Who better to ask than a receptionist," she added, holding her hand over the microphone.

She asked Sadler's receptionist if the psychiatrist had any time off booked, or if she was planning on travelling to the Scottish Highlands. The reply was as she suspected, no and no. "That's a negative on it being Sadler's travel plans."

"Before you go getting all gung-ho on me," Gupta said, pulling her enthusiasm back, "we'll need more than this to justify travel expenses to go to the end of the world. There's no way Franks'll sign off on this."

"But this is it. This is where Cara's going."

"Sure, we know roughly where she's going, but we don't have an exact address, or even know if Cara's planning on moving on after she's got there, do we? I'm just saying! We'll need more to back this up, that's all."

Nasreen put her hands on top of her head – fingers interlocking – in frustration.

She knew these were Cara's travel arrangements in front of her. Gupta typed in the destination on his mobile and waited for the results, while Nasreen paced back and forth.

"Look, according to Wikipedia, this place is a village and civil parish in the north-west Highlands of Scotland. It lies on the north coast of the country. The area's remote, and the parish is huge and sparsely populated. The population is dispersed and includes a number of townships. The parish is huge, do you see my point here, Nas?"

"I heard sparsely populated, as in not many doors to knock on."

"The population is dispersed and includes a number of townships, which means if Lucy is there, she could be in any number of these townships. Sorry, but I'm only saying what I know Franks will say."

As much as she wanted to argue, Nasreen knew he was right. It would be equally as frustrating being near Cara, yet not know where she was. They needed more. *Shit!* Nasreen took her phone out of her pocket when it rang.

It was Terrence. "Yep, they were lovers. I just phoned the coffee shop. According to Tara, Sadler seduced her while she was staying at a halfway house after she left Sadler's care. I've got to go, Nas, we're nearly at *The Telegraph's* offices."

Nasreen turned to Gupta. "We need to find Ravani. Sadler wasn't her target, Ravani is."

"Shit! We can't locate him. He could be anywhere."

The car's police radio crackled.

Gupta answered, listening to the message.

"Thought you'd like to know we've received an emergency call from a resident in a block of flats saying he can hear screaming coming from a neighbour above him."

Nasreen looked over at Gupta, her mouth open. "What's the address? We're on our way now."

"Thank you, sir," Gupta added. "Do we know the name of the above neighbour?"

"That's a negative. I've dispatched three patrols over there now."

"Careful, she's armed!" Gupta said. "We've reason to believe she's in possession of a .22 calibre pistol, sir. Can I suggest you send a fully equipped response unit?"

"Copy that," said the voice.

Nasreen wrote down the address of the block of flats, then thanked the chief inspector for letting them know. Gupta put the postcode into his GPS.

89

Karim's screams into his gag only made Cara dig the knife in deeper when she carved the letters into his chest and belly. GROOMER.

The letters were bleeding their message onto the bed sheet. "I've been dreaming about this day for as long as I can remember. Unfortunately, we don't have much time, so I'm going to go ahead and get it over with, okay?"

Cara sat on the edge of the bed and looked down at his pathetic manhood. She smiled at the thought, holding the knife. "I wish I could say this isn't going to hurt, I really do, but I'd be lying. This is going to hurt like a bitch." She delighted in his screams.

90

———

Nasreen hurried along the path leading to the block of flats, with Gupta close behind. When she reached the lift, she saw that it was up on the fourth floor, which was where she needed to be. After pressing the lift button two or three times, she had a bad feeling about what they would find up in Ravani's flat.

"It's coming down now," Gupta said, calmly.

"About bloody time." Nasreen paced.

When the door opened, she rushed in and pushed the button for the fourth floor.

She was restless to get to Ravani's flat.

91

"Please, Simon, Elliott, come in." Franks closed the office door behind them.

He'd spent the morning setting up surveillance operations for two criminal gangs his project had sourced.

It was frustrating that they couldn't just go in and bust the gangs, but they had to have a paper trail, a way of explaining how they had come up with the intelligence. "You say you have a lead in Clive's case?"

Franks sat down on what was Clive's chair and waited for Watts and O'Hara to get comfortable. Calling through to his assistant, he asked for three cups of coffee. "So, what've you got, Simon?"

"A partial print on a shell casing," Watts replied, his fat hand passing him over a report. "Elliott had an idea, which has paid off. We've had three incidents involving fully automatic firearms in the last week, which got Elliott to thinking they're probably linked. We contacted the chief constables at both forces investigating the shootings, and we think we've identified a person of interest."

The ballistics report showed that the same gun had been used in both the Clive Adams and Hughes shootings. There was no mention of the more recent Sandhu attack. He wasn't showing it, but he was worried the two detectives would link it to Garvey. "You have a suspect already?"

"Yes, sir," Watts replied. "But there's a problem there."

Franks accepted another piece of paper. When he looked at it, he saw it was a profile of Lennox Garvey. He cursed to himself. "There has to be some kind of mistake, Simon," he said, handing him the profile back, "Garvey's in protective custody. It couldn't have been him. I'm afraid you'll have to look elsewhere."

"That would explain why his file's been redacted," Watts said, accepting the profile. "But there's more."

For fuck's sake! He really needed this whole Garvey situation dealt with. He cursed Zack Astor for supplying him with such an incompetent assassin – if Astor's guy had done his job properly, and killed Garvey when he should, Franks wouldn't be here, now, trying to cover up Garvey's involvement in three shootings. "More? What've you got?"

"Here." Watts handed him a photo.

When he looked down and saw a photo of Garvey and another black man in a pub, his heart sank. Fortunately, Garvey had known where the camera was, and walked past it at a profile angle. Plus, the camera used was clearly analogue; the picture was grainy. "We can't use this," he said, handing the photo back.

"Sir?" Watts looked suspiciously at him.

"Look at it! It's grainy and in profile. We can't be sure it's Garvey. In fact, I know it's not, because, as I said, he's been in protective custody since he was arrested for drug trafficking last month. You'll have to go back and start looking elsewhere, Simon, I'm sorry. Garvey's not your guy."

The look of disappointment on Watts' and O'Hara's faces

was obvious, but he couldn't have them investigating Garvey. Franks needed Garvey dealt with internally, by his associates in the project. It was only a matter of time before they caught him, but the question was, how many more people would Garvey kill before they did?

92

Cara pressed the button for the lift and saw it was on the ground floor. Feeling positive and full of energy, she decided to take the stairs down instead. She headed for the stairwell door opposite.

93

Amelie walked into her regular coffee shop around the corner from her apartment. It was busy, but she noticed a booth looked like it would soon become available. Standing in front of the table, she waited for a young couple – in their early twenties – to finish putting their coats on. "Sorry, I'm jumping in your grave."

After the couple left, she pushed the tray of cups, saucers and plastic wrappers to the back of the table. Amelie took off her coat and placed it on the seat, along with her bag and phone.

At the counter, she picked up an orange juice and chocolate muffin, and waited in line to pay. Feeling a tap on her shoulder, Amelie turned around, and was greeted with a kiss on both cheeks and a small hug by her best friend, Zuzanna Lewandowski. She told Zuzy where they were sitting and watched as her friend took off her coat and came back over, picking up an apple juice and pain au chocolat, and handed them to her.

Amelie had been friends with Zuzy for ten years. A Polish immigrant, Zuzy moved to England with her boyfriend fifteen years ago, not that their relationship lasted long after they moved. Within a year, her boyfriend had disappeared and Zuzy found herself living on the streets, where she earned money, at first, by giving blow jobs. A year later, she'd ascended to full-on prostitute, walking the city streets looking for tricks.

When Amelie first met Zuzy, she had a hefty drug habit, which had taken its toll on her looks. Zuzy was wafer-thin, jittery and desperate, lying in a sleeping bag outside her block of apartments. Amelie being Amelie, bought her a cup of coffee and a cake from this coffee shop. She asked her questions about herself, and by the time they'd finished their conversation, Amelie suggested Zuzy live with her for a while.

Within two years of living together, Zuzanna had kicked her drug habit, fattened up a little, but not too much, and had a far better way of life fucking rich men and women Amelie introduced her to. Instead of walking the streets looking for tricks, Zuzanna had rich Johns calling her on her mobile, all thanks to Amelie, and her hard work entertaining them.

After much consideration, Zuzanna moved out five years earlier, into an apartment block down the road. She was Amelie's best friend, and confidant. Amelie couldn't think of a better person to ask a favour like this, than Zuzy.

Sat opposite each other in the booth, their drinks and cakes in front of them, Amelie asked Zuzy how she was, what she'd been up to, and a few other friendly questions. She loved how different Zuzy was now – she was confident, fun and loving life, which was all she'd ever wanted for her.

"So, what's up?" Zuzy asked, her Polish accent heavy. "You sounded like you had something to ask me on the phone."

Her English was flawless, which was something Amelie couldn't fathom. Most immigrants Amelie met used clipped English, missing off ends of words, or saying words in the wrong order, but not Zuzy – it was like she was born English.

Amelie leaned forwards. "I've got a favour to ask you, but I don't want you to do it if you don't want to. It could be dangerous."

"I'd do anything for you, you know that."

Amelie grabbed her bag and pulled out an envelope. She held it in front of her. "I need you to hold on to this for me. It's important that you keep it safe, until you need to post it."

"What's inside?"

"You don't need to know," she replied, still not relinquishing it. "If anything ever happens to me, I want you to post it in the nearest postbox, okay? I don't want to involve you in any of this, but you're my best friend and the person I trust the most in this world."

"And you're my best friend. I would die for you, Amelie. Of course I'll take the envelope. I'll keep it in my safe at the apartment. But what do you think will happen to you? Are you in trouble? Is this something to do with Lennox?"

Amelie tried to shush her friend politely, by holding her hands on the table. "I don't know what's going to happen. Hopefully nothing. But I need to know this is safe with you, and that you'll post it if I disappear or if I'm found floating in the river."

Amelie watched as Zuzy backed off.

"You're in trouble, aren't you? This is Lennox's fault." Zuzy moved forwards again. "I told you he was no good, didn't I? Not even a month in, and he's already dragged you into something dangerous. You need to leave him, Amelie, get out while you can."

"It's complicated. I can't go into detail, I'm sorry. The less you know, the better."

"Can't you go to the cops with it?"

"I can't, Zuzy, believe me. If you don't want to do this, I'll understand."

"No, I want to." Zuzy took the envelope and slipped it inside her bag. "But please be careful, my lovely. I love you; you're my best friend. I can't lose you."

"Hopefully you won't." Amelie cupped Zuzy's hands with hers. "This is just an insurance policy, in case things go wrong, okay?"

94

———

When the lift doors opened, Nasreen saw the stairwell door opposite close. She peered through the glass. Nothing. Her attention turned to Gupta, when he encouraged her to join him.

Outside Ravani's flat, Gupta knocked and shouted that he was with the police, to open up. He tried a further two times before he looked at her. "We've got probable cause. Your dodgy knee. Here, let me."

Nasreen stepped back.

Gupta drove his foot forward at full force, hitting the edge of the door. The wood split and the door flew open. "Police! Karim Ravani, call out, please! Karim Ravani?"

There was no sign of life in the flat. The lounge-diner was empty, as was the kitchen and bathroom. On the floor was a bloody towel.

"Damn it! We're too late." Gupta hit a wall with his fist.

When she joined Gupta in the bedroom, she saw Ravani's naked bound body spread-eagled on the bed. His stomach and chest were covered in blood – she could just make out the wording carved out. "Groomer," she said, out loud.

"She's letting us know he was her groomer."

"What's that in his mouth?" She looked closer, before it occurred to her. "Oh my!" Her stomach lurched at the sight.

"I'll call for the SOCOs." Gupta took out his mobile. "They're going to be busy today. Poor bastards, having to deal with this."

Removing her gloves, Nasreen put her fingers on his neck to feel for a pulse, not that it was likely he would have one, with the amount of blood the bed covers had soaked up. "He's still warm," she said, to a nod by Gupta, who was reporting the crime scene. "She was just here!"

Nasreen, her adrenaline kicking in, ran to the door, urgency hitting her hard. The stairwell door! Had Nasreen followed her instincts, she would have been more curious.

Without saying anything to Gupta, she charged along the hallway of the flat, out of the door, along the corridor until she came to the door to the stairwell. From there she flew down the stairs two at a time.

———

95

Franks closed the door behind Watts and O'Hara. When he sat back down at the desk, he turned to his computer. He had so many emails to sort through from various colleagues, four of which were from Harry. He sighed as he opened the first from his boss.

His disposable mobile rang in his uniform jacket pocket. He rummaged inside and brought it out, recognising the number as the private investigator's he'd assigned to observe Amelie Desmarais. "Dean, I've been expecting an update. Have you got anything for me?"

"Lots. She's a prostitute all right. And expensive too. Her apartment's worth over three quarters of a mill, so she'd have to have a pretty good job to afford that. As far as I can tell, she's officially a masseuse, but I've never met a masseuse who can afford an apartment like that, I don't care how good she is."

"Could it have come from an inheritance?"

"No, I've checked. Her father died back in the eighties in a mining accident and her mother was forced to sell herself to make ends meet. She died a few years ago, leaving Amelie with nothing. In fact, Amelie had to pay for her mother's funeral."

"Interesting." Franks stroked his chin.

"Wait, it gets better. I was just watching her in a coffee shop, where she handed an envelope to a woman she was with. They were having a deep and meaningful conversation about it too. I tried to get close enough to hear, but I didn't want to blow it, so I stayed back. I'm walking behind her now; looks like she's going back home."

"I wonder what was inside that envelope?" he asked out loud. He knew Amelie was hiding something – he didn't trust her.

"I don't know, but it looked serious. Amelie was whispering with the other woman, holding hands. It looked serious to me, anyway."

"Okay, keep on her."

"Will do."

96

———

S at in Sadler's Range Rover, Cara started the engine.

She had a gruelling nine-hour drive to the north west of Scotland ahead of her. She didn't mind driving, but not for long stretches, so she decided she might make a stopover somewhere in between, to break up the journey.

Cara pulled out of her space. She jumped when Nasreen Maqsood came flying out of the main doors to the block of flats. "Fuck, fuck, fuck!" Cara slammed her hand on the steering wheel again; it seemed she was doing that a lot lately.

Taking a deep breath, she focused on the road ahead. The pig hadn't seen her, yet.

As Cara drove away, the block of flats growing smaller, she kept an eye on the cop in her rear-view mirror. Cara breathed a sigh of relief when Nasreen was out of sight.

97

———

"Shit!" Nasreen scanned the front of the block of flats.

She stood and turned, going around and around, looking for Cara; she had to be around here somewhere. "Cara!" she shouted. Her breath was laboured after charging down the eight flights of stairs.

She was looking for a red-headed woman, either on foot or in a car. Scanning in every direction, hoping, praying to see her target, she saw people walking past. None of them fitted Cara's description. "Shit!"

Gupta emerged from the foyer. "Nas, she's gone."

"I know." She tried to catch her breath, bent over, her hands on her knees.

When she stood upright, her chest burned; she could also feel her knee throbbing. In all the excitement, she'd forgotten about her knee injury.

"We'll get her, don't worry."

"She was right here. That was her in the stairwell, I know it."

"Maybe, maybe not. It could've just been a resident."

"Trust me, it was Cara. And we let her get away!"

98

———

"Mr Rawlings, you probably know Lucy as well as anyone," Terrence said to the bespectacled editor of *The Telegraph* newspaper. "Where do you think she is now?"

Maxwell Rawlings' office was small but busy. He had bookshelves on every wall available. He even had shelves packed with books under the only windows letting in natural light.

Terrence watched his interviewee from across Rawlings' desk, which was covered in papers. He imagined the editor was probably a messy person out of work too, but what was it they said about being messy and intelligent? It was obvious the man was of way above average intelligence – Terrence could tell just by the man's tweed jacket with elbow patches.

"I wish I knew," Rawlings replied. "She was a fantastic journalist, and she's missed terribly in the office. Have you read any of her articles?"

Terrence only read *The Sun*, when he had the chance, but that wasn't to say he was ignorant when it came to current affairs – he watched the ten o'clock news most nights. "Sorry! Can't say I have."

"Maybe you should. It might help you understand her more."

"I don't need to understand her, Mr Rawlings. I just need to know where she is, so we can protect her from her ex-girlfriend, who's going through a psychotic break. Do you understand what I'm saying here? Lucy's in a lot of danger."

"I wish I could help, I really do, but she didn't tell anyone here where she was going. It was how she wanted it, a clean break away from everything, she said. I asked her to forward me her new address, but she told me she didn't want anyone to know where she was."

"And you're positive she wouldn't have told anyone in the office where she was going? There's no one here she was close to?"

"Feel free to ask around. I'm not hiding anything from you. Why would I? I want Lucy brought back alive and well – she belongs here."

"We're going to need to see her HR file," Terrence said, expecting a confidentiality argument from the man. "I take it that's not an issue?"

"Of course, I'll get my PA to fetch it for you," Rawlings said gracefully. "I still can't believe this is happening. When I heard the name Cara, I never imagined it would be Lucy's Cara – I thought she was still in hospital."

"You've met her before, then?" asked Bishop.

"Absolutely," Rawlings replied. "Lucy brought her to our annual awards ceremony three years ago, and my wife and I met Cara when we all had dinner together, maybe a year later."

"And what was she like?"

"That's what's so strange about it all; she was delightful. She was funny, smart, pretty to look at, the whole package. My wife commented on how lovely Lucy and Cara were, and my wife doesn't say that unless she really means it. And then it all changed."

"How do you mean, exactly?" Bishop asked.

"When Lucy came out of rehab and moved in with Cara, I'd never seen her so happy." Rawlings leaned forward. "She was practically glowing, she was so happy. And she stayed that way for a time, but then, slowly, her smile faded. When I asked her one time what was wrong, she told me she was having problems at home, that Cara was getting too clingy and needy. I just thought it was your typical relationship troubles, you know, but then one day I found her crying at her desk and asked her what was wrong, which is when she told me she was afraid."

"Of Cara?"

"Oh yes. She confided in me that Cara was stalking her. I said to myself that couples can't stalk one another, but apparently they can. Cara was everywhere she went, even when Lucy was here working, Cara was waiting outside. She'd turn up at work drinks, parties, and the like. It got so bad that Lucy didn't want to leave the building. And then, one day, about a week before Lucy was abducted, she told me that Cara had been texting her about honouring their suicide pact."

"Suicide pact?" Terrence said, things slotting into place in his mind.

"That explains a lot," Bishop added. "That's why she's going after Lucy; she's going to finish what she started. That's her endgame."

"So, what happened after that, Mr Rawlings?" Terrence asked.

"That's when I told her to call the police. When she left the office that evening, she couldn't see Cara outside, so she walked to a friend's house she was staying with, and that's when Cara pounced for the first time. The conversation got heated, the police were called, and they arrested Cara, but Lucy didn't want to hurt her, so she didn't press charges. After that, I ordered her to take out an injunction against Cara. Fat lot of good that it did; you know the rest: Cara breached the order, confronted Lucy and abducted her."

"How long was she missing for?"

"Three days in total, the longest three days of my life. We covered the story, helping the police with their enquiries. The police conducted a thorough search, and when the police arrived at the cabin, Lucy managed to talk Cara down, begging her to put the knife away."

"And Cara was arrested," Terrence added. "And then went on trial?"

"We all thought Lucy was mad." Rawlings leaned back in his chair. "She begged the judge to be lenient when sentencing, that Cara was mentally ill and needed psychiatric treatment; she had to press charges, but didn't want Cara to end up in prison. Lucy still loved her, if you can believe that? Even after all that, she still loved her."

"And how long after Cara was sectioned did Lucy leave?"

"About a week after it was all over, Lucy came and spoke to me about leaving. She said she felt she had to get away from everything for a while. She worked two weeks' notice and didn't leave a forwarding address, or anything; she just vanished. If you find her, please let her know she's missed, and has a job here waiting for her."

"We will," Terrence said. "Does Lucy have any siblings that you know of? We've located her mum and stepdad, but they're out of the country until April, and we have no way of contacting them."

"She has a sister." Rawlings looked skywards, like he was searching. "Katherine, I think. Yes, Katherine Reynolds – but I wouldn't go getting your hopes up there, they aren't close."

Terrence scribbled down the name, which he would look up

later. The door to the office opened and Rawlings' PA walked in with the file. Terrence liked the way she looked. She had the loveliest, most flawless skin. When she smiled at him, handing the file over, his heart fluttered. "Thank you, Miss?"

"Drayton," she replied, in a low husky voice. "Andrea Drayton."

"Thank you, Andrea, that'll be all for now." Rawlings nodded.

Terrence smiled at Andrea, taking the file from her, their eyes locking for longer than they should. He watched her walk out of the office. When she reached the door, she turned and smiled.

When the door closed, Terrence opened the file and read through the Human Resources information. "Do you know why they don't get on?" Terrence scanned the paperwork.

"No, she never really discussed her home life. I do know that their dad died back in the eighties in Northern Ireland, but other than that, her life before that is a mystery to me."

Terrence thanked the editor for his time. On their way out, Terrence asked Andrea Drayton to photocopy the file, which took about twenty minutes.

99

———

Franks dialled Zack Astor's number and waited for an answer. The office door was closed, so he could talk normally, even though he was about to discuss project business.

Something had to be done about the Garvey problem, and he knew how to do it. "Zack, it's Peter," he said, watching a colleague go past the window.

He stood, walked over to the blinds and twiddled the pole until they were closed.

"Good," Astor replied. "It's about time. We need a meet."

"I was thinking the same thing. Tomorrow evening at the warehouse, can you make it? Good, I'll leave you to phone around organising everyone. I'm busy, so I'll see you there at eight."

Without giving Astor the chance to object, Franks hung up. He waited five minutes with his phone out, waiting for Astor to call back, but he didn't. He knew exactly how to give everyone the boot up the arse they needed to find Garvey.

100

It was four o'clock by the time Terrence and Bishop located Francesca Neal, Cara's ex-girlfriend. Terrence watched as Francesca's car pulled into her driveway.

Getting out of their car parked across the road, he closed the door and walked to where she was getting groceries out of her boot. "Francesca Neal?"

"Yes? Can I help you?"

"Detective Sergeant Terrence Johnson." He then offered to help her carry in her shopping. "I need to talk to you about Cara Mooney."

Francesca rolled her eyes. "I wondered when your lot would be round."

"Can we come in and talk?" he asked, holding two Tesco bags of food.

"Would it matter if I said no?"

He shook his head and followed her inside, Bishop close behind, who had two bags in his hands. They walked inside and dropped the bags in the kitchen, where Francesca busied herself putting everything away.

A little boy came into the room and began trying to help his mum put the food away. He did everything but help. Terrence smiled at the little brat. "Cute kid," he said, with a smile. "How old is he?"

"Four," she replied curtly. "Now, what do you want to know? I've got a lot to do this evening, so please excuse me if I work around you."

"We won't keep you long," Bishop assured her.

"We're searching for Cara Mooney in relation to a series of homicides, that I'm sure you've heard about on the news," Terrence said. "Your name came up during our investigation, so I'd like you to tell us everything you know about Cara. You were in a relationship with her, I understand?"

"If you can call it that," she replied, holding a tin of baked beans. "We were together for a while, until she became obsessed with me. That's when I got the hell out of there."

"That's when you assaulted her, you mean?"

"I assaulted her? You're joking, right? She assaulted me. She put me in hospital for two weeks, she kept kicking me until I was unconscious."

That wasn't how Terrence had read it.

"I've still got the scars." Francesca put the tin down and turned round, showing him a scar on the back of her neck. Then she showed him a scar on her scalp, by parting her hair. "It took me years to recover after that beating."

"We read her psychiatric review and she says *you* beat *her*," he clarified.

"She would say that, wouldn't she. She's a psychopath, going around butchering people. She probably believes she broke up with me, but it's not true. I saw her unravelling in front of me, snorting so much coke, destroying herself. She scared me, so I ended it."

He waited for her to continue. She looked like she had a lot to say.

"I was a different person back then, you know." She leaned on the kitchen counter. "I was wild, into all sorts. I got sent to a borstal when I was fifteen, and when I came out I was sent to a halfway house, where I met Cara. We weren't good for each other, but I really liked her at first. She was attractive, fun and full of life when we first met. When we moved in together, after the halfway house, it was like my life had finally started. And a year in, everything started getting creepy. Cara would follow me around, never wanting to be alone."

It sounded like a familiar story.

"After a while of treading on eggshells around her, I decided enough was enough. I told her I was moving out and she went berserk, punching and kicking me. All I remember is curling up into a ball and waiting for her kicks to stop, which they didn't. I woke up in hospital with skull fractures, a broken collar bone and concussion. She's a powerful woman; I didn't stand a chance against her, I can tell you."

"We're so sorry for bringing up bad memories," Bishop said genuinely.

"I always thought one day she'd snap and have a meltdown. I remember reading about her abducting that poor journalist. I was so surprised to hear Cara was out so soon. You don't think she'll come after me again, do you? Is that why you're here?"

"No, we don't think that, so don't worry," he replied, wanting to make her relax. "We've reason to believe she's going after the journalist, Lucy Davis. We're trying to find her, but she vanished after Cara's trial."

"That poor woman," Francesca said. "I wish I could help you more, detective, I really do, but I haven't heard from Cara for years. And I don't want to ever again. Like I said, I'm a different person now; I'm married with a child, living the dream."

When Francesca's husband came down the stairs, startled to

see him and Bishop in his kitchen, Terrence decided they'd taken up enough of her time.

He thanked her for filling them in on Cara's history. "Congratulations," he said to her, winking at the boy looking up at him. "He's a cutie." As he was walking out, Terrence turned, took a card out of his jacket and handed it to Francesca. "If you think of anything else, please call me."

On the way back to the car, it felt like a wasted day. They were no nearer to finding Lucy or Cara, although he did have Lucy's sister to contact tomorrow. Rawlings said not to hold out hope on Katherine Reynolds, but he was. Terrence wanted so badly to apprehend Cara Mooney.

101

"You two have got to be the biggest idiots I've ever met," Maggie said to the two naked black men tied up in front of her. "Going into the kebab shop across from the restaurant. Have you ever heard of CCTV? Fucking idiots, the pair of you."

She watched them look at each other, fear in their eyes.

Behind her, she could hear whimpering cries.

She turned and looked at the gagged naked women, one white, one black, facing the two Jamaicans, with their wrists tied to their ankles with cable ties. "And you, my pretty darlings," she said, crouching down and looking at the women, "are just in the wrong place at the wrong time. Too bad for you, I'm afraid."

The abandoned warehouse they were in was perfect for these kinds of meetings. Darius had sourced it for its seclusion. When Maggie paced between her captives, she heard the rustling of the plastic sheeting beneath her feet.

There would be no evidence of what was to take place – she was free to do whatever she wanted with these animals and their girlfriends. "Where's Gypsy King?" she asked Darius, who stood behind the two bound men.

"He couldn't make it," Darius replied. "He sends his apologies. He asked if you're still coming to the fight tomorrow night. I told him you were busy."

"Phone him tomorrow and tell him I'll have two grand on blue."

"I already did. And don't worry about the mess, I'll deal with it."

Maggie smiled warmly at her lovely Darius. "I know you will, sweetheart."

When Darius said not to worry about the mess, the tied-up women had started crying louder, harder. Maggie noted the difference in size of the two men; one was muscular, the other quite slender. "You're in trouble." She bent down and stared into Muscular's eyes.

Now that she knew Scott was going to make it, she could focus her energies on retribution. This gathering would serve as her springboard. She felt such vile hatred for these two Jamaicans in front of her, some of whose bullets would have torn through her three boys, killing her eldest two and seriously injuring her youngest.

She wanted to take her knife out and slice them to pieces right there; at the same time, she wanted to savour the moment, make it last longer. "Right, you two horrible bastards, I'm going to give you the chance to make it easy on yourselves." She looked down at their wide terrified eyes. "Tell me where Lennox Garvey is, and I'll have Darius here put a bullet in each of your foreheads. Nice and quick, easy. If you don't, I've got all night to take you apart piece by piece."

"Please, we don't know where he is," Slender cried. "Honestly, we were asked to join Lennox by his uncle. We aren't a part of his crew."

Maggie bent down and looked him in the eye. "That's not good for you, is it?"

"Please, take my phone," he replied desperately, "I have texts from him. His phone number's in there. Please, spare the girls, they don't have anything to do with this. Don't hurt them."

With a knowing glance at Darius, he gagged both men. She didn't want them screaming when she did her duty. "Right, that's that," she said, taking a one-inch knife from Darius. "You've opted for the second option. Piece by piece it is."

Bending down in front of the white woman, who had pissed herself, she looked at her tear-drenched face, grabbed the back of her blonde hair and yanked her head back. "Is she his girlfriend?" she asked, looking back at Muscular.

"She is," Darius replied.

"Hello, my darling," Maggie said, to the crying woman. "Your man's been very bad, I'm afraid. He killed two of my sons, my eldest and middle sons. You see, I've had to watch my own flesh and blood die right in front of me. So, I think you'll agree that it's only fair I return the favour, before I kill them."

As soon as she'd finished speaking, she stabbed the woman in her cheek. Blood poured down the screaming woman's face and over Maggie's hand. She heard Muscular shouting into his gag. Then she stabbed the blonde repeatedly in the face, visions of her boys getting shot flashing in her mind.

Maggie stabbed the white girl's face a further fifteen times.

When she let go of the woman's bloody hair, the blonde fell to the floor, her face a bloody mess. Holes where she'd stabbed the blonde, littered her once-pretty face. One of her eyes was no more. The woman coughed blood.

Catching her breath, Maggie left the woman lying there, bleeding out. Although she hated getting messy, she had to admit that it felt good, felt right. Behind her, she heard Muscular crying, watching his beloved dying on the floor.

When she stood, still catching her breath, Maggie looked at Darius, who walked over to the fallen woman, bent down and sliced her throat. Blonde would've died anyway, yet Maggie wasn't a complete monster; she had to put her out of her misery. "It hurts, doesn't it, big guy?"

When Muscular spoke into his gag, she could tell he was saying, "Fuck you." Bending down in front of him, she stabbed him between two ribs, just once, not deep enough to kill him. "Say that to me again, and I'll cut your big dick off, do you understand me?"

Rage made her hand shake violently. She wanted to repeatedly stab him, over and over again, until he was just a pulpy mess. The only thing stopping her was his pain at watching his other half bleeding from a fatal wound to her neck. She spat in his face.

Trying to control the growing rage inside her, Maggie stood and took a walk around her captives, looking at each of them in turn. The other woman's crying was starting to annoy her. "You're up next, Princess."

102

"We've still got one or two leads left," Terrence said to Gupta, Nasreen and Bishop.

Nasreen looked at the whiteboard, which had photos of Sadler and Ravani tacked to it. Two more homicides to add to Cara's list. "Unless they tell us where Lucy is, we're not going to find Cara," she said, convinced their charge was on her way to the most north westerly village in the UK.

Since they'd arrived back at the station over an hour ago, Nasreen had listened to her colleagues discussing the case. It was so frustrating not being able to travel to the Scottish Highlands because their boss needed more evidence. Gupta hadn't even asked Franks if they could go; he simply told her that Franks would say "no".

There had to be a way of finding out where Lucy lived. There had to be a paper trail somewhere, either financial, or somewhere else. Even though Cara might not be going after Lucy, she had no doubt in her mind she was. And if she was, Cara would be on her way there now. They didn't have much time.

Gupta looked at his watch. "Look, it's late. I suggest we all go home, get some shut-eye, and come back tomorrow, see what we can see with fresh eyes, okay?"

Nasreen had to admit she was tired. With over eight hours being sat in a car with Gupta to her name, she wasn't surprised her eyes felt grainy and sore. And yet, in spite of feeling tired, she knew she wouldn't be getting much sleep tonight.

"I agree," Bishop said. "Let's meet back here first thing and see what's what."

"I'll go and meet Katherine Reynolds," Terrence said.

"Arjun, do you mind if I go back to Dawn Weaver's house tomorrow? I just want to make sure we haven't missed anything," Nasreen asked. "I still think she's the key."

"Yeah, I'll come with you, if Bishop doesn't mind going with Terrence?" Gupta replied, to nods from Terrence and Bishop.

103

"Maggie! Stop! She's done, stop!"

Maggie felt Darius' strong hands pull her away. On the floor, a longer bladed knife in hand, she observed the damage. In front of her lay the second woman, a pool of blood surrounding her. Maggie could see deep gashes in her belly, breasts and neck. But her face had borne the brunt of her fury. It was unrecognisable, just a series of deep stab wounds.

As she tried to catch her breath, she wanted to continue, but Darius kept her back. She looked over at Slender, who was crying like a little girl. Seeing him bawl made her want to cut him. They were next, the pair of animals she would put down for good.

Deep down, she knew it wouldn't bring her boys back, but it would help her sort through her emotions. She felt relief and joy that Scott was going to make it, while simultaneously feeling sorrow and utter despair that she'd lost her Frank and Vincent, not to mention her Phil.

Maggie felt such a deep loathing for these two animals that she shrugged Darius off, and flew towards Slender with the knife still in her hand. She couldn't see through the red haze in her vision, as she forced the blade into his face again, and again.

It was such a frenzied attack. After the first few stabs, his body was on the floor and she was on top of him, driving the knife up in the air, and back down into the animal's body.

"Jesus, Maggie," Darius said, pulling her off him.

Before she could attack Muscular, Darius had taken out his pistol and discharged it in to his forehead. She watched, as his body fell onto the plastic sheeting.

"Why did you do that?"

Maggie looked at Darius through the red mist; she felt like stabbing him too. "He was mine. You don't get to take him away from me!"

"You need to calm down," Darius replied, "take some deep breaths."

"I need justice!"

"And you got it," he added, keeping his gun by his side. "They're all dead."

On the floor, dead bodies surrounding her, she thought of all three of her sons together, laughing and joking with one another; she thought of her Phil, lording it over them in his playful way. A lump formed in her throat, a lump she couldn't swallow, couldn't extract either. That was when sobs escaped her.

104

—————

After nine long hours of driving, Cara found herself in the furthest north westerly village in the country. It wasn't so much a village, as a few houses built sporadically over a vast area of green land. She wouldn't find Lucy's house until the morning, so she kept driving until she came across a secluded spot to park.

She was still driving Sadler's Range Rover, which the police would be searching for. Although doubting the Scottish police would be very co-operative with their English counterparts, Cara couldn't be certain they weren't out looking for her, so she had to be cautious.

There was an air of excitement, knowing that she was one sleep away from seeing Lucy again, the bitch! Tomorrow Cara would be able to talk to her again. The thought kept going over and over in her head.

DAY 10

THURSDAY, 29TH MARCH

105

"No, Cara, please." Lucy was half in, half out of consciousness. Her dreams were so vivid, so scary. Every time she closed her eyes, she saw Cara's demonic face smiling at her. And then her smile faded, turned into a sneer, as a blade appeared in front of her eyes.

Lucy didn't want to sleep anymore; she wanted to do something, anything, that stopped her closing her eyes and seeing that evil face. Knowing she was awake, she saw Helena marching towards her carrying something.

"Come on, Lucy, we've got to keep the fever down. Lie back down."

She fought against Helena's wishes, not wanting to lie down. Lying down meant falling asleep. It was no use, Helena was too strong. Lucy let the chill moisture from the cloth cool her forehead.

Feeling hot and cold, she writhed under the duvet.

"Stay still. I'm trying to help you."

Even with her eyes open, Lucy could see Cara. She couldn't get away from her, neither awake nor asleep. She screamed for Cara to leave, to never come back.

"You're hallucinating, sweetheart," Helena said.

"She's right there, Helena." Lucy pointed above Helena's head.

When Helena turned to see what she was pointing at, Cara disappeared, her maniacal laugh ringing in Lucy's ears, lingering, festering.

"See? There's no one there." Helena went back to dabbing Lucy's forehead with a cloth. "It's just you and me here."

There Cara was again, at the back of the room. Lucy watched as Cara put her finger over her mouth, shushing her. Lucy didn't want to be shushed. "She's right there, Helena," she said again, this time pointing to the bedroom door.

"Okay, I'm taking you downstairs." Helena attempted to calm her.

Lucy felt an arm tugging at her. When she was forced to stand, her entire body ached; it hurt when she put weight on her feet. All she wanted to do was die. "Please let me die," she said, as she felt herself moving, but not voluntarily. She felt like she was flying.

She was flying down the stairs, one step at a time. Everything felt like it was in slow motion. Eventually she found herself on the sofa in the lounge. She lay back, feeling the cool sitting room air calming her burning skin.

"There you go, Luce." Helena placed the duvet from upstairs over her.

It didn't matter that she was downstairs, Lucy could still see Cara, only she was now stood in front of the television. "Helena, watch out!" Lucy buried her head in the pillow Helena had brought down for her.

106

Terrence sat in front of his computer, flipping through the file Andrea Drayton had photocopied. He hadn't had a chance to read it. As he read Lucy's personal details, he noted that there was a mobile number for her.

Thinking it wouldn't work, he picked up his landline phone anyway, dialled nine and typed in the number. After it rang twice, it automatically went to an answerphone, saying "the person you've called is not available". He guessed that it meant she was no longer using the number. "Shit!" he said, his hopes dashed. "It was worth a try."

"What was worth a try?" Bishop asked, making Terrence jump.

He looked up to find Bishop stood in yet another flashy suit. "I just tried a mobile number I found in Lucy's HR file." Terrence felt stupid that he'd even bothered.

"Too bad. We could really use a break on this."

"Tell me about it." Terrence rubbed his face with both hands. "Are you ready to go see Katherine Reynolds?"

"Give me five, will you? I've got to see Franks about another case quickly."

Terrence nodded and watched Bishop walk away. Going back to the file, he flipped over to the next page, when a loose Post-it note revealed itself. He peeled it off and inspected the writing. It said Andrea Drayton in pretty cursive. Underneath her name was a mobile number.

It must've been meant for him; she wouldn't have meant it for Bishop, surely? She hadn't locked eyes with Bishop; no, she'd shared a moment with *him*. Yeah, it had to be for him, had to be.

Looking at the note for longer than was allowable for a married man, he noticed how gorgeous her writing was. Putting the note in his desk drawer, a sudden feeling of guilt swept over him. He loved his wife, he kept telling himself.

Trying to take his mind off Andrea's smile, her lips, her hair... her smell. It wasn't working; he couldn't concentrate, knowing that her number was in his drawer.

He took it out and scrunched it up. He was married, for fuck's sake, he couldn't have sex with Andrea Drayton – those legs, that smell. No! He had a job to do.

He opened the drawer again and threw the ball of paper in there. He had to go and interview Katherine Drayton, no, bugger, Katherine Reynolds. He had to interview Katherine Reynolds, Lucy Davis' sister.

Having had enough, he stood and looked around for Bishop. When he couldn't see him, he put his coat on and walked through the open-plan office, along the corridor towards Adams' old office. He saw Bishop talking to Franks in the doorway. "Bishop, I'll meet you in the car," Terrence shouted loud enough for Bishop to hear.

On the way down in the lift, his mind focused on Andrea. Maybe the cold morning air would help; it would be like a cold shower. When he was outside, his wife phoned him, which really helped ground his imagination.

107

Lennox kissed Amelie goodbye. It would be the last time he saw her until tomorrow afternoon. He was staying overnight on the road. Tonight's mission was a big one, and his mind had to be on it, not pining for Amelie. "I'll see you tomorrow afternoon, yeah?" he said, letting go of her.

"Only for a couple of hours, though." Amelie stood with her hands on his waist. "I'm seeing Harry tomorrow night, remember?"

He'd forgotten. It wasn't all bad, though, she would hopefully return with more much-needed information regarding "Project Clean Sweep". "I'll try to make it back for three." He snuck in another kiss before closing her front door behind him.

As he neared the bottom of the stairwell, he heard Amelie call after him. He stopped by the fire exit door and waited for her. Amelie flew down the stairs carrying something.

"You forgot your phone, silly." She handed it to him before kissing him again.

To his surprise, she flew into his arms and they kissed in the doorway. It wasn't a goodbye kiss, it was more than that; it was an "I'm going to miss you, don't be too long" kiss. Eventually, after two more kisses, he had to jokingly order her back inside her apartment, so that he could get to his car.

It took him twenty minutes in morning traffic to drive to his lock-up. It was effectively a row of ten garages, with reinforced metal doors. The room was five metres by four metres, so big enough for him to store his arsenal, and other bits and pieces.

He opened the door, stepped inside and closed it immediately after him; he couldn't afford one of his neighbours to peek inside and see his cache.

Once he turned the light on, he found a chair, picked up a magazine and started loading bullets into it. When he'd loaded five, he heard a gentle tap on the door. He opened it and let Barkley in, handing him a magazine to load.

108

Nasreen knew they'd missed something in Dawn Weaver's flat.

There had to be something here that would give her Lucy's whereabouts, there had to be. She was looking for an address book, anything with an address, or at least a phone number.

She wouldn't believe that Dawn didn't know where her best friend was – it didn't compute for her. Lucy vanishing in the first place didn't sit right with her.

"Let's go through this one room at a time," Gupta suggested. "You start with Weaver's bedroom and I'll do the lounge, okay?"

"That's fine, and we'll meet in the middle," she added, walking away.

Although she liked Gupta, she felt he was keeping an eye on her. It seemed it was always her and Gupta in the field; she liked mixing the teams up a bit.

She hadn't really spoken to Bishop much yet, because she was always with Gupta, or Terrence, but she guessed that was because her being a detective constable meant she still needed supervising, which Bishop wasn't qualified to do. She got it, but she would like to know more about Bishop; he was interesting.

In Weaver's bedroom, she started by opening cabinets, wardrobes and cupboards. The crime scene had been catalogued, filmed, and anything that might have been touched by Cara had been bagged and taken away for analysis. Cara had rummaged through the cupboards, so quite a lot had been placed in evidence bags, but she was still hopeful they would find something.

Although the soiled bed covers had been taken in for analysis, it had soaked through to the mattress. Nasreen looked down at the patch of blood, which looked brown, not red. Poor Dawn Weaver, she thought, as she crouched down and started wading through Weaver's personal effects.

109

It was so fucking cold up north. Cara watched Lucy's small cottage through trees that were hiding her presence. She glanced at her watch and saw it was almost eleven.

To reach Lucy's cottage she had to walk a half mile from where she left the Range Rover, which meant she couldn't stay here after she made her move, in case the police turned up. She could always use Lucy's MG, which was the best idea, as there wasn't much petrol left in the four-by-four. Or, failing that, there was a white Transit van parked outside the cottage. She could use either vehicle when the time came.

She was so close to seeing Lucy, she could almost taste it, taste her. It felt like an eternity since she last saw Lucy, which would have been at her trial. Even through hate-filled eyes back then, she still loved the way Lucy looked, the way she smelt.

Crouching amongst the bushes and trees, Cara remembered her first time with Lucy; it felt like a lifetime ago. It gave her goosebumps even thinking about it.

Cara shook the thought away, needing her head on.

A figure emerged from the house, waking her from her daydream. It was a woman, slender build, short, dark hair, not unattractive, but not beautiful. She watched the woman open Lucy's car door, get in and drive away.

Lucy had to be inside the house. Cara stood, picked her way through the bushes until she was on Lucy's land.

Cara walked towards the side of the cottage, where there were no windows. When she reached the side wall, she crept around to the rear of the tiny house, where she saw Lucy kept two chickens in a coop; she'd always talked about buying chickens, but there had been no point for them owning any in a flat. She smiled, thinking that one of Lucy's dreams had come true. Cara still loved Lucy so much it hurt.

As she crept along the rear of the cottage, Cara peeked in through each window. There was no sign of life in the house. Then she crept around the other side: no windows.

It was only when she peered in through the front window that her heart stopped briefly. There she was! Cara could see the top of Lucy's head; she was lying on a sofa, covered with a duvet. The sound of a car startled her.

110

Turning in his seat, Franks looked at his monitor and wrote down a name on a piece of paper. His memory wasn't what it once was, and he found it easier to write names down prior to an interview.

He had a busy day ahead of him, not least because he had to be in the Midlands for the meeting that evening. He'd had his wife cancel tickets for the opera tonight, not that it bothered him; he went to keep her happy. But he would rather be watching the opera than meeting scumbag drug dealers, no matter how important they were to the project.

He had meetings to attend all day, before he took off at five for the main event – he had to be at the warehouse for eight. The first meeting he had was to interview a candidate for the role of detective chief inspector, who, if successful, would eventually be working under Faisal Bukhari, his new chief superintendent.

And then he had to interview another candidate for the role of superintendent, who, if successful, would be Faisal Bukhari's right-hand man, or woman. A combination of budget cuts and plain bad luck, had decimated the department, leaving him, assistant commissioner, doing the job of four people. It was just bad luck, he said to himself once more.

His mobile phone bleeped. He turned his attention away from the computer and took out his second phone – the disposable – and looked at the screen. His private investigator. "Dean, I wasn't expecting a call until later," Franks said, leaning back in his chair. "Please tell me you've got something?"

"I don't know if it's important, but I saw her with someone earlier. I'm sending photos over to you as we speak. And they're on their way."

Franks clicked on his email icon, as the Microsoft page appeared, loading his messages. When he was in his account, he saw he had a picture file. He clicked on it and waited for it to open.

His mouth hung open when he saw a familiar face leaving Amelie Desmarais' apartment block. Large as life, it was Lennox fucking Garvey. The next photo showed him kissing Amelie, but Franks could only see Garvey from behind. Amelie Desmarais was fucking Lennox Garvey! Franks had Garvey, finally! He felt like jumping up and doing an air five. He refrained.

"Is he of interest to you?" Dean asked.

"It's Lennox Garvey. Please tell me you're tailing him."

"No, why would I be? You're paying me to watch Amelie Desmarais."

"Shit!"

"Why? Is he important?"

"You'd better pray he comes back, Dean. He's a very wanted man. As soon as you see him again, call me, clear?"

"Got it! I'm not a fucking mind reader, Peter."

"Just do it. As soon as you see him again, call me and start tailing him."

When Franks hung up, feeling excited and hopeful, he

picked up his landline phone and asked his assistant to cancel all his meetings. The interviews could wait. He had to speak to Harry.

111

Cara crept along the side wall, keeping out of view of the driver, who killed the engine.

Putting her hand into her bag, she felt the handle of the pistol and brought it out.

When she reached the end of the wall, she glanced around the corner and saw it was the woman in Lucy's MG.

The woman was getting something out of Lucy's car.

Cara crept up behind the woman, her gun out, pointed at the woman's back, as she approached her. "Stay where you are, bitch!"

The woman jumped, startled, and then automatically put her hands up. Cara loved the power she yielded over people, more than loved it; she lusted after it. Watching this bitch tremble with fear was the best feeling, better than any drug. "Why are you driving Lucy's car? Who the fuck are you?"

"Do you want me to answer that?" The woman was shaking.

"Course I want you answer it. Thick bitch."

"I live with Lucy. I'm her girlfriend. I was just picking something up for her – she has flu."

"Turn around! Slowly."

When the woman obeyed, tears rolled down both cheeks, and she was shaking. She had a very elf-like face, which was quite attractive. Cara appraised her.

Facially she was attractive, but pass on the rest of her, Cara thought; she was very thin, to the point of looking anorexic, not like Lucy. Lucy had an amazing figure, full in all the right places, slim in all the other right places. This bitch didn't deserve Lucy! "Girlfriend?" she said, like she didn't believe it.

"Yes." The woman sniffed and closed her eyes, like she was about to get shot.

"You mean Lucy traded *me* in for *you*?"

She was hurt that Lucy's taste had dropped so far, going from her to this thing in front of her. She desperately wanted to pull the trigger, put her out of her misery.

"Cara, please, don't hurt us," the woman cried, her eyes open again.

"Oh, you think you know me, do you?" She raised the gun and rested it on the woman's forehead.

"No," she replied quietly, her eyes closed again. "Only from what I've seen on the news."

"Well, you don't! I'm here for Lucy. Show me inside."

Walking slowly behind the crying woman, Cara asked, "What's your name?"

"Helena." The woman, her hands up, walked slowly towards the house. "What are you going to do to us?"

"Keep walking."

Helena took her keys and opened the front door.

Cara nudged her in her back to keep moving. Once inside, Helena closed the door.

"Please, Cara, it's not too late to leave. If you go now, we won't tell anyone you were here."

"Shut up! Take me to see Lucy." She'd only just met Helena, and she already wanted to kill her. She had to bide her time, though, she would make use of Helena in her plan. "*Now!*"

Inside the old cottage were wooden beams – it was very rustic and cold. She could smell damp, or mould, whatever it was. The wooden floor added to the rustic feel. It was exactly as Lucy described in her dream home.

"Lucy, we have a guest." Helena showed Cara in to the sitting room.

Cara had to take a couple of deep breaths as she entered the room. She'd waited for what felt like forever to finally see her one true love again. When she cleared the door, she walked around the coffee table in the middle of the room and slowly turned until she could see Lucy lying on the sofa, on her side, facing away from her. "Lucy!"

Without thinking, Cara rushed over to be with her love, absent-mindedly setting the gun down on the glass coffee table. Cara bent down on both knees and stroked Lucy's shoulder, then her hair. "Lucy, it's me, it's your Cara," she said, hoping for a smile.

When Lucy rolled onto her back, her face was wet and she was shivering. Cara looked into her eyes, but they kept rolling back; she wasn't fully conscious. "Aw, baby, my poor Juicy's not well," she said, stroking her forehead. "I'm here now, I'll look after you."

Cara heard movement behind her. Then she heard glass being scratched.

"Get the fuck away from her, you demented psycho bitch!"

Without flinching, without moving, Cara looked down at her poorly true love. She stroked her hair, which was damp, yet lovely. She so adored that face, even with that burn scar. How could she ever have thought Lucy hated her? And yes, she did get her sectioned in an asylum, but it had done her good. Lucy loved her too, she was sure of it.

"Did you hear what I just said?" Helena growled from behind her.

Cara stopped stroking Lucy's hair. She'd finally got to her lover again, after a long time away. When she heard the hammer pull back on the gun, Cara rolled her eyes, stood, then turned to face Helena.

112

Nasreen cursed under her breath. She found an address book hidden in a cupboard in Weaver's bedroom, but it was old. It had Lucy's mum and stepdad's address written down as Lucy's, so it was very old – it didn't even have Lucy and Cara's flat listed.

After turning Weaver's flat over, she was beyond frustrated. She put her hands on top of her head and glanced around the room. Maybe she needed to see the crime scene in a different way. In her bag were the crime scene photos. She pulled them out of the A4 envelope and stood in front of the bed.

Flipping from one photo to the next, she stopped on one picture in particular. It showed Dawn Weaver's body on the bed, arms tied to the bedpost.

The poor woman. She couldn't begin to imagine the horror Weaver experienced just prior to being murdered. But it wasn't the body that interested her; it was the notebook next to the bed. "Arjun, can you come in here, please. I think I might have something."

Inside a minute, Gupta was looking at the photo she was holding.

"There." She pointed at the orange book. "We need to find that notepad."

"If it's not here, the SOCOs will have bagged it as evidence. There, can you see that? It has blood on it. I'll phone through and get them to find it for us. You know, it could just be a notepad; it might not have Lucy's address in it."

"I know, but it's worth a try, isn't it?"

Nasreen listened, as Gupta phoned the forensic testing lab, where the bagged evidence was stored and analysed. He knew people there, which was helpful in situations like these, where something in particular was required.

Gupta put his hand over the mouthpiece. "They're looking for it now. When they find it, I'll tell them to put it aside for later, when we pick it up."

"I'll go pick it up," she offered, wanting to be the first person to look through it. Gupta was right, though, it was probably just a scribbled on old notebook, but she had a gut feeling it would help them – she needed to learn to trust her gut feelings.

"You really think there's something in it, don't you?"

"I'm not getting my hopes up, if that's what you mean. But yeah, I want there to be something in it."

"Hold on," Gupta said, going back to his call. "Shit! Keep looking, would you! Call this number as soon as you find it." Gupta cursed. "They've lost – no, misplaced, it."

Nasreen didn't want to show she was equally as frustrated, so she went back to going over the crime scene photos again, not that anything sprung out at her. She knew their big breakthrough was hinging on the forensic team locating the notepad.

113

"Unbelievable! The one person we need to find, and she vanishes, just like her sister," Terrence said, frustrated. "Maybe it runs in the family."

"We'll find her." Bishop sat next to him in the passenger seat. "She's probably gone into town."

Putting the car into gear, Terrence accelerated forwards, not really knowing where he was going. They'd tried Katherine Reynolds' home and work. The woman at reception told him that Katherine had booked the day off as holiday. He asked the young receptionist if Katherine was off tomorrow. "No, just today," replied the receptionist.

"Where are we going now?" Bishop asked.

"Back to the station, I guess. There's no point hanging around outside her house after I've left a note on her door, is there? She'll call when she reads the note."

114

"Don't come any closer, or I'll shoot you where you stand, so help me God," Helena snarled.

"God's not going to help you, Helena," Cara replied, the glass table the only object preventing her from caving her head in. "Put the gun back down on the table, and I'll forget this happened." She took a step forward.

Helena stepped back, stretched her arm out further.

Cara noticed Helena's hands were shaking. She had to give Helena credit for having the balls to pick up the gun; she didn't see that coming.

"One more step and I'm pulling this trigger, Cara. I mean it."

Cara still didn't think Helena had it in her. She quickly put one foot on the glass table and pulled herself up.

Looking down at Helena, she could see what Lucy liked about her now.

"I'm pulling this trigger. I'm warning you!"

"No, you're not. You haven't got the killer instinct in you. Now, hand me the gun, and we'll get to know each other."

"I don't want to know you." Helena stepped sideways.

Cara jumped off the table, onto the carpet, two steps away from Helena.

The sudden movement made Helena flinch, but she didn't pull the trigger. "Go on then, if you're going to. Put one in my chest, Helena, if you have the balls."

"I will."

Having had enough listening to her threats, Cara lunged forward, grabbed the pistol and easily snatched it from the skinny bitch. She heard Helena scream, right before Cara struck her on the cheek with the butt of the gun.

Towering above Helena, catching her breath, Cara looked down at her vanquished host. First Sadler pulled the gun on her, and now Helena, of all people. "You know, Helena, you really should follow through on your threats. You could've put one in me by now. You could be sat here waiting for the police to arrive, safe. But here we are. What am I going to do with you?" She pointed the pistol down at her chest.

Cara wanted to be alone with Lucy for a while, before she put the last part of her plan in place. She wanted to spend some quality time with her Lucy.

With the gun pointing at Helena's chest, she ordered Lucy's girlfriend to get on her feet, which she did eagerly. Cara told her to walk to the bedroom, which she obeyed, one stair at a time, while rubbing her cheek and crying.

"Please don't hurt me, Cara," Helena begged, in front of the bed. "I haven't done anything to you, have I? I could've shot you, but I didn't."

"You couldn't, more like. The safety was on." It amazed her how many people fell for that – certainly Sadler had, and Sadler was an intelligent woman. Cara heard Helena curse. "Anyway, I need you out of the way, so be a darling and lie on the bed for me so I can tie you up."

"What? Why?"

"Because I'm the one with the gun, that's why."

She watched as Helena lay down, her arms above her, waiting to be tied to the bedposts. "Good girl," she said, using cable ties. "You do your first wrist." Cara heard the clicks of the cable tie.

When she was sure Helena was restrained, she tied her other wrist to the bedpost. "I still can't believe she chose you after me. It's so insulting. You know, I might have to kill you after all."

Cara laughed when Helena burst into tears. "Oh, come off it, I was joking. I'm not about to go and kill Lucy's new love, am I?"

115

It was four in the afternoon by the time the forensic lab phoned Gupta. Nasreen tried her hardest not to get angry at their incompetence in losing the notepad. Could their lab really be that badly run? She listened to Gupta speaking to the most senior forensic officer there, who was trying to suggest losing the notepad wasn't their fault. Her boss was having none of it though. Good for you, she thought.

"We've been waiting for hours. Get your act together and find me that bloody notebook, would you?"

She was as angry as Gupta. Instead of showing it, she kept on looking through Weaver's belongings. With how much difficulty they were having retrieving the book, she knew it would be the break they were waiting for. "Still nothing?" she asked, as if she hadn't heard him on the phone.

"Unbelievable! I don't know why we still use this lab." Gupta put his mobile back inside his jacket pocket. "I might suggest to Franks we find an alternative. This is the second time they've let us down on this case."

"Would it help if we went down there? We've seen as much

as we're going to here," she suggested, getting on her feet and peeling off her gloves. "We need that book, Arjun."

"You really think it's in there, don't you?"

"I *know* it's in there."

At first, she thought he would suggest leaving it, and wait for them to phone, but then he said, "Come on then, let's get on the road." She followed him out of Weaver's flat.

116

Terrence glanced at the clock on his dashboard: 16:46, before stepping out of his car. Bishop followed suit. He waited for two cars to pass before crossing the road to Katherine Reynolds' house. He'd spent the whole day waiting to speak to her.

Before he could knock on the front door, it opened, and he assumed it was Katherine waiting to greet him. She didn't look a bit like her younger sister. "Katherine Reynolds?" He held his warrant card up.

"Come on in," she replied, with a slight Irish twang.

She took him through the hallway, into the lounge, where a man, presumably her husband, sat on an armchair waiting for them.

"Detective Johnson?" the man asked, standing and holding out his hand.

Terrence first showed the man his ID, then shook his hand before sitting on the sofa, next to Bishop, who introduced himself and also shook the man's hand. "I hope I didn't scare you with the message I left, but we're desperately trying to find

Lucy, and no one seems to know where she is. I was hoping you might have her address?"

The faces the couple shared didn't fill him with hope.

They glanced at one another, like a couple with a shared secret they both wanted to tell. He waited for one of them to talk.

It wasn't long before Katherine initiated the conversation. "I'm so sorry you've had a wasted trip, but we don't really talk anymore, Lucy and me. We had a falling out a few years back. Every time we see each other, we row, so we just don't bother now, it's easier."

"I understand family dynamics, Mrs Reynolds, but now is no time for all that. We have reason to believe Cara Mooney is looking to kill your sister, so, if you love Lucy, even just a tiny bit, now's the time to help us."

"Course I love Lucy, detective, she's my little sister, but the simple fact is I don't know where she lives. Mum does, but she never told me; mum's had enough of us arguing, so she never really talks about Lucy to me now."

Making it clear that he was unimpressed by sighing, he stood and headed for the door. Then he turned, "We tried contacting your mum earlier."

"She's on a cruise," Katherine replied. "She could be anywhere."

"I don't suppose you happen to have a key to her house, do you?"

"Actually, I do." Katherine stood.

Terrence continued. "We're looking for an address book, anything that will give us your sister's whereabouts. Do you know if you have family up north?"

He told her which village he was referring to, but she told him, "None that she knew of."

Within three minutes, Katherine put her shoes on, took them outside, got in her car and they followed her in convoy to Derek and Siobhan O'Malley's house across town. The anticipation of possibly finding what they were looking for was palpable in the car.

117

Bored of watching Lucy sleep, Cara wanted to talk to her, to tell her the way things were.

Of all the bad timing, she would have to go down with the flu now, wouldn't she! For a good couple of hours, Cara had sat on the edge of the sofa, stroking her hair, occasionally singing quietly to her. It was boring.

Cara hadn't heard a peep out of Helena since she came downstairs.

Curious, she walked out of the lounge, up the stairs and into the bedroom, where Helena was still lying on the bed, tears tumbling down her cheeks. "Don't you ever stop crying?" she asked, irritably. "Look, you took your chance and bottled it. Crying won't help you."

"What are you going to do with us?"

Sat on the edge of the bed, Cara looked down at her captive and stroked her leg. "You know what? I haven't made my mind up yet." She took off her hoodie. "I wasn't expecting Juicy to be so out of it." She stood and left Helena crying.

Back downstairs, Cara looked down at her sick Lucy, who was lying on her side, her damp hair clinging to her flushed face. "Come on, Juicy, wake up!" Cara whined, wanting so badly for her ex-girlfriend to come around. "You know I don't handle boredom well." She sat on the edge of the couch, poking Lucy. "Poke!" Poking harder, then harder, anger welled up inside her. "Wake up!"

118

Franks boarded *The Albatross* at exactly 18:00. He'd spent all day trying to contact Harry, who'd been out of the office since ten o'clock, and no one knew where he was. Franks tried his mobile on several occasions, to no avail.

He had to cancel the meeting tonight, and rescheduled it for tomorrow night instead, not that it was a big deal, not now he knew who Garvey was shacking up with.

It wouldn't be long until the Garvey problem was eliminated once and for all. The thought cheered him up. With Garvey out of the equation, Franks could focus all his efforts on the project.

"What was so urgent, you had to drive down here?" Harry let him through to the lounge.

"We need to talk." He walked up to the bar and poured two glasses of whisky. "We've got a problem. And you need to sort it."

He watched his boss's reaction.

Harry took the drink he offered from his hand, walked over to one of the three sofas, and sat down. His boss didn't seem too bothered. "What is it, Peter?"

"It involves your 'friend', Amelie."

There was the reaction! Harry's face turned red and his brow furrowed. Franks needed Harry to be angry; it was why he'd come for a face-to-face.

"The fuck do you know about it?" Harry stood and walked towards him.

"She's a whore, Harry." Franks waited for the reaction. "But you already know that, right? You've been paying for her company, haven't you?"

"Is that it? Is that your big problem I have to sort out?"

His boss was nose-to-nose with him. "It's part of the problem, yeah," he replied, spilling the drink when Harry grabbed his collar and pushed him against a wall.

"Amelie's with me now. She's giving up the game, if you must know. Not that it's any of your business."

Franks held his arms out, unthreateningly. "That's good, congratulations."

The surrendering arms worked; Harry released his grip on his collar.

"Go away, Peter." Harry walked back to the sofa. "You don't need to worry about me and Amelie. You've just wasted your time driving down here."

Franks straightened his shirt, pulling it down, pointedly. "That's not entirely true, I'm afraid. I haven't told you the reason I'm here."

He watched Harry shrug. He could tell his boss wasn't interested, so it was his responsibility to make him interested. "She's fucking Garvey," he said with no warning.

"Get the fuck out of here," Harry said, almost laughing. "That's bullshit. She's not fucking Garvey. No fucking way!"

"I'm sorry for being the bearer of bad news, but it's true." He reached under his coat and pulled out photos he'd had blown up. "I have evidence." He walked over to Harry and handed him the pictures.

"What the fuck?" Harry flipped through the pictures one at a time.

"I am sorry, Harry. I didn't want to come here like this. But she's been helping Garvey – we need to sort this out, and soon. We need to know how much she has on us."

His eyes met Harry's, as his boss looked up.

"Oh, wait a minute," Harry said, "she's a prostitute, which means she fucks other guys, right? Garvey's just another one of her clients, I'm sure."

Franks shook his head. "I don't think so. The private detective I hired to follow her, saw her hand an envelope to a friend in a coffee shop. He said the conversation looked serious. She has information on us, and we need to know what she knows, and act accordingly. The project's at stake here."

"Don't come in here and patronise me, Peter! I know what's at stake! Amelie can't have anything on us from me. I haven't talked to her about it, or anything."

"Has she been in your office? Has she been left alone in here before?"

"No, never." Harry flipped through the pictures again, shaking his head. "And I can't stop her making money, can I?"

"She's never been in your office, are you sure?"

"Yes, course I'm sure. And that envelope could've been anything – it could've been a letter to a friend, for Christ's sake. You don't know it had anything to do with the project. It could've been anything."

Franks cursed under his breath.

"Oh, wait." Harry looked straight ahead, but not at anything in particular.

"What? What is it?"

Franks watched as Harry stood, took a set of keys out of his pocket and walked out of the lounge, towards the office. He followed his boss into the small study and waited while Harry's laptop booted up. Stood behind him, looking over Harry's shoulder, he saw the files appear on the screen.

"I told you she didn't get anything from me," Harry said.

Franks observed the dates on each of the files under Project Clean Sweep. He noticed that one didn't correspond with the others. He pointed at it. "Open the personnel file."

"I opened this. Oh, wait, the dates don't add up."

The file said it had been opened in the early hours of last Saturday. Franks waited for Harry to do the maths. Even he knew Amelie stayed over last Friday, because he met her on the Saturday morning, as she was leaving. She probably had a USB stick in her bag as they spoke. He felt like kicking himself. But he would bet his life on the fact that Harry felt infinitely more stupid than he did.

"That fucking bitch! She's been stringing me along all this time?" Harry was getting angrier by the second. "I'm going to kill that lying bitch! She probably thinks she can steal more off my laptop when she moves in here."

"She's moving in here?"

"I asked her last Friday. I could tear her apart with my bare hands. These hands. Limb from limb, I swear."

It was the first time Franks had seen Harry angry, which wasn't surprising; it wasn't like they were good friends, or even had a good working relationship. He endured Harry – he had to, it was the chain of command. "When are you seeing her again?"

It took Harry a couple of seconds to process the question. "Tomorrow night, at eight." Harry turned and looked at him. "She's coming over. I've booked a ride for her."

"You know we need to deal with this, don't you? If word of this gets out–"

With a reluctant nod, Harry replied, "Yeah, I know."

"She could really fuck things up. I can have a couple of our friends meet her here, instead of you? It would give you an alibi, if she was ever found."

It was the first time he'd actively spoken to his boss of having someone killed, not that it was overtly said. Since they'd first discussed the project, months earlier, they'd always said it was for a good cause, to clean up the streets, to make them safer.

Neither of them ever envisaged the need for having anyone killed in the project's name. Franks couldn't believe he was suggesting such a thing now. "I know how hard this must be."

"No, it's all right. I'll meet her here."

"Are you sure? You don't have to do this on your own. I can have a couple of Astor's guys here to help you."

"No, I'll do it. This lying bitch is going to get what's coming."

"If you're sure." Franks wasn't; he didn't think Harry had it in him.

He wouldn't be able to murder someone, just like that, not unless they'd done something heinously evil to him, or at least that was what he hoped. He'd become a police officer to help people, and here he was talking in code about having Amelie Desmarais murdered. Life was strange.

"She shouldn't be sniffing around." Harry closed down his laptop. "I'll take care of Amelie. She won't be interfering in our business again, trust me on that."

119

"Come on, where is it?" Nasreen was frustrated that she couldn't find the notebook.

When she looked at her watch, it said: 20:12. She and Gupta had hunted for the book for hours, painstakingly searching through the lab's shelves, cupboards and every other nook and cranny they could find. Nothing. It was so important to find it, which was probably why they couldn't. Sod's law, she thought, bitterly.

"Here, help me with this, Nas." Gupta pulled a shelving unit on one side.

Nasreen took the other side and helped Gupta pull it out far enough to see what was behind it. Nothing. There were four more identical shelving units in the room. Carefully, one by one, they yanked them out. Nothing.

She was beyond frustrated. Then, when she looked down, she saw a flash of orange in front of one of the shelving units. "I think I've found–"

Letting the sentence trail off, she walked up to the unit, bent down and inspected the orange object. Squashed beneath the unit was the notebook.

Nasreen asked Gupta to tilt the unit back, so she could slide it out. She pulled the book out and stood with the evidence bag in her hand. She didn't open it straight away.

"Here," Gupta said, "I'll open it. I know how much hope you have riding on this."

Nasreen let Gupta take it off her. If it was another dead end, her hopes would be as empty as the pages in the book. "And?"

"Nothing. Just an empty book."

She listened to Gupta curse and kick the shelves, while she glanced through the empty notebook. It was as empty as Gupta said. "Shit!" Taking one last look, she flipped through the empty pages from the back to the front.

On the last page, she stopped when she saw that a page had been torn out. There was the tiniest guilty slither of paper left. "Arjun, can you find me a pencil, please." She found a table to rest the book on. Looking at it now, up close, she could see that the front page had indents in it. "Thanks." She took the pencil from her boss.

"Please be an address," Gupta said, crossing fingers on both hands. "Please don't be last week's shopping list." She listened to him pace, while she shaded in the whole page with the pencil. "Well?"

"It's an address, and mobile number," she replied, looking up at him with a smile.

120

Terrence waited patiently while Katherine Reynolds hunted through her mum's kitchen drawer. He watched as she took everything out, placed it all on the kitchen surface and waded through the old notebooks and pads that had accumulated over the years.

Katherine found three ancient address books.

Terrence was getting annoyed.

"It could be anywhere." Katherine looked up at him. "Do you mind checking the lounge? Try by the landline phone by the main door."

Terrence walked with Bishop into the lounge, where he found the telephone, but no address book. "Typical! When you need to find something–"

"I found it! Her address and phone number are here!"

Marching into the kitchen, he took the book from Katherine and copied the address and phone number into his own notepad. He had to phone Gupta and Nasreen first, before he even thought about calling Lucy Davis. "Arjun, I've got the address. Nas was right, it looks like we're going to the Scottish Highlands."

He listened as Gupta explained that only half the team could go, because it wasn't definite Cara was even going there, although it was a safe bet she was.

Gupta told him that he'd speak to Franks about flights there. Terrence suggested that they drive, but it wasn't a short journey – it would take twelve and a half hours by car, via the M6. It would take anywhere between an hour and twenty and four hours to fly there, depending on which operator they went with. There were no more flights out that night. They'd have to wait until morning.

Not wanting to miss out on the action, Terrence suggested that he drive with Nas there tonight, and suggested that Bishop and he follow them out tomorrow by plane. It would give them time to establish if Cara was there. Gupta wouldn't hear of it; he told Terrence to stay put, that he and Nas were already on their way.

Reluctantly agreeing, he jabbed the red icon on his phone with his finger.

"What did Arjun have to say?" Bishop asked.

"We're grounded. It looks like they're grabbing all the action. Arjun wants us to stay put, in case Cara's not there. This fucking sucks!"

"She's there all right – I'd bet my life on it."

Terrence sighed. There was nothing he could do; he had to wait for the green light from Gupta. He wasn't as brave as Nasreen; he wouldn't have gone running into that bunker like she did. He would go home and wait for the official nod.

Thanking Katherine for helping them find her sister's address, he left with Bishop. When he sat in the driver's seat, he sighed. He needed to be there when they took Cara down; he didn't want to miss out. "What do you say we make a move now?" he asked, only half-joking. The thought of staying behind bothered him.

"You mean drive to Scotland?" Bishop asked.

"You said it yourself, she's there. Find directions on your phone. I'm going to call my wife, tell her I won't be home tonight."

121

Lennox had sat in the passenger's seat for hours, tailing Omar Almasi, the Midlands dealer Franks had chosen. Back when he'd worked for William Rothstein, he had dealings with Almasi, so Lennox knew the kind of man he was. Taking Almasi out tonight would be doing the world a favour; and an added bonus.

With his Uzi in hand on his lap, he watched Almasi's silver BMW M2 fifty metres ahead. The M42 was busy, meaning Barkley had to weave in and out of the fast lane to keep up with Almasi's sporty coupe. "Shit! They've made us," he said, chambering the Uzi.

Lennox wanted this so much, he could barely keep his hand from shaking. Omar Almasi was the worst kind of dealer; he used vulnerable women and children as mules, sending them to smaller towns to widen his narcotic grip around the Midlands.

A third-generation Iranian immigrant, Almasi was a born Brummy, who'd proven his intent to society by being the sole distributor of gear to his secondary school. He'd managed to complete his education without being caught, when he'd chosen his successor to carry on his reign of dominance over the younger users.

From there, it was only a small step from local school kingpin to the huge drug network he controlled now. It wasn't that he dealt drugs that Lennox disagreed with, it was the manner with which he conducted business that left a bad taste in his mouth.

It was generally agreed among the varying gangs that children were off-limits – it was bad for business to sell illegal substances to minors, but Almasi saw them as an untapped source of income. That alone was worth a bullet in the head.

Almasi wasn't only into drugs; he had a tight grip on human trafficking too. Almasi brought desperate immigrants into the country, their ages ranging from four upwards.

These poor women were inevitably sold to the sex trade, where the helpless victims would be subjected to daily rapes to break them in before they were finally sold on the black market.

Lennox was surprised Franks had chosen Almasi to be part of the project, given his crimes against the very people Franks wanted to protect.

Out in the open, spotted, Barkley stepped on the accelerator, as Lennox felt the power of the engine drive the Mercedes they were in closer to Almasi's BMW. With adrenaline coursing through his entire body, he wound down his window, a blast of cold air stinging his face. "Closer, Bark, we need to get closer."

Lennox watched the BMW weave in between cars on the slow lane and middle lane, trying to keep away from them. As he held the machine pistol out of the window, preparing to unleash hell on Almasi, the rear passenger's window wound down. That was when Lennox saw the first muzzle flash.

122

Cara stepped out of the shower, took a towel from the rack and dried herself, while she walked through to the bedroom where Helena was crying. "Do you ever stop crying?"

"Fuck you!" Helena replied, through the sobs.

Laughing, Cara dropped the towel and got changed into her jeans and hoodie again. She would change the T-shirt, knickers and socks later. Right now, she wanted to go and see if Lucy was awake yet; she'd grown bored of poking and prodding her. "I'll be back later. Don't get up, I can see myself out," she added, smiling.

Downstairs in the living room, Lucy was still asleep on the couch. She was lying on her side, her face finally visible. Cara squatted and stroked Lucy's cheek. "Wake up, sleepyhead," she whispered softly.

Her attention was broken when she heard a mobile phone ringing from behind her. Cara got up and searched for it. It was somewhere in the adjoining dining room.

After a brief search, four rings on the mobile, she found it and picked it up, looking at the caller ID. It was a UK number. She was in two minds whether or not to answer it. "Hello...?"

"Lucy Davis?" came a female voice.

"Yes." She tried not to give away the fact she didn't have an Irish accent.

"My name's Detective Constable Nasreen Maqsood."

123

Bullets thudded into the side of their car, smashing the rear passenger window, sending shards of glass into Lennox's hair. Crouching in his seat, Lennox pulled the trigger on his Uzi, as a short burst hit the BMW's side. He had to be careful not to hit any other cars caught in between them, although the gunman in the Beamer didn't seem to care.

Cars in between them pushed their brakes on hard, trying to get out of their way. Barkley, a skilled driver, swerved towards the BMW, giving Lennox an opportunity to fire at the front of the car. The driver's window smashed, but he failed to hit the Iranian driver. "Shit!"

Another burst of gunfire tore into their side, one bullet narrowly missing his head; he felt it whizz past him, and into the windscreen. The Beamer was slightly behind them, so Barkley broke to level them off.

Cars around them braked, not wanting to get caught up in the gunfight. Lennox saw cars in front of them swerving to avoid a hail of bullets. It made Barkley's driving even tougher.

"Shoot the fuckers already!" Barkley tried to avoid the cars approaching him.

"What do you think I'm doing?" He pulled the trigger once more.

The next burst of hot lead tore into the driver's door. A single, stray bullet found its way into the driver's neck. Very briefly, Lennox saw blood spatter inside the car, as the BMW pulled sharply to the left and hit the motorway barrier.

Lennox saw it as a win. The BMW was a mess in the background, smoke billowing into the dark night air. The driver was dead, although it probably wasn't Omar Almasi. Lennox would have to find another way of getting to the Iranian dealer.

They had a more pressing matter: ditching the bullet-riddled Mercedes and getting out of here. "Pull off on the next exit, we're ditching this ride."

124

"If it isn't the lucky pig," Cara said. "This is an unexpected surprise."

Her heart pumping at a rate of knots, Nasreen looked over at Gupta, who was busy driving. She put her hand over the mouthpiece. "It's Cara, she's there." She took her hand away. "Cara! I wasn't expecting you to pick up."

"How's your tit now? Does it hurt still?"

Nasreen put her hand over the stab wound. It did hurt, as it happened, but not as much as her knee. "It's fine, thanks for asking."

"How does it feel to know you're only alive because I let you live?" Cara sounded very pleased with herself.

"I remember it differently, Cara. You couldn't finish the job, you were interrupted, remember?"

"I won't be interrupted next time, Pig. I still owe you for Beattie. Anyway, it's great to finally talk to you."

Nasreen could think of so many things she would rather be doing than conversing with a psychopath. She could be at home, reading Mina a bedtime story, or be praying at the Mosque, or practising her kickboxing at the gym. Anything would be preferable to this. "Likewise. Where's Lucy? Is she okay?"

"Oh, she's fine. Just lying down having a nap. We'll be on our way soon. I have big plans for Lucy and her girlfriend."

"I'm sure you have. Look, Cara, you don't need to do this, you know? If you let them go and hand yourself in, we'll do everything we can to help you. You're as much a victim in all this as anyone else."

There was a long pause.

"Victim? Victim? I'm no fucking victim! I'm a bird of prey–"

"A bird of prey? Oh, come off it, you were born a victim. You've been let down by everyone you ever knew." Nasreen continued despite being unsure if proceeding was the best way. "By everyone, from your paedophile dad to your druggie mum, by Karim Ravani, and hell, even your psychiatrist betrayed you. They all used you; they all threw you away, like you were nothing, Cara. It's not your fault. You can still have a happy ending; you just need some help."

"You think you know me?" Cara's voice was getting angrier by the second. "You think because you've read my psych notes you know what I've been through? Fuck you! You don't have a fucking clue what my life's been like. You don't know anything. My dad raped me for so long I started thinking it was normal; I resented my sister when he switched his attention to her, when I should've protected her from him. I was raped every day for six years by Karim and his friends, do you think you know what that's like? Fuck you, Pig, you don't have the first fucking idea."

"Cara, you can still have a good life." She tried her best to calm her down, by keeping her voice soft and soothing. "It's not too late for you."

"Who do you think you're trying to con? I'm not going to any prison, you can count on that. I'm going out my way, on my terms, not yours."

"Okay, so you can go out on your terms. If that's what you want to do, fine, but don't take innocent people with you, please. Let Lucy and her girlfriend go; they don't deserve any of this."

"Me and Lucy made a pact. And we're going to honour it."

When Nasreen spoke again, there was no reply. "Shit! She hung up on me. She's there with Lucy and the girlfriend. She's going ahead with the suicide pact. Shit!" They were still hours away from the village.

"Call the local police there. Get them to go over to Lucy's house."

Nasreen looked up the local police district number for Lucy's area on her mobile and dialled.

125

"Hurry up and get dressed." Cara cut the cable ties binding Helena. "We're leaving, and you're helping me with Lucy."

After she'd dressed herself, Cara forced Helena down the stairs at knife point then made her get Lucy up and off the sofa. Helena put a thick winter coat around Lucy, making sure she was warm enough. Cara heard Lucy groaning; she wasn't asleep, wasn't awake – she was somewhere in between. "Quick! Take her other arm." Cara put one of Lucy's arms around her neck. "Where are the keys to the van outside?"

Before helping Lucy, Helena went into the dining room and picked up the keys for her van. Then she went back and helped Cara with Lucy. It took both of them to hold Lucy up, and get her into the passenger seat of the Transit van.

In the back of the van, Cara had her knife and gun out, ready for whatever came her way. She warned Helena that any mischief would be dealt with harshly. If they got pulled over by the police, Cara told Helena that if she didn't act normal and get them through it without incident, she would use the gun and knife on both her and Lucy.

"Where're we going?" Helena asked, starting the engine.

"You don't need to know. Just follow my instructions and we'll be there in no time. Drive normal, got it?"

It was dark in the back of the van; Cara could see through to the driver's seat. She could feel every pothole, every rock that they came across. The back of these vans weren't designed to be ridden in. She knew exactly where she was going, having found the perfect place for her and Lucy's endgame.

DAY 11

FRIDAY, 30TH MARCH

126

"You mean to tell me she came to see you and you sent her away?" Gupta shouted. "She told you she was being stalked by Cara, and you just ignored her? You can bet I'll be talking to your chief constable about this. I'll have you back in uniform before the day's through, you lazy arrogant piece of shit; if you'd listened to her and put some officers in her home, we wouldn't be in this situation now, would we?"

"It's not my fault you couldn't catch her in time," Oliver McGrath replied. "We're stretched thin at the best of times. We can't just put officers in a house as protection, in case a psycho turns up. Do what you want, my chief constable will have my back."

Nasreen listened as the gruff Glaswegian, with his heavy hard-to-understand accent, argued with Gupta. Her boss probably wouldn't come out on top, not being within his jurisdiction. The Scottish officers didn't want an English detective inspector coming in and challenging their authority.

She turned and looked around the lounge. There was a duvet on the sofa, which probably meant someone was sick. It had to be either Lucy or her girlfriend. Nasreen saw some flu remedies on the kitchen counter too.

Leaving Gupta to argue with the Scottish detective, she walked up the stairs and looked around the first floor. In the bedroom, she found two cut cable ties on the floor, evidence of Cara's presence.

There was no blood in the house that she'd seen so far; that was a good sign in itself – there were also no bodies, which was a first for Cara's crime scenes. One question stuck out in her mind, though: why was she taking Lucy's girlfriend with her? What plans did she have for her? Whatever they were, they weren't good.

Scenes of crimes officers were busy dusting for prints and various other duties, even though there were no bodies. When she and Gupta arrived, McGrath and uniformed officers were busy searching the house. Uniforms found Sadler's Range Rover about a half mile up the road, and Lucy Davis' green MG convertible was parked outside. McGrath informed them that, according to the DVLA, Helena was the registered owner of a white Ford Transit, which was missing.

It was 08:08 by her watch, and light outside. More and more uniformed officers from villages and towns nearby were ascending on the cottage's grounds, waiting for instructions to go searching for Lucy and Helena house by house, which could take hours, or even days.

Downstairs, Nasreen joined Gupta, who was still tearing chunks out of McGrath. She only met him half an hour ago, and she already disliked him; she didn't care for his gruff attitude.

If he'd taken Lucy seriously when she went to him with legitimate concerns, they might have Cara in custody by now. Nasreen wanted to chip in; instead, she left it to Gupta to issue the reprimand. "It's definitely Cara."

Nasreen handed him one of the cut cable ties she'd bagged

upstairs. "We need to start the search now. I spoke to Cara hours ago; she could be anywhere by now."

"She'll be around here somewhere," McGrath said, confidently. "It's so remote; it's perfect for what that psycho wants. I've requested help from other townships. We can be mobilised and searching within half an hour."

"And now you want to help?" Gupta said sarcastically.

"Look, Detective Gupta, we're not in your big city now," McGrath added. "We're in the rural Highlands, where murders and rapes, and whatever the fuck else happens in your cities, don't happen here. This village only has four uniformed officers and two detectives."

"We can argue amongst ourselves on the way. We need to get going. Lucy and Helena might not have long left, if they're not dead already." It was a gloomy comment, but true nonetheless.

"You heard the lady," Gupta said. "Get your lot together and we'll get to work."

Nasreen walked outside to find twenty uniformed officers waiting around. Gupta joined her, and they stood and waited for McGrath to organise the troops.

After a couple of minutes, McGrath, with his fat belly overhanging his trousers, found a map and placed it on the bonnet of a police car. The uniforms gathered around him, while he explained the situation to them, loudly.

"You've all been given your grid squares," McGrath said. "Now get out there and find this psychopath. And radio in if you find her."

Nasreen coughed, loudly, trying to get McGrath's attention.

"What is it, Detective Maqsood?"

"She's more than likely armed with a small calibre pistol," Nasreen said, after everyone turned towards her. "Your officers should be calling for a fully equipped armed response unit, not tackling her themselves."

She saw McGrath look down at the floor, mutter something, before he addressed the uniforms. "You heard Detective Maqsood, when you find Cara Mooney, call for the armed response unit, who will be on standby. Now, get going!"

While the uniforms were getting in their vehicles and driving away, McGrath came over and joined her and Gupta.

"You really think she's that dangerous?"

"Yes," Nasreen replied. "She *really is* that dangerous."

"Let's go find her then."

127

Lennox was freezing and pissed off. He and Barkley had ditched the bullet-riddled Mercedes a couple of miles away from the crash site. They'd heard the sirens when they walked away from their car into some woods in the middle of nowhere. After a couple of hours of walking in the cold damp darkness, they managed to find an old disused barn to use as shelter overnight.

"Where the fuck are they?" Barkley shivered.

"They'll be here in a minute." Lennox looked down at his mobile, which miraculously had two bars on it, astonishing considering where they were.

"That's what you said an hour ago."

"They'll be here." Lennox wanted to smack his friend in the mouth. "But they've got to find us first."

"What a complete fuck-up."

Lennox turned to his childhood friend and frowned. "If you'd stayed further back, they wouldn't have spotted us, would they?"

"Fuck you, man." Barkley turned away. "We had to get in closer. They'd have seen us sooner or later anyway."

He didn't want to argue; he just wanted to get some shut-eye. He hadn't slept all night, but Barkley had, so he'd been forced to listen to his friend snore louder than a freight train. "Here they are!"

Stepping out from behind the trees, onto the tiny dirt track, Lennox flagged down the car carrying Bembe and Khenan, who he hadn't seen for days. He was forced to call them, interrupting their surveillance of James Foster, the project's South East dealer.

When they were safely inside the car, and on the move, Lennox told Bembe to turn the heating up full. His feet, hands and face were freezing. He leaned back in his seat and rubbed his hands together, using the friction to warm them. "Thanks for this," he said to his two saviours.

"Getting Foster out in the open's going to be tougher than we thought," Bembe said, after half an hour of silence. "We've been on him for days – he doesn't have a routine he follows."

Lennox had met James Foster several times, during his time working for Rothstein. Foster was the entrepreneur of the project's dealers; he owned several successful businesses, and used dealing as an addition to his income. Foster owned a couple of pubs, a nightclub, a couple of restaurants, a security firm and a garage, which he used as the HQ for his stolen car ring.

Younger than Rothstein, Foster looked up to his dead former boss. Rothstein had taken James "Jim" Foster under his wing back in the day, but Foster had proven over time that he was a far better businessman than Rothstein.

Crime wasn't the be-all and end-all for Foster, unlike Rothstein, who had revelled in being the top dog; in fact, Foster was fast becoming wholly legitimate, bar from the dealing and car ring, which both earned him a small fortune.

"It's okay, Bembe, we'll do him together. Move on to Zack Astor – we'll leave Jim until last."

"I know he's a friend of yours." Bembe looked at him in the rear-view mirror.

"He's not a friend." He turned and looked out of his side window. "I only met him a few times. Anyway, he's with them now, which makes him our target."

Closing his eyes, Lennox thought of Amelie, of arriving home, showering and getting into bed with her. His thoughts generally returned to Amelie, which was how he knew he liked her.

He couldn't bring himself to say "loved her", not even in his head; he wasn't there yet, but he knew it wasn't far off. This was the most serious he'd ever been about a woman. What more evidence did he need to convince himself he loved her?

Bembe broke the silence. "Hey, man, if we're going after Astor now, who are you two going after next?"

Lennox turned back and looked at Bembe in the mirror. "Matthew Walker's next."

Walker was the South West dealer. Lennox had never met, or even seen Matthew Walker before. The man was a mystery, which none of the others were; it could be a problem, but it probably wouldn't be. Once Lennox found his target, he could usually find a way to get to them.

128

Terrence closed his car door. He looked at the house, saw the police tape and immediately knew that they'd missed everyone. It was just gone nine. He was exhausted, but the adrenaline kept him awake.

Bishop stretched. "Are you calling Arjun, or do you want me to?"

"I'll do it." Terrence wasn't looking forward to the reprimand he was bound to get for disobeying Gupta's direct orders.

He took out his phone and dialled, noting that he had two bars, which was better than he thought he would get. "Sir, it's me. We're at Lucy Davis' house now. Where do you want us to start searching?"

Surprisingly, Gupta didn't sound pissed off; he even sounded pleased for the help. Why would he want to stay back in the city after they had all put in so many man-hours hunting Cara Mooney? "Cape Wrath? Are you kidding? What kind of shit name is that? It doesn't sound ominous at all. Okay, we're on our way."

Hanging up, he looked up Cape Wrath on his mobile, which

was getting 3G, but not 4G. He had to wait for his phone to load up Google.

When he did finally see the page, it told him that the only way to get to Cape Wrath was via a foot passenger-only ferry, which would take ten minutes to cross the Kyle. From there, they would need to take a minibus, which would take an additional hour to reach the most north westerly point of the country.

It was possible that they might not need to go – if the ferry operator hadn't seen Cara, or Lucy, then they wouldn't be at the lighthouse. Then he read additional information, which told him that hikers could trek across moorland to get there, if they so wished.

He sighed when he realised they had to go and check. He really didn't think Cara would take Lucy there, but they had to be certain. "Let's get going," Terrence said to Bishop. "Looks like we're going sightseeing."

"Sounds like fun. I've always wanted to visit Cape Wrath."

"Getting paid to tick off your bucket list." Terrence got in the car. "Now that can't be bad. I can think of worse ways of spending my time; it's just a shame I hate boats."

Franks was on his way to the Midlands, where he planned on killing two birds with one trip. He had "The Meeting" at the warehouse at three, which didn't seem as pressing now that he knew where Garvey was staying, and a mini conference before that at lunchtime – he hoped the conference wouldn't overrun.

He was listening to the radio in his car, when his mobile phone rang. It was his burner, so he knew it was about the project. He pressed the hands-free button and said, "Yeah?" loudly, trying to speak over the sound of the car bombing along the motorway.

"Peter, it's Zack. Did you hear Garvey's just tried taking out Almasi? He killed Omar's driver. We need to sort this out for good."

"Yeah, I heard," he replied, concentrating on the road. "It's all in hand. I found out yesterday where Garvey's staying. When we have eyes on him, I'll call you and let you know where he is?"

There was a quick pause.

"Under the circumstances, I think it'll be better if you give Garvey to Maggie. It's the least we can do, given what she's lost."

"Duly noted. I'll call Maggie and let her know. Is that good enough for you?" It was the best solution all round, but he didn't like being undermined, especially by the likes of Zack fucking Astor. If Franks had had his way, they wouldn't be using known drug dealers like Astor; however, this was the way Suzanne Embry, the Home Secretary, and Harry wanted it done. "Was there anything else?"

"If you say we've got Garvey, that's good enough for me."

Franks hung up. His uniform, his shirt mainly, was digging into his neck. He fiddled with his collar and undid the top button with one hand while steering with the other. As he drove, he thought about how good it would be once he knew Garvey had been taken care of.

He could properly relax; he could get stuck into organising the raids that were to follow, but all the while Garvey was out there, executing his partners, he couldn't relax. Franks hadn't relaxed in months. Still, it was coming, soon.

130

———

Cara forced open an old rickety wooden door, attached to a long-since-abandoned accommodation house, which had been used as a makeshift home for workers on the radar station. When she stepped inside, she could tell the house – a long thin red-brick building – had been used recently. There were newly discarded tins, plastic bags, sweet wrappers and all sorts of other debris littering the cold stone floor.

It seemed that whoever was living here had left, which was good for them. If she came across anyone, she would kill them. This was her last stand, her last refuge before the endgame – Cara knew she didn't have much time left, but she was going to make sure she made the most of it while she could.

She knew the police would be out in full force looking for her by now – there was only one thing stopping her from carrying out her plans: Lucy wasn't awake yet; she couldn't do anything until Lucy was conscious.

When she arrived at the radar station, she found the best place for her, Lucy and Helena – it was a concrete room built into the land they were on. From above, the World War Two planes that the station once monitored wouldn't have been able to spot them, which was the point, she guessed. The room they were in was like something out of a horror movie, with drab grey concrete walls with mould growing over them, the floor littered with debris, again, just like this room. It was a fitting place for what she had planned.

She was looking for chairs for Lucy and Helena to sit on. She'd left them sat on the floor in the middle of the room, tied together back to back with cable ties. There had to be a couple of chairs around here somewhere.

It was light outside, but the building had been boarded up, so it was dark, save for the cracks between the wood nailed across the windows. It was dusty too, the sun showed her, highlighting it in the thin rays of sunshine the cracks allowed in the room.

It was only when she entered the last room that she came across two old chairs. They were wooden, rotting, but they would do. She picked them both up and turned around to go back, when her attention focused on a dark blob in the corner.

The blob was moving, sleeping. It was a dirty old tramp; the room she was in was probably his bedroom. She put the chairs down and took her knife out of her bag. It was too bad for the old boy, she thought, as she crept towards him.

As she knelt down, she touched his grey grubby coat.

The tramp suddenly sat up, as though he'd been awoken from a dream and was trying to orient himself.

"Take it easy, old man," she said, the knife in her hand, ready to strike. "I'm not going to hurt you. Go on, back to sleep." She couldn't understand why she hadn't stuck him with the blade. She should've struck him by now.

Cara listened to the vagrant mutter something, but she couldn't understand what he was saying. It wasn't because he was Scottish, either – even a Scot wouldn't have understood him.

Then she watched him lie back down, covering himself with newspaper.

She stood, went and picked up the chairs and walked back the way she came until she reached the doorway. A voice in her head, the voice of reason, spoke to her. She set the chairs back down and took out the knife again, walking back over to the tramp. She turned him over and sliced his throat, deep.

Towering over him, she watched the old boy claw at his neck, gargling blood.

His eyes watched her, asking her why?

He reached up to her with one hand, until the blood loss was so great that his energy levels were depleted. His arm dropped to the floor, and his eyes stared straight up, dead.

131

Terrence stepped onto the dock and asked for a moment of the ferry operator's time. "Have you seen this woman today?" he asked. The boatman was preparing for a trip across.

As expected, the ferry operator shook his head. It was obvious that Cara wasn't over at the lighthouse with Lucy, but there was still a chance they might have gone on foot.

He was reluctant to spend the next few hours conducting a fruitless search, when they could be joining in on the mainland, with at least some chance of apprehending Cara. "Or this woman?" he asked, showing a picture of Lucy.

"I know her, but I haven't seen her today."

"How do you know her?"

"She's been across a couple of times. What's this about?"

"The first woman I showed you is a wanted fugitive. She's murdered several people, and we have reason to believe she's abducted Lucy Davis, the second woman. We believe the fugitive may be taking her to the lighthouse."

The boatman nodded his understanding. "Jump on board. As this is a special situation, I'll leave now, get you there quicker."

"Thanks, I appreciate it." Terrence signalled for Bishop to follow him on board the small boat. "How long does it take to cross?"

"About ten minutes normally, but I'll get you there faster. Hold on!"

132

———————

Lennox thanked Bembe and Khenan for getting them out of a tight spot. He shook their hands and opened his door. They'd already dropped Barkley off. He'd asked his friend to meet him at five at the lock-up. "And I'll see you both at five, yeah?"

His two saviours agreed to meet him, before driving off. Lennox walked to the rear door of Amelie's apartment block and used his copied key to let himself in. He walked up the stairs and along the corridor until he reached Amelie's front door. He used his key to let himself in, where he heard Amelie in the kitchen.

Looking at his watch, he saw it was lunchtime. He was starving; he hadn't eaten since last night, so he'd missed breakfast. "What's for lunch?" he asked, wrapping his arms around Amelie's waist. "You smell so fucking good," he added, his nose in her neck.

"I've missed you." She turned to face him.

"Me too."

When he felt her hands trying to unbutton his jeans, he pulled her jumper over her head and dropped it on the floor, while she let his jeans drop around his ankles. He reached under her skirt and pulled her knickers down, taking her arse in his hands and lifting her onto the kitchen counter.

Amelie's phone vibrated on the counter.

"Shit!" cursed Amelie. "To be continued, yes? It's almost time to eat anyway." She pulled her knickers up, made herself look respectable, and walked over to the counter, where she picked up her phone. "It's Harry," she whispered.

Lennox pulled up his jeans and sat at the kitchen table, listening to Amelie reassure Harry that she was still coming to see him tonight. He smiled at the thought of the most senior policeman in the country being so clingy. "It's still on, then?" he asked, when she hung up. "What a pussy!"

"Here, you can have mine." She shoved a plate of scrambled eggs on toast under his nose. He picked up the ketchup and smothered the eggs with it. "Are you not eating?" He shoved some on his fork.

"I'm not hungry, after all. I'm really nervous about tonight; I don't know why. I've got this feeling he knows."

"He doesn't know shit! None of them have a clue, I promise." It was a bold statement, and one he was confident of being true. Apart from Almasi spotting him on the motorway, none of his targets knew he was coming after them. "Here, share this with me. It's so fucking good."

"I don't know! I've got a bad feeling and I can't shake it." She sat on a chair next to him, as he held out some eggs for her to eat. "No, really, I'm not hungry. Thanks."

"You know you don't have to go through with it, don't you?" he said, mid-mouthful. A piece of egg escaped his mouth and landed on her hand. "Sorry!"

Amelie brushed it off and wiped her hand on her jeans. "No, I'll go. We need that information, and I'm the only one who can get it."

"If you get the feeling he knows, leg it, okay?" He held her hand. "I feel bad for putting you in this position. If you suspect anything, you run!"

133

Franks shook hands with a colleague, the Chief Constable of the West Midlands. He knew George Epsom well enough, which was to say that he'd met him on a few occasions. The seminar they were about to attend was about Policing Standards, with particular emphasis on best practises.

He'd already nodded to the West Midlands Police and Crime Commissioner, signalling that he would chat to him later about the shooting of Omar Almasi, which had happened on the outskirts of the city. But it would have to wait, as he had to get to the warehouse for his meeting with his partners.

"Peter, I was hoping you'd make it."

When he turned around, he saw Julie Sayers' smiling face. His one mistake, his one indiscretion stood smiling in front of him. She was as pretty now as she was five years earlier. "Julie. It's been a while."

"Thought you were avoiding me. It's been, how long? Four, five years?"

"Yeah, how are you?" He wasn't really interested; he wanted to get away from her before they ended up in some hotel room, like before.

He loved his wife, loved his kids. When he looked at Julie, he was reminded of how he'd betrayed them, how he gave in to temptation, and how weak he was. It made him feel bad to look at Julie's pretty face. He had to stop thinking about her. He looked around the reception room, for anyone he could attach himself to.

"I'm great, thanks," she said, smiling.

There was a long excruciating pause.

Why couldn't he move? And why couldn't he stop looking at that face, at those full lips? Why couldn't he stop thinking about that awful, awesome night five years ago? He remembered how he felt leaving the hotel room.

"And you?" she asked.

"Can't complain. Nobody'd listen anyway, right?"

"I'd listen." She didn't blink.

He heard a voice shout that they were going inside the conference room for the hour-long seminar. Without making it obvious, he breathed a sigh of relief. The senior uniforms started moving towards the double doors. "It was good seeing you again." He tried to walk off, but she blocked his move.

"We should catch up properly, Peter. How about after the seminar? We could find a nice pub somewhere and have a drink?"

"I'd love to, but I have a meeting to attend. Sorry. Another time, perhaps?"

He really hoped she took the hint. It wasn't that he didn't want to, because he did. He would love to take her out for a drink, then take her to a hotel room again, but he wasn't going to do that to his wife, not a second time.

"Here, take my card." Julie handed him her work card. "Really, Peter, I'd love to catch up with you. It's been too long."

Part of him was flattered that a younger, lovely-looking and intelligent woman, such as Julie, was interested in him; the other part was warning him to steer clear of her – she was trouble of the divorce kind. He pocketed the card, making a mental note to himself to discard it as soon as he left the seminar.

As he joined the crowd of senior officers, his burner phone rang. He took it out of his pocket and stayed back, while his colleagues moved forward. "Yeah?"

"Peter, it's me," Dean said. "He's back at Amelie Desmarais' apartment."

A massive grin crept over Franks' face. "Keep on him. Do *not* lose him, do you understand? I'm going to chat to some friends and have them collect him." Franks hung up. He had Lennox Garvey!

134

Lucy's head was pounding.

She tried to open her eyes; even the dull light hurt them. When she tilted her head back, it collided with something.

"Lucy, are you awake?"

She tried saying yes but it came out as a groan. Her head was fuzzy. Finally, she opened them, and they focused after a few seconds.

Sat on the floor of some dungeon, Lucy scanned the room. The only way to describe it was like a basement in a slasher horror movie. She was in a concrete walled room, with debris all around her. The walls were filthy, with mould, graffiti, and God only knew what else. It smelt of piss. "Where are we?" she whispered.

"We're in the radar station. Cara's here."

Lucy thought she was going to faint. "Cara's back?"

"Yeah. Don't you remember her talking to you at the house?"

"No. I've been seeing Cara everywhere since she texted me. She didn't hurt you, did she?" She wouldn't forgive herself if Helena was hurt.

"Relax, I'm fine, but we've got to find a way out of here."

Lucy tried moving her hands, but the cable ties dug into her wrists.

"They're tight," she said, giving up the struggle.

There was a long silence. Lucy thought about Cara, about how her ex-girlfriend had tried to kill her over a year ago, before the police had found them in the log cabin.

She'd managed to talk Cara down then, maybe she could again? She wanted to feel hope; all she felt was dread at seeing her again. "So, what do we do now? We're trapped."

"I don't know, I'm thinking."

Lucy was so tired. She closed her eyes, feeling her head drop. Before it dropped properly, she bolted back, her head hitting Helena's.

"Are you falling asleep?"

"No," she lied, her eyelids drooping.

"Stay awake, I need you."

"I'm trying."

As her head fell, she was immediately jolted awake by Cara's voice. Lucy could hear something scraping in the distance.

"Oh, Helena." It was Cara. "I've got something for you."

Lucy wanted to close her eyes, but they wouldn't let her – they had to see Cara.

"Pretend to be asleep, Lucy. Put your head down and pretend. Do it now, before she sees you're awake."

Obeying, she let her head fall, as though she was asleep. She closed her eyes. Lucy thought maybe she could see Cara if she opened her eyes slightly, just a crack; she was curious to see how she looked.

Lucy listened as Cara arrived in the room with them.

She heard Cara pacing around, doing something.

Opening her eyes, just a little, she saw Cara with two chairs, and watched as she dusted them off.

"These will be more comfortable for you." Cara took a knife out of her bag.

Still pretending to be asleep, Cara went out of her vision.

"I'm going to cut these cable ties off now. If you try anything; if you try to run, I'm going to slice Juicy, do you understand?"

"I won't, I promise."

Lucy felt something cold against her wrist, then felt the freedom that followed. Her wrists were released, but she was supposed to be asleep, so she kept her head down.

"Give me a hand with her," Cara ordered.

Lucy felt arms pick her up, while she let her body go limp. She was lifted up and placed on one of the chairs. Cara grabbed her wrists and tied them to one of the slats of the back rest. Then she heard Helena sit. She heard the cables tie, that unforgettable clicking noise, as Cara tied Helena to the chair.

135

Terrence looked up at the lighthouse. It was tall, white, with a black top. It had a white building attached to it, and an outhouse over the way. The best thing about it was the view from the top of the cliff it was built on. The lighthouse was underwhelming, though creepy. He looked to the top of the building. Thick grey clouds loomed over them.

He watched Bishop taking photos with his phone. The area was so isolated; that was why it was so creepy. He hadn't seen a single person for the past half-hour. He and Bishop had searched the area, including inside the two buildings.

As he'd suspected, there was no sign of Cara or Lucy. They'd just wasted the morning. "Are you ready, Bishop? We need to get back to the mainland."

Bishop took one last photo, apologised for it, and joined him on the walk back to the minibus, which would drive them back to the west point pier, where the ferry operator would pick them up.

Terrence was disappointed they hadn't found Cara – part of him had hoped Cara and Lucy hiked it over. He genuinely hoped Nasreen and Gupta had had more luck. He checked his phone for how many bars it had: none.

Gupta shook his head. "Where the bloody hell is she? We've been driving around for hours, and for what? Nothing."

Nasreen sat in the back of McGrath's Range Rover, staring out of the window. Not one person they'd spoken to all day remembered seeing Cara or Lucy. Three interviewees knew Lucy, or at least remembered seeing her around the village at some time or other.

Nasreen, McGrath and Gupta went from house to house speaking to the owners, showing them photographs and asking if they could look around their properties; none of them minded, given that it was a manhunt. She thought most of them were grateful to have police making sure a violent fugitive wasn't lurking in one of their barns or sheds.

The main problem they now had was the vastness of the area they had to search, and there was no telling if Cara had stayed local, or not; she could be on her way back to the city by now, for all they knew.

Since they left Lucy and Helena's cottage, they'd not heard a thing from any of the uniformed officers out searching. It was like Cara had dropped off the face of the planet.

"How far out are we searching, McGrath?" Gupta asked.

"About fifty miles." McGrath stared straight ahead, concentrating on the road. "Finding her in all this rough terrain's going to be difficult at best, especially given her head start. I still think she's heading back to England."

"No, she's not," Nasreen interrupted. "She has a plan, and she needs to do it before we find her."

"This suicide pact you spoke about earlier," McGrath said, in more of a question than a statement. "Do you really think that's what she's going to do?"

"Yes, I do," she replied, "unless we can find her before she acts on it."

"Nas spoke to Cara on the way up here," Gupta explained. "She also had a run in with her at a victim's house; Cara nearly killed her; she threw Nas off the first floor of a block of flats, then stabbed her in the chest. So you can forgive her eagerness in finding her."

"Jesus," McGrath said, to no one in particular. "And you're okay? What was that, a twenty-foot drop? That must've hurt."

"Something like that," she said, "and I messed my knee up when I landed, but apart from that, I'm fine." She was far from fine, but she wouldn't let McGrath know that.

"And she stabbed you? Where?"

"In the chest." Nasreen pointed at her left breast. "I wouldn't say stabbed exactly. It only went in an inch. Any further and I might be saying something different."

"Much further and you wouldn't be saying anything, Nas," Gupta said.

There was silence in the car, as McGrath steered them towards their next house. Nasreen could barely contain her frustration. She had to find Cara, and soon.

137

"Darius, I need a word." Franks beckoned him over.

Franks' partners, the remaining living partners anyway, were spread throughout the warehouse. He had already spoken to Astor, who was there with his son and an entourage of loyal soldiers, and he'd spoken briefly to James Foster, who warned him that two black men had been spotted around his area, not that Foster knew who they were, or if it had been Garvey, or not.

Finding a quiet spot, away from everyone else, Franks stood and looked at Darius. He noticed how stocky the man was, with big brawny shoulders. "I thought you should know we have Garvey under surveillance," he said, expecting a positive response. Nothing. "So, I thought, given the circumstances, we'd let Maggie have first shot at him. What do you say?"

"I'll let Maggie know," Darius replied. "She'll want to be part of this."

"After this meeting, I'll give you Dean's mobile number so you can confer with him." Franks looked at his watch. It was just gone three. "But please be careful with Garvey; he's not to be underestimated. I need this problem put to bed, Darius. Promise me you'll see to it that Garvey won't come back to haunt us."

"You don't need to worry about that," Darius said. "When Maggie gets hold of him, there won't be much left *to* come back and haunt you. Leave it with me; I'll handle it. And there's another issue I need to speak to you about, and everyone else too."

Franks called the meeting to order. The dealers gathered around; most of them knew each other, either as allies, or enemies, but it didn't get in the way of business.

There were representatives present from every area, except the North West, and the Midlands, for obvious reasons, which was why Franks called the meeting in the first place. "I don't want to keep you long, so I'll make it brief. We've had problems with Lennox Garvey, as you know, which I'm pleased to say will be resolved tonight, however, it does mean that we need to move things around. Right now, there's no one controlling the North We–"

"I speak for Maggie, and Scott, when I say that the Hughes family will take the North West," Darius said, interrupting him before he'd even finished.

"You've got no muscle anymore," said one of Almasi's representatives, a short Iranian man wearing a baseball cap and black leather jacket. "If anyone should get the North West, it should be Omar."

"He just got shot to shit yesterday, for fuck's sake." Darius snorted derisively. "He won't be able to move, not when it's raining bacon on him, like it is now. The Hughes family still has the reputation. Frank and Vincent were never the muscle for the family. Scott and I are, and Scott's still alive, expected to make a full recovery. We'll take it, Peter."

Listening to both sides, Franks was more inclined to side with Darius. Plus, he didn't like Omar Almasi, not that he'd heard much to make him dislike the man; he just didn't, there was something off about him. And he didn't like the scowl on Almasi's representative, either. "All right, Darius, the North West is now Hughes territory."

Muttering and objections came from Almasi's crew, not that Franks cared. This wasn't a democracy; it was an autocracy, and his word was final. This was *his* project, and he managed it how he managed it. "Hey, stop this dumb crap," he snapped, at the baseball cap-wearing Iranian. "It's my decision, and that's that!"

Franks continued with business for another ten minutes. When he concluded the meeting, he took Darius to the side again, gave him Dean's number and made him promise not to let him down on the Garvey issue, that it had to be resolved tonight, to which Darius, again, gave him his word that Garvey would be dealt with.

Lennox looked over at the alarm clock: 16:08.

He groaned; he wanted to stay in bed with Amelie. He'd arranged to meet Barkley, Bembe and Khenan at five, although Bembe and Khenan were renowned for being late by at least a half hour.

"I guess I'd better get ready." Amelie unwrapped herself from him.

"It's Harry tonight."

"Now I'm moving in, I'm hoping he'll give me more freedom to move around the boat."

Lying there, watching her as she sat up, he rubbed her bare back, feeling her smooth soft skin. "Just be careful."

Amelie got off the bed and leaned forwards to kiss him. "Always," she said, with a smile. "And you'd better get up too. You're meeting the others soon, aren't you?"

Lennox groaned. He grabbed her hand and pulled her in to him. "I'd rather be here with you." When she fought him, he let her go.

"Come on, beautiful, I've really got to get ready. I need to take a shower, after everything we've done this afternoon. He'll smell it, you know."

She was right. They'd spent the afternoon in bed. Lennox loved that she was so uninhibited, which was par for the course, he guessed, in her line of work.

He watched her walk to the doorway. "I love you," he said, surprising himself. What the fuck was he thinking? He must be going soft in the head.

Amelie turned back to him. "I know," she said, with a knowing smile. "I mean, how could you not?"

Lennox laughed. While Amelie was taking a shower, he got up, put his clothes on and went to the kitchen. He fixed himself a sandwich, while he waited for her to finish in the bathroom. When the door opened, Amelie walked out wrapped in a towel. He stepped inside.

"Did you mean that?"

"Mean what?" he asked, turning to her and grinning.

"What you said just now," she replied, with a scowl that said, "you know what I'm talking about. That you love me?"

"Oh, that. Nah, I was just saying what I thought you wanted me to say." A grin spread across his entire face.

"You're a terrible liar, Lennox Garvey." She grabbed his nipple through his T-shirt.

"Okay, okay, I meant it," he said, pretending it hurt. "I love you. Are you happy now you've turned me soft in the head?"

Amelie leaned in and kissed him. She smelt amazing, even though he knew it was just the expensive shower gel she used.

"Very happy, thanks." She winked and walked through to the bedroom.

He looked up at the clock on the wall. He had to get going; Barkley would be picking him up soon. As he sat down on the toilet seat, he thought about their next target: Matthew Walker.

Of all six project dealers, he was the least known. Lennox would need to do some surveillance on Walker before they moved in for the kill.

139

———

Cara stared at Lucy, who still had her head down.

She couldn't believe how long she'd slept for; it wasn't normal, even for a sick person. When she moved closer, she could see beads of sweat running down Lucy's pretty face. Cara bent down and put her hand on Lucy's forehead. "You're burning up."

"Please, Cara, we need to get her to a hospital." Helena had stopped crying. "Take me in her place if you want, but let her go. Please, you're in control here. If you love her even a little bit, have some compassion and help me get her to a hospital."

Cara was taken aback. Something in her head just didn't compute, couldn't. "You'd do that? Take her place, I mean?"

"Course I would. I love her. I'd do anything and everything for her. Why, wouldn't you?"

"What, die for her?" Cara had to consider that question. Would she sacrifice herself for Lucy? Would she die if Lucy could live? "Fuck off! That's shit, you wouldn't do that for her, that's just stupid."

"I'm in love with her, Cara. It's what you do when you love someone. You value their safety and happiness above your own."

"Enough!" The knife in her hand was calling her. "You're talking shit now."

"Please, Cara, look at her; she's so unwell."

Stepping towards the annoying lying bitch, all Cara wanted to do was stab her in the eyes. Love didn't mean sacrificing yourself, what a load of crap. Her eyes narrowed. "I tell you what." Cara walked behind Lucy and crouched down. "I'll let Juicy go." She used the knife to cut one cable tie, then the other. "There you go, if she wants, she can leave."

Cara stood back, pleased with herself.

"Now, Lucy!"

Stunned, Cara watched as Lucy sprang from her chair, and ran towards the exit.

It took a few seconds for what had just happened to register. When it did, her face changed. Gone was the pleased-with-herself smirk, replaced by an angry sneer.

With knife in hand, she ran after Lucy, who had a head start.

Cara was superior to Lucy in every way; she was taller, fitter, stronger, and, arguably, more intelligent, or so she thought.

When she was out of the underground bunker, it didn't take her long to spot the out-of-shape figure of Lucy, hobbling to nowhere, screaming for help.

She sprinted, full pace, until she was right behind her ex-girlfriend. When she was within range, she leapt on her from behind, bringing her down, hard, careful not to stab her with the knife. That came later. "You tricky bitch!" She punched Lucy on the back of her head, twice. "How long have you been awake, bitch, huh?"

When Lucy didn't answer, Cara turned her over, so she could see her treacherous face. "How long, Juicy?"

"Long enough," Lucy replied. "You killed my friend, you killed Dawn. I hate you so much!"

140

Looking at his watch in the dull light of the lock-up, Lennox cursed. "Where are they? I said five, didn't I?" Bembe and Khenan's disrespect was becoming a pain in his arse. How difficult was it to be on time? They were forty-five minutes late, which was unacceptable.

"Friday night traffic, maybe?" Barkley sat on a chair, loading bullets into a magazine.

"Nah, they don't live that far away." Lennox went back to his chair.

Apart from Barkley, there was no one he could rely on. Maybe now he could rely on Amelie, but his past experience couldn't make him sure of that; women were flaky at best. He could be in love with Amelie now, but give it a few months, he might rue the day he met her. He didn't trust his feelings, especially when it came to love.

There were two knocks on the door.

Lennox got up, mumbling. He stepped up to the door, pulled the wires back, as the door opened from the bottom to the top. He watched the two sets of legs grow bigger, saw the bodies, but didn't recognise the faces.

It was the handguns the two men were carrying that made him freeze.

"As I live and breathe," said the taller man. "Lennox Garvey."

Lennox took a couple of steps back.

"No sudden moves now, boys," the uninvited guest said, raising his pistol. "Let's make this as quick and painless as possible. Someone's very eager to meet you. I can't say it'll be a pleasant meeting, but hey."

Lennox wanted to make a dash for his Uzi, but he couldn't move. Two of their colleagues came in carrying hoods. He was fucked!

Before he knew what was going on, there was a hood over his head. There were no holes in the fabric, so he was blind. He felt a pistol in his back, as he was forced to walk forwards.

141

———

Lucy, tied to the chair, tried in vain to break her bonds.

It was hopeless, the cable ties were too strong. "Please, Cara, you don't have to do this. You could let us both go." Lucy watched as Cara leaned against a wall, glaring at her with the knife in hand.

Trying to use friction to break the plastic cuffs, she watched Cara. "What're you going to do to us?" Lucy was desperately trying to keep her ex-girlfriend busy talking while she fought with the plastic ties.

Cara stepped up to her and looked into her eyes, while she struggled. "You remember the promise you made me? Back in the cabin?" Her once pretty – no, gorgeous – face was gone, replaced with an evil twisted and tortured one.

"I didn't promise anything."

"What promise? What's she talking about?" asked Helena.

"You lie! You said when the time came, you couldn't live without me," ranted Cara, the knife mere inches away from her face. "You said we'll both go together. It's romantic, you said. Now's the time, Juicy. We're going to take a leap of faith off that cliff out there. You and me together, the way it's supposed to be."

142

Maggie stepped out of the car and felt the cold breeze against her cheeks.

She wrapped herself in her thick winter coat, sinking her head into it more. Her driver – an associate of Scott's – got out of the car, joining her as they walked towards the derelict warehouse. She was eager to meet her sons' murderers, the real culprits, the organisers.

It was approaching seven o'clock, so it would be dark in half an hour. The warehouse was huge, once used to manufacture perfume for a well-known brand, not that she could tell now; the walls were covered with graffiti and all the windows were smashed. The floors were awash with all kinds of junk trespassers had left behind.

She heard something crunch under her foot, looked down to find she was standing on a used needle. It made her cringe with disgust. Her family may have dealt class A drugs, including heroin, but that didn't mean she liked it. She'd warned her sons to steer clear of H, the big one. Smoking cannabis and snorting cocaine was one thing, but injecting heroin was quite another. It was a one-way ticket to an early grave.

"Maggie," Darius called, "they're over here, all prepped and waiting for you."

She joined her darling Darius, kissed him on his cheek and walked with him through a long room until she came to a doorway. She stopped, took a deep breath, and entered.

Once inside, she came to a room with lots of old machinery. She could hear muffled shouts coming from behind the redundant factory equipment. Next to a huge mechanical monstrosity were two large oil drums. Gypsy King was here.

"King's waiting for you now." Darius walked slightly ahead of her.

Maggie slowed her pace, savouring the moment she came face to face with Lennox fucking Garvey. She'd dreamt of this moment for days. She only hoped the satisfaction she received was as in her dreams, although she doubted it would be. She'd killed them, tortured, and broken them until they begged for mercy in her dreams, and nothing could compare to that.

When she cleared the machinery, she saw a naked Garvey and another of his associates, both with their arms tied behind their backs, wrists to ankles.

Both had rags stuffed in their mouths, and both had hulking muscular bodies. She knew instinctively which was Garvey; he was more confident, more upright. Looking at him made her want to stab his eyes out. That confident stare sent waves of anger crashing over her, threatening to make her lunge at him with her knife.

She looked behind him at the two empty oil drums. She looked back at Garvey. "Your tombs, boys. You're going to die tonight. But not before I get my justice."

143

___

Frustrated, pissed off, that they hadn't found Cara or Lucy, Nasreen put her money on the table and walked out of the White Heather Café, where Gupta and McGrath were still finishing their cups of coffee. "I'll be outside," she said to Gupta.

It was approaching half seven when she stepped out into the cold night air. It was so isolated out here, so creepy. The A838 was a quiet road; everywhere was quiet up here at the top of the world. Everyone was friendly, though, she had to give them that. There was no way she could live in such an isolated place.

Looking across the road at the fields ahead, she suddenly had a feeling that Cara was nearby; she couldn't explain it, couldn't verbalise it, she just knew her charge was here.

Gupta joined her outside the café. "Are you ready?"

"Cara's here!" Nasreen said, pointing, "I know it. I feel it."

"She's not here," McGrath said. "It was the first place we checked. There was no sign of anyone."

"What's over there, anyway?" Gupta asked.

"The old Smoo Radar Station," McGrath replied. "It's just a load of old ruins now. There's derelict accommodation buildings and a couple of old bunkers, nothing, really."

"She's there." Nasreen looked over at Gupta, her eyes serious. "Arjun, believe me; I know it."

Waiting for Gupta to make the call, she started walking over the road. She would walk over there herself, without backup if she had to. "Phone Terrence and Bishop! And the armed response unit. Cara's here!"

144

Amelie handed the taxi driver her usual tip. She opened the door, got out and started walking along the marina pavement, towards *The Albatross*. It was cold still.

Wrapped in her long thick winter coat, she took in her surroundings. She loved the marina. Actually, she loved the town, now a city, full stop. It may have been the gay capital of Europe, but it had the best nightlife around, even better than her city's, in her opinion.

When she reached *The Albatross*, Harry was waiting on deck to greet her with his huge smile. He stood aside and let her pass, then kissed her on both cheeks, before leading her through to the lounge, where he poured her a glass of wine.

Expecting some chatter, she was confused when he was really quiet. "Is everything all right, Harry?" She put her glass on the table in front of the sofa. "You're not very chatty tonight. Do you want me to go?"

His face changed all of a sudden, from sullen to angry.

He grabbed her arm and pulled her up to her feet.

"What are you doing? You're hurting me." She tried to

release her arm from his grip but it was no use; he was intent on dragging her somewhere.

When he stopped outside his office, next door to the bedroom, she knew he'd found out what she'd done. Harry used his key to unlock the door, pulled her inside until they were at his desk. "What're you doing?"

"You know full well what I'm doing, Amelie, if that's even your real name. I should've known better than to get involved with a whore!"

When he clicked on the mouse, the screen showed Harry's project files. She watched as he brought up the personnel file's date and time of its last opening.

"You tell me how that opened itself last Saturday morning." Harry showed her the date and time. "You can't, can you? Because you opened it, and copied it, didn't you! You fucking bitch!"

Amelie gulped. She didn't have anything to come back with. She'd been rumbled; she hadn't even thought about the laptop giving her away like this. She was screwed! "Get your fucking hands off me!" She struggled, trying to free herself. "You're a bent cop, the worst kind of scumbag, hiding behind your respectability. You fucking arsehole."

She kicked his shin, hard, causing him to groan in pain, and then kneed him in the groin, forcing him to let go of her wrist and crumple in a heap on the floor.

When she turned and ran, she heard him call her name.

Without looking back, she ran through the rooms of the boat until she was in the lounge. Then from nowhere, Harry pounced on her from behind, forcing her to the ground.

Face down, with Harry sat on her back, she felt him grab her head, pull it back and smash it into the carpet, twice.

"I trusted you!" he snarled. "I brought you into my home,

offered you a way out of this life. I would have given you everything you ever wanted, and this is how you repay me?"

Harry smashed her head into the carpet again, before turning her over and forcing her onto her back, while he sat on her belly. Amelie looked up at his enraged face. His eyes were wild; they scared her.

Then she felt his hands around her throat, squeezing so hard, the pressure behind her eyes was excruciating. Every molecule of her being fought for survival; her hands reached for him, clawed at him, tried to stop him from killing her.

145

It was almost dark by the time Nasreen and Gupta reached the first accommodation building. The door had been left open. Nasreen switched on the torch McGrath had given her, and she scoured the rooms one by one. The only light came from the torch.

There was nothing but detritus on the ground, years of neglect making each room more forbidding. As she came to the last room, her torch shone light on a lump in the corner of the room. At first she didn't know what it was, but then. "Hello? Sir? Are you awake?"

Gupta crouched down beside the body. "I don't think so, Nas."

Nasreen shone the torch on the ground beside the head. It was blood. She saw the trademark gash, saw the look of fear in the tramp's dead eyes. "She's been here."

Lennox realised that with this gag in his mouth, he wouldn't be able to tell them about his insurance policy. If they slaughtered him where he knelt, all would be lost. He shouted into his rag, until he coughed.

"It looks like he wants to say something, Maggie," said the taller of the men.

"I don't care." Maggie waved the knife dangerously close to his face. "What's he going to say, 'sorry'? It's a bit late for that, don't you think?"

She was looking at him when she said it, which made him shout even harder. He had to get them to take the gag out.

"Let's start with this one," said Gypsy King, a man Lennox had used for body disposal before. He was as tall as he was wide, a huge beast of a man with great big slab hands. He was wearing bloody overalls covering a jumper and jeans.

Lennox shouted when Gypsy King bent over and picked Barkley up and over his shoulder, as though he were a bag of flour, not the seventeen stones he was. Shouting still, he watched as Gypsy King dumped Barkley in one of the oil drums.

Then Lennox felt strong arms pick him up and carry him over to where Barkley was frantically trying to free himself inside the oil drum.

In the background, Lennox heard a rumbling sound. Gypsy King wheeled in a cement mixer. He screamed for them to stop, when Gypsy King started filling the oil drum with quick setting cement, covering Barkley in the lethal paste.

"This is going to hurt, I'm afraid, mate." Gypsy King continued to use the spade to fill up the drum.

"You watch this, you bastard!" Maggie snarled at him. "You're next."

Tears rolled down his face when Gypsy King finished filling up the drum, leaving just Barkley's head uncovered. He could see that Barkley was finding it hard to breathe already. Lennox fought with his captors, trying to free himself from their grip.

"You see, Garvey, the cement is setting, and as it does, the exothermic reaction heats up the molecules in the cement, solidifying them, bringing them closer together. Around about now, your mate here will feel the excruciating pain of being heated up, before being squeezed to death. I'm sure there's a better way of putting it, but you get my point."

Lennox cursed into his gag, threatening to kill them all, but they weren't listening. They were too busy watching Barkley die, watching and listening to his cries in agonising pain. He could see Barkley's breathing slowing, his face turning purple. It wouldn't be long now.

Where the fuck were Bembe and Khenan? Without being allowed to speak, he had to rely on an intervention from his friends. Where were they?

"Look, you can feel how hard it is now," said Gypsy King, touching the cement.

When Lennox looked at Barkley, he could see he was dead.

The level of guilt he felt was overpowering; he'd asked his friends to help him, he'd involved them in this. Tears continued to roll, as he watched Gypsy King shovelling more cement over Barkley. He watched until Barkley's head was completely covered.

That was when Lennox felt the strong arms pick him up.

Cara had had enough of arguing with Lucy. It was clear to her that her ex wasn't going to come with her voluntarily. And if Cara had to hear Lucy beg her to let them go once more, she would stab Helena in the throat.

With the knife in hand, she squatted and stared into Lucy's lovely big eyes, which were moist with tears. "Enough! I'm going to give it to you straight, Juicy. You either come with me now, of your own volition, or I stab Helena in the throat and drag you there myself." She watched a tear drop down Lucy's cheek. "And don't think I won't."

"Don't you do it, Lucy," Helena replied, defiantly.

"Shut the fuck up!" Cara leapt on Helena, her knife under her chin. "It's now or never, Lucy. If you don't agree to join me, I'm going to carve her up, do you understand?" Cara could see Helena trying to swallow.

"All right! All right, I'll do it. Just don't hurt her, please. This is between you and me. I'll go with you now. Please, just leave her alone."

Cara slowly withdrew the knife from under Helena's chin. When she released her grip on Helena, Cara stood back and looked down at her Lucy, who still looked deathly sick. "Right, we're up, gorgeous."

A noise came from behind her.

Cara scrambled, looking for the rags she'd gagged the girls with earlier.

Spotting them, she picked them up and stuffed them in their mouths, but not quick enough to prevent Lucy shouting out, "Help! Help us!"

She ran over to a corner of the room and waited for whoever was coming in, knife in hand. She could see torchlight flickering.

A big figure walked through, shining a light on Lucy's face.

Waiting until he was fully inside, Cara stepped towards him with stealth, careful not to make a sound. He was a big guy by the look of his silhouette. She would have trouble with him.

Before she could reach him, he turned round.

The silhouette momentarily stunned, Cara seized her chance, and rushed him, the knife held aloft, until she drove it into his neck.

After yanking the blade out of his throat, Cara watched the fat man with a moustache fall to his knees, trying to cover the wound with his hand.

He fell face down onto the ground, blood pooling.

Cara didn't have to guess he was a police officer; she knew instinctively. But pigs never travelled alone, so she didn't have much time. She had to move quickly.

Using the bloody knife to cut Lucy's ties, she grabbed Lucy by her hair and pulled her towards the exit. Helena screamed into her gag, calling out for Lucy.

The pressure in Amelie's head was so great, she thought it would explode.

Her vision grew darker with each passing second. She could see Harry's contorted face glaring down at her, spit dripping from his lips, the intent in his eyes obvious.

Reaching up, her fingers found his face. She grabbed it, using her thumbs to find his eyes. She could feel him trying to get her hands free, but she held on, her thumbs plunging into his eye sockets. With as much effort as she could muster, she pushed her thumbs in deeper, hearing him cry out in pain, but not releasing his grip.

It was only with one last plunge, that he let go of her throat. The relief was overwhelming, as she tried to take in as much air as she could.

She let go of his head, watching as he staggered backwards, trying to recover. He was blinded, temporarily; she hadn't gone in as deep as to permanently scar him.

Amelie pushed herself along the carpet using her legs, to get away from the wounded animal. It was the dangerous time, when animals lashed out.

When she'd sucked in enough air, she pulled herself up, looking down at Harry, who was still clutching at his eyes. "You fucker!" She caught her breath then ran forwards, kicking him in the groin, as hard as she could.

Harry fell back, his hands on his crotch, crying in pain.

Amelie rushed at him again, kicking him in the belly, followed by his head. "You come anywhere near me again, I'll kill you, do you hear me? You bastard!"

Exhausted, she picked up her bag and coat, staggered up the stairs and out onto the deck. When she was safely off the boat, Amelie staggered along the dock, holding her bruised neck. She could see people up ahead. If she could get among strangers, she would be safe, for now.

Having to decide what to do next, she took a moment to gather her thoughts. If Harry knew about her, then she had to assume his assistant did too. Lennox had told her how dangerous Peter Franks was. One thing she did know, she had to go back to her apartment and get her laptop.

Outside the twenty-four-hour supermarket, she found a black cab taxi, opened the door and got in, telling the driver where she needed to get to. She passed fifty pounds through the hole in the plastic partition. She asked him to double-time it.

Nasreen came out of the abandoned building to near total darkness. She walked quickly in the direction McGrath went, Gupta not far behind her. A bad feeling in her gut told her he might have already found Cara.

Turning her walk into a run, Gupta following suit, it wasn't long before they found the opening to the underground bunker. Not another one, she thought, remembering her descent into the Harrison Farm bunker. This time she was careful and had backup. As she entered the black hole leading to the room, she heard sirens in the distance.

Using her torch, she shone the way until they were in the room itself.

On the floor in the middle of the room was McGrath's fresh body, the blood still pooling. "Shit!" She turned to Gupta. "We've just missed her."

"She can't be far," Gupta replied. "Go! I'll see to Helena."

Running, using the torch to show her the way back, Nasreen made it out of the bunker and onto the uneven grass.

She looked for Cara and Lucy.

In the distance, in silhouette, she could make out two figures at the edge of the cliff. "That's them!" she shouted, hearing Gupta close behind her. "I'll keep Cara busy. You grab Lucy."

While running towards their charge, Gupta argued with her, saying he should take on Cara. Nasreen shook her head. "I've got a better chance than you."

"In that case, take this." Gupta handed her his cosh. "I think you'll need it."

Grabbing it from him, Nasreen pressed the spring release button on the side of the handle, as the cosh extended into a long metal bar. Having an extendable metal baton would come in useful, especially against a psychotic bitch like Cara Mooney.

As she approached Cara and Lucy, she heard them arguing. "Cara Mooney! Put the knife down, you're coming with us."

"You!" Cara snarled, letting go of Lucy.

"It's over! Let's both put our weapons down, yeah?"

"I'm going to fucking kill you." Cara ran at her with the knife.

Maggie looked down at Lennox Garvey with a smile on her face, while Gypsy King used his spade to start filling up the drum with concrete.

So far, it was just above Garvey's knees. There were so many ways she could kill him, but this was as good as the next. "Wait! Let me do it." She handed the knife to Darius and took the spade from Gypsy King.

Putting her back into lifting the concrete, she enjoyed covering him more and more.

She stopped suddenly, when Darius reached down and took the gag out of Garvey's mouth. "What the fuck are you doing? Put that back in!"

"Please, you're making a big mistake. I've got all the information I need to expose the project. I know who's involved, where the warehouse is, which police officers are involved, everything."

Maggie, not listening, threw some more concrete in the drum, leaving Garvey up to his waist. She didn't want to listen; she needed to watch him die. "No one fucking cares, Garvey. Shut the fuck up!"

"Hold on, Maggie," Darius interrupted. "If he's telling the truth, it could all be over for us. We need to hear him out."

"It *will* be over for you," Garvey added, "if something happens to me. I've given strict instructions for an envelope to be delivered somewhere if my source doesn't hear from me soon. Don't make a mistake. And get me out of here before this stuff sets."

"Maggie, I've got to speak to Franks about this," Darius said.

"It's at Amelie's apartment," Maggie said. "Send someone round there to get it."

Maggie was delighted by the look of surprise on Garvey's face. "What? You didn't think we knew about your little whore girlfriend? How do you think we found you?"

Shovelling more cement in, she stopped again. "And don't worry, we've got another drum reserved for her. She'll be joining you soon."

While Darius was away, phoning Franks, Maggie used the time to keep topping up the concrete, until Garvey was up to his neck.

She put the shovel down and retrieved the knife.

It wouldn't be long now, until it set and he couldn't breathe.

It would be getting really hot for him.

"Quick! Get him out!" Darius put his phone in his pocket.

"No fucking way!" She stood between Darius and Garvey. "He stays where he is. He owes me a death; he's not sliming his way out of this."

"I mean it, Maggie, stand aside. I've got to get him out of there."

Knowing she couldn't fight Darius off, knowing he would easily overpower her, Maggie spun around, took the knife with both hands above her head, and drove it into the top of Garvey's head with as much force as she could gather. The blade embedded itself into his skull three inches deep.

She smiled down at Garvey's instantly dead face.

There was stunned silence.

No one moved; no one spoke.

"That's just fucking great, Maggie," Darius fumed. "What the fuck are we going to do now? We don't know if he was telling the truth, we don't know where he'll send the envelope, nothing. We fucking needed him."

Maggie wasn't listening. "You can fill him in now," she said, trying to pull her favourite knife out of Garvey's skull.

It was wedged; it took all her strength to remove it. "Darius has the money; he'll give it to you before we leave," she told Gypsy King. The satisfaction was good, but not great; the main point, though, was Garvey, the last of her sons' murderers, was dead. Justice had been served. She turned to Darius, barged him out of the way and walked towards the exit, hearing him call after her.

151

———

Cara came at her, but it only took one forceful swing of her cosh to knock the knife out of her hand. Nasreen stood there, the cosh ready, opposite an unarmed Cara. "It's over! Come on, Cara, give it up. I'll smash you to pieces with this."

"What's the matter, are you scared to face me without your stick?"

Nasreen, considering the question, pushed the tip of the baton inside its sheath, threw the handle to her right, and changed her stance. With her fists up in front of her face, her legs altered to offensive stance, she said, "I've taken down bigger bitches than you before."

"I doubt it." Cara put her fists up in front of her.

"Come on, Nas, take this bitch down." Terrence had joined them, unknown to Nasreen. "Do it for all those people she's butchered."

Looking back at Cara, Nasreen moved her feet, edging closer to her opponent, who was edging her way nearer too.

In the distance, the sound of sirens grew louder.

"You hear that? Armed police officers. It's over. This is your last chance."

"Fuck you, Pig," Cara snapped. "I already told you, I'm not going to prison, or any fucking psych ward."

Nasreen's first move nearly cost her the match.

Cara caught the front kick so easily, that she pulled Nasreen closer and punched her in the face.

Nasreen spat blood and shook her head. "Lucky catch." She felt the pain and adrenaline, a powerful combination.

Cara made the first move this time, which was defended by a kick to her stomach by Nasreen. Cara grunted in pain. Seizing her chance, Nasreen attacked with a series of punches and kicks that stunned the untrained Cara. The last punch knocked out Cara's left central incisor. She felt satisfaction at watching Cara spitting blood.

When Cara looked to her left, Nasreen followed her gaze, and saw Gupta approaching Lucy. A sudden feeling of dread crept over Nasreen.

"Lucy!" Cara shouted.

Trying to intercept her, but failing, Nasreen watched as Cara ran towards Gupta, picking up the knife along the way.

"You're not taking her away from me!" Cara ran at Gupta.

Nasreen wasn't far behind her, but Cara was faster. "Arjun, watch out!"

It was too late. Cara took the knife and threw it at Gupta, the blade sticking in his shoulder. She heard him groan. "Arjun!" Every part of her tried to reach Cara before she caught up with Lucy, but her shorter legs were no match for Cara's.

Still running, Nasreen passed Gupta and asked him if he was all right.

On his back, the blade stuck in his shoulder, he told her to "get that psycho". Nasreen continued running until she was only a few feet from Cara and Lucy, who were stood at the edge of the cliff. "Cara," she cried, "please stop. You don't want to do this."

Edging closer to her quarry one step at a time, Nasreen

noticed they were perilously close to the edge. The last thing Nasreen wanted was Cara taking them both down. "You love Lucy," she said, softly. "You don't want to kill her."

Cara had the knife under Lucy's chin. "We made a pact, don't you understand that?"

"We never made a pact," Lucy snapped. "It's what you wanted. Don't you see? There's nothing romantic about killing ourselves."

"Shut up, Juicy. It's the most romantic thing ever. We're meant to be together, don't you understand that? In life and death, we're one."

Nasreen saw how close Cara was to the edge; one more step back and it was over. "Stop, Cara, you can still have a life."

Nasreen heard the sirens stop, followed by voices. Had she turned around, she'd have seen eight heavily armed police officers running towards them. "They're on their way. Please, let Lucy go. You don't want to hurt her, not really. You love her too much."

"Save it! You can't talk me out of this."

When Nasreen saw Cara take another step back, wobble and start to fall, she lunged after Lucy, who was going down with Cara. Landing on Lucy's legs, Nasreen held on to her for dear life.

Cara, dangling on the side of the cliff, holding on to Lucy's wrists, looked up at her ex's face. Why hadn't she fallen with her? Anger swept over her. Lucy had agreed to end it with her. She couldn't renege on such an important promise.

With her legs hanging, Cara used her hands to try to pull Lucy down.

Lucy looked down at Cara's hate-filled face. She felt every yank on her arms. If the policewoman wasn't strong enough, she would fall. Lucy had never been so scared. Every part of her was fighting to live, fighting to get away from Cara.

Lucy heard noises in the background.

"Shoot her," she heard the policewoman shout. "If you don't shoot her now, she'll drag us all down with her. Do it now!"

154

Nasreen couldn't see them, but she knew there were armed police nearby. She saw two feet next to her, but her concentration was on holding on to Lucy.

Lucy was crying. Nasreen felt arms around her. It was then she knew that Terrence and Bishop were holding on for dear life too. There was no way Cara would bring them all down. "Shoot her! Do it now!"

Lucy, tears streaming down her face, watched Cara below her. Her eyes were dark pits of pure hatred. That was when she heard the two gunshots. Lucy saw the bullets enter Cara's forehead and cheek. Her ex-girlfriend's grip on her arms released, and she watched Cara fall into the darkness below.

156

Nasreen pulled Lucy back until she was well away from the cliff edge.

"Lucy!" She heard from a distance, knowing it was the girlfriend, Helena's voice. There was a desperation only worried loved ones carried.

Pulling her up, Nasreen hugged Lucy tighter than she'd ever hugged anyone before. The embrace lasted an indeterminable amount of time, right there on the grass. Helena, held back by Terrence and Bishop, kept shouting.

"Thank you so much." Lucy was crying.

"You're welcome." Nasreen pulled away from the embrace and looked at Lucy. She was shivering, sweating and looked pale, even in the dark. It was over! They'd caught and dealt with Cara Mooney, the most savage and impressive killer Nasreen had ever gone up against. Had their fight continued, given Cara's superior strength, she would have won, Nasreen knew. But now she could return home, sleep for a week – a good eight hours, anyway – and see her Mina.

Amelie looked behind her before opening the rear door to her block of apartments.

Everything looked clear. Her nerves were heightened; she was so scared, even going into her lovely apartment. It made her sad to think she wouldn't be staying. She loved the place so much.

As she ascended the stairs, she kept an eye out for any suspicious figures lurking. She knew this was a dangerous time. Looking to her left, then right, she opened her apartment door, not seeing anyone.

Inside, she closed the door and leaned back against it, breathing in and out deeply. She felt safer in here than out there. Without hesitating, she walked through the dark lounge, keeping the lights off, just in case, until she found her laptop in the dining room. She disconnected it and took it under her arm, trying to think where her rucksack was.

When she turned to go back into the lounge, Amelie saw a figure blocking her way. She gasped. The figure doubled. She had no choice but to confront them. They were blocking her only escape route.

One figure lunged for her.

Grabbing the computer from under her arm and, with superb timing, she swung it at the figure's face, hitting it hard. The figure fell back.

She jumped over him, wedged between the two. She knew the fallen silhouette would be back up soon, so she had to get past the one in front.

When the remaining shadow lunged for her, she screamed. He grabbed her by the neck and forced her against a wall. She raised her knee, managing to connect it with the intruder's crotch. She'd been taught by her mum, if in trouble, aim for the balls; it worked. Both figures were down on the floor.

With the laptop under her arm, she ran out of her apartment, along the hallway and down the stairs, hearing at least one of them behind her. Her fight or flight instincts kicked in, and she chose flight.

When she reached the ground floor, she flew out of her building, through the car park, to the riverbank. She heard footsteps, running, right behind her.

FIVE WEEKS LATER
FRIDAY, 4TH MAY

158

"Detective Maqsood, please come in and have a seat." Chief Superintendent Faisal Bukhari stood aside and let her inside his office. "We've got a lot to discuss."

Nasreen did as she was told. She took a seat and waited for her new super to sit down behind his desk. When he finally sat, she studied him. Bukhari, whom she'd heard of by reputation only, was a good-looking man. He was taller than she'd imagined, when she found out he was taking over from Adams. It was Bukhari's chiselled cheekbones, strong chin and dark eyes that drew her to him.

"Firstly, I need to apologise for not introducing myself earlier. I've been here for almost a fortnight, and as you can imagine, it takes time to settle in, especially taking over the investigative unit."

"It's fine, sir," she replied, her hands clasped neatly in her lap. "We don't normally have much to do with our supers, not as high up as you, anyway. I only had dealings with Chief Superintendent Adams because our department was plagued with injuries and sickness. He ended up doing four people's jobs, the poor guy."

"Yes, tragic what happened. We'll get whoever's responsible, don't worry about that. Now, on with the formalities: I understand you're still on your probationary period?"

"Yes, sir. The IOPC extended it after my indiscretion. But since then, I've followed all the rules; I helped bring Cara Mooney to justice; and since then I've worked on two more cases–"

"You don't have to justify yourself to me. I've read your file, detective. And I have to say how impressed I am by your performance, especially after your... little indiscretion. I can see here you didn't exactly have a good working relationship with Superintendent Adams?"

Nasreen coughed, then apologised. "Erm, no, not really. After I broke so many rules and regulations, he wanted me off the force. He had his reasons..."

"Which is why he didn't promote you to sergeant?"

"Yes, sir." She couldn't take her eyes away from him; he was delicious. Nasreen felt uncomfortable staring; she looked down at the floor.

"I think after your successes post the Harrison Farm case, it's only fair to promote you now. Congratulations, Detective Sergeant Maqsood, you're no longer a probationary constable. Welcome to the team officially. I've submitted your paperwork. Your ID with your new title will be with you soon. It's very well deserved."

Nasreen was speechless. When he stood and extended his hand, she reciprocated. "Thank you, sir. I don't know what to say."

"You don't need to say anything; you should've been promoted by now." He sat back down. "I think you showed a lot of courage going into that bunker by yourself. It was ill-judged, perhaps, but courageous nonetheless. I don't agree with Superintendent Adams' assessment of you. You'll find we work very differently. Unofficially I actively encourage free-thinking, whereas others unfortunately like their officers to follow rigid rules. So..."

The telephone on his desk rang.

Nasreen waited while he spoke to the caller, diverting her gaze every now and then. She was conscious of her stare. It seemed they had another case, if his conversation was anything to go by. When he replaced the receiver, he apologised again.

"You and Terrence have a case," he said, handing her a piece of paper with an address on. "A body's been found in a skip on a construction site; there's the address..."

"On my way, sir," she replied, taking one last look at his beautiful face.

THE END

ACKNOWLEDGEMENTS

I'd like to thank, first and foremost, you, the reader, for taking a chance on reading my book. Without you picking up and reading it, there would be no need for me writing it, or the publisher releasing it. So, thank you. If you enjoyed Bird of Prey, please consider leaving a review. And if you'd like some behind the scenes information, please follow me on Instagram: @dcbrockwell or my Facebook page: DCBrockwell Author. In addition to writing, I like gardening and making cocktails, so you'll find quite a mixed bag on my Instagram account.

I would also love to thank the team at Bloodhound Books. Betsy and Fred, for taking a punt on my story, thank you so much for this opportunity to showcase my work; it's more appreciated than you know. Morgen Bailey, my editor, for shaping it up, ready for publication. Also Heather Fitt and the publicity team. Thank you all for your contributions. I hope I don't let you all down.

And I can't sign off without thanking my beta readers, who often pull me up on poor choices with storylines. You helped give me the confidence to submit my first novel 'No Way Out'. Thank you!

Finally, if anyone wishes to join my team of beta readers, please email me at duncanbrockwell@hotmail.co.uk.

DC Brockwell can be found here:
Instagram: @dcbrockwell
Facebook Page: DCBrockwell Author
Twitter: DCBrockwell